EXQUISITE
Betrayal

A.M. HARGROVE

Hannah —

It was awesome
meeting you at
Penned Con 2015!

Love —
AM Hargrove

Cover Design by Sarah Hansen at Okay Creations

Cover Photo by Kelsey Keeton at K. Keeton Designs

ISBN-13: 978-1494296889

ISBN-10: 1494296888

Table of Contents

Chapter One	Fallon	1
Chapter Two	Ryland-Thomas	11
Chapter Three	Fallon	19
Chapter Four	Ryland-Thomas	35
Chapter Five	Fallon	47
Chapter Six	Ryland-Thomas	61
Chapter Seven	Fallon	70
Chapter Eight	Ryland-Thomas	82
Chapter Nine	Fallon	92
Chapter Ten	Ryland-Thomas	105
Chapter Eleven	Fallon	113
Chapter Twelve	Ryland-Thomas	127
Chapter Thirteen	Fallon	137
Chapter Fourteen	Ryland-Thomas	146
Chapter Fifteen	Fallon	153
Chapter Sixteen	Ryland-Thomas	163
Chapter Seventeen	Fallon	174
Chapter Eighteen	Ryland-Thomas	185
Chapter Nineteen	Fallon	195
Chapter Twenty	Ryland-Thomas	213
Chapter Twenty-One	Fallon	230
Chapter Twenty-Two	Ryland-Thomas	243
Chapter Twenty-Three	Fallon	255
Chapter Twenty-Four	Fallon	265
Chapter Twenty-Five	Ryland-Thomas	274

Chapter Twenty-Six	Fallon	279
Chapter Twenty-Seven	Fallon	288
Chapter Twenty-Eight	Ryland-Thomas	299
Chapter Twenty-Nine	Fallon	308
Chapter Thirty	Ryland-Thomas	324
Chapter Thirty-One	Fallon	328
Chapter Thirty-Two	Ryland-Thomas	340
Chapter Thirty-Three	Fallon	350
Chapter Thirty-Four	Fallon	360
Epilogue		364

Sometimes an Exquisite Betrayal leads to

Better Ways...

BETTER WAYS ©

Before you carry me to safety
Before I get what you deserve
Before we drink and blame the alcohol
Before I bleed to make you hurt

I'm choosing better ways of proving I'm not afraid

We'll just stop in for the night
We'll just set things all right
Be sure this time
If we're falling off the ride
If I sing you a lie
Be sure this time

Before you rattle our mementos
Before I wish that I'd gone home
Before we scream and blame the amplifiers
Before I decorate our ghosts

I'm choosing better ways of proving I'm not afraid
I am choosing better ways of proving I'm not afraid at all

Further down the way, I'll forget the reasons
I could never stay, I could never sleep in
Further down the way, I'll forget the reasons
I'm choosing better ways of proving I'm so afraid

We'll just stop in for the night
We'll just let these wrenches fly
Be sure this time

If we're falling off the ride
If I'm singing 'goodbye'
Be sure this time

We'll just stop in for the night

Music and Lyrics by She Said Fire
Copyright © 2013
Joshua Hawksley, Peter Strzelecki, Chris Moss and Christina Vitucci

One

Fallon

Ever since this bucket of metal called a plane left the ground, I've been asking myself if spending my last nickel on this trip will be worth it. Even though it means going without food at times, I stashed away every tip I earned to save for this. My mountain of debt is enormous, but then again, I keep telling myself, you only live once, right?

When the plane suddenly lurches, I know it's going to roll completely over at any minute. I want to get off this carnival ride so badly I can taste it. My fingers tightly clench the armrest and I'm pretty sure if I ever deplane, my imprints will be left behind forever.

I feel a light patting on my arm and then I hear, "It'll be just fine, dear. Those are only crosswinds from the desert. We always have those in Vegas." The flight attendant announced moments before that we've been cleared for landing, but from the motion of the plane, I fear we won't make it.

Glancing to my right, I see the tiny, elderly woman sitting next to me. My nerves are so shot, my attempt at smiling is an epic fail.

Fallon, sweetie, always remember to keep your chin up. Negative thoughts will only bring you down.

Dad's words come back to me, a soothing balm to my tattered nerves and empty bank account. God, how I wish he were still here. I wouldn't be in this damn mess of debt right now. It's been six years, but sometimes the pain is so raw that it feels like yesterday.

"Honey, is this your first time flying?" The voice next to me breaks me out of my daydreaming.

"Hmm? Oh, yes, ma'am," I squeak.

"Ah, I see. Well, this is all part of flying and very normal."

"Really? I feel like I'm on a sideways Tilt-A-Whirl at the county fair."

"Oh no, honey, this is smooth. I've been on some real doozies, I tell you. So what brings you to Vegas? Are you going to lose all your money to the slots?" she laughs.

"Huh?" My anxiety has me so edgy, I'm not following the conversation for a second and then it hits me. "Oh, no, ma'am. I'm here for the Wicked Wench's Conference." I don't have a spare nickel to spend on the slots as it is.

She nods and eyes me for a second. "So, are you a Wench then?"

"Oh no! I'm a blogger," I tell her, glad for the distraction from the chaotic flight.

The noise of the engines has picked up so she is leaning closer to me now, trying to hear. "A what? A booger?"

"No! Not a booger! A blogger!"

"Oh, a blogger. I've always wanted to see you girls dance. Do you have those fancy clicking shoes? Can you kick your legs high up in the air? I bet you can. You look like you could be limber like that."

By the time I start to explain that I'm a blogger and not a clogger, the plane rolls to a stop and the seatbelt light goes off. For an elderly woman, she moves like lightening as she shoots out of her seat and flies down the aisle. I sit and stare at her with my mouth hanging open. Obviously she knows the ins and outs of flying much better than I do. I'm lost in the sea of shoving people as eager as I am to get off of that death trap.

As I'm pushed along the jetway, I finally emerge into McCarran International Airport. The place is huge! Taking a deep breath, I knock the monster of intimidation back and follow the signs to Baggage Claim, eager to meet my fellow book bloggers for the first time.

We are a gang of five that met online over our love for romance novels. We teamed up through Twitter first and then Facebook. As we found ourselves chatting and becoming friends, our interest in the same genre triggered the idea for us to start a book blog where we could review and post about our favorite books. I think it was Kat's idea originally, but it took off like a forest fire in a Santa Ana wind.

We decided to celebrate our first anniversary by attending the Wicked Wenches Con in Las Vegas together. It would finally give us the chance to not only meet each other in person, but also some of our favorite authors of romance. Kat Graham, Amanda Cook, Mandy Henderson and Andrea Simpson are my partners, though I look at them as my family. They've done more for me in the last year than my mom has in the past five. Honestly, if they had purchased me a paper clip, they would've done more than my mom, however that's another story.

I finally locate the conveyer belt thingy and watch for my bag when my phone dings. I look to see it's a text from Kat.

Kat: *I'm here. Are you?*

Me: *Yep...just waiting on my suitcase.*

Kat: *Where?*

Me: *Carousel #15*

Kat: *On my way!*

Five minutes later, the bags start to roll down and mayhem ensues. I've never seen anything like it. From what I can tell that belt keeps going around in a big circle and eventually it's going to get back to me again. I can't figure out why those people are in such a frenzy over it.

Suddenly, I hear a giant screech followed by a squeal and turn around to see a blur with long, light brown hair flying towards me. It comes as no surprise that we both end up on the ground, hugging and laughing. As women tend to do, we find ourselves talking a mile a minute and eventually notice the area around Carousel #15 has cleared out and mine is the only bag still circling on the belt. We laugh for another few minutes before standing up to collect it.

Kat takes one look at my bag and breaks out in peals of laughter. She's hugging her sides and bent over while I'm worried she's going to topple on her head.

"Stop already!"

"I'm sorry, but damn, Fallon, where the heck did you get your luggage? From duct tape's anonymous? You need to go to duct tape rehab."

I shrug as I give Kat the evil eye, but then I break down in giggles. My suitcase does indeed look like

4

something the Tin Man from The Wizard of Oz would carry since it's mostly silver. Granted, underneath the strips and strips of tape, there is a black bag somewhere, yet I'll be damned if I can see it now.

"Okay, you win. It is awful, isn't it? I didn't have a choice, though. It was either that or less money for shooters and the shooters won."

Kat nods. "Excellent choice. Come on, let's go hunt down Amanda."

We head out of Carousel #15 and don't have to look far. Walking towards us and shouting at the top of her lungs is a gigantic hot dog nestled inside of a bun, complete with squiggles of mustard and ketchup. The only thing human about it is the face and it's yelling out, "Where's the Virgin for Vegas? Where's the Virgin for Vegas? Have I got a wiener for you!"

I take one look at her and do a one-eighty with the intention of running away. However Kat grabs my wrist before I get the chance. "Oh, no you don't. You have to take this like a woman!"

"Oh my God. You can't do this to me!" I'm ready to drop to my knees and beg.

"Oh, yes we can! Now smile and look pretty," she laughs.

I can't believe this. What are they doing? Amanda approaches, dressed up like a fully loaded hot dog and hands me a tequila shooter. "How 'bout a nice shooter for the Vegas Virgin?"

At this point, I down the tequila and want to crawl inside my bundle of duct tape. "Please, you all. Don't do this." I frantically look around to see if anyone's watching.

"We're not doing anything except for kissing that dreadful virginity of yours good-bye," the wiener announces.

"Shit, shit, shit!"

"Don't worry, Fallon. It'll get better with more tequila," Kat assures.

I poke out my arm and say, "Then give me some more and make it fast."

Amanda hands me another shooter. "How 'bout a nice, juicy wiener to go along with that, ma'am?"

"Oh, dear God." If anyone ever died of embarrassment, I was sure it would be me. Like right this minute!

Kat puts her hand on my face. "Amanda, I think we need to cool it. Her face is on fire and I'm not sure if it's the tequila or you."

"It's her." I grab my hunk of duct tape and march straight outside.

Behind me I can hear, "Little Virgin, wait up. Little Virgin, we have to meet Mandy and Andrea!"

I frenetically wave my hand behind my butt. Right now, I only care about one thing and that's getting away from the giant wiener that's determined to get me drunk on tequila shooters and announce to the world that I'm a 'Little Virgin'. I continue to shoo them away as I turn to check if they're following me when I barrel into something quite firm and hard that sends me flying flat on my ass. The concrete is scorching and my thighs instantly feel like fried eggs hitting the frying pan on sizzling butter.

"Aiyee," I scream as I try to stand back up. By this time my ass is in the air as I roll to my hands and knees. Now my palms and knees are on fire. "Dammit! Shit, that's hot!" I say as I jolt to my feet, arms flailing while I try to straighten my skirt.

I finally glance up to find two, deep, emerald green eyes gazing at me. Well, that's not exactly true. They're slowly scanning me from top to bottom until they then stop and lock onto my cleavage. The reason for this is that my left nipple is more than half exposed. Okay, it's completely exposed.

"Oh fuck!" I squeal as I tug my bra up and adjust my top. Why does this crap always happen to me?

I look back to see that Amanda and Kat are just awestruck. Not at me, but at green eyes because, glory-freakin-hallelujah, he's one beautiful man. And why wouldn't he be? Only I would fall down, ass in the air, boob hanging out in front of a gorgeous man. It wouldn't happen in front of a wrinkled up, old, toothless man. Nope, never. I go for full on nipple exposure with the well-built, rugged, green-eyed blond that looks like a sex god, orgasmic-producing Eden.

"I'm sorry," I say. "Forgive me. I should watch where I'm going."

"Are you all right?" he asks and then scrapes his teeth across his lower lip right before he bites down on one corner.

Holy-put-my-panties-in-a-wet-wad! That voice and mouth. Green eyes has a sexy British accent to match the rest of his perfect self. Heart meet pink sparkly toe nails.

My head tilts a bit, as if I'm trying to figure out what he just asked me. "Huh?"

"I asked if you were okay. You took a good fall there on your bum. Just wanted to know if all was okay there?"

Somehow my hand starts unconsciously rubbing my butt. "Oh. Yeah, I guess so. All's good on the bum here." My voice has gotten all throaty on me.

Tall with unruly dark blond waves falling over his forehead, he stands there and stares at me. Then those magnificent orbs slowly rake me from head to toe again. Even though it feels like it's a hundred and fifty degrees in the Las Vegas August heat, chills break out over my entire body. Every single hair—even the microscopic ones that I so diligently try to keep waxed—stand at attention, reminding me of their existence. An overwhelming urge to grab and kiss this hunk of sexiness charges into me, and I have no idea who he is. I can't stop ogling his face... his bottom lip is full, and when he runs his tongue along it, I have to clamp my lips together to keep myself from moaning.

"So it looks like you're here for a visit then?"

"Yes, a long weekend." My voice still sounds funny to me, all husky and throaty.

"Well, perhaps I'll see you around the strip then." And again, those magnetic greens of his inspect me from head to toe. "Have a nice day then," I hear him say.

I can't move. I'm as still as a marble statue until the girls each grab one of my arms.

"If Vegas is full of those, I'm never going home," the giant wiener claims.

We walk back inside to meet the other two of our gang, while I'm still addled by my encounter with green eyes.

We collect Andrea and Mandy and then seek out our transportation to the hotel. As we wait in line for the bus to take us there, the chills I had earlier have morphed into rivulets of sweat as they stream down my body. Not a single thread of my clothing is dry. This place is a freaking oven. When they talk about desert heat, they aren't kidding. The only good thing to come out of it is Amanda had to ditch the giant wiener outfit. I think she would've died if she hadn't.

"Did you all realize it was gonna be this damn hot? I feel like I'm in Hell," Andrea says.

"Hell can't be this hot, and if it is, well then, I'm gonna start really doing some serious prayin' cuz you all, this is crazy!" I say. "I think I just sweated off my right butt cheek."

Our bus finally shows up and we about knock the other people over to get on board. I'm ashamed to admit I'm not sorry in the least for that ghastly behavior of mine. It's either that, or walk around with only one butt cheek, and the way I am thinking, it will be really hard to lose my virginity with only one butt cheek.

At least the ride to the hotel doesn't take very long. When we pull up to it, though, we're kind of disappointed. "Well, they sure made it look a lot nicer online," Andrea harrumphs.

We all agree with her, but there isn't anything to do except go inside and check in. So that's what we do.

The lobby is a bit outdated and has a space odyssey look to it, but it's clean with a casino and bar. What more can we ask for, right? The other nice thing is it is only a couple of blocks from the conference and all the cool hotels. The Space Nugget will do just fine for the next five days.

We had booked two adjoining rooms so we could share two bathrooms. The rooms are tidy, but they're seriously lacking in decor.

"Well, it's clean and cool and what do we care about anything else, right?" Mandy asks.

"Yeah, it's not like we're gonna be in here a lot anyway," Kat replies. "I'm happy if the air conditioning works."

So we all unpack and decide what to do that night. The convention kicks off in the morning, so that leaves tonight open. Tomorrow night is our big party with R. T. Sinclair.

Everyone starts tossing around ideas of what to do and our excitement mounts. We're in the world's largest adult playground and we have a plethora of places to choose from.

Amanda has a look in her eye that I'm beginning to understand. She once talked about hitting the male strip clubs and I'm all for that, but right now my stomach is telling me it wants some food. I'm relieved to hear her say, "Hey, what do y'all say we hit the town? Grab a little food, hit a casino and then do some shooters!" she shouts.

Everyone is on board with her suggestion, so we all get ready for our first night out on the town.

TWO

RYLAND - THOMAS

Whoever that gorgeous girl is that rammed into me, I'd like to get to know her. No, scratch that. There's no liking about it. It's more like a *need*. I wish I didn't get so bloody freaked out around members of the opposite sex because that one is fucking hot. I'm not talking about this bloody desert heat here, either. My body immediately got fired up when I'd gotten a good look at her. It was nearly impossible to pull my eyes away.

I felt bad when she landed flat on her arse, but damn what a pretty sight it was when she rolled over. Then the poor thing burned her palms on the walkway. When she treated me to that show of her lovely nipple, however, it was all I could do not to put my mouth on her. Too bad both of her lovely buds didn't poked out. Guess I'll have to be happy with just the one. Now she's triggered an urge in me... one that I haven't felt in a long time.

Shaking my head to clear the encounter, I enter the airport to collect my sister, Tilly. She's already texted me, so I head on over to the baggage carousel and hunt for her. I finally spy her over a sea of heads and piles of black, rolling bags. Why does everyone insist on buying that silly luggage that looks the same? Don't they realize how difficult it makes it to find your bag when it plops down on that conveyor belt? I guess not because everyone keeps on buying it.

"Tills," I yell over the din of the crowd.

Her head bobs around, trying to seek me out.

"Tills, over here!" I yell as I wave my arm above my head.

She glances my way and waves. It's so good to see her. I squeeze through an opening and finally make it to her side.

"Ryland Thomas," she squeaks as I crush her in a hug. After she releases me, she gives me one of her thorough inspections. "Bloody hell, look at you. You're a damn twitchy mess. You need a woman, Ryland Thomas. When was the last time you got laid?"

"Lay off, Tilly. Besides, that's not an appropriate thing to ask your brother, for Christ's sake."

"It is, too. It's been far too long and you know it. You're entirely too tense. You won't even talk to women, much less hook up with them."

I fold my lips into my mouth and bite down simply so I don't explode on her. I know she means well, however this isn't doing me a bloody bit of good. "Where's your satchel?" I ask.

"I brought more than a satchel and I'm still waiting for it," she huffs. Then she adds, "There it is."

I look in the direction she's indicating and see a gigantic purple and pink polka dotted trunk. "Bloody hell, Tills, how long are you planning on staying here?"

12

"A week or so."

I eye her suspiciously. "What's going on?"

"For your information, Mr. Nosy, someone is meeting me here after the conference. We're going to take a mini vacation."

"Ah, I see."

"Is that it? Don't you want to know anything else?"

"Not really."

"But I'm your sister... your twin at that."

"I know, but Tilly, your sex life is your own business."

"What if I were to tell you it's more than just sex? What if I were to tell you that I'm in love?"

"Then I'd say good for you. Let's get out of here." I look around for a Sky Cap because there's no way I'm going to lug that gigantic piece of luggage around. It's a huge, rectangular trunk on tiny wheels. I could fit my bedroom furniture in that thing.

One finally sees us and I tell them I'm going to get the car.

After getting Tilly and giganticus loaded into my car, we head for the Bellagio.

"So, you're prepared for this, right?" I ask. I always get a bit antsy before these things.

"As usual. When are you going to stop worrying about all of this? I pull it off like a charm and you know it."

"You do make it work quite nicely, I will say. But, Tills, I simply get a bit nervous. Can't help it. My sales would go to shit if my readers ever found out."

Out of the corner of my eye I see Tilly look at me. Here it comes. Her sympathy speech. "Look Ryland Thomas, you're a fabulous writer. Your fans would love you anyway. Besides all of that, don't you think it's time to let the past go? Release all that anger and start living again?"

My hands clench the steering wheel as I stare straight ahead. Tilly can't understand and never will. We were only eighteen when our parents died in the train crash. It was an unfortunate thing, everyone said. They were traveling in France and the train derailed, leaving most of the passengers critically injured or dead. Our parents were killed instantly, leaving the two of us behind. Luckily, we were extremely well padded financially, but the emotional scars left us both a mess for a while.

Tilly stumbled around a bit and I did my best to shield her from everything, like a good brother should, but she had great friends who were always there for her. I, on the other hand, wasn't so lucky. At the time, I thought differently. It was the usual story, the one where the beautiful blond comes to the rescue, saving the poor guy from the pain he's in.

Yeah, right. Turns out, the only thing she was interested in was my best mate. For a while I tried to lie to myself by covering up all the obvious things; her staying out late by herself, not showing up at restaurants when she said she'd be there. The final blow hurt worse than I ever thought possible, though.

I came home early from class one day, as I was still in university, having forgotten my creative writing notes, so I jogged back to my flat to grab them. When I walked in, I heard voices, one female and the other male. As I stopped to listen, the sounds turned into things I shouldn't be hearing, things that I knew shouldn't be coming from my bedroom, especially since *I* wasn't in there.

Walking on silent feet, I stood in the doorway and watched him going down on her as she sucked him off. Since she was on top, I couldn't get a good look at the bloke's face, and I didn't care much about that either. Or so I thought.

"Well, isn't this interesting?" At least they paused for a moment.

The look on her face wasn't what I expected. I thought I'd see remorse, or even shock. She smiled instead and asked me to join them. Then the bloke lifted his head and said, "Didn't know this was your type of thing, mate."

It was my best friend. He knew bloody good and well it wasn't my thing. He didn't stay my best friend after that, of course. I may have been blind and naive, but I wasn't stupid.

"Yeah, and how many years have we known each other?"

"About ten now, I guess," he groaned. She'd resumed giving him head by then.

"Then you should know I'm pretty damn disgusted by this. Now get your fucking piece of shit arses out of my flat." I didn't yell or scream; however both of them knew I wasn't joking.

They just looked at me and I finally had to say, "Now!"

Feet hit the floor as they scrambled to get dressed. They left in such a hurry that she had left her handbag behind. I tossed it out on the street and really didn't give a shit about it. I never went to class that day or the next. The fact is, I stayed in that flat for two and a half weeks until Tilly came to get me.

15

She cried when she saw me. I know I scared the crap out of her. I hadn't bathed in all that time and I'm pretty sure I had suffered some kind of a breakdown. I had fooled myself into believing that Iris loved me and I'd lied to myself all along, telling myself she truly cared. It was all smoke and mirrors, though. It was too much to bear after losing my parents, and now Iris and Will.

My best friend's betrayal was even more difficult to take over the long run because he understood me and had known me for my whole adolescent and adult life. Talk about getting buggered. Never thought it would happen to me by my best mate.

Tilly picked up the pieces of me and glued me back together. It took her awhile, but she didn't give up. I dropped out of university for a term, yet did go back and finish, thanks to my sister.

She tries; I'll give her that. She never gives up, either. Despite that, how can I tell her that I'm wary of opening up to another woman again? When you've been dealt a double whammy like that, you just don't let it go and move on. The only person I'll ever trust is Tilly.

"So how do you want to handle it?" she asks.

"What?"

"Have you even been listening to me at all?"

Guilty as charged, but I don't dare tell her that. "Well, sure."

"Then tell me, dear brother, what did I just say?"

"Oh look, we're here!" I exclaim as I pull into the Bellagio.

"You're not getting out of this, Ryland Thomas," she promises. Whatever 'this' is.

I hand my keys to the valet and a bellman follows us inside with my bag and giganticus as we go to check in.

16

I've booked two suites for us, next to each other, as requested. Tilly needs her space and so do I. The clerk gives us all our information and off we go.

"Ryland Thomas, we need to talk about tomorrow night. I'm going to unpack and then I'll be over in thirty minutes."

"Fine," I say in my grumpy voice. I hate playing this duplicitous role, but it is a necessity for my sales.

As promised, thirty minutes later, Tilly knocks on my door.

"Have you chatted with Sam?"

Sam is my agent and a good friend as well. "Yes and he thinks this will be great publicity for me. Thanks again, Tills, for doing this."

She narrows her eyes. "You'd make me a lot happier if you'd get off your bum and get a social life. I worry about you, you know."

"I'm fine," I insist, wondering if it's true as the words leave my lips.

"It's been years already. Are you going to mope around forever?"

"Tilly, if you don't stop bringing this up, I'm going to get really pissed. And I don't want to do that."

"Maybe I want you to get pissed."

She's confusing me now. Why would she want me to get angry? I give her one of my looks, the one that tells her she's exasperating me.

She laughs. "Go ahead and get mad because I don't give a shit. I've had it with your surliness over Iris and the nasty crap she pulled on you. Get over it! Hear me, Ryland Thomas? I'm done with your silly moods already. And if you don't start behaving like a man your age should act, I'm gonna quit doing these appearances for you."

"You're joking."

"No, I'm promising. I'm done. Understand?"

"Tilly! You can't mean that!"

"Oh, but I do. Now, pull yourself together and get out in the world. Get laid, or whatever. Bloody hell, I'll hire you an escort if that's what you want. But you need some female company for Christ's sake."

She sees my wallet on the table and hands it to me along with my phone. "Here," she says before she puts her palms on my back and pushes me out the door. "Have fun tonight."

I'm left standing in the hall of my hotel, staring at the door to my suite.

Three

Fallon

"I'm not so sure about that tequila, but these lemon drop shooters are really good," I yell over the thumping of the music. We're in a club called *Dance NOW*. Men are swarming everywhere, and I have my eye out for *the* one except I'm terribly dissatisfied.

"Yeah, I agree," Kat yells back. "I like these a lot better than tequila."

Amanda, Mandy and Andrea are out on the dance floor perfecting their moves. I'm not sure exactly what kind of moves they are, but I have to say, Amanda is all kinds of flexible. That girl can flat swing her legs around and then drop it down low.

Kat and I are taking in the scenery when I glance up at the bar and notice the sex god from the airport. I give my head a hard shake, ensuring it's not the lemon drops making me see things. When I open my eyes, there he stands, tipping a glass of amber liquid into his mouth. Would I ever love to be that glass right now, tucked tightly against those luscious lips of his.

I hear Kat saying something to me, however I'm not paying her the least bit of attention. "Fallon?" she hollers.

Then she must've followed my gaze because I suddenly hear her say, "Mother fucker, it's him." Now this is coming from a girl who never swears.

We both must look like two hoot owls in the night sitting on a tree limb, unblinking, as we ogle Mr. Pretty, yet neither of us can do a damn thing about it. He really is that freakin' gorgeous.

That glass that I envy so much is taking another trip to his lips and the iceless fluid tumbles gently into his mouth. I moan. Hearing myself, I clap a hand over my mouth. My movement must have distracted him somewhat because my eyes are suddenly in the direct line of fire of his.

"Oh shit," I mumble under my hand. "What do I do now?" I ask to no one in particular.

He simply stares at me. Those green eyes are so intense I briefly wonder if he's a vampire. Then I chastise myself. Everyone knows there are no such things as vampires.

So now what? I wonder as his eyes continue to bore holes into mine. It's as though he's running an assessment of me, like I'm a car he's thinking of test-driving. If that's the case, then I'm more than troubled when he pulls his long, sinewy frame away from the bar and saunters towards me. His clothes are molded to him; he's wearing jeans that ride low on his hips and a black shirt that clings to him.

"Oh crap," I say.

"He's coming for you, girl," Kat says as she moves away.

No, no, no! What is she doing, abandoning me like that? She knows not to do that.

"Aren't you the girl I knocked over at the airport earlier today?" he asks, his voice dripping over me like cream.

My head tilts back, six inches or so because Green Eyes is at least six-foot-three. I should know because I'm five-nine. "Ah, er, well, I think I actually ran into you. But yeah, it's me." I stick out my hand to shake his. "My name is Fallon McKinley, and I'm sorry about that." I am mortified because he did, after all, see my ass and nipple. Oh shit, the gorgeous piece of humanity has seen my nipple! My face suddenly feels like a blast furnace.

"Yes, well, Fallon, I thought it was you. Name's Ryland. Nice to meet you then. May I buy you a drink?"

"Oh no. I'm good here. But thanks."

What the hell is wrong with me? I force myself to calm down and talk to the man like a mature young woman. "So Ryland, what brings you to Vegas?"

He stiffens a bit before answering, "Yeah, well, I just thought I'd pop over for a few days of gambling. You know, try my hand at the tables. And you?"

Unable to hide my excitement, I grin and say, "Oh, we're here for the Wicked Wench's Convention."

His eyes widen at that. I laugh, telling him, "Don't worry, I'm not a stripper or anything. It's a convention and book signing for romance novelists and book bloggers. I'm a blogger so I'm here with my blog team. We're also here to meet one of the authors we sort of help promote. She's giving a private party tomorrow night, so we finally get to meet her face-to-face."

While I'm talking, he starts acting like I have the plague, and with my last announcement, he nods and then says, "Well, have fun then." And just like that, he's gone.

I have no idea what I've said to discourage him so, but he disappears like nothing I've ever seen before. I cup my hand over my mouth just to make sure I don't have skunk breath. I think that maybe he's gotten a whiff of something bad and has decided to get the hell outta Dodge. However, my breath smells like nothing more than lemon drop shooters. Not bad considering I've eaten spaghetti, too.

Kat pushes her way back over and wants to know the scoop. And well, dammit, there really isn't any. I can't help feeling more than a little disappointed. I've never run off a man so fast in my life!

"What do you think I did?" I ask, confused over his odd departure.

"Maybe it's not you. Maybe his bowels started acting up."

"Kat! Be serious!"

"I am. Why would he run off so fast if it weren't something embarrassing like that?"

Well, she did make a good point. Maybe he's eaten some beans for dinner and he needed to save us all.

In any event, I am extremely disappointed, and even though I'm not short on dance partners for the rest of the night, my mind stays occupied with green eyes and a mouth that promises sinful treats.

In the morning, it's a mad rush for the shower because we all want to sleep in as late as we can. The conference begins at seven-thirty with breakfast and an opening session with none other than our favorite author, R.T. Sinclair. We are all about to fall over ourselves in anticipation over tonight's Meet and Greet party with her.

I'm not sure any of us believe we're actually going to get face time with her, but that's what the invitation said, so we're going with it.

It's now seven-fifteen and we're beating a path to the conference as the August heat of Las Vegas has us all looking like we just climbed out of a swimming pool.

"Why the fuck did I take a shower? Somebody tell me why I bothered to take a fucking shower. Look at my shirt. There ain't a dry spot on it," Amanda spouts out.

Poor Andrea is red-faced and looks like she's about to have heat stroke. She's from London where it never gets this hot. At least the rest of us come from the south where the summers are steamy. Granted, this takes it to an unprecedented level, but still, my sympathy is with Andrea.

"Andrea, are you okay?"

"I will be once we get in the air conditioning again." Her voice is so breathy and weak that I worry.

"Almost there," Mandy promises.

I look at my thin cotton t-shirt in dismay. It's completely see through. "Oh no!" I exclaim. "I look like I'm entering a wet t-shirt contest."

"Oh crap!" Mandy yells. "Me, too."

I look at her and sure enough, she's in the same boat as I am.

"We all do, dammit. Fuck Vegas," Amanda curses the town as she walks more determinedly.

"I don't give a bloody damn right now. I just need some ice," Andrea cries.

Who knew that five minutes of walking at seven-fifteen in the morning could turn five perky women into five dripping, angry, whining bitches?

We walk inside the convention center and the AC smacks us like a freezer. In minutes, we're all shivering because our clothing and hair are soaked. We look at each other and shake our heads.

Kat looks down at her chest. "Don't say it. Just don't." She's referring to our chests. We all have our brights on.

"Aw fuck," Amanda and I say simultaneously. As a team, we all enter the large room with our arms crossed over our chests.

"How are we going to carry our coffee and croissants?" Mandy asks as she shakes from the cold.

"I'm not eating," Andrea replies.

"Neither am I," I agree. "Let's just grab a seat. Maybe when we dry off, things will flatten back out."

We find seats as close to the front as possible, which is about a third of the way back, and plop our wet and now frosty butts down. I want to huddle close to both my neighbors as I shiver, but of course, I don't.

"Bloody hell, I'm freezing," Andrea mutters.

"I know, right?" Kat answers as she scans the room, taking in the faces of the other guests.

Hopping to my feet, I announce, "Headlights be damned. I'm going for some coffee. Can I get y'all some?" Four sets of greedy eyes look at me, begging for some java. "Okay, I'll do my best."

I hurry to the coffee stand and quickly make five cups. Making sure to put the lids on tightly, I stack them up and slowly head back to the room. Not paying attention to where I'm going because I'm juggling five towers of java, I do the unthinkable and bash into someone.

As I stumble, the cups tip against me and coffee starts to dribble out of the openings and then they go all topsy-turvy on me. I watch in horror as the catastrophe unfolds before my eyes.

The lids fly off and then I'm screeching as the scorching fluid hits my skin. My hands let the rest of the cups loose and fly to my chest as I attempt to stop the burning.

"Shit," I hear and then someone is dragging me to the bathroom and putting cold towels on me. I'm not paying attention to anything except the stinging of my skin. The cold water begins to ease the pain. I wave my hands in front of me and then get a good look at the damage. My white t-shirt is now caramel colored and the V of my chest is bright pink.

"Does it still burn?"

Oh no! That accent. I'd recognize it anywhere. I lift my head and lock onto Green Eyes himself.

Shit, shit, double shit.

"We really have to stop meeting like this," he says, trying to inject a bit of humor into the situation. The door bursts open then and in walks a man. He looks at me then at Green Eyes then at the urinal, not quite sure what to do.

Making it easy on the man, I make that decision for him. "We were just leaving." Green Eyes grabs another wad of towels and dampens them before we leave.

"Well, just another day in paradise for Fallon," I sigh.

"Fallon?"

"Me. I'm Fallon. Remember? Last night?"

"Right. Well then, Fallon, are you okay?"

I glance at my chest. It's angry red, like I've spent the day in the sun. "I think it'll be fine. Just a minor thing, like a sunburn. You're Ryland, right?"

"Yes, Ryland. That's me. You remember?"

Like I could forget?

"Uh-huh. So, what are you doing here?" I try to divert my attention away from the burning pain of my chest. It really is stinging now.

"I'm a freelance writer and I do some reporting for *Romance Times*. I'm going to do an article on the convention."

"Cool! Tell me; do you get to meet all the authors?"

He eyes me strangely. "No, not as many as you'd think."

"Well, that's a shame."

"So, how's your... er?" he asks as he makes a circular motion with his hand around his chest. I notice his eyes have drifted south.

"I should probably get some ice." I fan my hand to move the air across it.

"Maybe you should have a doctor look at it," he suggests.

The thought of that sends my brain into freak mode. I can see the bills mounting up. I can't afford any more debt and a trip to the hospital would add hundreds to my pile of "unpaids." This trip has maxed out my credit cards as it is and the last thing I need is an additional bill to add to it.

"No-no. I'm fine, really. My friends are waiting for their coffee, though, and then I need to go back to my hotel and change. Damn, I was really looking forward to this session, too. I *love* R.T. Sinclair."

"That a fact?"

"Oh God, yes! I've read everything she's written at least ten times. She's the best thing to hit the shelves. I wish she'd write faster."

The corners of his mouth turn up, making me wonder if he thinks I'm merely one of those goofy women that hides in the fantasy world of romance novels. I don't really care if he does because what does he know, right?

"She probably does, too."

"Why do you say that?"

"Well, I was thinking that she'd want to make her fans happy... you know, fans like yourself."

"Oh." I brighten. He has a great point, one I have never thought of before. "Well, I better go and fetch that coffee before they think I ran off somewhere. Thanks for saving me."

He nods and then I head off to the coffee station.

When I get back to the girls, they look at me in alarm. I can tell my chest must look like a tomato by their expressions. Kat immediately digs in her bag for some unnamed ointment and tells me to smear it all over the burn. It has become quite painful, so I don't bother to argue. Then she hands me some ibuprofen.

"Thanks, Mama Hen. I'm gonna head back to change."

They all say, "But you'll miss R.T.'s opening speech. She's supposed to give clues about the award finalists."

"I know." I hang my head. "But look at me."

"Go after. I'll go with you," Amanda volunteers. I agree and settle in to wait on R.T.

When R.T. concludes her talk, I'm so happy I stayed to hear it. She gives us a little insight about the awards night and also about what's coming next for her. What's even better than that, though, is she's one of the most

27

engaging speakers I've ever heard. It's just an additional confirmation of why I'm such a huge fan of hers.

That night, we're eager to meet our favorite author, so we head over to the Bellagio—the fanciest hotel in Vegas. She's set up a room there for her Meet and Greet.

We marvel at the beauty of the place when we walk in the lobby. The fountains outside were a show themselves, but the flowers and artwork in this place are a far cry from the Space Nugget.

We're all gazing at everything with our mouths hanging open when Amanda says, "What do you reckon a night in this joint costs?"

I shrug. "I don't have a clue, but I bet it would make six monthly payments on my student loans. Or maybe even a year."

"I know, right?"

Kat nods to her left. "That painting over there would probably pay off my mortgage."

"At least you have a mortgage. And a job."

"You'll get both, Fallon. Hang in there," she says. "This is supposed to be your celebration, so don't get whiney on us."

"You're right." I don't want to get whiney, though damn, sometimes I can't help feeling sorry for myself, especially when I'm surrounded by all this luxury. "Hey, maybe I need to hang out here with the rich folk."

Amanda doesn't hold back. "Now you're talking."

We figure out where we're supposed to be and head that way. I'm a bit nervous about meeting the famous R.T. Sinclair, but I squelch the feeling and think about the excitement of getting her autograph.

We get off the elevator and find ourselves in front of some fancy double doors. We all look at each other.

Mandy acknowledges what we all are thinking, "I think I underdressed."

"It's too late to worry about that now," I say before banging on the door. It's opened by an attractive woman, maybe in her forties, who asks us to identify ourselves. We tell her who we are and then she gives us a huge smile and welcome.

And then our jaws hit the floor. This room is loaded... and I mean *loaded* with champagne, food and all sorts of alcoholic beverages. We just hit pay dirt. I grin.

A man walks up to us, wanting to know what we want. I'm pretty sure tequila shooters aren't appropriate, so I order a cosmopolitan. The others follow suit. Then we walk around and look at all the opulence surrounding us.

R.T.'s books are everywhere. I am in a frenzy, grabbing and opening and looking and touching. I hear a gurgle of laughter, and turn around, having one of those embarrassing fangirl moments. I squeal. Outrageously loud. I promised... I even pinky swore I wouldn't do it, but damn, I couldn't stop it from rushing out of my mouth. As soon as it does, my hand clamps over my lips and I mumble how sorry I am.

R.T. laughs again, and in her amazing British accent says, "Don't ever be sorry for that. I love my fans." And then, *oh my gosh*, she hugs me! Then, I do something even worse than the squeal. As she's hugging me, I start jumping up and down.

I finally catch myself and look at my girls. They are all giving me the I'm-going-to-shoot-you-dead eye. Oh damn. I can't help it. They're going to kill me later.

"I'm so sorry, but you're my most favorite author ever, and I'm just, well, you rock, R.T.! And that was an amazing speech you gave this morning."

After that embarrassing fiasco we all introduce ourselves.

"Well, thank you, Fallon. And I'm so glad you could come to the party, girls. I've wanted to meet you for so long now and I owe you so much. So before everyone else gets here, I want to give you some things."

She heads over to the other room, motioning for us to follow. On a table are these huge gift bags lined up with our names on them. We look at each other and smile as she passes them out to each of us. The bags are chock full of awesome things; signed hardbacks and photos, custom necklaces and bracelets that her characters wore, t-shirts, gift cards, mugs, dinner vouchers, and finally, an iPad Mini for each of us. We are speechless.

I finally say, "This is too much. Way too much."

"It's not nearly enough. You girls have done so much for me that I don't think I can ever repay you. Therefore no more talk of this. Let's simply have some fun."

So that's what we do. We eat and drink, entirely more than we should, and then after all the other guests leave, she asks if we want to go dancing.

"Hell, yeah," we all say.

A short time later, we all head over to Rock the Night Away in a limo. Once there, more drinks are ordered and we start in on the shooters. I lose track and spend most of the time on the dance floor. I'm already in love with Vegas. And what's not to love? Yeah, it's a desert here, but the damn place is raining with men. Men offer to buy me drinks and hit me up for dances constantly.

As the night progresses, I should be surprised to see Ryland there, but I'm not, when I look to see him next to me on the dance floor.

"Are you stalking me?"

He laughs. "I was going to ask the same of you."

We dance some more until a slow song comes on and I start to leave the floor.

"Where are you going?"

I turn and stare as he pulls me roughly against him. My body heats as flames fan across my skin.

"How's your burn?" His voice is next to my ear and I can feel his breath on my neck. Goosebumps prick my skin everywhere, a contradiction to the heat that continues to burn me. His arm has me hooked around the waist and I'm held snugly against him. His jeans rub against my thighs, making me heat up in places I'm not used to being heated in.

"M-my burn?" I'm confused at first; my mind is focused on another part of my body right now.

"The coffee today. You burned yourself."

"Oh, yeah. It's fine. Still stings a bit. Thanks for asking."

He nods while his fingers are laced with mine and his thumb is rubbing a circle on my first knuckle.

"You look lovely tonight, Fallon."

"Thanks. So do you."

He brings my hand to his mouth and leaves a kiss on it, right as the song ends. He doesn't release me as a quick-paced song with a driving beat comes on and we become surrounded by dozens of dancers.

Those eyes of his are so green that, even in the dark of the club, I can see gold streaks in them. They're compelling eyes. And they're staring right into mine. I don't dare blink. I don't want to miss a second of them. We're swaying to the hard beat with his arm defining our rhythm while his mouth is moving incrementally closer to mine. I can feel his breath on my lips. I want to feel his lips on my tongue. I want to know his taste. Our noses are touching, and finally, when our lips are about to meet, he releases me and steps back.

He raises my hand to his mouth, presses a kiss to it and says, "Thank you, Fallon, for the lovely dance." Then he backs off the floor, leaving me gaping at the empty space like a fool, feeling the distinct loss of his warm body against mine.

I'm in the crush of the crowd, so no one seems to notice except for my scorched body. I inhale, trying to puzzle this whole thing out and lower my heart rate at the same time. I decide I must have bad breath and make a mental note of changing my toothpaste and picking up some mouthwash as well as gum the next day. Why else would he leave so abruptly? Unless he realized, that up close, he wasn't attracted to me after all. Numbly, I push my way off the dance floor in search of another drink.

When I reach the bar, I spy my girls laughing and hanging out with R.T. They finally notice my crestfallen face.

"What's up with you?"

"Just tired." Now all I can think of is going home. "Would you all mind if I took off?"

"As in go home?" Mandy eyes me suspiciously.

"Yeah."

"You okay?" Amanda asks.

"Uh-huh."

R.T. is staring at me. She appears to be assessing me. In her cute British accent, she says, "Come on, Fallon. I'll get you home now."

"No, I don't want to spoil your evening."

"Well, darling, I won't have you leaving by yourself." She turns to the girls and hands them a wad of bills. "This should cover your cab ride home." Then her arm comes around me and out we go. The limo pulls up and she ushers me inside.

"I'm sorry. I didn't mean to cut your night short."

"No worries. You looked like you'd seen a ghost back there. What happened?"

"Oh, it was nothing. Just a dance."

"With a certain someone?"

I look at my sparkly toenails and nod.

"Well, it seems it was more than just a dance."

I groan. "I thought it was going to be, but then all of a sudden, he leaves me standing there. I think I have halitosis or something. That was the second time he did that to me. He's giving me a severe case of whiplash."

"Really? The same bloke?"

"Yeah. I'm hitting the store tomorrow for some mouthwash."

"Fallon, do you really think it was your breath?"

"It was either that or up close he thought I was ugly."

R.T. howls with laughter. "Now that's a good one. You? Ugly? You're about as ugly as a puppy."

I take a good look at R.T. and smile. She's gorgeous. I mean truly perfect. Blue eyes that could swallow you whole and blond hair that's soft and shiny. I wonder if she's ever had to worry about a stupid thing like losing her virginity.

"Well, coming from you, I take that as a compliment."

She laughs. "Why? Don't you think you're pretty?"

"I'm decent enough, I suppose. And I don't go around worrying about my looks, if that's what you're wondering. But I also know I'm certainly not on your level."

"Why is it that we women find it so hard to see what's right about ourselves?"

"Oh no! Not you? You're perfect."

"Ha! That's what you think. Under this mask of artfully applied makeup, there are many imperfections, my friend. I guess we all have our scars to bear."

"You can say that again." We arrive at the Space Nugget about that time. "Thanks so much for a fun night."

R.T. scrunches her brows for a second. "Are you staying until Sunday then?"

"Well, yes. Tomorrow night after the closing ceremony, we want to party it up. What about you?"

"Same here. Care if I tag along?"

"Seriously?" I can't believe R.T. wants to hang with us!

"Yeah. You Yanks are a blast."

"Well, we're not all Yanks. We have Andrea."

"Right. And she's a blast, too! Let's hit the clubs after the closing ceremony tomorrow. I hear they're going to have a Hot Man Abs showing for us."

"Ooooh! I'm so on board with that."

"Catch you tomorrow, then."

FOUR

RYLAND – THOMAS

Everywhere I go, she's there. I should've expected it. As a blogger, and one who loves my books and supports me like crazy, I should've known she'd be everywhere that Tilly was. At the Meet and Greet I had to hide the entire time. Thank God, Tilly finally corralled them all and left. I figured they'd go home and then Tilly and I would have some drinks at the club. When I saw Fallon standing there, I was helpless to do anything other than grab her and dance.

The smart thing to do would be to stay away from her. It's the only way I'll be able to keep my real identity hidden, but when I'm around her, I lose my bloody common sense. I don't *want* to get close to her; I haven't wanted to get close to any woman since Iris. Being close to one, especially one as gorgeous as she is, can only spell trouble for her and me. Besides that, I find I'm out of sorts when I'm around her. She has a way of jumbling up everything in my head.

So now, I'm positive she must think I have some mental disorder. Every time I'm near her, after a few minutes, I haul ass. No question, the gorgeous girl addles the hell out of me. But why wouldn't she? She's everything I've never dreamed of. A tall, redheaded American with a southern accent. I always thought, if I ever pulled my head out of my arse long enough to actually go after a girl, I'd end up with a blond Iris-look-alike. But this one with her gray eyes and full lips I want to lick and suck until I hear her moan… well, damn… this writer here is suddenly at a loss for words.

This potential complication is one I must avoid. I can see myself falling head first into those gray eyes and never climbing back out. And that damn body of hers. When I close my eyes I can imagine the way her skin would feel beneath my fingers and it traps the damn air in my chest. Why the bloody hell does she have to show up here, and looking like that no less? I would pay her to let me slide my thumbs across those nipples of hers. Or better yet, mold my hands around the perfect cheeks of her arse.

Hell, I need to go home and take a cold shower. That girl has me way too jacked up for my own good. I feel like writing erotica instead of a romance novel right now. It would probably be a best seller, too, if I kept her on my mind the whole time.

Since the temps had dropped somewhat, I decide I'd rather walk the few blocks to the hotel versus taking a cab. Maybe it'll help calm my dick down and clear my head. As I enter the lobby, my phone vibrates and I see it's Tilly.

"Why did you abandon Fallon?" Her voice is harsh with disapproval.

She knows. I didn't realize old hawk eyes had been watching.

"Tilly, doesn't anything I do get past you?"

"Nothing. Answer me, Ryland Thomas."

"Bloody hell, I didn't abandon her. I simply left after the song ended."

"Well, she thinks she has bad breath."

"What?" Then I laugh as I think about it. It really does make perfect sense.

"So you have to apologize to her."

"For what? Making her think she has bad breath. It's funny, Tills. Come on."

"It's not. She's a lovely girl with hurt feelings."

"Because she thinks that I think her breath stinks when it doesn't? That's rubbish." It's a wonder I ever sold any books. The mechanics of a woman's mind escapes me, so how the hell do I ever write romance?

"No it isn't. What if someone told you your teeth were wonky? Wouldn't that hurt your feelings?"

"No. I don't care what my teeth look like!"

"Bollocks! You do care. You're always flossing and brushing. I've seen those bleaching whatchamacallits in your bathroom, too."

Oh God. I groan. "Okay, so I care about my teeth. But I don't care if *others* think they look bad."

"Then, why do you bleach them?"

"Come on, Tills. This is crazy. Why are we discussing my dental care?"

"If you don't tell that poor thing you're sorry, I'm going home tomorrow morning."

"You can't do that. You're up for an award tomorrow night. What if you win?"

"It's not me, you bloody fool! It's you and you'll just have to accept it, like you should've been doing now for the past three years."

I harrumph and scowl at my phone. I can't possibly reveal the true identity of R.T. Sinclair and risk everything I've worked so hard for over the last three years.

"Okay. You win. I'll find her tomorrow and apologize."

"That's not enough. You'll take her out tomorrow night and act the perfect date, too."

"Seriously?"

"Absolutely. And if you run off with your tail tucked between your legs, I'm done with this whole charade of yours."

She isn't kidding. I know Tilly as well as I know myself. We're two peas in that stupid, rotten pod. "Damn you, Tills. Your fucking chain is squeezing the damn life outta me. Loosen it up some."

"Not until I see some humanity back in you."

Tilly is magnificent in her acceptance speech. She nails it once again. I have to hand it to her, she's come a long way since the first one of these conventions we attended three years ago. Her poise, her calm in front of the audience and the way they hang on her every word has even me convinced she penned those novels.

Thinking back to the first one we attended with Sam on hand to guide us through the steps, I laugh to myself. We were both so damn green. Tilly wanted to know if she should wear a disguise, and Sam and I laughed because I was the one whose identity needed to be kept a secret.

Tilly was so scared and nervous; ever since then I've promised her I will always be by her side for these events.

As applause breaks out again, she blows kisses to the crowd then leaves the podium. She catches my eye and we head towards the exit.

"You'd better meet us there," she eyes me.

"Um, what do you mean?"

"I'm bringing all the girls with me."

"Shit, Tills. How's this gonna work?"

"You'll stumble into her and then dote on her all night long, just like you promised."

I huff, but head over to said meeting place.

This is not my kind of scene. As I wait at the bar for a drink, at least three women approach me and ask if I'd like some company. By the time the third one asks, I actually snap at her. I know I'm being an arsehole, but whatever. I finally get my whiskey, neat, and let the amber fluid ease the tension in me.

My eyes scan the room and there they are, walking in the door. Damn, I can't stop looking at her, either. The thing about Fallon is, most redheads have ghostly pale skin. Not her. Her dark auburn hair is paired with bronzed skin with barely a freckle in sight, and it only makes me want to run my palms all over that delicious flesh of hers. She's wearing a gold halter-top that exposes entirely too much skin. Then there's her skirt. Well, damn it all, her legs run all the way to her neck. Jesus, I need some privacy to go and adjust myself.

As I stare at her, her head swings my way and those smoky eyes of hers lock onto mine. When her lips part, there's only one thing I want to do and that's not possible in a public place. What the hell is wrong with me? I haven't had feelings like this since Iris. Well, to be honest, Iris never evoked a response like this out of me. This girl has me charged.

She drops her head and one of the other girls says something to her, grabbing her attention. Tilly is scanning the crowd for me so I decide to text her so she doesn't spend all night rubbernecking the joint.

Me: *I'm at the bar, straight ahead. I've already made eye contact with her. Getting ready to make my move.*

T: *Be nice.*

Me: *I will. Promise.*

I throw back the rest of my whiskey, knowing I'll need it, and order another. Then I head her way.

When I make it to where she's standing, I lean over her back and whisper in her ear, "You look lovely this evening."

She turns and says, "You know, you're really a weird guy. I think it best if you just leave."

My eyes widen because, clearly, this isn't what I've been expecting at all. Then I flash her a smile. "I know you must think that, but I have my reasons."

"Like what?"

Now I'm stuck. What do I tell her without making her look like a fool? "I wasn't feeling well."

"Seems to me you don't ever feel well."

"Yeah, I've had some, er, issues since I got to Vegas." Okay, it's lame, but whatever.

"Oh really? What kind of issues?"

Bloody hell! What do I tell her now? "Yeah, I've had some weird kind of stomach thing going on. Kind of embarrassing actually."

She eyes me as she cocks her head. "Uh-huh. Well, Ryland, I hope you get to feeling better soon. Maybe you ought to lay off the whiskey." Then she turns away.

Talk about busting my chops. She has moxie, that's all I can say.

"Yeah, you're probably right. But if I do that, then I lose any chance of running into you."

Her head whips around and her eyes land on mine. She clearly hasn't expected that response. Now she's really inspecting me, assessing me. Those damn eyes of hers dig into me, and I swear to God they're reading my bloody mind. I know in thirty seconds, she's going to know every single secret I've ever had; things Tilly doesn't even know.

"May I buy you a drink while you continue to mentally examine me?" By this time, her friends, courtesy of Tilly, have moved away.

Her eyes narrow, but then she nods. "Yeah, okay."

Linking my hand with hers, I guide her to the bar where she orders a tequila shooter and I laugh. "You don't waste time getting right down to it, do you?"

"Nope. This is my last night here so it's party time for me."

"I see."

She throws her shot back like a pro, but her grimace shows me she's a novice. I bite my lip.

"Another, or something else?"

"One more and then I'll take a vodka and soda." I get her what she wants and she smiles.

"So, Fallon, where's home?"

"Spartanburg, South Carolina."

"And where exactly is Spartanburg, South Carolina?"

"It's in the upstate of South Carolina between Charlotte and Atlanta."

"I see. Sounds lovely."

"Oh, it is."

"Is your family there as well, then?"

Her eyes darken and her smile fades. "Nope. Just me." She tries to act nonchalantly, but there's a bit more to this. My brain tells me I shouldn't, yet my heart pushes me to dig a bit deeper. There's something about this girl that makes me want to learn more about her.

"So is your family elsewhere?"

"Yeah, my mom lives in Atlanta." That's all I get. She's so abrupt, I can tell she's not into her mom and doesn't want to talk about it, so I change the subject.

"What do you do in Spartanburg?"

"Boy, you're a nosy one, aren't you?"

"No, just curious about the gorgeous lady I'm talking to."

"Slick."

"Excuse me?" She surprises me with that.

"That's a slick line."

My voice deepens. "That's not a line, Fallon." And it isn't. I'm not one to use lines on girls. The fact is, I don't hang in bars and pick up women, at all. It's not really my scene. It actually makes me quite uncomfortable and it truly is the last thing I want to do.

Her lips part and I have to quash the urge to put mine on them. I tense with the effort it takes, briefly pondering these feelings. She's raw beauty standing in front of me and she's exquisite. There's nothing made up about her. All the pieces of her fit together like nothing I've ever seen; those deep red locks I'm itching to wrap around my fingers, silky smooth bronze skin that I could spend hours touching and kissing, eyes that shift from slate to silver when she's annoyed. It's her mouth, though—that luscious plump, sexy mouth—that's my nemesis and I know it will lead to my ruin. But I don't care... I'm past caring. I can feel the scars of my past launching from my chest as I stare at her. My heart is beating so loud in my ears that I'm sure she can hear it.

"So, are you going to tell me?" I'm so much more than curious about her now.

She clears her throat. "There's not much to tell."

How can that possibly be true? Someone that looks like her has to lead an exciting life.

"Oh, come now. You don't expect me to believe that? For starters, I bet you have a remarkable love life."

She laughs derisively. "Oh yeah. That's a good one."

Now I'm perplexed. "I find it hard to believe that you don't."

"I don't really give a damn what you believe." She crosses her arms.

"No, it's apparent you don't. So what do you do then? Your career?"

"You're really trying to make me feel good, aren't you?" she snorts.

She's difficult to figure out. "I'm just trying to get to know you."

"Maybe you should stop asking me questions then."

She's quite touchy. I've hit on a sore point, however I don't know why. "It's kind of hard to get to know someone if you don't ask them questions." Her expression softens a bit and then her shoulders slump.

"I'm sorry. I'm being a jerk. I guess I was put off by the way you left last night and then all of a sudden you show up all nice and everything. I don't usually act like this. The thing is, I don't have a job right now. Well a real job. I do have a temporary job waiting tables. I just graduated from college, so I'm looking for a permanent

43

one… you know, a career kind of job, but I'm not having much success."

Ah, she's a little out of joint because she needs a job. I get that. "I'm sure you'll find exactly what you're looking for."

Her brows shoot straight up. "I doubt that. That's not the way my luck runs, so I don't think it's gonna start happening now. I'm just hoping for something soon to help me start paying off my student loans."

"And your degree? What's it in?"

"Creative writing and English Lit."

"So what's your dream job?"

Her eyes soften and she smiles. I can't help smiling in return. That's how I want to see her look all the time.

"I would love to become a professional book reviewer or critic. I've always loved reading and writing. That's one reason I started blogging," she explains.

Now it all makes perfect sense. I get why her reviews are so well written and on point. She understands the process of the novel itself.

"I'm assuming you've sent your resumes to all the right places then?"

"Sure. But those jobs are close to impossible to come by. I'll have to earn one of those. In the meantime, I'll do anything to work my way into one. Still, it's tough getting a foot in the door."

My brain starts churning ideas. I have some connections through my agent and publisher, though I can't let on the real reason for *how* I have them. "I'm a freelancer, you know. Maybe I have some contacts that might be able to help. I can look into it. Are you able to relocate?"

"Yeah. Anywhere."

"Let me see what I can do."

"Why? Why would you do this for me?" She eyes me with suspicion.

That was a good question. I never do things like this for anyone. "Because I like you Fallon." That admission shocks the bloody hell out of me.

And it seems to shock the hell out of her, too. Her mouth opens and closes several times, as if she wants to say something, but then decides either she has nothing to say, or can't find the right words. In the end, she half smiles and nods.

"How about a dance?" I ask.

She agrees, so we walk out and move to the fast beat. Her arms are in the air and her eyes are closed. I'm more than glad because it means I can stare at her, uninterrupted. She's facing me at first while her chest and hips have me in a trance. Or so I think. When she spins and her back is towards me, I get the full view of her lovely arse and feel the wind gush out of my lungs.

Before I know what's happening, my arms reach for her hips and I pull her against me. My body is electrified by her touch. If she's shocked, I can't tell because she stays with me and we finish the song that way. I can't release her afterwards, though. I hold her tight against me with her ass rubbing my dick, and it's almost too much for me. I'm sure she can feel it through my jeans. It's wedged between the cheeks of her bum; I still can't force myself to release her, however.

My hand fans over her stomach and it's all I can do not to slide it beneath that flimsy shirt of hers. I can smell her perfume, all citrus and flowers, as I breathe her in. The groan I want to release is being held back with every ounce of control I have, but it's so bloody difficult.

The music changes again, this time to a slow song. I spin her in my arms until we face each other. Her eyes lift to mine and it's all there for me to see. However it's those parted lips that reel me in more than anything. The heat and want are pouring out of them. My head dips and I'm licking them before I'm even aware of it. Her breath takes mine in as she inhales. I know I am so screwed. The reality is, I knew it before, though I didn't admit it.

Fallon

Why does he always end up wherever I go? It's impossible to avoid him. Even though he's perfect and all, if he keeps pulling this crap of getting me all worked up and then running out on me, I'm going to lose it.

When he spins me around, those green eyes of his consume me and I want to tear his clothes off right then and there. I can feel the strength of his arms as he pulls me close. His touch sends fire scorching across my back that dives straight between my legs. My panties become damp. Shit, that's never happened to me before. I can't stop staring at his mouth, those full lips that I'm dying to suck, because I know any second now, he's gonna let me go and walk away. This time turns out different, though.

I'm suddenly tasting whiskey and peppermint as his tongue plunges into my mouth. And, hot damn, it's a heady combination. Not a bit of my mouth escapes untouched, either. I never knew a kiss until Ryland. My arms don't creep, they don't inch, they suddenly latch around his neck like it's a lifeline and I'm drowning. In a sense, I am. I'm immersed in him… in his lips and tongue as they move, suck and kiss me as though he means it. He's not playing nice; he's pulling out all stops here.

I clench him to me and my hands are in his hair, tangled in dark blond waves of thickness. When the music stops, I only know it because he breaks off the kiss. We're still wound together like twines of a rope as he whispers to me, "I think we need to move away from here. We've drawn a bit of attention to ourselves."

"Huh?" I couldn't care less, but I look up to see dozens of eyes on us.

He threads his fingers through mine and then we head to the back bar where he orders us up another round. I can't speak, I'm still blown away. He is so fuckable that he has me tied up in knots; my body on the verge of imploding with the sensations I'm experiencing. My vision is distorted by his extraordinary sexiness. Every nerve ending screams for his touch while the hollows of his cheeks beg for my lips to kiss them. His eyes are like magic the way they tunnel straight into my soul.

My heart thrums and electricity shoots through me as he plays with my wrist by skimming his fingers back and forth. I shiver. His hands could have me on my knees, begging, in seconds if he only knew.

"Cold?" He hands me my shot and my drink.

I shake my head and thank him.

"You're beautiful. Almost unbelievable."

His words are unexpected and I nearly choke on my shot.

"You're surprised."

It's not a question but a statement. I nod. My dorkiness emerges and I can't speak due to the burn of the tequila. What I want to do is scream, however then I'd really look like a moron.

"You okay, love? Your face is quite red."

"Yes." It comes out as a hiss and he starts laughing.

"Tequila a bit rough then?"

I nod and he laughs again as he pats my back.

"Whew," I'm finally able to get out. I down quite a bit of my vodka drink, beginning to feel the effects of the liquor as my buzz kicks in.

"So, where'd you learn to kiss like that?"

The question catches me off guard, so I throw it back. "From you."

Green eyes widen and then he lets loose a good belly laugh. "Then I must be a bloody good teacher."

"Or a good leader and I'm a good follower."

His eyes darken and those thin, golden striations brighten as he stares at me. My fists are clenched because it's taking that much restraint not to run my hands through his thick, wavy mop of hair, or to slide them under his shirt and feel his muscles tighten beneath my fingers.

His tongue swipes his lower lip and then he takes it between his upper and lower teeth. That's exactly what I want to do to it. He reaches for my glass and sets it down. The next thing I know, his hand is wrapped in my hair and I'm tasting him all over again. His arm hitches me against him and I can feel the hard length of his body from my knees to my chest.

It's my most fervent desire to be naked with this man. I would gladly hand my virginity on a platter to him right here, if he'd take it. So, to let him know I'm willing, I press myself into him and melt. I can feel the vibrations of his groan. Oh hell, didn't that just make me feel good now?

He pulls away and says, "Little Fallon, you're a dangerously sexy woman. I could do all sorts of dirty things to you right here."

I bite the corner of my lip. "Like what?"

His knee is nudging my legs apart; not very wide because I have a skirt on, but just enough for his leg to fit between. Then he hikes me against it and we're dry humping. I freaking moan. Out loud. I end up putting my face against his shirt to muffle the sound, though *hot damn*. His hand on my ass and his leg rubbing me in that spot are going to make me come if he doesn't stop.

"You have to stop, Ryland."

"Tell me you don't want me to," he breathes in my ear, "and then maybe I will."

"Oh God, I don't want you to," I say.

He stops, but his mouth claims mine again, like he is the sole owner of the damn thing. And I love it. When he releases me, my knuckles are white as my fingers are gouging into his arms.

"That's the kind of dirty I was referring to."

"Fuck." There are no other words that come to mind. When he then throws back his head and laughs, I want him to kiss me instead. I'm shaking with need.

He hands me my drink and I down it before I look at him, and over his shoulder, I see we're about to have company. Damn, just when things have heated up too. Talk about bad timing.

"There you are. We've been looking all over for you," Mandy says.

"Um, yeah. We've just been over here. Everyone this is Ryland." I hope I don't sound as breathy as I think I do.

Although, they're all looking at me and giving me the eye, so I guess I do. They all tell Ryland their names as I look on. R.T. merely stands there and grins like she has a huge secret. What's that all about?

After the introductions, Amanda orders another round of shooters. This time it's Redheaded Sluts for everyone. I know she's sending me a message, so I try my best to shoot daggers at her. I was never good at that, the nice in me overriding everything bad. We down those and I look up to see her hand me another one with a wink. This is going to be very bad indeed.

My eyes land on Ryland and he's wearing a lopsided grin. I'm not sure if it's natural or alcohol induced—on his part or mine—because, at this point, everything is lopsided to me. We all head to the dance floor where the music is blaring as we sing. I can't tell what song is playing, I only know we're singing. Lord help those that are next to us.

The rest of the night turns into an alternating round of dancing and doing shooters. When my lips go numb, I know I'm in serious trouble.

I look around, not seeing my girls, only two Rylands. I'm perfectly happy with that because, while one Ryland is gorgeous, two are stupendous. Unfortunately, I don't get to enjoy two Rylands too long. The last thing I remember is trying to decide which Ryland to dry hump on the dance floor before my lights go out.

The jackhammer wakes me up and I can't figure out where the noise is coming from. Wherever it is, I want it to stop, and fast. It's splitting my head right open and my brains are spilling out. I inch open my eyes and slam them back shut. The brightness kills me. It sends my stomach churning and the pain in my head worsens. I realize it's not a jackhammer after all. It's the throbbing my own skull is producing.

I moan and roll to my side. That tiny movement causes the most violent surge of nausea to roll over me that I've ever experienced in my life. I've got seconds to get to the toilet. I move to jump out of bed, but I only manage to get my legs tangled in the sheet. My face slams into the floor as I erupt like Mt. St. Helens. I'm not sure what hurts worse now… my throbbing head, my stinging face or my guts. I heave again and then I hear that British accent.

"Bloody fuck, not again. I thought we were over this by now. Thank God I moved the rug."

The rug? What's he talking about. Where am I? I give one last gurgle and heave again, and this time it's nothing more than saliva. I'm now in the dry heave stages of a hangover. I've never been this bad before. Truth is, I've never thrown up from drinking before, and the way I feel now, I don't ever want to do it again. I groan in agony. I seriously don't know which way to turn, I'm that miserable.

"Hang on, I'm getting a cloth."

Moments later, a cool cloth appears and is bathing my face. It feels nice. But when it leaves, I moan in its absence.

"Better now?"

I nod, careful to move my head slowly.

"Come on," he starts to untangle my legs, "let's get you in the bath."

When my legs are freed, he helps me stand before we walk towards the bathroom. I still have no idea where we are.

"Where am I?" I croak.

"In my hotel room at the Bellagio. You were quite plastered last night, love."

My thoughts shift back to the night before and my stomach seethes with the simple reminder of those redheaded sluts. Damn Amanda. Or maybe it was Mandy. Hell, I don't remember anymore, Fact is, I can't remember a freakin' thing.

Ryland leads me into the bathroom as I blindly follow him, not daring to open my eyes to the blazing light. If I do, I know I'll be facing a searing pain so severe that I'll scream. He picks me up and sits me on the counter, then strangely, I feel cool air wash over my skin. How odd.

I crack open one eye and squeal. I'm topless, my boobs playing show-and-tell and proud of it, too. My nipples are pointed and happy as can be. I swear I can hear them giggling. What the fuck?

He hears me squeak and nonchalantly says, "Sorry, love, but you puked all over your shirt. I had to get it off you and you were braless." Then he shrugs like he hasn't a care in the world. And why should he? He's not the one with his boobs laughing and joking with each other. I slap my hands over them, trying to quiet them down. "A little late for that, don't you think?"

I don't know what to think. All I know is that I'm half naked in Ryland's hotel room at the Bellagio. Holy schmoly. For a second, I wonder if I lost my virginity, but I realize that's a stupid thought because my panties are still on. Panties. I'm in my panties. Thong panties. Sitting on his counter. And that's all I have on. Holy fuck. Why me?

He notices my face. I'm sure it's scarlet, but it feels like it's going into a nuclear meltdown right about now.

"It's okay, Fallon. Everything's gonna be fine. Don't worry."

"Who's worried? I'm not worried. I'm embarrassed, Ryland. Look at me." Why the hell did I just say that? "No, don't! Don't look at me. That's why I'm embarrassed."

He grins and, damn, he's hot. "And you're really something to look at, Fallon. Even if you have thrown up all over the damn place and passed out cold on me. This magnificent view was worth that price."

My face is going to melt right off. I cover it with my hands.

He hands me a toothbrush covered in toothpaste and I start to brush away. He does the same. When we finish, he looks at me thoughtfully. "I need to get you something to eat and drink. You'll be sick if I don't."

"I've been sick. A lot, it seems."

"Right you are. But it'll be worse. You need something back in your stomach."

He picks up the phone in the bathroom—we are in the Bellagio after all—and orders room service. Coffee, orange juice, coke, ice water, toast and pancakes are on the way.

When I feel his fingers hook under the elastic in my panties, my eyes fly open.

"What are you doing?" I sound like a three-year-old on steroids.

"Relax. You've been sick. It's in your hair— everywhere, really. I was going to get you in the shower."

54

"Oh."

By this time I figure, what the hell, the man has seen most of my bits, all except for my hoo-hah. A shower won't reveal that unless I'm planning on doing some fancy acrobatic moves, which I'm not. So I let him strip me and carry me to the shower. I almost choke when he drops his britches and follows me inside.

"Fallon, you spewed all over me, too."

It's hard not to look at him in all his naked perfection. I read a lot. Way too much, probably. Every romance novel describes the guy as having chiseled this and cut that and the V to heaven. Well, Ryland is chiseled, cut and his V goes straight to a mouth-watering hard-on that, even in my hung-over state, has me wet between my legs in zero point two seconds.

Before I even know what I'm doing, my hand closes around him and I say, "Ahh," just like you do in the doctor's office. By now, I'm positive he thinks I'm a nutcase. But what the hell, I'm leaving today, so I may as well go for it. My eyes search his out and his green ones connect with mine.

"Fallon," is all he says before his tongue is in me. The soap is smoothed all over me and I do the same to him, making sure I spend extra time on his dick because it's so amazing. It's the first time I've ever touched one and I'm mentally kicking myself for waiting this long. "Bloody hell, Fallon." He pulls my hand off him. "Darlin', you have to give me a second." His chest heaves as he struggles to gain back his breath.

Then his eyes narrow and he flattens one hand against my stomach, pushing me against the marble wall. My butt makes a slapping sound, but I don't care. I'm only concerned with what his mouth is going to do. When he drops to his knees and buries his mouth against me, I cry out as this is a whole new thing for me. And praise to all hot mouths!

With one hand, he spreads me apart while the other is on my ass and his tongue is playing with my clit like it's never been played with before. Teasing and then sucking it, he goes round and round, back and forth, until I explode into an orgasm of epic magnitude. Holy wow! Ryland takes me on a magic tongue ride and I want it to last forever.

He kisses his way back up to my mouth. I can taste myself on him.

"Christ, you're amazing. Tell me you like the way you taste on my tongue."

"Yeah. I do." I'm surprised by that, too.

It makes me want him more. Like now. I grab his dick again, but he brushes my hand away. Now his head dips down and starts having sexy time with my nipples. I thought the meltdown I just had when I came was fabulous, then he introduces me to something totally different, although equally as erotic. My nipples are as hard as diamonds and I'm scorched as desire bursts through me like a raging inferno. My voice catches in the back of my throat as a guttural sound emerges.

"I want you, Fallon. Can we...?" he asks.

So this is finally it. "Yes."

"Don't move."

He leaves and then comes back, rolling on a condom. We crash together in a fiery kiss as he walks me up against the wall again. He takes my hand and slowly raises it above my head as he entwines his fingers with mine. Then he tugs my thigh up and brings it around his hip.

56

"You're beautiful, love, all wet like this. That mouth of yours could make men move mountains."

He kisses me again and then I feel him inching into me. I tense for a second, but his mouth takes my mind off it as his tongue takes over. And suddenly he thrusts into me and I yelp, "Ow, ow, ow!"

He immediately stills. "You're a virgin?" His breathing is erratic.

I nod. The pain is easing now. I squirm my hips around, wanting him to continue, but he doesn't. His eyes drill into mine, making me uncomfortable.

"Why didn't you tell me?" His tone is terse. "Warn me at least?"

He's upset. I didn't expect this reaction. "I didn't think it was a big deal." Our moment is slipping away.

"Bollocks! If it weren't a big deal, you still wouldn't have been one." Point well made, Ryland.

He starts to back out of the shower and I say, "Wait. Don't go."

He stops and looks at me for a second and then turns and walks away.

I watch him leave as my stomach feels like someone put a blender in it. This time it's not because of my hangover, though.

The water runs down me as I stand there, rinsing the last bit of suds away. So much for my precious virginity. A bitter laugh escapes from me before I clamp my mouth shut, cutting it off. His reaction is tearing into me and I honestly don't get it. Confusion crowds my mind. I'm lost in the flood of it. How should I handle this? Should I apologize? Did I actually do something wrong? Losing one's virginity didn't seem like such a dramatic thing before all of this. At least, I'd never heard any of my friends describe any kind of reaction like this.

I lean against the same wall that, only minutes ago, was the hottest place I'd ever been. Now I'm shivering even though the water that pours over me is burning hot. What I'd like to do is stay right here and hide forever, but I know that's not possible. So I open the shower door and scan the room for a towel, but I don't see any. The rack and the counter are nothing except empty spaces. Then in the bathtub I spy a pile of them, but they're all dirty. He must've used them on me last night.

Leaving me no choice other than to walk around naked, I stiffen my spine and head out the door. When I enter the room, he turns and looks at me. I try not to flinch, however his eyes are so penetrating that I feel myself unraveling, so I cross my arms over my chest. I wish I could simply disappear.

"Um, there weren't any towels and I don't know where my clothes are." My voice catches in my throat. The last thing I want to do is cry, so I swallow the threat of tears.

He hands me a robe and says, "You soiled your clothes to the point that they're ruined. I'm sorry. Can I go back to your hotel and pick up some things for you?" Clearly, that's the last thing he needs to do.

"Uh, what time is it?" I remember my flight is at one.

After a quick glance at his watch, he says, "It's eleven."

"What? Eleven? My flight's at one!"

"You're going to need to call the airlines and change it. You'll never make it."

I plop on the bed, my head in my hands. "Do you know where my purse is?"

"Purse? You didn't have a purse."

My head pops up so fast it spins. "What do you mean I didn't have a purse? I did have a purse. It was a little gold clutch that I could wear across my body. I had it on last night."

"No, you didn't. It wasn't on when you got sick. I would've remembered that."

"Oh, shit, shit, shit." I'm on my feet now, frantic, wringing my hands. "Everything was in my purse… my wallet, credit cards, cash, driver's license, phone; my whole life. What am I gonna do?" I wail.

He wasn't concerned a few minutes ago, but he is now. "Okay, calm down and let's think. I'll call the club to see if anyone turned it in."

He made the call and the answer was a big no. "Can you call your friends?"

"I don't know their numbers. They were programmed in my phone." Now I'm in a full-blown panic. "I can't get on the plane! I don't have any ID!"

"Bloody fucking hell!" He storms out of the room and I stand there, not knowing where to turn. Then I think about Facebook.

"Ryland! Can I use your computer?" I yell.

"Why?"

"Facebook. I can send them all messages on Facebook and they'll answer because they all have the mobile version."

"Yeah. Give me a sec."

He boots his laptop up and opens up Facebook and then logs out. I get into my account and leave them all a SOS. Then I wait. About five minutes pass and I get a hit from Kat.

"Where the hell are you? We've been worried sick! You wouldn't answer your phone."

I give Kat the rundown, which she can't believe, and she tells me they don't have my purse. They're all headed to the airport and have checked out of the hotel already. They left my suitcase at the bell stand. She asks if I want her to come back, but I tell her no. She has to get home to her family and go back to her teaching job, so she can't deal with my issues right now.

I collapse back into the chair and then I sob. I'm stranded in Vegas with no money, no credit card, no phone and no ID. What the fuck am I going to do?

RYLAND - THOMAS

She crumbles to bits right in front of my eyes. She's in the biggest mess, if I've ever seen one. Feeling helpless isn't a good place to be. Especially since she spent the night puking all over the place and now her clothes are ruined. The poor girl is totally wrecked. I'm also sure that little sexcapade of ours didn't help, either.

"Look, why don't I give you something to wear and we can go to the club and look for your purse."

Those incredible eyes of hers lay into me. They're so filled with panic that I'm at a loss of what to do or say. "I don't want to be any more of an imposition. If you don't mind, I'd like to borrow some clothes, though, and I can just walk back to my hotel."

"And do what? Sit there?"

Her lovely lips form and O and then her face crumples.

"I'm sorry," I say as I rub my face. "At least let me help you look for your purse."

She finally nods. I rummage through my drawer and pull out a pair of jeans and a T-shirt. She thanks me and pulls the shirt over her head. The loss of that spectacular view causes a feeling of such deprivation that I almost ask her to take the damn thing back off. Next, she pulls on the jeans. They're huge. She rolls up the legs and turns down the waist, however it doesn't help much.

"Those aren't going to work. Why don't I run down to one of those boutiques in the lobby and buy you something?"

Her eyes widen and her head starts to shake. "Oh no! I could never let you do that. Besides, I have clothes in my suitcase. I only need to wear this to the hotel and then I'm good." As she bends down and puts on her sandals, there's a knock on the door. Room service.

"You need to get some food into you first. Then we can go."

"I'm pretty sure I can't eat right now."

"At least try."

She agrees and I tear into my breakfast while she picks at hers. When we're finished, we head down to the lobby. I watch as she struggles to keep my pants on, which causes me to let out a chuckle because she looks cute as hell, but she tosses me a nasty look.

"What? I can't help but think it's funny. And you look rather cute."

She must not agree because she ignores me. I hand the valet my ticket and we wait for my car. When it arrives, her eyes bug out. Growing up in England created a love for Aston Martins, so I always told myself, when the time was right, I would buy one. And that's what I did. I bought the V12 Vantage and it's quite dishy, if I say so myself.

The valet opens the door for her and she slides in, allowing herself to be hugged by the leather seats. "Nice ride."

"Thanks. So, where to?"

"The Space Nugget."

"The what?" I've never heard of that hotel.

"Take a left and it's about six blocks on the right," she says.

We get there and I can't hide how appalled I am. "You stayed *here*? For several nights?" The place is atrocious.

"Well, yeah." She sounds like there's nothing in the world wrong with this eyesore of a dump.

"Thanks for the ride. And for, um, taking care of me while I was sick. Yeah," she says as she gets out of the car.

"Wait, we need to check the bar for your purse."

"I can take it from here." Her stubbornness is poking its head out now.

"Fallon, please let me help you. You have no money, credit cards, nothing."

"I'll be fine. Really."

She gets out of the car and somehow ends up twisting her ankle to the point that the strap on her sandal snaps. "Ouch, oh hell," she yelps.

I leap out and run around to help her. Apparently, when her sandal broke, her foot slid out of the shoe and she stepped on a rather large piece of glass that's now stuck in her foot. Bugger. What'll happen to her next?

"Let me have a look at that. It may need medical attention."

"No! I don't have insurance, so I can't do that." Her voice is edged in panic.

"I'll pay for it," I huff, "but I think this needs to be sewn up."

"Naw, it'll be fine." Her hands are trembling and she's looks like a ghost.

"Fallon, this is a deep cut. The glass is stuck in your foot. I'm afraid to pull it out, it's in that deep. Christ, you're bloody stubborn."

She sinks back into the car, defeated.

"I'm sorry to be so harsh, but you're acting the fool. Now where's your luggage?"

"Kat said at the bell stand."

I nod and go inside. The Space Nugget is deplorable. At least it's clean, but how could they stay here? I see the bell stand and one bag next to it that's nothing except strips and strips of duct tape. "Does that bag belong to Fallon McKinley?"

"Yes, sir."

Handing him a twenty, I collect it and roll it to the car. We get back to the Bellagio and when we get to the room, I have the concierge send a doctor up.

Thirty minutes later, one arrives and confirms my fears. Fallon needs stitches in her foot. The glass went quite deep and she stares ahead, blankly, as I'm sure she's now trying to figure a way out of her quandary.

"Stay off that foot for the next three days. After that, if you don't see any bleeding, you can put some weight on it, but not a hundred percent. The stitches should come out in ten days." He then hands me a slip of paper with the name of a medical supply store on it so I can get crutches for her.

When he's gone, I ask her if she's thirsty and she breaks down and cries. She's hugging the pillow to her face. I walk over to her and pull it out of her hands then drag her into my arms to let her have a good cry. What will I do with her? I was leaving today.

"What am I gonna do?" She sniffs.

"Can you call your parents?"

Something passes over her with those words. Her eyes darken and she says, "Not unless your cell service reaches the afterlife."

Shit. "Oh, Fallon, I'm sorry. Both of them?" I only ask because I think of how strange a coincidence that would be.

"No, just my dad."

"What about your mum?"

A bitter laugh escapes from her. "I could be in the ICU somewhere and she'd tell me it was my problem and I need to figure it out on my own."

"Oh, come on, Fallon." It's difficult for me to believe any parent can be like that. "Just call her and tell her what's happened. She's bound to help."

Her jaw clamps shut and that little muscle in her cheek is going click, click, click. "Hand me your phone, please." Her eyes are rapid fire blinking, and I think she's doing her damnedest not to cry again.

I hand her the phone, she dials her mum and puts it on speaker. While she talks, I can hear her mum's voice on the other end saying exactly what Fallon had predicted. She's loud, abrasive and uncaring. I'm incredulous.

"Fallon, that's what you get for going to Vegas. You should've been more responsible in the first place and not

65

lost your pocketbook. I bet alcohol was involved, wasn't it?"

"Yes, ma'am," Fallon responds.

"How many times have I told you to be more careful? You obviously have paid no heed to my advice. So since you thought so little of what I've told you, you're on your own. You can figure out what to do. You're a resourceful girl, or at least that's what you keep telling me. Let's see how you manage this debacle."

She hangs up and then slaps my phone back in my palm. "Happy now?" she asks as her voice splinters and tears begin again.

I pull her into my arms, wondering if I'm comforting her or if she's comforting me. I'm so saddened by what just happened. How can a mother leave her daughter stranded like that? In Vegas of all places? What's wrong with people?

I take it upon myself to call the concierge and ask them for advice. They immediately put a call into the LVPD and I get a call back. I put Fallon on the line so she can describe her purse. At least now it's reported.

Her bag is delivered to the room while she's on the phone. Once she hangs up, I ask her if she'd like to change into something of her own.

"Honestly, right now, I'd just like to sit here for a minute. My head is spinning and I don't know where to turn. I'm paralyzed without my purse. How could I have lost it? Why did I have to get so damn drunk last night? Why did I come to Vegas?" Her fingers are knotted into her hair, as though she wants to yank it all out by the roots.

I don't know what makes me ask, but I simply find myself saying, "What happened to your dad?"

I regret it the second the words leave my lips. When those gray eyes of hers stab mine, I want to die. Her pain is so raw it pierces my heart. I walk to her and blanket her in my arms yet again. It takes me back to those days after I lost my own parents. I tell her it's okay, only I know that's not true and the words ring hollow in my ears.

"No, it won't ever be okay with him gone. He meant the world to me. He went to help his friend cut some trees down on a piece of land he owned. The chain saw tripped up and, well, it was pretty bad. They told me he died instantly. My parents were divorced and I lived with my dad. I was sixteen at the time. I had to move in with my mom after that and life didn't go so well then." That tells me things were bloody dreadful for her.

"Fallon, why don't you get comfy on the bed here. I'm gonna take a run to the club. Just to make sure they didn't miss anything when they checked. I'll comb over the place and then I'm gonna pick up those crutches for you. I'll be back in a sec."

She nods.

At the club, I find nothing. Not even in the bathroom. When I'm there, I call the LVPD and ask for the officer that called earlier. I leave him my name and number, just in case they find her stuff after I leave the hotel. I have to go home either today or tomorrow and I have a feeling I'm going to have a houseguest when I do.

Next I call Tilly to see if she can help. Now she's involved, which doesn't bode well for me. Fact is she's giddy over this whole thing. I head straight to her suite where she has that devilish look on her face that tells me she's up to no good.

"Tills, you hafta lay low so she doesn't see you. I've no idea how I'm gonna maintain my cover with all of this." She laughs at me. "It's not funny, dammit!"

"Is, too. It's the best thing that's happened to you since Iris pulled her shit on you."

The blood drains from my face. I hate it when she brings Iris up. It's more than Iris this time. And Tills senses it.

"What are you hiding Ryland Thomas?"

"Nothing!"

"Out with it. I can read you like those damn books you write."

"Nothing. She's just torn up."

Tilly's not going for it. "Uh-huh." Her eyes lay into me. She's always been able to see right through me. "You slept with her!"

Now my face is heating up. "I did not." Technically that is true, but at the same time, it isn't. "Well, I did sleep with her, yes, but she was knackered and passed out cold."

"Bollocks. You shagged her. I can see it in your eyes."

Fuck! How does she do that?

"Admit it."

"Okay, I sort of did," I say sheepishly.

"What the hell does that mean?"

"Tills, I'm not gonna give you the sordid details of everything I do," I huff.

"Out with it, Ryland Thomas."

She pesters me until I break and tell her everything. Well, not everything, though the basics, anyway.

Tilly punches me in the arm. "I can't believe you… you arse. No! You're a fucking arse! How could you do that?"

"What do you mean? I'm the one that got duped!"

"Aw, poor Ryland Thomas. Takes a shower with a lovely girl and things get steamy, so they decide to have sex, and when he finds out she's a virgin, he fucking walks out on her! How you write and ever sell any books I'll never know. What a douche-face! I can't believe I'm related to you. Oh, to think that evil virgin duped you. How awful of her, scheming wench that she was. I'm sure she does that all the time. Plays men like that."

Now, don't I just feel like a shit?

Tilly orders me to take Fallon home with me. That really is the only solution to all of this when I stop and think about it. I can offer her money, however that wouldn't go over well. She would look at it as payment; the ultimate insult. If I take her home, I can make something up to smooth her ruffled feathers. There's no way I can abandon her here without a quid to her name. Not only is it a ridiculous notion, it's dangerous. So I march back to my room to break the news to her and hope she's not going to throw something at me.

Fallon

When Ryland returns, I'm sitting on the bed, trying to figure out what to do while still praying he's found my purse.

"No purse?"

"'Fraid not. But I have a suggestion for you."

"What?"

"Come home with me, and before you say no, listen to what I have to say."

My good southern manners take over, so I nod. My guts are getting ripped up again and I'm only half-listening, trying to think about what to do.

"I can make some contacts to help you find a job and you can send some resumes out while you're at my place." It's lame, but I try to smile.

"I have a better idea. I stay here, call the South Carolina Department of Motor Vehicles and get a replacement driver's license so I can fly home."

"Not bad, but I have to leave today. I have work to do and deadlines to meet. You can call them tomorrow from my place to have your replacement sent there. Then you can call the airlines and tell them you're sick or injured and can't fly."

"But—" He doesn't let me finish.

"I'm going to play the decision maker here and I'll be quite blunt, too. You're up against a brick wall. You've nowhere to go. You have no money for a hotel. Or even food. I'm offering you an out. Take it, Fallon, 'cause I can't leave you here."

I drop my aching head in my hands and rub my throbbing temples. "I don't have much of a choice, do I?"

"Not the way I see it."

"When do we leave?"

"As soon as we can get packed up. I think you may want to change as well. But you need to cancel your credit card first."

He's right. The credit card needs to be canceled, though it is maxed out, so no one can really charge anything. Besides, I'm still wearing his jeans, sans panties, and his T-shirt, braless no less. I nod.

"May I use your phone?"

He hands it to me. "I'll give you a bit of privacy."

I laugh a bit maniacally. He glances at me. "A bit late for that, don'tcha think?" I retort.

He shrugs and walks into the next room anyway.

After I talk with the bank and take care of canceling my credit card, I have a new one sent to the address Ryland has given me. Next, I call the airlines and tell them my fiasco. Between my purse missing, and having to stitch up my foot, the attendant is very understanding. He does confirm, though, that I'll still be charged a fee for changing my flight. That's great… just more good news for Fallon.

71

Then I drop to the floor from the bed, since I wasn't supposed to put any weight on my stupid foot, and crawl to my lovely duct-taped bag. Grabbing some soft, stretchy yoga pants and a tank top, plus some underthings, I sit there and get dressed. When I tug off his jeans, I notice the crotch area is spattered with blood.

At first I'm confused because I didn't have my period. Then it hits me and I'm beyond appalled. After our brief interlude and my stellar loss of virginity, it never dawned on me that I would bleed. What classic Fallon fuck-uppery! I shouldn't be surprised because everything I do ends up either backfiring or humiliating me to death. I should be used to it by now, but this one really digs in deep.

Ryland returns and I must have been sitting on the floor like this for a while. I'm still holding his jeans in my hands, staring at the bloody crotch, naked from the waist down.

"Ready?" He looks at the bed and then sees me on the floor. "Sorry, I forgot you couldn't walk." He brings me the crutches and then notices that I'm still half naked. "Are you okay?"

"Peachy." I will *not* cry in front of him over this. But damn, my voice is so freakin' squeaky and high pitched that I sound like Minnie Mouse.

"What happened?" He pulls his jeans out of my hands and notices the blood. He doesn't say anything, but tosses them aside and hands me my panties. I put them on, followed by my yoga pants. "Up we go," he says as he picks me up. I'm grateful he doesn't mention the stained pants.

I should've saved that thought. "Fallon, don't be embarrassed about starting your period."

My breath rushes between my thinned lips. "It's not my period, Ryland. It was my fucking virginity."

"Oh." He stops.

"It's not a big deal. We should go."

As soon as those words are out there's a knock on the door, saving me from continuing that humiliating discussion. The bellman is there to transport our luggage down. My lovely and fashionable duct taped bag is perched right alongside his designer whatever. Can this get any worse?

I'm glad when we get to the car and Ryland disappears to check out. I don't even know where he lives, but at this point, what difference does it make?

On our way to wherever, we stop at a convenience store to stock up, as Ryland says.

"Where do you live?" I ask once we are back on the road.

"Lake Tahoe."

"How far away is that?"

"About seven and a half hours."

"Seven and a half hours?"

"Yeah, but this car is a smooth ride and the route I take has great scenery. You'll love it. Besides, if we get tired, we can stop for the night somewhere."

"Okay. It's not like I have anything else to do." I snort. Then it hits me. I'm supposed to be at work on Tuesday. "Oh no!"

"What is it?"

"My work. Back home. I wait tables at a small cafe. Zack is gonna fire me."

"Can you call him?"

"They're closed today. I'll have to call tomorrow. The shit show just keeps getting even better." I rub my eyes and temples for the thousandth time that day.

For the first time since he left me in the shower that morning, I feel a warmth flow from him as he turns to me and takes my hands. "Fallon, you're right. This has turned to shit for you, but I'm gonna help you straighten things out. Sometimes, things turn to shit for a reason. Maybe you came here to change the direction of your life. Who knows? But things will get better, I promise." He gives my hands a gentle squeeze before he releases them. Then he lays on the gas and the car comes to life as we speed down the highway. At that moment, it hits me. What happened to the dickhead from this morning?

"Thank you, Ryland, for helping me out of this jam. I'm not sure what I'd have done here without you."

My head bobs against the window and wakes me up. My mouth feels like the southbound end of a northbound skunk.

"Have a nice kip?"

"Huh?"

He laughs. "Nap. Kip. Same thing."

"Oh. I did. Thanks."

"Thought so. You were snoring like a champ."

Great. This guy really knows how to stroke my ego. "You really do know how to make a girl feel good about herself, don'tcha? Do you practice this or something?"

"Ouch."

My breath oozes out in a slow sigh of regret. "I'm sorry. I'm not usually this snarky. I… honestly, in certain

74

situations, I'm the one that usually let's people walk all over her, so I don't know what's gotten into me."

"Why do you do that?"

"Do what?"

"Let people walk all over you?"

Jeez, here we go. Lecture time. "I just do."

"No, there's a reason for it."

"I'm sure it has to do with my mom."

"Maybe you need to…"

Cutting him off with a tone that's both terse and exasperated, I say, "I *know* what I need to do. I need to tell her to stop trying to run my life, to treat me like an adult and to respect my feelings. I need to tell her that after my dad died I needed her more than ever, but she was never there and she left me, a sixteen-year-old, to deal with it by myself. I need to ask her why she tossed all of his precious belongings without thinking about asking me. There are a million things I need to tell her, but I won't ever do it because it would be the biggest waste of my time.

"She won't listen to me. She's selfish. No, she's worse than that. She's narcissistic. Do you wanna know what the last birthday gift she gave me was? It was a freakin' card. When I turned sixteen. Six years ago. Last year, she emailed me the day after and told me she was sorry she'd missed my birthday, but she had appointments all day. So maybe that's why I let people walk all over me. Because she's done it to me my whole life!" Whoa… where did that diarrhea of the mouth come from? I never discuss my mom with anyone. No one except my girls from the blog know about her.

His voice is soft when he responds. "I'm sorry, Fallon. I'm bloody sorry you have a mum like that."

"So am I, but I'm more sorry that my dad's not here. He would've been on the first plane to come out and help me if I'd called him. I wouldn't be a burden to you right now if he were still alive."

"You're not a burden."

"Now that's a lie, Ryland. You called me a liar earlier over the whole virginity thing. Well, I'm hitting you back on this."

He is silent for a moment with his lips clamped together and then he asks, "Why didn't you tell me? About being a virgin? The truth, Fallon?"

I shrug. "Because I wanted you so bad that my thoughts weren't on being a virgin at that time. They were on us and how... Does this really matter now?"

"Yeah, it does."

His passion surprises me. I take a good look at him now, staring openly. His hands are fisted around the steering wheel, knuckles almost popping through his skin.

"Why?" I whisper.

"Because it should've been a special moment for you. One where I was gentle with you, where I took my time and not up against a shower wall, thrusting into you like an animal."

"This is about you and not me, isn't it?"

He takes his eyes off the road for a second to look at me and then goes back to focus on driving. "No, it's about us and what happened. You don't get it, do you?"

"I'm not following," I answer because I am confused.

"This was all a big game to you, wasn't it?"

Now that sort of stings because it had started out that way, hadn't it? My silence gives him his answer.

"You were playing me, weren't you?"

76

"No! You're wrong. Everything that happened between us this morning in the shower was real, Ryland."

"What about before?"

"I barely remember the night before."

"How about before that?"

Inwardly, I groan. I can't tell him one of my Vegas trip goals was to lose my virginity. He won't go for that at all. How can I get around that?

He glances at me and asks, "Why was it that everywhere I went, you seemed to be there?"

Now, while it was odd, I have no clue. "Coincidence? I don't know. Why don't you tell me?"

"Uh-uh. I asked you first."

I gasp. "You think I was following you?"

"Well?"

I seethe. "If you think I'm some kind of a stalker chick, you're dead wrong. I've never chased, followed or even initiated a conversation with a man on that level. I'm uncomfortable flirting, if you want the truth." By now, my voice is almost at an all-out yell. "I'm twenty-two-years-old, and until this morning, I was a virgin for Pete's sake."

"Then I'm confused."

"Over what? That you turned me on and I wanted to have sex with you? What's so confusing about that?"

"That you would want your first time to be that way."

"Jesus, Ryland, you're acting like a girl."

Now that got his attention. He first sputters and then he gets pissed. "Oh, because I was concerned about how we went about it? That I wanted it to be more romantic for you?"

"Right. So you pull out and leave me alone, in the shower. Yeah, that was romantic all right."

His face turns so red I think it's going to ignite. Shit. Maybe I should've kept my mouth shut. What if he pulls over and dumps me out here in no man's land?

However he shocks me when he says, "You're right. That was a shitty thing to do to you and I'm sorry." I smile to myself until I hear him say, "I shoulda just fucked your eyeballs out and then left you standing there."

That stings so badly it feels nearly physical. I suck my breath in with the impact. "Of all the dirty things—" He doesn't let me finish.

"Seems to me, you're the dirty one, Fallon. What else do you want to play at here?"

With all the meanness I can muster, I say, "How 'bout you quit acting like a stupid shit and shut the hell up for a bit." My hand flies to my mouth, shocked that I just said that. I peek at him and he looks frozen in place. I hope he can drive safely like that.

I truly don't understand why this whole virginity thing is such a huge deal for him. Isn't it the girl that usually acts all hurt and everything? All I wanted to do was have fun, and when I met him, I thought it had become a little more than that. Yet, here he is, acting like an adolescent. I'm getting angrier by the minute.

"You certainly aren't acting like someone who's been stepped on her whole life. In fact, if I were a guessing bloke, I'd say *you* were the one who does the stepping. No damn wonder your mum treats you the way she does."

Now *that* was uncalled for. He's just pissed me off something fierce. Off come the boxing gloves 'cause I'm getting ready to go thermonuclear on this motherfucker. "Why you slimy, teasing cockblocker. You wanna know something? I thought you were the hottest thing these eyes have ever seen. And while you think slamming me against that shower wall wasn't romantic, in my book, it was hot as fuck. Yeah, you heard right. I wanted you to slam your dick into me like that. I wanted it bad and I was all about you that way. Did you ever stop to think about *that*?

"Why the hell do you think when you asked if we could do it, I said, 'yes?' Because I wanted it that way, you jerk-faced moron. It was hot, gritty, steamy sex. But what do you do? You pop my cherry and then get offended. What the hell is wrong with you? Are you from another planet? If I'm not all weepy about it, what gives you the right to be? It was my goddamn cherry and I had a right to do whatever I wanted with it. So stop whining about it already and shut the fuck up."

"Wait a bloody minute. You think simply because you waltz into my life, you can demand exactly how we have sex and how you lose your virginity. I have a say in this, too. It's my damn dick that's involved here."

If I don't get out of here soon, I'm going to cram that holier than thou dick of his somewhere the sun never shines.

"Stop the car! I can't deal with your idiocy anymore," I yell. This guy is a lunatic and what has me more concerned is that I'm riding in his car, alone; going to his home, alone. He is positively nuts.

"No!"

"Stop the fucking car or I swear to God I'm gonna jump out of here!"

"You wouldn't do such a thing."

I open the car door. Okay, that's not such a good idea as we're traveling at about seventy miles per hour. The door nearly wrenches my arm off. I can't hold onto it much longer as I keep screaming. He slams on the brakes and we come to a screeching halt.

I unbuckle my seat belt and jump out of the car. I forget about my stupid foot and tumble flat on my face, kissing the hot pavement. My palms break my fall, but I get road rash in the process and my chin takes a hit, too. I don't give a crap about that, though. I'm up and moving, trying to get away from Psycho-Ryland. This dude is infuriating and annoying as hell, and I can't deal with this right now.

I hear his footsteps behind me, and when I feel his hands on me, I start screaming, "Get your stupid hands off me!"

"Bloody hell. Stop yelling." His hands release me and I start moving again. He's right next to me asking, "Where are you going?"

I don't answer. I want to pretend he's not here. He's a vile creature. And to think that, only this morning, I was panting and moaning with his mouth on my hoo-hah. Holy hell! I shudder at the thought.

"You can't stay out here, Fallon. It's going to be dark in an hour and then what?" Somehow, his words penetrate my addled mind. What *will* I do? "And your foot; it's probably bleeding again. Come on. Get back in the car."

I stop and look at him square in the face. This whole interaction has hit me so hard I'm trembling. "I can't get back in that car with you. You freak the shit out of me. You're crazy. And you're mean. Plain old mean and nasty. And stupid. Yeah, you're stupid, too. And extra dumb." I'm yelling at him, panting.

His lips pinch together. He says nothing, though he does bob his head up and down one time. So we stand there, looking around like two idiots. I don't want to break the silence because I'm afraid of what our next confrontation will be like. Why does he make me say these crazy things? In fairness, he's not the only crazy one. I'm acting bat-shit crazy, too. I don't ever scream at people like this. I rub my neck, roll it on my shoulders and groan.

"So, ah, what do you suggest we do?"

I look at him. I honestly can't come up with a thing.

"I don't know," I mutter. One thing's for sure. My foot is bleeding. The pavement's melting. I'm hot and thirsty, too.

EIGHT

RYLAND - THOMAS

Why are women so damn hard to figure out? Now I've freaked her out. Like I'd ever harm a bloody fly. Me, the kid who brought all the wounded animals home and nursed them back to health. And now she's afraid I'll hurt her. If this situation weren't so damn bizarre, I'd laugh.

Finally, I persuade her to get back in the car, however she's so suspicious of every move I make, I want to laugh. "Fallon, I promise, I'm not going to hurt you."

She shakes her head. Her body is quivering like a trapped creature. It's difficult to distinguish whether it's from fear or anger, but I don't dare ask and risk her trying to bail out of the car on the open highway again. She's extremely pissed off at me. I wish Tilly could see this. On second thought, scratch that. She'd flay me alive for the way I spoke to her, particularly that comment about her mum. That was the lowest possible blow.

The cooler is in the back so I rifle through the ice and hand her a bottle of water while she keeps her eyes on me like I have a weapon and I'm going to stab her or something.

"Fallon, I'm not gonna hurt you. I swear it."

She grits out, "Okay, let's get this straight. I'm not afraid of you. I'm pissed off as hell. You are a first class, psycho assface. I'm sorry I came to Vegas. I'm sorry I lost my purse. I'm sorry for a lot of things. Most of all, I'm sorry I ever met you."

And that is it. She never says another word for the rest of the night, so I give up trying to engage her after several attempts. I figure it's better this way. At least we've stopped wounding each other with our spiteful words.

It's after midnight when I finally pull into my driveway. Fallon is asleep and I'm half tempted to let her sleep the night in the car. My conscience won't allow me to do that, yet it's a nice thought anyway. I walk inside and check out the guest room, just to make sure everything is in order before I carry her up. She never stirs, even when I tuck her into the cool sheets. For a few minutes, I stare at her and allow myself to imbibe in her astonishing beauty.

She's curled on her side with her glorious hair fanning out across the pillow. Unable to resist, I pick a lock of it up and rub it between my thumb and index finger, delighting in its silken texture. If only we could start over, I'd make her first time memorable and filled with gentleness and not pain. The sound of her voice screaming, "Ow," reverberates through my head. It chills me and makes me sick to my stomach that I caused her pain.

Why can't she see my side of things? If only I could explain to her the amount of bloody self-control it took to pull out of her. Christ, the way she felt. It was like a slice of paradise I've never known.

Eventually, I back out of the room and close the door.

The morning comes all too soon. When I hear a tapping at my door, it confuses me for a moment. "Yeah?"

"Um, do you mind if I use your phone?"

Shit. I'd forgotten all about Fallon. "Not at all. Help yourself."

"I don't know where it is."

As I scrub my face, I say, "There's one in my office. Main level, off the great room."

The clicking and thumping of her crutches down the hall tells me she's gone. A doctor should probably examine her foot today, as I'm sure she tore her stitches out. Then it strikes me. Oh shit! She's going to see everything in my office! I zoom out of bed and head down the hall before I realize I'm stark, bollock naked. Backtracking, I get dressed and get to my office in record time.

Too late. She's standing there with a dazed grin that stretches from ear to ear. I've never seen her smile like this.

"Why didn't you tell me you were a fan?" She's awed.

Fan? I want to laugh. "I don't know. Probably because most men don't read romance novels?"

"Oh my God. I'm so freakin' jealous. You have every book, every release, paperback and hardback. Are they all signed?"

"Sadly, no." Why would I keep signed copies of my own books?

"But still, you have a treasure trove here. I mean, I would trade anything for this. Do you mind?" She is gaga over them and is asking permission just to touch them. Jesus, I know she loves my stuff, but this is an over the top kind of love.

"Have at it."

"This is my favorite. *Lovers Between the Sheets.*" She picks it up and holds it reverently in her arms. "Oh God, I can't tell you how many times I've read this. Probably a dozen at least. At the end, when he hands her the sheet of music with his proposal written in the song, I so lost it. I think I went through an entire box of tissues."

"You liked that, huh?"

"Liked it? Hell, no! I *loved* it. I freakin' adored it. It was the most romantic thing *ever*. That book stayed with me for *weeks*. I couldn't sleep at night thinking of Willow and everything she had been through. And then Jack." She takes this giant breath and sighs. "R.T. Sinclair is positively brilliant. I live and breathe for her books, I tell you."

Now I have a new appreciation for the way a fan loves an author. I can only smile at her because I realize her fresh and honest words, straight from her heart, have made me happy.

"What?" She's giving me a curious look.

"What?"

"You're laughing at me, aren't you?" Her eyes cloud with suspicion and that fresh-faced sweetness that was there is covered up with something called distrust.

"No, I'm not laughing at you at all. I'm admiring the way you're so passionate about this. I think it's quite refreshing."

She relaxes a bit, yet that beautiful creature who is so in love with my works, is now shielded from me. I want her back. "I love R.T. Sinclair, too. And I agree. *Lovers Between the Sheets* is her best work. I'm hoping for a sequel." I'm trying to hint to her that I'm writing that very sequel right now.

"*No*, that would be so wrong! It ended on such a good note. I don't want it ruined by all that angst and tension between the two characters. With that book, I want the characters to march into the sunset, get married, have lots of babies and live happily ever after."

My face falls. That's not anything close to what I have in mind for Jack and Willow. If she only discovers that Jack cheats and Willow leaves him, she'll die and hate me forever. Maybe I need to change my plans.

"You okay?" Now she's the one looking at me with a curious expression. Tilly always tells me I wear everything on my face and I guess Fallon has picked it up.

"I'm fine. I was just thinking you need to call your state agency for your ID."

"Oh, yes! Phone."

"Over there," I direct her.

She makes the call and they inform her they need certain documentation to send her a replacement.

A couple of days pass and our unspoken truce has now developed into more of a friendship of sorts. We're sharing laughs and becoming more and more comfortable around each other. It's funny when I realize it's all the result of her love for my books. We truly do have a lot in common as we begin to open the doors to this odd relationships of ours.

Her foot's been re-doctored by my physician and I'm keeping her off it while she waits for her new credit card to arrive, but still no word on her purse. When she called her boss at the deli, he said he'd hold her job for a week, but then he would have to fill it.

"Thanks for all the help with everything, Ryland."

"My pleasure." And it really is. "Can I ask you something?"

She nods.

"And I know this is quite touchy for you, but does your mum have the money to give you? I mean, if she would want to?"

Fallon shrugs. "I don't honestly know. I've asked her so many times for help, but she's always refused. She lives in a nice, fancy house. Not anywhere near as fancy as yours, but it's nice. And she has everything she's ever wanted. But, I don't know. I don't ask for anything anymore. She was always like that. As far back as I can remember. Her life always came before anything else."

The crushing debt Fallon is in over student loans appalls me. Since I hail from a wealthy background, I've never faced financial woes before. The happy face she's able to put on every day simply amazes me. It's not just the debt, either. That bitch known as her mum dumped her and then she lost the hero in her life only to have to go back to the mum who didn't want her. I can't get over the difficulties she's faced, yet she finds a way to move forward. She hasn't lost hope. She really is nothing like the girl I glimpsed the other day.

"Thanks for the contacts you've given me for the resumes," she says. I've called in a few favors and hopefully it will pan out for her in the form of a job.

"Happy to do it. I hope it works out for you. So, you really don't think there should be a sequel to *Lovers Between the Sheets*?" This has bothered me ever since she told me.

"No, I don't. I think it would lessen the impact of the first book. That book was so heartfelt and genuine; I think readers would look at it as a way to make money. It can't possibly be true to the characters. What will R.T. do? Make Jack have an affair and then have Willow leave him? That would be so out of character for either of them, it couldn't possibly work. If she wants to write a book like that fine, but do a completely different one. I'm sure it will rock... they all do."

I'm gaping at her because she reiterated my plot in one sentence and then annihilated it. When she says it, though, it makes perfect sense.

"You're right. I didn't look at it that way." I'm deep in thought when she interrupts me.

"Why all the obsession about this, anyway?"

"Oh, I don't know. Just curious, I guess."

A thought pops into my head. Maybe I ought to hire her as my personal assistant. I need one, badly. Mine resigned a month ago and I still haven't found a replacement. Fallon would be awesome because she knows all my books already.

"You're really fumbling around in that head of yours tonight, aren't you?" Her head tilts to the side as she studies me.

"Yeah, sorry."

"No worries."

"Would you like to sit outside?"

She nods and then we head that way. I love this place and I can tell she does, too. It seeps into my bones and relaxes me like no other place I've ever been. The mountains are spectacular, but the lake, it's really something else. Lake Tahoe is a four season place with things to do all year long.

We settle in and I ask, "Do you snow ski or board?"

She laughs. "Naw. I always wanted to try 'cause it looks like so much fun, but I never had the extra funds."

My heart aches a little at her response, knowing everything has been a financial struggle for her since her dad died. "Maybe someday then."

"What about you. You live amongst all of this. You must be a good boarder or whatever they call them."

"Yeah, they're boarders. And yes, I do both. I started skiing when I was growing up. We used to go to Switzerland on family holiday."

Her eyes get huge. "Whoa. I bet that was amazing." She has this entranced look on her face and her eyes are sparkling so much I want to touch the place beneath them, just to prove to myself they're real.

"Uh-huh, but the states are better for skiing, in my opinion. They really do it right here."

"Yeah?"

"Yeah."

"So you've been skiing since you were a little kid?"

"Yeah."

"Do your parents ski."

"They used to, but they died when I was eighteen."

Her face morphs into one of utter shock. "Holy shit. I'm so sorry, Ryland. Both of them?"

"Yeah. A train derailment in France. It was dreadful. My sister and I were left behind to deal with it. Good thing we had each other."

"You two are close then?"

"Don't know what I'd do without her."

When I look at her, she has the sweetest smile on her face; she looks like an angel. "It's so great you have her, you know."

"Yes. I do. We were lucky we were eighteen when our folks died 'cause we'd have been sent to live with other families. Like your foster care here. I would've died had we been separated."

"Wait, are you twins?"

"Yeah."

"Oooh, I'm so jealous. I always wanted a twin brother to look out for me. And to take up for me around my mom."

"Why is she so rotten to you?"

Her lips press into a thin line and she shrugs. "She loves everything else more than me."

She bites the corner of her lip to stop it from trembling. This is clearly a topic she doesn't want to discuss. I think back to that nasty comment I made to her about how she deserves the way her mum treats her and it shreds my guts. I move to her side and pull her into my arms.

"Fallon, I'm so sorry for all the hateful things I said to you. They were terrible and I didn't mean them. I don't know what came over me or why I said such dreadful things. I'm also sorry that you have such a shit for a mum."

"I'm sorry, too. For all the crummy things I said." She lets me hold her, and before long, I feel a heat growing within me. Of course, I can lie to myself and deny it's been there all along, yet what good is that? I've wanted her since I saw her in that blasted airport with her sexy nipple exposed.

My hand reaches under her chin and I lift it so I can see her eyes. They're smoky and full of heat, just as I'd hoped. At this point, my tongue has a mind of its own and it seeks hers out. I'm putty when she moans into my mouth. I'm completely lost. My fingers, which have been yearning for days now, plunge into her hair and weave themselves into it, relishing in the softness of her waves. I cradle her head as I pull her into my chest and continue to play with her lips and tongue. I tease her as I suck and nibble, making her sigh.

Her hands crawl across my waist and sneak beneath my shirt. When I feel their coolness contrasting with my hot skin, my body twitches so fiercely, it shocks us both.

"Fallon, you're bringing me to my knees with that mouth of yours. And your hands are…"

"What Ryland?"

Our foreheads are touching and our mouths are mere inches apart now. It's far too much for me. "I want you. I said some terrible things to you in the car the other day and I'm sorry as hell for that. You probably want no part of me, but yeah, I want you so bad I can almost taste you. I want it to be right this time, though. And hear me out. Please."

She nods.

"Slow and soft is how I want it for us. Gentle and sweet. With skin touching skin and our mouths together because I want all of you, Fallon, every last drop this time, until you're begging for me to take you."

She lets out a huge puff of air. "What are you waiting for?"

That's all I need to hear; my arms lift her and I carry her to my bed.

Nine

Fallon

My body burns for his as he carries me up the long flight of stairs. The fingers of one hand are twisted in the hair at the nape of his neck and the index of the other is hooked around the collar of his shirt. I run it along the edge, wanting to feel the heat of his skin. I brush his collarbone, longing to lay my lips in the triangle it creates next to his neck. He smells of woods and clean air, and I'm dying to bury my face against him.

We reach his bed and I feel the loss of him when he sets me down for a moment before he's back with me, pulling me to the edge of the bed and spreading my legs apart. He wedges himself between them and simply sits back on his heels to look at me.

His eyes tear into mine, setting an army of butterflies loose in my stomach. I'm frozen in his gaze, but my fingers lock onto his, and it's that slight movement that sets into motion his kiss.

This one is nothing like the ones we shared before, it's searing and passion filled; filled with emotion. Maybe it's because there was so much wrong that happened the other day and he's trying to make it right. Or maybe he's trying to change everything. It doesn't matter what the reason is. I'm so wrapped up in him right now my head is whirling.

Without breaking our kiss, he lifts my shirt and I feel the cool air hit my scorched skin as goosebumps ripple across me, causing me to shiver. The back of his hand skims over my belly, rubbing me with his knuckles as I arch into him, trying to get closer. My body is aching with need, and though I hardly know what this need is, I'm wet with want for him.

Releasing my lips with one last lick across my lower lip, he leans back on his heels. "Fallon, you're a dangerous girl," he rasps.

My breath is moving in and out so fast I have difficulty speaking. "Wh-what?" I swallow.

"Hmm." His eyes are devouring me while I lick my lips. "Exactly."

He's not making sense, although I don't have time to consider this before his mouth is on mine again. He doesn't kiss me long, and this time, when he stops, my T-shirt comes off, but he doesn't remove it all the way. He traps my arms with it behind my back. I look at him in question, yet he says nothing.

His mouth lowers to my chest and he starts to suck my pearled nipple through the thin fabric of my bra. The combination of the material sliding against me, and his mouth sucking and teasing me has me whimpering. I want so badly to sink my fingers into his dark blond waves, but my hands are trapped. When he moves to my other nipple, I cry out his name. I'm not sure if it's frustration, desire or both, but I have such a throbbing ache between my legs now, I'm sure if he continues this torture, I'm going to climax.

He must've read my mind because he pulls his mouth away and I feel him unbutton and unzip my shorts. When my legs are freed, he doesn't waste a second before his mouth is on me; tasting me, licking, sucking, taking. His hands are clenching my thighs, fingers digging almost painfully into my muscles, enhancing what I'm feeling. It shatters me. I come apart, screaming his name.

"Take off my shirt!" I yell. He laughs at first, but I scold him. "I'm not kidding. I need to hold you, Ryland."

He moves so fast, I'm engulfed by him. He covers me with his body, every inch of my naked self as I loop my arms around his neck, tucking into that little bit of heaven I wanted to kiss earlier.

My voice is all garbled against him when I say, "I don't like not being able to touch you when you do that to me."

"What was that?"

So I lift my head and repeat myself.

"Hmm. I like hearing you say that," he says.

"Ryland, why are you still dressed?"

I feel him shake. "I got a bit distracted."

"Get undistracted."

"Not possible." His voice is husky with need.

I grab his face and kiss him. Hard. "Now."

He stands and takes off his shirt and pants while I watch, transfixed. He's arresting in his perfection. There are things about him I hadn't noticed the last time, and I'm taking my time to enjoy all of him now.

He has lovely ink, bits of it here and there, mostly script. I want to lick every word. His shoulders are honed, rippling when he moves. I lick my lips in anticipation of feeling their firmness beneath the wetness of my tongue.

"There you go again," he murmurs.

"Huh?' I'm confused for a moment.

"Dangerous. That look you give me."

I'm pulled to a seated position as he unhooks my bra and stares. "Now you're savagely dangerous." The backs of both hands brush against my nipples, and they pebble instantly in response.

"If they could talk, they would debate that and say you were the one that was savagely dangerous."

He flattens the palm of his hand against my chest and pushes me backwards until I'm flat on my back. My hand reaches for him because I need to feel that hardness of him in my hand, which apparently surprises him. His eyes don't leave mine as I stroke him. He's silk and steel, all in one. I want all of him... every last inch.

"Is this right?" I want to know how to do it. The only thing I know is what I've read.

I can see his throat working before he answers, "More than right." His voice is guttural, throaty. It plows into me like a wrecking ball. My mouth crushes his as I melt into him.

My hand leaves him, then both hands end up tangled in his hair. He frames my face and breaks off the kiss. He brushes my hair off my cheek then says, "The night we came back here from Vegas, I watched you sleep for a while. I had a hard time leaving your side because I was so..." He stops and shakes his head a couple of times. "I felt like such a shit for how things turned out that day, and as I watched you sleep, I became incredibly *aware* of you... your loveliness and how utterly gorgeous you are. It was difficult to leave your side."

His voice gets so quiet I have to strain to hear him. "Thing is… as I stood by you, I was ripped open when I remembered our time in the shower. You asked why it troubled me so much and it was…" he squeezes his eyes shut for a second, "it was because of the way I hurt you… caused you pain. Every time I think of how you were in pain, of the sound of you crying out, it just…"

I have to stop him. "Hey. Ryland. S'okay. I'm all good here. See? Look at me." I smile softly at him and stroke his cheek.

"It's not supposed to hurt like that, Fallon. It's supposed to make you feel like this… like it did when you came."

"Then make it right this time, Ryland. I need to feel you inside of me. Show me now."

Reaching in his night stand, he pulls out a condom and puts it on before he rolls to his side and lifts my leg, spreading it wide. Then he moves between them, supporting his weight on his elbows. His lips touch mine, but only for a moment then his hand is moving on me, feeling me. "God, you feel so sweet, love."

I can feel his tip against me and then he's inching inside of me before moving back out. Back and forth, going deeper each time, stretching me until I don't think I can take any more because I'm so full. He pulls out and then starts again. When we're finally hip to hip, he lifts one of my legs up, puts it around him and then slides his hand beneath me.

His breath catches as he says, "Fallon, *this* is how it should've been." Then he starts rocking in and out, slowly, never taking his eyes off mine.

My lungs empty of all air as I lose myself in him. With absolute clarity, I know he's right. Has been right all along. It should've been like this the first time; all soft, sexy, slow and pure.

It's building inside of me, and he sees it. How do I know this? Because he starts rotating his hips now and putting the perfect amount of pressure on that sweet spot of mine. The hand under me moves and grabs mine. He laces our fingers together as he raises it above my head at the same time his mouth drops to my breast again. He only licks me this time and then stops. Then he surprises me.

He takes my other leg and wraps it around his waist and then sits back. I feel an emptiness, a loss without him in my arms, but it doesn't last long. He takes my arms and pulls me into his chest, positioning me against him. We're face to face again, me on his lap, and we resume our movement. He's so deep now. I want to scream with the intensity of it all.

"Does this feel okay? I want you to feel good, Fallon."

My eyes are half closed when I manage a smile. "Far more than okay, Ryland. It's wonderful," I finally gasp out. I'm not sure how because I'm having trouble finding enough oxygen here.

Somehow his hand is between us while his thumb starts to circle my little pleasure button. In about ten seconds, I'm coming all over the place, writhing on his lap and maybe screaming. I'm not sure anymore. It's a never-ending orgasm.

"Bloody hell, Fallon. That was sexy as all fuck," he says. I want to laugh. I'm giddy, but I'm so weak I can't do a thing. He's still rocking into me until, all of a sudden, he makes the most erotic sound imaginable and I feel him throbbing inside of me. The expression on his face is so amatory, I want to start all over again, simply so I can see him climax.

"Ryland, I think you just beat me in the sexy department."

"Impossible." His breathing is still ragged.

We're sitting, facing each other with his arms encircling me as he kisses me.

I have to tell him. "You were right. This should've been our first time. It was beautiful."

"Yeah, it was. But sometimes, when you go through the rough spots, the beauty shines through, and when it does, it's much more appreciated."

I don't know why I ask this, but I do. "Have you ever been in love?"

He stiffens, but answers with a "Why do you ask?"

"Curious, I guess."

"Yeah. You?"

"Nope. Thought I was headed there, but he turned out to be a class-A jerk-hole."

For some reason, he must like that answer because his mouth pounces on mine without hesitation. I give him back everything he wants. It's mouthwatering, heart pumping and leaves us both panting.

He looks at me oddly, like he's searching for the right words, yet he ends up saying nothing at all. I feel the same. I mean, what do you say when you've just had the most amazing sex ever?

Well, me being me, says just that. "That was the most amazing sex ever."

He laughs. Really hard.

"What was so funny about that?"

"Since the only other time you had sex, I acted like an utter arse, I would hope it was the best you ever had." He nudges me with his nose.

He has me laughing at that. "So, think you can top this?"

Those amazing emeralds squint at me. "Hmm. I've always loved a challenge."

He moves me aside and I groan. "Where are you going?"

Laughing, he heads towards the bathroom. "Don't worry; I'll only be a minute." A moment later I hear the commode flushing and he's back. He reaches for my hand. "Come on."

"What?"

"I'm going to cook you dinner and then, when we're finished, I have a challenge to meet."

We dress and go down to the kitchen to prepare dinner.

I learn something about Ryland that night. He loves to cook. I help him assemble seafood kabobs, which I love. As a South Carolinian, I'm a born and bred seafood lover.

He has scallops, halibut chunks and swordfish pieces, seasoned perfectly. He serves them with skewered vegetables on a bed of rice pilaf. We sit down to a sunset over the mountains, sipping a chilled glass of wine and eating our delicious dinner. It couldn't be any better.

After about the third bite, my appetite for food shifts, and I'm thinking about Ryland's mouth on me, instead of on his fork as I watch it slide into his mouth. Now I'm drooling.

I don't realize I've stopped eating until he asks, "Is something wrong?"

"Huh?"

"You haven't really touched your food."

A rock of desire has formed in my throat so I bite my lips together and try to swallow it. I realize his plate is empty, so I've been staring at him for quite some time. I shake my head and lick my dry lips because all the moisture in my body seems to have migrated south and landed between my thighs.

He sets his fork down and pins me with his eyes. The lids are half closed and his lips are open slightly, just enough to let his tongue peek out and dab at his lower one.

"Fallon," his voice is laden with desire, "what are you thinking about over there?"

"You." I couldn't get another word to come out of my mouth right then.

"What about me?"

Damn, I wish he hadn't asked me that. "How sexy you look."

The corners of his mouth lift. "That so? What would you like to do about it?"

"Kiss you."

"That all?"

"No."

His hand locks on my wrist and then I'm suddenly in his lap, an inch away from that scrumptious mouth of his. I trace the outline of it with my fingers, but don't get too far before he grabs my hand and takes my index finger in his. "Tease," is all he says before he slides my finger into his mouth and begins to suck on it, softly at first, but then hard. Sweet heaven, I'm moaning all over the place.

"Fallon, you didn't think I would stop at that, did you?"

Truth is, I can barely think at all right now. His finger is sliding down my chest now, from my throat to the button of my shorts. I'm on fire for him. My body sways towards him, wanting more, but he doesn't give in. He undoes my shorts and slips his finger down the front until he finds exactly what he's looking for. He knows it because I'm one giant, moaning, squirming ball of fire by now.

He slides his finger into me and says, "Ah, Fallon, you're drenched, love." He starts to move in and out as my hands grip his arms. Then he stops and I cry out in protest. I watch as he takes his finger and slips it all the way into his mouth before pulling it back out and licking his lips. "Mmmm, sweet and salty."

His hands grab my hips and I quickly find myself on the edge of the table as he pushes the plates out of the way.

"What are you doing?"

"Having my dessert." He flashes me a wicked grin.

"But the dishes."

"I don't give a bloody damn about them," he says as he tugs my shorts off, tossing them aside and then he spreads my legs wide.

His mouth finds me, ready and willing for him, and the sight of him tasting my most intimate bits hypnotizes me; I can't pull my eyes away. My hands are in his hair as he moves over and around me, his tongue and fingers working me to perfection. I'm sure I sound like the coyotes in the hills back home, but I don't care. This man is amazing and I've never felt anything like this. He's working my body as it's never been worked before, and I can feel myself getting closer to a climax.

Suddenly, I'm there, crying out his name, my body rigid with tension before it explodes and cascades around me. I'm so sensitive now, however he doesn't stop, even though I beg him to. It's almost painful, yet he's relentless in his pursuit of something; whatever it is, it's pushing me over the edge again. This time, it's an endless cascade of spasms. It lasts for a very long time, and when it finally passes, I fall back on the table, spent.

I'm not on the table for long, though. He pulls me up and strips off my shirt then begins a tongue journey across my body, the likes of which I've never imagined. My skin is fire and ice, heat and shivers.

He grabs a handful of ice from the pitcher of water on the table, and I suck in my breath when it lands on my stomach. Each cube ventures off in a different direction with the guidance of his hand and tongue.

It's when he moves between my legs with them that I'm reborn. I burst into life again as heated desire engulfs me. His tongue pushes a cube deep inside of me. The combination and fire and frost makes me want to scream, yet I'm not given the chance because I'm suddenly on my feet as he spins me around and bends me over the table.

I can hear his zipper go down and his shirt being whisked off then I feel his heated chest against me and his hot breath against my ear. "Fuck it all, Fallon. You are way more dangerous than I ever gave you credit for, love. We're going to fuck this way, it's going to be rough and you're gonna love it, I promise."

I hear him putting on a condom and then I can feel him pressing against my opening. At first, he inches inside, but then, when he knows I'm ready for him, he thrusts all the way in and, oh God, he feels so damn good that I cry out. "Ah, I want more."

He gives it to me. I can hear and feel him slamming into me, and I'm loving every plunge, every bit of him. He's stretched my arms out and one hand is holding mine while the other is wrapped around my waist, holding me tightly against him.

"Are you good?" he wants to know.

"Yeah, b-better than good." I'm moaning so much, it's hard to answer.

The way he flexes his hips, pushing himself in so deep that he reaches a point that feels so damn right to me. Then he takes his hand and starts to move it over my clit, and before long, I come again. Just like that. My little muscles inside start to clench and squeeze him.

"Ah, bloody hell, Fallon." He makes that throaty sound. I can feel him throbbing inside of me.

"Ryland, I really want to kiss you now and hold you."

"I got you, love. Give me a sec." He's out of breath while I wait.

A minute, maybe two later, he pulls out and I regret that. I whine over the emptiness I feel.

"I know, babe, I feel it, too, but I have to get this condom off before we make a mistake we both don't want."

"Um, Ryland, I'm on the pill, and obviously, I'm safe since you're the only one I've ever slept with. I don't know your past, but…"

"Fallon, I haven't been with anyone in quite a while, but yeah, I'm safe, too. I've been tested and, well, it's a long story. Maybe later. Right now, I want this to be about us."

"Yeah. Us."

He takes the condom off, and puts it somewhere, I guess. I'm still on my stomach on the table so I'm not aware and I don't really care. Then he lifts me up and walks me to a lounge chair where he lies down and pulls me on top of him. "Good?"

"Yeah," I say as I snuggle against him. "Perfect." Then I kiss him. "I feel like a noodle right now."

"I hope that's a good thing."

"Hmm, yeah. Very good."

We're quiet for a while with me settled on top of him, touching him everywhere my fingers can wander. I love burrowing next to his neck where I can lick and taste him, yet also smell him. There's a tiny part of me that wishes I could find one imperfection on him, just something that would make him look less like a sex god and more like a human, but I can't.

"So?" he asks.

"Huh?" I'm completely lost, deep in my thoughts. I pull myself back to him.

"The challenge?" He nudges me with his nose.

"Oh, yeah. That was good, too." I cup his face with my palms and rub his scruff. I love that bit of scruff he wears.

"No better?" He acts surprised.

It makes me laugh. "Ryland, now I find that funny. Both times were spectacular, but that thing you did with your tongue, well, that defies description."

He flips me so fast I find myself staring at him as he hovers over me. "Wait, are you saying you think I'm better with my mouth than I am with my d—"

105

"Wait! No, that's not what I meant at all." I think I just insulted him by the wounded look in his deep green eyes.

"Because if that's what you think, let me disabuse you of that notion right now."

Dear Lord.

He's nudging my legs apart and I feel his erection against me. Wait, amend that last thought. It's now pushing hard against me as I strain to get closer; I want him inside me now, so I let him know.

"Yeah, Ryland. I want you again… now."

His eyes widen slightly and his lips part as he sucks air into his lungs.

Ten

Ryland - Thomas

"How can you do this again? I thought that… well, that you couldn't so soon after…"

Her question makes me stop and think. "I thought so, too, but apparently, my body has different ideas where you're concerned." And my body *is* reacting to her in many ways that surprise me. My mind flashes back to a place I don't want it to go and, for a moment, I see Iris's face before me. Then a thousand images fly passed and I can't keep up with any of them. I push them away and bring myself to the present.

"No condom?" I need to be sure before we continue here.

"No."

Ah, fuck. One word from her in that husky tone of hers makes me want to groan.

She's all hot and sweet, but fiery at the same time. It's all I can do not to release right then. What the bloody hell?

I press on home and hit heaven. Jesus, how can a woman feel so damn good? I hook my arm beneath the crook of her knee and lift it high as I continue to pound against her hips with mine. Ah, she's so tight; I can feel every nuance, every movement of her. And I want to crawl all over her. Those eyes of hers suck me into their smoky depths and I end up in a hazy dream of her. One where she's all mine. When she calls out my name, well, bloody hell, doesn't that just make me go all to pieces in her?

That mouth is calling my name and I don't want it to stop that sweet music, but I have to taste her, I need to have that tongue of hers against mine. I feel her warm breath rush into my mouth as our lips come together. I don't remember ever loving kissing this much. It's like fucking crack, not that I know what crack's like, but whatever. Then I can feel her coming and it pushes me off the edge.

"Holy wow, Ryland. Why the hell did I ever stay a virgin so long?"

My eyes grab hers, and I say something that surprises us both. "It's not always like this, Fallon." And it never was before... not with Iris... not with anyone.

She's trying to puzzle me out while my belly is doing backflips and somersaults like crazy. She affects me. Only Iris has affected me like this, or at least, I've tried to convince myself she has. What's going on here? Suddenly I feel like I can't breathe, like the world is shifting too fast and I'm losing control.

I have to move before something happens, before I say something I'll regret. I look at her sadly and then push to my feet.

"Ryland? What's going on?"

I can't speak; my voice is jammed in my throat. What the hell is wrong with me?

I turn and look at her with a smile. "Nothing at all," I mumble. Then I scramble out of there before I do something crazy. I make it to my room before the panic hits.

The vise around my neck is cutting off my air, yet luckily, I'm able to talk myself through it and stop the attack before it takes over my entire body. What the hell precipitated that? I haven't had one of those in years, ever since Tilly found me. I didn't even know I had an issue with them anymore. Now how am I going to face her? What will I say?

I don't have to worry about it for too long because, moments later, there's a pounding on my door and I hear, "Ryland, open the door, and let me in or I'm coming in anyway."

Shit. Here we go. "It's open."

When she stomps in, her eyes resemble a thunderstorm getting ready to unleash its savage power on me.

"What was that all about? What—do you think you can just fuck the hell out of me and then walk away? Huh?"

Words escape me and all I can do is stare at the red-haired, gray-eyed beauty that has every right to hate me at this moment.

"Then, let me *disabuse you* of *that* notion, mister. You just succeeded in making me feel like a fucking whore, so thank you very much. If that's what you intended, well con-fucking-gratulations! I certainly hope it made you feel like a big man. Now I understand why I stayed a virgin for so long and I wish to God I still was one!" She turns and marches right out of the room.

I feel the finality in her words. She's not just marching out of my room; she's marching out of my life. All because I had a rotten panic issue for some unknown reason. No, that's not exactly true. I can lie to myself, but what purpose does it serve? I know why I had that attack. It goes back to Iris and my fears of getting emotionally entangled with anyone else.

A million reasons flash through my mind, and then there's that small matter of her finding out who I really am. So now, I've done the very thing I know will push us apart and solve everything for us. I won't have to worry about getting involved with her and she'll never know the truth about me. No harm no foul.

Two days later Fallon's replacement credit card arrives. We aren't speaking. At all. I feel like a shit and every time I look at her, my guilt threatens to eat me alive. It's become a living, breathing thing... a giant beast that destroys my sleep at night and ruins my work during the days. It resides in my gut, my mind, my bed and everywhere else I turn. Every time I think about speaking with her, the words get jammed in my throat and I freeze. What the fuck is wrong with me?

My office offers no haven because, every time I go in there, I picture her and how she looked when she held my books in her hands. The deck is no better, for I have graphic images of us having passionate sex out there and on the table, with her moans driving me fucking mad. The kitchen isn't safe because I see her helping me assemble those damn kabobs. I can picture her hands skewering the pieces of fish, and I feel as though it's my heart that's getting pierced instead.

We avoid each other, or rather, she avoids me is the more accurate description. If she sees me even coming close at all to her, she diverts her course and oftentimes, she simply stays in her room all day. I've noticed how haggard she looks with the purple crescents beneath her eyes and how puffy they are all the time. I'm the schmuck that made her look like that and doesn't that just make me proud? What would Tilly say if she could see us now?

So it was that, late one morning, my dear sister decides to pay a surprise visit on me. Since I haven't returned any of her phone calls, texts or emails for the past week, so she takes it upon herself to make the drive from San Francisco—where she lives—to my place.

Fallon was walking out of the kitchen and I was in the main den, which was unusual, when she barges in.

"Ryland Thomas, where have you been? You haven't answered any of my calls…" She stops when she sees Fallon standing there.

Fallon stares at Tills as though she's seen a ghost.

"Fallon! What a surprise!"

"R.T. What are you doing here?"

I have to hand it to Tilly. Her shock is masked immediately by a smile. "Well, Ryland and I go back a ways. We knew each other back in London. He does some freelance work for me and I also have him write a lot of my press releases. We've been friends for quite some time."

"That's right," I add.

"Oh. Well, it's nice to see you again. I'll just leave the two of you to talk then."

Tilly eyes her as she climbs the stairs. Then her eyes turn to me and I know I'm in for it.

We move to my office and the barrage of questions begins. "What the hell, Ryland Thomas. I've been trying to reach you for days! You are an ass."

"Yeah, well, get in line. There are plenty of others who think the same."

"What's going on?"

I shrug.

"Ryland Thomas, I'll camp out here until you tell me. I swear I will."

Knowing Tilly, she will do just that, too. So I dive in and give her the story, minus all the gory details.

"Jesus, Ryland Thomas. What the fuck are you doing to the poor thing? Scarring her for life? I'm surprised she hasn't taken a knife to your bleedin' heart while you sleep at night. Damn, you're a rotten bastard."

"Yeah, well, I couldn't help it."

"Liar." She turns, heading out the door.

"Where are you going?"

"To tell that girl just what kind of fucked up asshole you are, that's where."

"What about me?"

"What about you? Listen to me, you butthole. You don't have crazy sex with a girl, who was a virgin before you got your damn hands on her, and then get up and walk away from her the way you did. That's worse than a slap in the face. You pretty much told her she wasn't even worth that. At least a slap is an emotion. What you showed her was nothing. Emptiness. You're a rotten fuck,

112

you know that? I used to feel sorry for you. I don't anymore."

She's right. I am a fuck. A mountain of one, too.

Now there are two women staying with me that won't speak to me. At all. Tilly won't even look my way. One afternoon I overhear them talking. Fallon wants to know how Tilly got away with just moving in here and ignoring me. Her explanation is that we've been friends ever since university; we're like brother and sister. All I could think of is, *Oh what a tangled web we weave.*

When Fallon's replacement driver's license finally arrives, Tilly arranges to drive her to the airport in Reno. She makes me pay for her plane ticket home, but tells Fallon she's the one that paid. Fallon argues about it, however she finally accepts it because she recognizes she has no other choice. She promises Tilly she'll pay it back as soon as she can.

When I tell Tilly how much debt Fallon is in, Tills nearly faints. She can't speak for a very long moment and then she says with a glint in her blue eyes, "Well, Ryland Thomas, you need to do something about that."

Now what the hell am I supposed to do about it? Sometimes I think Tilly is losing her mind.

As the day arrives for Fallon to leave, my heart feels like someone just pulled it out of my chest and stepped on it. I wish I could figure this thing out.

Tilly has discreetly disappeared, leaving Fallon and I alone in the den. We look at each other and I'm so taken with her, I want to tell her not to go, but the whole idea is preposterous. She hates me and I don't blame her. I'm the asswipe who treated her like shit.

I want to come up with something clever to say, something she'll remember forever, yet my tank is empty. So instead, I merely say, "Fallon, I'm sorry things turned so wonky for us. Take care of yourself back there in South Carolina."

Her eyes gouge into mine and I flinch. She doesn't say anything, just nods. Then she spins around and walks out of my life.

I knew when I met her that she was special, and it's been becoming increasingly clearer to me just how special Fallon is. Because right now, watching her leave, I feel like my life has just been steamrolled. I can't breathe for a very long moment. I had hoped, but now…

I hear Tilly's car roar to life before the noise of the engine fades away. I climb the stairs and walk into her room. Looking around, I hunt for something, anything, she may have left behind. I'm crushed when I find nothing. Only the remnants of her scent linger in the air, so I plop on the bed and let them fill me. It'll be a long, long time before I can forget Fallon McKinley.

Eleven

Fallon

Two Months Later

It's taken me a bit, but I'm beginning to breathe easier. After being drawn and quartered by the douche-face Ryland, my life felt so damn dim. All the girls were after me to get out more so I could meet someone else that would steal my heart. How is that possible when my heart's had the shit beaten out of it before it's ever had a chance to begin with? How could one stupid stunt in Vegas turn into such a fiasco for me? Was I the only stupid girl to fall for the first guy I ever slept with? That was the one thing I have stayed strong over. That and the fact that I'm not going to let some sleaze ass talk me into sleeping with him. That sure flew back and smacked me right across the face.

I thought it was bad enough when that dickface, Bryce Mason, tried to make me think he had feelings for me. Yeah, I was humiliated beyond words. He played me like a stupid video game. The way he had me walk in on him getting that blowjob in front of all his d-bag fraternity brothers. And my friend Adam trying to get me to leave. I thought *he* was the one being the jerk when he was only trying to get me out of there.

But no, Bryce asked me over because he said he had something special he wanted to show me. It was special all right. I still shudder when I think about how I barged into that room, and there he stood, his pants around his ankles, the guys in a circle around him so I couldn't really see what was going on.

"Come on in, Fallon," he had said.

"What's going on in here?" I was laughing, thinking they were playing a drinking game or maybe smoking weed. Nope. Nothing could've prepared me for what happened next. The circle opened up and one of them pushed me into the middle and said, "Bryce tells us you need a little lesson, so we thought this might be a way to do it."

I looked down and there was some blond chick going down on him like a freakin' piston then Bryce closed his eyes and started moaning.

I clamped my hand over my mouth because I thought I was going to be sick. I tried to leave, but they wouldn't let me. I'm not sure who it was, but someone held my arms and forced me to watch. They wouldn't let me go until they were through with their little game. It was unbelievably gross.

I stumbled out of there, shaking, and my face streaked in black from my mascara running all over the place. They laughed at me because I was crying. Adam was outside waiting. He took one look at me, and didn't say a word. He simply took me by the arm and drove me home. I never spoke to Bryce The Dickface again.

That's one of the reasons I wanted to lose my virginity in Vegas. Why I decided I was over this crap of being the goody-two-shoes. It had gotten me nowhere other than in a mess and I was tired of it. I wanted to experience what everyone has been yapping about. I wanted to prove to myself that I could make my own choices and decisions about this. This is what I wanted, wasn't it? Well, serves me right. I got what I deserved.

My old boss, Zack at the deli, calls, so I go visit him.

"Fallon, I'm sorry, hon. You know I couldn't hold your job for you," he says. His eyes are filled with remorse. He's a great guy and I know he's being sincere.

"It's okay, Zack. You have a business to run here."

He nods. "Listen, if something opens up here, I'll be sure to give you a call."

"Great." I give him a weak smile.

"Hey, you okay?" he asks.

"Yeah. Sure."

He's not buying it at all. "Any luck on the job front?"

"Not yet. If you hear of anything…"

"You know I will," he promises.

So now I'm working as a temp at the local medical center, writing press releases and things of that nature. It pays minimum wage and I don't make any tip money, so it's been even rougher than before. Not to mention, I hate it. Happily, my books take me away from all this boring fuckery and I still blog on the side with my girls.

Speaking of my girls, they all pitched in and bought me a new cell phone. What would I do without them?

I get home from work, check my snail mail and email, and try not to freak. Bills. I'm in a state of panic every time I get another one. I open my computer and go straight to my email, praying for some kind of message, telling me that I've landed a real job. As I scan them, I find one from Critics Abound, one of the most prestigious literary critique agencies.

Initially, I think it's for a blog post, but as I delve into it, it's a hit from a job application I sent them. They want to interview me next week. They're located in San Francisco, so I'll need to fly out there. My heart falls through my second story apartment and lands smack in my neighbor's den. There's no way I can afford a plane ticket. My credit card is maxed out and my savings are zapped. I'm so damn broke, I can barely afford to eat anymore.

My first inclination is to sling my piece of shit laptop out the front door, however I refrain. Instead, I inhale and walk into my room to change clothes. I need to run and get this craziness expunged from my head. I'm reaching my breaking point, and if I don't do something, I'm gonna scream.

So I put on my music and head on down to my favorite spot—a quiet old neighborhood with stately homes surrounded by large oak and maple trees—and run my legs off. The leaves have turned and fallen, and darkness has settled on this town, yet I don't care. Fact is, I'm relishing in it that no one can see me now because the tears I've refused to shed are now rivulets lining my cheeks.

Anger, frustration, self-pity, doubt, sadness and humiliation make a nasty combination of emotions, but the release is even uglier. As I listen to one of my favorite songs, *Sleeping Through The Revolution*, by She Said Fire, I plod through the streets, unaware of anything except that I need to get a grip on my life. Something has to give or else I will. I can't hold out much longer. I'm just going to have to break down and beg my mom for money. As much as I despise the thought of it, it's the only chance I have of getting to that interview. I think about the song and how I need a revolution in my life right now. Maybe my mom will finally relent and be my own revolution for once.

When I get home, I take a quick shower and decide to make the call. Before I do, I read the email again, just to make sure I have all the necessary information because I know she'll interrogate me. As I go through it again, I notice a phrase at the end, "Please contact us immediately so we can make your travel arrangements."

"Holy shit!" I'm jumping up and down, screaming at the top of my lungs, over and over. Five minutes later, my neighbor is knocking on my door to see if I'm okay.

"Never been better," I tell her and then I head back to my computer to compose my message.

Of course I can fly to San Francisco for an interview. And yes, I'm available next week. Please let me know what other information you may need from me... blah, blah, blah.

Then I text all the girls to let them know and we have a "squee" party on Facebook. I explain how at first I didn't think I was going to be able to go because of the cost of travel, but then how I discovered that they were handling that. They're super excited for me and my spirits are soaring as high as they've been for some time. My mind is running a hundred miles an hour and I can't sleep so I decide to reread my favorite book ever, *Lovers Between the Sheets.*

At three in the morning, I finally turn off my e-reader and fall asleep.

The next morning, I check my email constantly, allowing for the time change, and around one in the afternoon, I get a hit. It's from Kristie Whitley at Critics Abound confirming my interview for the following week on Tuesday. My travel arrangements are attached in another file. I open the file and see that I'm flying out on Monday and they're putting me up in a hotel for two nights. I'll be coming home on Wednesday.

Excitement pours through me. The urge to run home and call everyone I know almost takes over, but I'm at work until five so I have to rein myself in. My manager smiles when I tell her why I won't be in next Monday to Wednesday. At the end of the day, I rush home to call the girls live. I chat with Kat first.

"That is so awesome! They're really flying you out there?"

"Damn straight."

"Holy crap, Fallon. You could be moving to the City By The Bay."

"Huh?"

"You know, that old Tony Bennett song? My mom used to sing it all the time. Something about leaving his heart in San Francisco."

I harrumph. "Well, he should've sung that I left mine in *Lake Tahoe*."

"Yeah, but you're on your way to a bigger and better life. You're gonna land this one. I just know it."

All the other calls go the same way, but I can't Skype with Andrea because of the time difference. I email her instead and we decide to go for it on Saturday.

The only spoilsport in the whole thing is that woman known as my mother.

"I don't know why you're wasting your time traveling out there. You're never going to make it with a big company like that," she tells me. She sure knows how to make a girl feel good about herself.

Right as I finish my uplifting call with her, it is time to talk with my British connection. Andrea raises me back up with her positive thoughts.

"That bloody witch. I've a mind to come over there and knock the lights out of her," Andrea says.

She makes me laugh.

"You're gonna do fantastic, now, you hear? You go out there and blow them away."

Yeah, my blog girls know exactly how to pump me right up.

The plane lands and I head down to baggage claim, even though I didn't check one, because that's where they told me someone would meet me to drive me to my hotel. Imagine that! I've never been driven anywhere like this before, so I'm feeling very special.

The driver is standing there holding up a sign with my name on it. It's a bit weird, but I follow him to the car and off we go. Even though I'm tired, my excitement fills me and I take off for a walk around the hilly streets of San Francisco after checking into the hotel. Other than that disastrous trip to Vegas and then Lake Tahoe, I've never been anywhere outside of the southeast. So this is a real treat for me.

My budget is minimal. No, that isn't exactly true. It's nonexistent. I don't have enough money to buy a meal, but I can get a little something each day from a convenience store. I'm hoping that, since my interview is scheduled for ten in the morning, I'll get a lunch as part of the deal.

This place is amazing. I walk and walk until I hit the wharf. I can't believe all the activity and restaurants. It reminds me of Myrtle Beach back home. I giggle. All these tacky shops that sell souvenirs and stuff are everywhere. I stop often to take tons of pictures with my phone. Then I see a cable car and want to jump on it, but I'm too scared because I'm afraid I'll get lost. I think I end up walking ten miles that afternoon into evening.

As I'm walking past a huge bookstore, I stop and look through the window. My forehead is pressed against the glass as I ogle all the lovely books inside. By now, I'm sure I'm drooling. I want so bad to walk through those doors, yet I don't dare because it would be torture not to be able to spend a dime. Knowing me, I would spend the ten dollars I've set aside for food on a book instead and then I'll be starving for three days.

As I'm standing outside, staring at the display of books in the window, I hear, "Fallon? Is that you?"

I turn to see R.T. standing there.

I grin. "R.T.! How are you?"

"What are you doing in San Francisco?"

"Oh!" My hand flies to my chest because I didn't even think about that. No wonder she's so surprised to see me. "I have a job interview tomorrow with Critics Abound." I'm grinning now.

"Whoa! They're the best, Fallon. I mean, the very best. I'm so thrilled for you."

"Thanks, but I don't know. I probably won't get it."

122

"Don't say that. Of course you will. You write the best reviews ever!"

My face heats with the compliment.

"So, where are you staying?"

I tell her and she says, "Well, that's not far from here and it's not far from where I live. I'll walk with you. Better yet, have you eaten?"

I'm so embarrassed about not having any money that I tell her yes. However, right after I say the words, my stomach lets out a humongous growl. Of course I haven't eaten since this morning, so I'm starved.

Her eyes narrow as she looks at me. "When was the last time you ate?"

"Wh-what? Why?"

"Just answer me, Fallon."

"This morning before I left home."

"Come on. We need to catch up anyway."

She latches onto my arm and drags me to this amazing restaurant where we catch up. In the middle of dinner, she finally asks about the gray elephant sitting on my lap.

"So, how you've been? And stop beating around the bloody bush."

"Great. Well, if I get this job, I'll be great. Otherwise, not so good, if you want to know the truth."

"Go on."

I look at my hands that are clasped in my lap. I don't think it's a good idea to look at R.T. right now because, if I do, I'm sure the old Hoover Dam will burst right open.

"Yeah, well, I lost my job at the deli after I got home, and well, things are pretty rough financially." That's all I want to tell her, however she keeps prodding me until I give it all up. "I'm working a temporary job, but it only pays minimum wage. I have my school loans to repay, but since I can't really make ends meet, my credit card is maxed out and I'm behind on my rent. So I'm hoping that this works out 'cause, if it doesn't, well, I'm pretty much fucked."

"Why didn't you call me?"

"For what?"

"Help."

I shake my head. "Oh, I would never do that."

"You don't think after everything you've done for me that I wouldn't want to return the favor? I could help you, Fallon."

"Uh-uh. I won't take that kind of help."

"What about a loan?"

"Maybe after tomorrow, this discussion won't be necessary." I didn't want to talk about this with her. It was embarrassing enough to live it, but to have to talk about it is awful.

"Okay. But if for some reason—"

"Yeah, okay."

"So, have you spoken to Ryland at all?"

This dinner has just gone from sheer humiliating to straight fucking hell. I pinch my lips together and shake my head.

"He never called you?" She seems shocked.

Sometimes, you think you're getting over something, and that your life is taking a turn for the better, but then someone comes and throws you a fucking curve ball that flies at you so fast that you don't have time to get out of the way before it smashes right into your skull, blinding you with the pain. That's what this conversation is doing to me.

"Jesus, Fallon. Don't answer. And I'm sorry I brought it up. I only thought..." She shrugs.

I smile weakly and nod. "It's okay. All's good." I sniff and bend my head so she won't see the tears that bubble out of my lids. I push them back, yet a few escape, much to my chagrin. I despise feeling weak and thoughts of Ryland bring me to my knees. Fuck him for making me feel like this. I hope his stupid wiener rots off!

The next day, I meet with Ruth Conner, Kristie Whitley and her team at Critics Abound, and we mesh from hello. Well, I mesh with Kristie. I'm not so sure about Ruth. She's another story altogether; as in, aggressive and pushy. I get the feeling she's really hard to work for, too. Ruth is only there for the first half of the interview, though.

"Um, at the risk of blowing any opportunity I have for employment here, how close do the literary critics actually have to work with Ms. Conner?" I need the answer to this because I know in my heart that woman would eat me alive.

Kristie assures me my contact with her would be minimal. "I'm her direct report, Fallon. You would have very little to do with her. All your work would be done with and through me and my team."

"Good to know." I smile and breathe easier. It's like I've been made for this position. After the Ruth part, there isn't really a formal interview.

"Fallon, I have to say, when we got your resume, I was expecting the routine thing, but you're a nice surprise. I'm more than impressed. I've gone back and looked at all your reviews and they're professionally done, hitting on everything we like to see. We want you on our team. *I* want you on this team."

It's hard to hide my surprise. I'm prepared to sell myself, however now I want to laugh and then hug her.

"Really?"

"Really. So when can you move out here? I know it's a lot more expensive in San Francisco than it is in South Carolina, so we're prepared to help subsidize your rent. We'll even help you locate a place to live. How does that sound? Oh, and I almost forgot. Let's go over our offer."

I sit there, hardly able to absorb what she's saying because I'm blown away.

"Fallon, you're looking at me like you're in the weeds. Is everything okay?"

"My wheels are spinning." Then I laugh hard, like I haven't laughed in months.

"I take it that's a good sign?"

"A very good sign."

"So, how does January third sound for your starting date? That would give you a chance to gather up your things, close out your home in South Carolina and make the drive after the holidays are over."

"It sounds perfect!" I have to grasp the arms of the chair to stop myself from leaping up and doing one of those cheerleading jumps. I'm that excited.

Then Kristie looks at me and asks, "I know your favorite author is R.T. Sinclair. It's obvious from your blog. I'd like you to do a feature on her, if you can. Do you think that's possible?"

I know it's possible, but I'm confused. "I thought I'd be doing reviews."

"You will, but this is something new we want to try... sort of a spotlight on an author. I'm sure you've

126

seen them before. We want to start doing this every month. We're thinking of adding this later in the year, and I thought it would be a good chance for you to spread your creative and journalistic wings, so to speak. You game?"

Hell, yeah, I'm game. I leave out the small detail that I'm a friend of R.T.'s and that the interview shouldn't be a problem. On the way back to the hotel, I text her to share the good news. Then, I tell the world that I'm moving to San Francisco.

R.T. takes me to dinner again that night, but this time it's to celebrate. It's a different atmosphere from last night's; more festive and fun filled. That is, until I bring up the interview.

Her face morphs into something odd; something I can't discern. There's something off about her now, and I don't know why.

"You know, when I started this whole thing, I didn't want to get into the interview thing. That's why you never see me on those TV shows and all. And if I tell you no, I'll feel like I'm hurting a dear friend."

"Oh, I didn't know you felt so strongly about it. I would never ask you to do something that goes against your grain. Don't feel bad if you can't do it." I'm disappointed, although I understand.

She looks at me and shakes her head. "You know, Fallon, I want you to do really well in this job. And if this interview will help, then everything else be damned. I'll do it, but you can't ask me about my love life. How does that sound?"

"Perfect. But R.T., I want you to know something, I honor our friendship and everything you tell me outside of that interview will always stay that way. I'm not the kind of person that will run to the press and blather on about you. Besides, my boss said it was something they would start later in the year. So let's see what happens. It may never even come to anything."

"Okay. I know I can trust you. So tell me about your moving plans."

For the rest of the meal, we chat about what I'm going to do for the next month. When I leave, I promise to call her before I head back this way. I'm excited, but a bit anxious about my big move here. Isn't that the way it's supposed to be? I shove those thoughts away and head back to my hotel.

RYLAND – THOMAS

Three months later and I still can't get her out of my head. My life's gone to shit without her and I deserve it for the way I treated her. I can't seem to pull it together to write a damn consistent paragraph, either. I feel like Jack Torrence in *The Shining*, writing, *"All work and no play makes Jack a dull boy,"* over and over and over. Maybe I should write an entire novel saying repeatedly, *"R.T. Sinclair is a dickface and fucked over the nicest girl in the world."*

Ah, bloody fucking hell. Who am I kidding? That wouldn't help, either. I'm a shit. All this time and I thought Iris and Will were the jackholes, but who's the king of them all now? I walk over to look in the mirror and my gut contorts with disgust.

Staring at my reflection does nothing for me, so when the phone rings, I let it tear me away from my own pity party, glad to see that it's Tilly.

129

"Yeah."

"Stop whining. I'm sick of you already and you only said one word," she tears into me.

"So hang up."

"Sod off. Listen, the turkey day thing is next week and I have some brilliant news. Wanna come to Cali?"

"I'm in Cali."

"You know what I mean. You need to get a life and get over yourself already. Honestly, Ryland Thomas, if you feel that badly about it, then call her. You sit there and pine away like some Jane Austen character, but you don't do a damn thing about it. Oh, and by the way, your writing's gone to shit. So get out of your self-imposed prison and come to my place for a few days."

"You can be a pain in my arse, you know?"

"Yep. So?"

I groan, but give in. If I don't, Tills will drive me insane. "All right. I'll be up on Tuesday."

"Perfect. And be prepared to have some fun."

Tilly is so completely exuberant. I can't figure her out. She greets me as if she has something positively exciting to share, hugging the life right out of me.

"What the bloody hell, Tills?"

"I've missed my brother. That's all. Can't I hug you anymore?"

I shrug it off as one of her crazy moments.

"So where's what's his name? The love of your life?"

"Who?"

"You know. The Vegas guy?"

"That ought to tell you something now. We broke it off back in September. The bloke was a jealous freak."

"Ah."

"That's it? Ryland Thomas, do you even realize you barely speak to me anymore? I haven't seen you since August. You're my only living relative for Christ's sake. What the hell? You need to pull your head outta your arse and get it together."

I squeeze my eyes shut and scrub my scruffy face. "I'm trying, Tills. I really am."

She cocks her head and stares. "That bad, huh?" she whispers.

"Worse."

"Well, damn it all. Why didn't you say something?"

"I don't know. Couldn't. Didn't want to." I scrub my face again.

"Are you in love with her then?"

My breath's gone in a rush. "I don't know that, either. We were together for just those few days and the whole idea seems ludicrous. But she did something to me that…" I try to swallow the brick that's formed, although it takes a few tries before I finally succeed. "I don't *want* to be in love, I do know that."

When Tilly laughs, my head snaps towards her. "That's wickedly brilliant, coming from the master of romance novels."

"What's that supposed to mean?"

She laughs again. "Come on! You write all those books about relationships and here you are trying to figure out your own shit. Take a good, long look at your feelings. Do you miss her? Do you want her back in your life? Would you do anything to change the way things turned out? Have you ever kissed anyone that made you feel the way she did? Can you ever imagine kissing anyone like that again? What about the sex? Did it turn you inside out? The answers to those questions will tell you what you need to know."

"But I only knew her for a few days!"

"Who cares? Is there some kind of a time stamp on love? Did someone come out and report that a study showed ninety-nine point nine percent of those people that fell in love only did so after two hundred and sixty eight days? We're talking about your feelings... your emotions, Ryland Thomas. Don't let your bloody stubborn head get in the way of your heart."

I let her words tumble through my brain for a few seconds and then suddenly I realize it's all hopeless. "Oh, hell, Tilly. Who am I trying to fool? With the way I treated her, she wouldn't give me the time of day now. And I don't blame her."

"You won't know if you don't try. And really, Ryland Thomas, do you want to stumble through life thinking, 'What if?'"

She makes a solid point.

That's when my evil sister dumps it all on me. "Besides, Fallon's moving to San Fran in January."

My heart thumps so viciously I'm sure Tills can hear it. My eyes drill holes into hers. "What did you say?" I whisper.

"You heard me. She was hired by Critics Abound."

I can't move. Fallon will be on the west coast, not that far from me; only about three and a half hours. Jesus C, help me.

"What the fuck, Tilly! Why didn't you tell me? What should I do? Am I supposed to call her? And how long have you known this?"

Tills is laughing. "Do you really need to question whether you're in love with her? Look at yourself. You look like a bloody, lovesick fool. You won't even give me a chance to answer."

Her words nail me.

I don't want *to be in love*, I tell myself again. It only leads to pain and suffering. Heartache and misery.

She watches me and sees the change in me. I'm guessing she does because she scowls while her lips stretch into a thin line.

"You know what? You're a bloody, fucking moron. That's what you are." Then she's gone into her room.

After her door slams shut, I sit and think. The bottom line is, it doesn't matter what I want. If I love her, then I love her. It's not like I can do anything about it. Besides, how will I know if I *do* love her if I don't seek her out to find the answer? Oh, I suppose I can go on about my business the way I've been, miserable and aching on the inside. However, if I don't give it a chance, then how will I know it wasn't meant to be? Apart from that, I need to give Fallon that chance, too; that is if she'll even have me.

Of all the things, why me? Why am I the one to fall in love at first sight? And really, after Iris, I'm the cynic. It's only that experience that's allowed me to write all those sad romances, but I always change the endings to make them happy ones because I can't stand the thought of someone, even a fictional character, going through what I did.

I knock on Tilly's door.

"I need your help." I tell her my plans, but she has an even better one. I can't help smiling at her and agreeing with her idea.

Exquisite Betrayal

The Americans love their turkey, so Tilly does her best to stuff one, but every year it ends up raw on the inside and burnt on the outside. This year's no different. As a backup, she has some chicken, so we eat that instead with the smashed up potatoes and gravy and other things she's prepared. Tilly hasn't inherited Mum's knack for cooking like I have, so the food is merely okay, but I dig in like it's the tastiest grub ever.

"Eck," she says around a mouthful of some vegetable concoction as she makes a face.

"Know what? Next year, I say we go out."

"Great idea and so much easier, too." Her exuberance over my suggestion makes me want to laugh.

We carry on with our efforts to eat, but after a few more forkfuls, we both laugh and give up. The food is tossed in the trash and we make arrangements to eat out. I hug her and say, "I'm proud of your efforts, though. That was a lot of hard work."

She shudders. "Yeah, but it was disgusting."

An hour passes and then we're getting ready to head to dinner when Tilly's phone rings. She looks at it and gets an odd expression on her face. "I don't know this number," she mutters as she answers.

I watch as Tilly's face falls, and I know something's amiss by the conversation. She hangs up and tells me that Fallon was in an accident and totaled out her car. "That was the hospital calling. She's fine, but she's suffered a broken foot and a concussion."

"Oh shit!"

"They're going to let her go home later, so she must be okay."

"Call her, Tilly. Now."

"No. Let's give her some time to get home."

Thoughts are zipping through my mind, but the main one is that I need to go to her. Minutes seem like years as they tick by. Tills wants to strangle me after half an hour because I keep insisting she call. She finally gives in.

As soon as she ends the call, I ask, "Well?"

"She's a mess because she only had collision insurance. She's in financial straights and now she's worried about how she'll make the drive out here."

"Is she okay?"

"Physically, yes. Mentally, she's a wreck."

"Fuck!" I slam my hand against the counter.

"Think, Ryland Thomas. If you showed up there, you'd upset her even more."

"Yeah, you're right." I think about it for a second and then say, "I'm gonna give her a ring."

Before she can stop me, I grab Tilly's phone.

When Fallon answers, my heart skips a beat, but I don't let it stop me. This woman needs my help and she's going to get it, no matter what.

"Hi, R.T."

"Fallon, it's not R.T., but I guess you didn't need me to tell you that now, did you?"

"Ryland?" I can hear the catch in her voice and it rips into me.

"I wanted to check on you."

"I'm okay."

"Well, from what R.T. said, you could use a hand."

"What are you doing at R.T.'s?"

"Er, I came to eat a horrid turkey that was quite raw and disgusting."

She laughs a bit and it eases me somewhat. "Well, you two have fun."

"Look, if you need anything… anything at all, you call us. You hear?"

"I will."

I end the call, look at Tills and say, "You're going to Fallon's. To help her. Do you know anything about that part of the country? We need to book you a flight and it's not gonna be easy, it being Thanksgiving and all."

"Uh-uh. But here." We walk to her laptop and look it up. Charlotte looks to be only about sixty miles from Spartanburg where she lives. In a matter of moments, I'm on the phone again and I've got a flight booked for Tilly the next morning as well as a rental car reserved, which is equipped with GPS.

I call Fallon back from my own phone this time and she picks it up after only one ring. "Ryland."

"R.T. will be in late tomorrow. What's your address?" She rattles it off while Tilly writes it down. "Don't wait up on her. She has GPS so she'll find you, Fallon. Understand?"

"Yeah, I hear you." Her voice is soft so I have to strain to hear.

"Fallon, we'll get this fixed. And by the way, congratulations on landing the big job."

There's a pause before she answers, "Thanks."

"Good night and don't worry about a thing."

We sit at dinner, Tilly's shoveling food into her mouth like she hasn't eaten in a month.

"Tills, when was the last time you ate?"

She stops and gives me an eat-shit look. "I'm starving. So what?"

I laugh.

"Hey, I could make a ton of sarcastic comments about you, but I'm refraining. I'm just glad to have my brother back."

I put my fork down. "I'm scared as hell."

"Of what?"

My brows go sky high. "Don't act like you don't know. My heart's so screwed right now, but when I see her, I know I'm done for."

"Maybe. Maybe not. But hey, what's so bad in that anyway?"

I'd like to shake my sister right now, but I refrain. "Oh, nothing, other than it scares the piss outta me."

"Right then." She scrunches up her face. "Is it because of the Iris thing?"

I shrug. "I suppose so, though I honestly can't say for sure. It's the hurt part, I think. I loved Iris, yeah, but the hurt was so bloody awful; the betrayal and that feeling of destruction. You saw me afterward. That's the reason, you know. Why I've refused to get involved with anyone. I don't want to go down into that darkness again. I can't explain how bad it was."

"Was it Iris or was it Will that hurt you so badly? And why do you think you'll get hurt this time?"

I laugh. "Oh, I don't know. It's in the stars, maybe?"

"Now that's a load of crap. Ryland Thomas, you got your balls kicked in by your best mate and girl, but don't let it ruin you for the one you deserve, the one who can truly bring you happiness. You need to leave all that emptiness that haunts you behind... let it go. Release it once and for all. I hate seeing you this way." At that, she grabs my hand and squeezes it, hard.

"I love you, Tilly. You're always here to patch me up, aren't you?"

"Well, you did a damn good job of patching me up after Mum and Daddy died. You know I'm here for you."

"Damn, I want to go to her so badly, it's killing me."

"No, you can't do that. Fallon would freak. She's so vulnerable right now. She needs to deal with you when she's at full capacity, not weak."

"What if I want her weak?"

"Ryland Thomas, that's the last thing you want and you know it. You'd always question whether she came to you freely or because she needed rescuing."

The truth is, I don't give a damn how she comes to me. I'll take her any way I can get her.

The next day is the longest I've ever lived.

I drop Tilly off at the airport and then wait to hear that she's arrived at Fallon's. When she finally calls, she tells me that Fallon looks like hell and is wearing one of those boots for her fractured foot. It's all I can do to keep myself in California. I want to hop on the next flight there, yet the sensible side of me knows that won't work. We have the plan laid out, and Tills is going to work through it. My part will come in when Fallon moves here. Then maybe, just maybe, I'll be able to win her back little by little.

Fallon

When the morning sun wakes me, I hear R.T. making coffee in my tiny kitchen. I try to hurry out of bed, but my soreness as well as that cumbersome boot I have to wear hinder me.

"So, tell me what happened in your car crash," she says as I grab a cup of coffee.

"I thought I did."

"No, not that... what led to it."

"It was Thanksgiving and I was angry, like I usually am over any holiday. My mom... well, you know. She always makes everything so difficult. I thought I'd wait to tell her about my job on Thanksgiving because she'd be around her squirrely little husband and maybe for once I could make it through unscathed. I was wrong. She berated me, and it was back to me being worthless again.

"She has this thing about me staying away from men who want me for my money. I mean, honestly, I think most men would run from me if they knew my financial status. So, I'm not paying attention and here comes this guy and he T-bones me. I don't remember getting hit, really, only waking up in the ambulance.

"The next thing I know, I'm in the hospital. I call my mom and she blames me for not being vigilant on the road. And that's it. They had to call a cab for me because all my friends were gone and I didn't have a way to get home. I didn't know the hospital even called you until you called me back."

"Fallon, look at me."

I do.

"I'm glad they called. If I'd known you suffered through this alone, I would've been so hacked."

"Well, now that you're here, I have to say I'm really glad you came." I hug her, refusing to let the tears fall. After a few minutes, I take a giant breath and step away. "You've been such a great friend, R.T. I don't know what I'd do without you."

"I have an idea. Why don't we shower and get dressed. Then let's hunt down some brekkie. That'll make buying you a car all the more fun."

I look at her like she's lost her marbles. "Uh-uh. You're definitely not buying me a car."

"Of course I am. You don't think I've come all this way to pat you on the back and then leave, do you? And don't you give me that evil eye. You know what will happen if you do. I'll just go out on my own and buy you something terribly elaborate that'll make you extraordinarily guilty. So come on."

Knowing this is a no-win situation, I give in and go take a shower.

We stop for breakfast and afterwards, at her insistence, I direct her to the medical center. She leaves me in the car while she goes in to pay the bill. Now we're moving on to buy a car for me. I'm a bit nervous because I don't know how to handle all of this. Since I only had collision insurance, the little bit of money I'll get from my car will be from the salvage of it so it won't amount to much.

"Have anything in mind?" she asks.

"Only that the damn thing will get me to California."

"Okay."

It doesn't take us long because all the car dealerships are lumped in one spot. She finds a nice, used Ford Fusion, which I'm comfortable with. I would've gone for something even less expensive, but she won't hear of it. As she fills out the paperwork, I leave because it makes me uneasy. Lucky for me, it's my left foot that's injured, so I'm okay to drive. We head to the grocery store on the way back home so I can cook dinner since R.T. really is pitiful in the kitchen.

"I can understand what Ryland meant about your turkey. You're not into the cooking thing, are you?"

"Not at all, unless you call enjoying the end result into it. I do so love to eat. You can probably tell."

I make a grunt-like noise. "Don't even go there."

"S'true. But I'm cool with it. I've gotten over the part where I'll die if I'm not perfect. Besides, if they don't like it, fuck 'em."

I laugh because she has a great attitude. "You're right. But you look great." And she does.

"But it's not like *you* have anything to worry about." R.T. eyes me.

141

I shrug. "The real reason is stress and lack of money to eat out. I run to get rid of my tension."

"I don't know how you do it. I can only run to my fridge and back."

We both laugh at that while I put our salads in two large bowls and serve it up with the wine she bought. We sit to eat at my dinky table then she toasts me and laughs. "Quite a little romantic dinner we have here."

"Oh, yeah. I have them lining up by the dozens. Oh, wait. I think I hear one knocking now."

She pauses and looks thoughtful. "I would think that's your reality."

An image of Bryce The Dickface flashes before me. I shudder and blink, although R.T's so observant, she catches it.

"I don't mean to pry."

"Not at all. I was the girl who wouldn't put out. I guess word got out and..." I shrug and then roll my shoulders back to ease the tension that's grabbed them.

"Was it just one guy?"

"Naw... but my finest moment was with this guy I'd been seeing and thought he cared. I told her the story and watched her scowl.

"Jesus, Fallon. What a bloody cretin."

"Here's the thing. My dad always told me to look for clues about people. You know, little things that reveal their true nature. The Dickface had been leaving nuggets of information about himself all over the place, but I chose to ignore them all. So, I suppose I got what I deserved."

"Stop it. You think you deserved to be treated like that? Are you joking? Fallon, the guy was a piece of crap. So you ignored a few things about him, but come on. He

142

stood there and let some chick blow him and *forced* you to watch. That's not only mean, it's perverted and abusive. He should have the bloody shit beaten out of him."

"Yeah, well, it's over and done. I'm past it and—"

"Then what about your little Vegas thing? If you were really past it, why were you so hell bent on losing your virginity?"

I'm suddenly very ill-at-ease discussing this. R.T. knows the basics of what happened with Ryland, but I'm not in the mood to have a therapy session with her.

"Please don't take this the wrong way, but I really don't want to talk about this."

"Right, you don't because you weren't over it, were you?"

"No, that wasn't it."

"Then what?"

"I was tired of hearing everyone go on and on about sex. I read about it all the time. And dammit, I just wanted to *feel* it for once in my life. I wanted to be the girl to have the fun, too. With Dickface, it never felt right. I mean, he always made me feel like I *had* to give it up; always pressuring me. I wanted to do it on *my* terms, you know? In Vegas, I figured I could do that. And then, when I saw Ryland, there was this… this, I don't know." I pinch the spot between my eyes.

"What?"

"This fucking attraction that was stronger than anything I'd ever felt in my life. And I wanted for once to experience something just for me. For the first time, I felt the impulse to have sex. And I wanted it bad. I thought he was on the same page. I mean, we mended our broken bridge after that disastrous ride from Vegas to his house, but..." a fierce thought strikes me then. "You know, I just realized something. I must not be able to read people very well and I must be a crappy judge of character. Maybe that was God's way of letting me know that, besides punishing me for doing something so damn stupid."

"Now that's the dumbest thing I've ever heard. You're not being punished and you're not a poor judge of character."

"Oh really? Then explain to me how I end up in these situations."

"If I were to guess, I think the thing with you and Ryland was a huge misunderstanding."

I laugh, yet it isn't a humorous one.

"Yeah, well, tell that to my bruised ego, and please keep this between us. I know y'all are close, but I don't want him to know any of this stuff."

She reaches across and pats my hand. "I won't say a word, and I know how hurt you were. I was there afterwards, remember?"

I nod. "I'm glad you came when you did. Those last few days would've been boob crushing."

"Boob crushing?"

"You know. Guys are always talking about their precious balls. Well, have you ever had your boob smashed?"

"Whatever do you mean?"

"This wreck I was in... my seatbelt had somehow slipped down across my boob and when it snatched me back during the impact, my damn boob got crushed and it hurt worse than anything else on my body. It's still killing me. So those guys that whine about their little gonads all the time oughta have their boobs smashed. Just sayin'."

R.T. starts out with a tiny giggle, though soon, her whole body is shaking as she holds her sides. "Oh, dear, I don't mean to laugh, but that was damn funny!"

"Tell that to my boob. Damn thing is swollen and purple. Looks like an eggplant. How would you like to have an eggplant for a boob? I'm freakin' lopsided."

Out of the blue, she says, "He'd kill me if he knew I said this, but he looks like hell and has been an arse ever since you left. Wouldn't take my calls for months. This was the first time I've seen him since you left. He knows he fucked up... knows what he did to you was wrong, but that's all I'm gonna say, 'cause I've already said too much."

I mumble, "You know what? I'm glad he's hurting because he really cut me down and I'm not sure I'll ever get over that. We'd just shared something amazing, and he abandons me there, like I was a speck of dirt. Nothing more than that. And then I even go to him, hunt him down to... ah hell, what's the use in hashing it all over again. What's done is done, and I don't want to see him again. I can't afford to have my heart get trampled on like that another time."

"I understand. What shall I tell him?"

"I don't care. But make sure he has no false illusions of us hooking up 'cuz it ain't gonna happen."

"Fair enough," she says, nodding.

We sit in silence and continue to eat. I can tell she's thinking, though, by the glances she keeps giving me.

"Stop that. I know you're conjuring up something in your mind."

"Not really. I'm simply trying to figure out how it all could've gone so wrong between the two of you."

"Why does it matter so much?"

"I want to see you happy, Fallon."

"Glad to know someone does."

"Can I ask you a personal question? Aside from the Ryland issue?" she asks.

Why the hell not. I mean Ryland was the most intimate. "Sure."

"What happened with your parents?"

"Oh. My dad died and my mom's crazy." I tell her the story and she sympathizes. "Thanks, but my mom is who she is. I keep hoping, but... it'll never change. I wish I could move on, yet you know, she's my mom and it's just difficult. Dad was the best and now that he's gone, so she's all I've got. I'm not sure she does me any good, though."

"Why don't you spend Christmas with me? You can come out to San Francisco early and get moved in right afterwards. You'd have a few days to get to know the city. What do you say?"

There isn't an adequate reason to say no, so I accept her invitation. "Why are you doing all this for me?"

"I like you. You're a great person and friend. I hope you feel the same."

"R.T., honestly, I don't know what I would do without you."

With that, she squeezes me in a tight hug.

"Hey, watch the boob!"

"Oops! Sorry. I'm going to love having you in Cali. I hope these next couple of weeks fly by."

Between my final week of work, limping around in that silly boot and packing to move, the last two and a half weeks are a blur. Before I know it, I'm on I-40, heading west towards San Francisco.

I'm so excited I can almost taste it. Everything feels fresh to me; from my new, used car to my old clothes and meager belongings tossed in the back and trunk of the car.

In the end, instead of renting a trailer, I decide to leave my old bed and chest of drawers behind. The bed was an ancient hand-me-down and the chest was something I found at a yard sale. I'll just buy something else when I can afford it and I can always sleep on a blow up mattress until I can afford a bed.

It's going to take me a few days to get there, but I don't care. I'll spend the night somewhere along the way when I get sleepy.

My excitement is crazy through the roof because I've never done anything like this before. I'm so happy that I can visualize that mountain of debt shrinking when I think about being able to pay off my student loans.

It's a foggy evening when I pull into San Francisco and locate R.T.'s house. My body is fatigued from the drive, but I'm super psyched to be here nevertheless. She lives in a lovely Victorian in Cow Hollow with a driveway, which is an absolute impossibility to find in this city.

I hike up the steps to her porch and admire her Christmas lights and decorations everywhere. When I ring the bell and the door opens, my jaw drops as I stare right into that incredible set of green eyes I left behind several months ago.

FOURTEEN

RYLAND - THOMAS

Her face tells me everything her voice doesn't. I'm the last person she expects or wants to see.

"Fallon." My throat tightens as though someone is squeezing it while I stare at her for a minute and absorb her. The scent that lingered in her room for so long washes over me and I inhale it as I close my eyes before I give myself a mental shake and pull it together.

"Please come in." I smile. I want to hug the shit out of her, she looks that good. Then I notice the boot she has on. "Good Lord, let me help you." I grab the things out of her hands, but she doesn't move. I'm sure she's shocked to see me, so I blurt out, "R.T. had to run out for something, but she'll be back in a sec. Not to worry. You're not stuck with me for long." She still hasn't said a word. "Fallon. Everything okay?"

Her eyes are stormy. "Hell, no, it's not okay. You stand there like... like... like I'm supposed to be overjoyed to see you. Well, I'm not." She crosses her arms over chest and glares at me.

Shit. I was hoping for a bit of a better response. "Right then. I don't suppose you are, me being the arse that I am, but it's damp and chilly out, and I know you're knackered from the drive, so come on in and I'll get you something to drink while you get settled in. You don't have to speak to me if you don't want."

Those damn eyes of hers always nail me, but this time, I feel like I'm five-years-old and being scolded for eating all the cookies in the jar. The guilt she evokes in me forces me to look away from her.

I shutter my eyes from her penetrating gaze and say, "Please, Fallon. I feel like an absolute shit as it is. I know I deserve to be strung up by my balls and then some, but come in for Christ's sake. You can't stand on the porch all night. You'll catch a chill."

At last she nods. Once. And then limps passed me, head held high. The slight breeze she creates is filled with her scent, and all I can think of is burying my face in her hair. My dick jolts and I suddenly have the hard-on from hell. "Fuck," I mumble.

"What's that?"

My voice is firm as I answer, "I said fuck. As in me. I'm a fuck, Fallon. Through and through." I've come this far, so I might as well continue.

She's stopped by now and is studying me, her head tipped to the side.

"I deserve every nasty and ugly word you can send my way because I treated you abominably. And I'm sorry. More than I can say."

Tilly barges in the door right then, interrupting my apology. I don't know whether to be pissed or happy.

"Fallon!" The two girls hug and Tilly is trying to hop around.

"R.T., don't forget about Fallon's foot."

"Bugger, I'm sorry. I forgot about your boot thing. Shit, Fallon." She peers at Fallon for a second and notices something's up. "So, how was the drive?"

"Long. I'm glad I'm here." It's a half-hearted comment.

"Um, did I interrupt something?"

Fallon and I answer at the same time. Of course, she says no and I say yes. Tills looks confused.

"S'okay. I was going to fix us all drinks anyway. So what can I get everyone?"

They both want wine so I pour us glasses of merlot.

We sit for a very uncomfortable five minutes, then I excuse myself and go in the kitchen to cook. I can hear the girls chatting for a bit before it sounds like they're moving up the stairs to the bedrooms. I know I should help, but I think they need their privacy more, so I continue cooking dinner.

Tilly walks in later and I'm not comforted by the look on her face. "She's not happy you're here," she whispers.

"No shit. She didn't even want to come inside."

Tilly nods. "Ryland Thomas, I think we need to tell her about us... who you really are."

"What?" I'm not prepared for that.

"If you have deep feelings for her, this will open another door for you. You know, tell her that you trust her with this... that sort of thing. We can tell her over dinner and then I'll discreetly disappear and let you two talk things out. But one thing... keep your hands off her."

"What the bloody hell is that supposed to mean?"

"Exactly what you think it does. You're eye-fucking her. Not touching her will be hard, but don't do it. Not even on the arm. You want her to almost have to beg you to touch her. Got that?"

I'm confused, though I agree. Why would I touch her when she looks like she wants to stab me? I doubt she'll ever get close to begging me to touch her. The way I see it, she'll be begging me to stay away from her.

Fallon's picking at her food, and Tilly feels the need to kick me under the table.

I clear my throat. "So, Fallon, we have something we need to talk to you about. It's something that will require your, um, promise to keep it close and not breathe a word of it to anyone."

She looks at me suspiciously. I kick Tills and she continues, "Fallon, what Ryland is trying to say is that there's something we want to share with you and it's something important to us. Only one other person knows this, therefore can we have your promise you won't share it with anyone?"

She nods. "Yeah. But what's so important between the two of you that you... oh my God. Are you two married?"

"What? No! God no! Holy fuck! You can't think *that*. Ew!" Tills is almost turning green now. The thought of us doing *that* makes me want to laugh, so that's what I do. I laugh. Really hard.

When I finally pull myself together, I look at Fallon. "Fallon, she's my sister. R.T. is my sister. And her name is Tilly. Well, it's really Rose Tilly."

Now she's looking at me like *who cares* and all that.

I go on. "Fallon, I'm the real R.T. My name is Ryland. It's Ryland Thomas." I'm quiet for a moment so it can all sink in.

Her mouth works around for a few moments and then she says, "But I thought..." And then, "You're not R.T.?" Then points an accusatory finger at Tilly. Tills shakes her head.

"I'm the stand in. I do write, as a freelancer. Everything that Ryland Thomas told you is reversed. I freelance and he's the novelist. I do all of his public appearances and only his agent knows that he's the writer. Everyone else, even the publisher, thinks he's a woman."

"But how...?"

I answer this time. "The same way we did it in Vegas. I wanted to keep my identity a secret because most women don't think a man is capable of writing heavy romance novels. So we thought, since you and Tilly were so close, and that you and... well, you know... we thought you should know the truth. And honestly, this bloody facade was getting right confusing. I'm really sorry we didn't tell you sooner, Fallon."

She nods and keeps looking between Tills and me. Then her expression changes completely. *"You* wrote *Lovers Between the Sheets."* It's a statement, and from the tone of her voice, it's difficult to tell if she's disappointed, shocked or disapproving.

I slowly nod and watch her shoulders slump. This isn't good news for me. We finish eating in silence and my heart feels worse than it's felt in weeks. I guess I expected her to be neutral about this, yet her disappointment in me has forced me to the lowest point in my life.

152

When everyone is done, I gather up the plates in silence and carry them to the kitchen. There's really no need for Tilly to give us time to be alone because, at this point, I have nothing to say. I tidy up the kitchen and fill a glass with water. I decide today's been enough for me and call it a night. As I head towards the stairs, I hear Fallon call my name.

"Ryland, may I speak with you?"

"Sure, and about my name. You can either call me Ryland or Ryland Thomas, now that you know the real me."

"Which one do you prefer?"

"Actually, Ryland Thomas. I know it's a bit long, but it's what those who are closest to me call me. My folks called me that. It's what Tilly calls me. I'll leave it up to you to decide."

"Okay. Ryland Thomas it is."

I follow her into Tilly's den where we sit.

"Thanks for sharing your true identity with me. So, you're both R.T.'s, aren't you?"

"Yeah, we are. Twins, you know. Tills was named for both grandmothers and I was named for both grandfathers. Funny that they were both R's and T's."

"Pretty neat, I think. I always thought it was strange how you seemed to be around her all the time."

"I know. And that first day in my house when you went to use the phone, I wanted to tell you then, but I was afraid. And Tilly needed to be in on it, too, because she's been a part of it from the start."

"I can understand that."

"I hope you're not too angry with us. We didn't hide it from you out of malice. It was a decision we made at the start; that no one would ever know. When I wanted to

153

tell you, I couldn't because we're almost like a partnership in this... Tilly and I." I drag my hand through my hair.

Fallon nods. "I see that. I just want you to know that I still think you write the best books, and just because I know who you are now, won't change that fact."

It eases my heart somewhat, so I bow my head in acknowledgment. We need to talk about us, however I'm not sure if this is the right time. I look at her and she's gazing at me like she's expecting something.

"I'm sorry for everything, Fallon. If I could change how I behaved that day on the deck, believe me, I would. I swear to God I would. I was the biggest jerkass around."

"I won't disagree. I know there are things we need to talk about, but my body is screaming for sleep, so do you mind if we continue this tomorrow?"

"Not at all. Do you need help up the steps?"

"Naw, I've got it."

"Okay then. Good night, Fallon. Sleep well."

I watch as she takes it one step at a time and my heart feels the burden has been lightened somewhat. I'm aware that I have a long way to go, but at least she's willing to speak to me now.

Fifteen

Fallon

Ryland is R.T. and his twin sister is Tilly! And she's not the author. Good lord. What a night of surprises. And he's tripping all over himself, apologizing. Even R.T.—I mean Tilly—said he was completely freaked about everything. I'm not even sure what to think, but I do know this. I'm going to make that man work for it. I will not cave into him at all. I don't care how damn hot and sexy he is. For right now, though, I'm so flippin' tired I can't keep my eyes open. I barely make it into the bed before I'm asleep.

I wake up and I'm burning hot… and no damn wonder. Ryland—I mean Ryland Thomas—is wrapped around me like a steaming hot crepe. His arms are holding me against his hard body and I can feel his chest hairs brushing my skin. I'm incredibly aware of him, flames fan across me like an inferno and that place between my thighs aches with a need so strong I'm sure

I'm going to detonate any second now. How did he slip into my bed without me knowing?

I try to move and I feel him shake as he says, "Oh, no, you don't." Then hot lips are scorching my neck and his tongue begins a descent that soon has me squirming. As if he can read my mind, one of his arms lowers to my belly and his fingers move to that place I want him to touch. When he finally does, I moan and put my hand over his, trapping it there. I hear his deep laughter again and his finger slides into me. Soon, I'm coming apart all over him. He doesn't stop, though. He doesn't give me a moment before he moves between my legs and spreads them wide.

He looks up at me. "I've missed this so much." Then his tongue is on me, inside of me, licking and sucking while my hands fist his hair.

"Ryland Thomas, I need you."

He doesn't stop, just continues to relentlessly nibble and lick me until my head is spinning. The orgasm that vibrates through me defies description. It begins in small waves, but then crashes into me in epic proportions, beginning at my core and radiating throughout my body, ending in the arches of my feet. I'm like jelly. But no, he's not finished. Now he's thrusting into me, pummeling me and I'm making that climb all over again.

He slides his finger into my mouth, whispering, "Taste this. It's nirvana to me." Forest green eyes with the dark gold striations stare back at me as he touches his forehead to mine. "It should always be like this. And it will always be like this. I love you, Fallon."

I unravel in his arms, deliciously, deliriously and he joins me as he groans, calling my name. We're both tangled up in each other, our sweat making us slippery. It's beyond sweet.

"God, I missed you," he says as he curls up against me, lacing his fingers with mine. "Don't ever go away again."

I fall back to sleep, tucked into his neck, breathing against his skin and trying to absorb what's just happened between us.

When the sun awakens me, I stretch out my arm, trying to touch Ryland Thomas, but I only find an empty space. I sit up to find I'm alone. Lifting the covers, I check to see if I'm wearing the PJ's I put on last night and sure enough, I am. Holy shmoley! Was that a dream I had? If so, it was some kind of dream. I slip my hand down the front of my panties to find them damp. I'm dripping as well. I've never had a wet dream before. The damn thing was so real! I lift up my shirt to find my nipples looking like they're getting ready to head for the moon. Jesus, I need to get a grip here.

My head takes me back to that dream, and images zoom before me... images that I want to be real. Before I know it, my hand is back in my panties and my hoo-hah is getting some relief because there's no way in hell I can walk around like this all day. Dayum. I've got to pull it together.

Knowing I need to get up, I head to the bathroom and the first thing I do is plow into Ryland Thomas. I almost land on the floor, but he saves me in time by grabbing my hand... my damp hand with its wet fingers.

"Good morning, love. You look quite adorable this morning."

"Um, I'm sure." My hair probably looks like a herd of squirrels are living in it.

Then, to my utter horror, he lifts my hand, takes my fingers, slides them into his mouth and sucks them. Fuck me running!

"Mmmm." He releases me, winks and walks away.

I can't move for a few minutes, yet when I do, I haul butt into the bathroom, my heart doing the fifty-meter dash and setting a world record. This is so embarrassing. I can only imagine the looks he'll be giving me today.

As I shower, I keep going back to that dream. Who dreams like that? I mean it was so damn vivid. I could have sworn it was real.

I'm finally dressed and heading down to join the others. It's Christmas Eve today and I've no idea what they have planned. I still want to talk to Ryland Thomas because we certainly have piles of unfinished business between us.

As I enter the kitchen, Tilly is at the table drinking coffee and working on her email while Ryland Thomas is cooking something.

"Good morning," I say to them.

Tilly mumbles back and Ryland Thomas flashes me a wicked grin. I grab some coffee and ask if he needs help. He merely raises a brow.

"What are you making?" It smells so yummy. My stomach gives a rumble.

"French toast. Do you like it?"

"It's one of my favorites."

"Excellent."

Watching him cook, I remember how he has quite the knack for it. He plates everything up and hands me mine while he carries his and Tilly's.

We sit and eat. It's so delicious I can't help from grinning.

"What?" he wants to know.

"Mmmm. This is so good." I shove in another forkful. "I mean really, really good. How'd you learn to cook like this?"

"My mum taught me."

I harrumph. "Lucky you. My dad was a crummy cook. Oh, he tried, but never could get the hang of it. And my mom, well, she was only worried about her things and such, so I never had a teacher. I'm okay I guess, but I can't make this kind of stuff. You know... family recipes that are passed down."

He looks at me and then says, "I can teach you. It's easy. If you're interested, that is."

"Oh yeah. I'd love that."

Tilly finishes up hers and says, "I thought we could do a little Christmas spirit stuff today."

Now I get a bit uncomfortable because I don't want to be a third wheel in their family traditions. "Look, if you two have things you want to do, don't let me keep you from them."

"Well, bugger, Fallon, I was hoping you'd want to spend some time with us. You know, it's just been the two of us forever so we've been kind of looking forward to having you here," Tilly says.

"Yeah?"

"Yeah." She smiles.

Ryland Thomas adds, "Tills, were you thinking about doing one of those car trips where you ride around all day and look at decorations?"

"Yeah. Why?"

"Because Fallon's been in a car for days and I think the last thing she wants is to spend another day in one."

"Right you are there, brother. Didn't think about that, now, did I?"

"No, I don't suppose you did."

Tilly brightens up again. "Well, then, how about a walk instead?"

I'm about to break out in giggles because watching the two of them is hilarious. Ryland Thomas looks at Tilly like she's just grown another head. "Bloody hell, Tilly. She has a broken foot. Are you daft?"

The giggles win the battle and finally take over as they look at me and join in. Tilly admits that it wasn't her most brilliant idea ever. Then we laugh some more. Ryland Thomas finally says that maybe a brief drive and a brief walk, just to get us all out of the house and then we might want to watch some old classic Christmas movies. We all agree and get ready to leave.

Tilly goes upstairs to do whatever, leaving Ryland Thomas and me alone. He gets a smirk on his face. "So, did you sleep well last night?"

"Yeah, I…" I begin to wonder if he knows of my dream. "Did you…" But there's no way he could've been there.

"Did I what?"

"Never mind."

He has such a sexy grin on his face. I feel my body reacting, and damn it all, that's the last thing I need.

"What, Fallon? Tell me."

"It's just that, well… were you in my room last night?"

"No, but not because I didn't want to be."

Damn that voice of his. Then I do the stupidest thing of all. I look straight at his mouth and catch a glimpse of his tongue peeking out and taking a lick at his lips. Shit, I am so done for.

When I shiver, he notices and the corners of his mouth lift. He knows he's affecting me, so what does he do next? He steps right in front of me, so close I can feel the heat rolling off him. However he doesn't touch me. Instead, he says in that deep sexy voice of his, "It's not just your room I want to be inside of, Fallon." His tongue slides across his lower lip, like he's tasting the most delicious thing in the world. I'm dying here.

Now I'm wondering just who's going to be working more for it, him or me, because right now, I feel like dropping straight to my knees and begging him to take me up upstairs and do the dirty to me. Slow, hard, fast; however he wants it.

"Are you ready?" Tilly asks as she comes into the room. *More than ready*, I say to myself. In fact, right now, I'm so damn achy I could scream.

I look at Ryland Thomas, who is gazing at me like we're in bed. I nearly groan before I catch myself.

"What are you two waiting for?" Tilly asks. That's what I'd like to know, too. "I'll go start the car," she says before heading out the door.

As Ryland Thomas is handing me my coat, I'm not sure what comes over me, but one minute his hand is reaching out to me, and the next, I'm slapping my coat away as my hands fist the lapels of his coat and jerk him against me. I crush my body close to his and kiss him like the world is going to end. I finally get some amount of control over myself and force my mouth to break contact.

He smirks and whispers, "That's my girl." Then we walk to the car like nothing ever happened.

Right before we get in, I lean into him and hiss, "You're still gonna have to work for it, buddy."

He chuckles as he shuts the door.

This has been the most torturous day of my life! My body is so tightly strung I don't know which way to turn. This heightened response has to be wrong because I certainly can't go through life like this. I'll be the bat-shit crazy lady everyone talks about. We've watched a couple of movies, but I can't sit still for anything. Tilly is giving me odd looks and Ryland Thomas has been wearing a slight smile, so I know he gets that I'm squirmy for one reason only. I want to strip my clothes off and rub my body all over his, however that would be wrong on just way too many levels. Well, maybe not exactly wrong, but it wouldn't be smart.

Thank Heavens it's time for dinner. We head out to our reservation. It's only around the corner so we walk and I purposely put Tilly in the middle, but it doesn't last. Somehow, Ryland Thomas ends up next to me, which makes my body fire up like all the Christmas lights we're seeing everywhere. I'm pretty sure I could glow in the dark right now. I'm so hyperaware of him, it's starting to make me fidgety.

"Do you have ADHD?" Tilly asks. "You sure are jumpy."

"Just nervous about my new job, I guess."

My ears perk as I hear his deep chuckle. My nerve endings answer back. "Stop that," I say to myself more than anything. They both look at me.

"You okay, Fallon?" Ryland Thomas asks.

It finally hits Tilly as I growl at him. She grins so wide I want to smack her.

Hoping to calm myself down, I drink way too much at dinner, but my misguided attempt has me singing— rather badly, I might add—Christmas carols on the way home. They laugh at me because I'm so terrible and I'm enjoying my little audience. When we make it home, Tilly puts on some music and then comes back with some presents.

"Oh, no. No, no, no. You weren't supposed to do this." I've been adamant about no gifts.

"I know, but get over it, darling. It's Christmas. Well, almost anyway."

Ryland Thomas is smiling as I take the small gift. I open it and grin. It's a gift card for a new bed from the two of them. Then, I immediately start crying.

"Is it an ugly gift card?" Tilly teases. Ryland Thomas doesn't speak. He simply stands there and watches.

"No, you goof ball. It's just that, well, since my dad died, no one's been so damn good to me. But it's way too much. You've already given me much more than I can ever repay you for. I can't possibly accept this."

"You're repaying us with your friendship. Besides, you can't sleep on the floor, Fallon," Tilly says.

As I stand here, I'm at a loss. What I want to do most is hug them both, but that means I'll be wrapped in his arms and I'll never want to be out of them again. How the hell did I go from not wanting to talk to him a day ago to not wanting to be away from him? What the hell is wrong with me? My resistance needs to hold firm here. How can I be such a caver?

Tilly hugs me and I squash her. I've grown to love her like my best blogger friends. When she lets me go,

163

he's standing there. His arms open up and I've no choice except to walk into them. Oh. God. He. Smells. So. Fucking. Good. I. Want. To. Lick. Him. All. Over. My face is in that special place where his neck meets his shoulder and I want to die like this. Or stay here forever, frozen in time.

"Um, hello, you two. I'm over here," Tilly says, her voice forcing me out of my trance.

My cheeks grow warm so I know they're flushed.

Ryland Thomas rubs the back of his hand across one and says, "You're blushing." I only nod, since my voice has abandoned me, exactly like my damn resolve to stay strong. Fuck! I'm so screwed here.

RYLAND -THOMAS

Oh, was Tilly ever right. This thing about not touching Fallon is working. I'm not having to do a thing except perhaps cast a glance her way. And it's hard not to simply ogle the woman. This morning, when she ran into me in the hall, it took every bit of resolve not to push her back into her room, strip her cute little nightclothes off and kiss her all over.

And what the hell was going on in her room last night? Whatever it was, she woke me up out of a dead sleep with her moans. She was calling out my name, like we were having the best sex ever. She must have been dreaming, and damn, I wish I could have had that same dream. I ended up in the damn bathroom, taking a cold shower at three a.m. The poor girl is as addled as I am.

When she told me I was going to have to work for it, I wanted to throw my head back and laugh my arse off. What she doesn't know is we're both going to end up

165

working, although it'll be working to keep our hands *off* each other. I wonder how long we can last.

My body is so jacked. I've never met anyone that makes my heart flip like she does. When she opened that little gift and then started crying, I wanted to let her know everything would be fine and that she didn't have to pay anything back. It bothers me that she's burdened with the debt of her student loans and that she's so worried about it. One day I'd like to have a nice little chat with her mum and let her know exactly what kind of a piece of shit parent she is.

Tilly went to bed shortly after my comment about Fallon blushing.

"I think you look lovely with roses in your cheeks," I tell her.

"Thanks again for the gifts, but you know I can't accept the bed. It's just too much."

"Tilly was adamant, Fallon. It wasn't all me."

She looks at me for a moment. "The car? Who was that?"

"Both of us. We knew it could kill your chances of getting out here. I mean, what else would you do?"

"Yeah, and that's something I want to talk to you about. I'd like to work up some kind of a repayment plan. Just like if I were paying back the bank."

It's obvious she's serious about this idea. "Okay," I agree. "I can go with that. But about the bed, Tilly will blame me if you don't take it. And really, it's not that much. You have no idea how difficult she is when she's pissed, too."

That gets a smile out of her and then a nod.

166

We both fumble around with more words for a few minutes and then tell each other Merry Christmas before we head to bed.

Since my plans are to get up early and fix a big Christmas breakfast for the girls, I hope I can sleep tonight. I want to spoil them. I have a special gift for Fallon and I'm excited to give it to her.

I'm sound asleep when I'm awakened by a banging noise against the wall. I lie there for a moment and then I hear Fallon's voice. She sounds like she's injured herself, so I hop out of bed and pull on my jeans. Wondering if she fell out of bed, I open her door and come to a screeching halt as I take in the scene before me. She's on her knees in the bed, her hands on the headboard, and her ass is in the air while she's moving back and forth, groaning. Fuck. Me. She has to be dreaming again because her head is thrown back and she's into it.

"Ah, ah yes, Ryland Thomas. Harder."

Bloody hell. My dick is getting ready to explode in my jeans and I can't move. The scene in front of me enthralls me. My body moves without my awareness and my hand is on her ass, moving her panties aside, rubbing her and damn, she's slick with need.

"Wake up, Fallon," I say next to her ear as I run my tongue down her neck.

Her body stops moving in her dream and I can tell she's awake now. My hand is moving back and forth and then I slip inside of her. Now she's moaning again, but it's because she's awake and I'm there. I nibble her neck, that place she loves and I hear her respond. She moves against my hand, wanting more, so I comply.

I can't stand it any longer, so I flip her over and pull off her panties. Gripping the insides of her thighs, I

167

spread them wide and my mouth finds home. She's so sweet and salty all at the same time. The sounds she makes are my undoing. I want inside of her like I've never wanted anything before, but I won't go there yet. This is all about her and will be for a while. I can feel the muscles in her legs tensing, my clue that her orgasm is on the horizon. I pick up my speed and plunge another finger into her. Those little muscles of hers tighten around my fingers as she calls my name with her hands in my hair, pulling me to her. And bloody hell I love the way that feels. When everything passes, I kiss the insides of her thighs as she pulls on my hair. I lift my head and she grabs my face as she sits up.

"Come here."

Crawling up her luscious body, making my way to her lips, she kisses me, turning me inside out. As she's kissing me, she's tugging me against her so now I'm stretched on top of her. Her mouth is paradise, and I've been denied it for too long. I seek out every tiny hiding place I can, memorizing them. I want to remember this kiss forever.

Suddenly, it becomes abundantly clear to me that a kiss with her is more intimate than the act of sex itself. There is something so incredibly emotional and personal about it that I know I'll never think of kissing in the same way again.

When I pull away I can only stare into her silver gray eyes. Her lips are soft and I can't keep mine from touching them again. I suck on first her top lip then her bottom one. Then I run my tongue along them. I touch nothing else on her other than her mouth with mine. And it's divine.

"Every time I kiss you, Fallon, I feel like I'm handing you a piece of my heart." The words are whispered, but they're honest and true.

Her thumb runs along my bottom lip. "You don't even know me, Ryland Thomas."

"I know you better than you think I do. I know that you make me feel things I've never felt before. You do things to me that I can't explain. Things seem... different with you. I didn't care about things before you. And I know I'm a bloody fuck up, but I'm going to work hard to prove to you that I can be the man you need and want in your life."

Her hands tighten in my hair as her mouth seeks mine for a kiss filled with passion and urgency. We come together with such need for each other it's impossible to deny any longer.

My hand runs into her hair. I love the feel of its silken texture. I don't ever want this moment to end because in it is something so loving and peaceful that it makes me realize how right things are with her and how well we mesh. It also brings home how fragile we are and that the tiniest of things can destroy us. If anyone knows how uncertain life is, it's the two of us. Knowing this only makes me want to be an even better man for her.

When we finally stop to breathe, I smile. She smiles back for a moment then asks, "Why did you come into my room?"

Chuckling, I answer, "Your headboard banged against my wall. Then I heard you cry out and I thought you hurt yourself. But when I got here, I found quite a picture." I describe it and she buries her head in my neck and groans. I laugh again. "It was worth it."

169

"I had this vivid dream of you last night, too. I really thought you were in bed with me."

"I wish," I snort.

She sighs. "Ryland Thomas, what are we gonna do?"

"Do? Why do we have to do anything? Can't we just take it a day at a time?"

"I suppose we can."

Standing up for a second, I pull off my pants. "Scoot over, love." I slip under the covers next to her and wrap her in my arms.

"What will your sister say about us sleeping in the same bed?"

"She'll be wondering what took us so long. She's wanted this almost as much as me. But Fallon, we're not going to do anything except sleep in here tonight. We're going to take things slow, like we should've from the start. There's an undeniable attraction between us, but we still have some sorting out to do. And there are some things I need to tell you, too. But right now, I want you to get some sleep, love." I kiss her neck.

"Okay. G'night Sinclair."

"'Night, love." I chuckle at her use of my surname.

Waking up with a raging hard-on is just as bad as trying to go to sleep with one. I quietly roll out of bed, so as not to disturb the true sleeping beauty next to me, and tiptoe out of her room. I get in the shower and take care of things. Christ, it seems like that's all I do since I met Fallon. After I get dressed, I head to the kitchen to get my big brekkie started.

I make bacon, sausage and get the hash browns going. I pull out the scones that Tilly bought and stick them in the oven to warm. The coffee's made and I get the juice and iced water in the pitchers. I mix up a batch of Mimosas and a batch of Bloody Marys as the girls finally make their way downstairs. Fallon's showered, but Tilly hasn't.

Tilly says, "Oh, I smelled all the yummy goodness and couldn't wait to eat."

"What's your poison, ladies?"

They both start with coffee while I put the eggs on. I am making scrambled eggs with fresh herbs and Parmigiano-Reggiano grated on top.

We sit down and enjoy our full breakfast before we get into the Mimosas, at which point Tilly announces that it's present time, so we head over to the den where the Christmas tree is located. I put on the Christmas music and she starts handing out her presents.

Fallon is crestfallen when she gets more gifts.

"Hush now. This is so much fun for me and it gives me an excuse."

I just smile because all I want to do is watch Fallon open her gifts.

She does and smiles to see some earrings, a bracelet and a new leather handbag that she can use as a briefcase for work.

"Tilly, this is too much!"

"You'll need it for work. It can hold your laptop and all your papers that you'll have to carry back and forth. Come on, Fallon, you need to look professional. You can't go in to work carrying a ratty old backpack you used in college."

Fallon is quiet for a second and finally agrees.

"Good."

Tilly hands me my gifts and I open them to see a new MacBookPro. My old one was starting to run a bit slow. "Tilly, this is great. Thanks!" I hug her.

"That's awesome," Fallon says. "That's a dream machine."

"It is," I agree.

I give Tilly her gift, and when she unwraps it, she squeals. "Oh my God, are you kidding me?"

"What is it?" Fallon asks.

"It's a trip to Vietnam for two weeks. I've been dying to go there." Tilly jumps up and hugs me. "Thank you, Ryland Thomas. This is perfect."

"I hope you noticed it's for two. I bought it when you were still with what's-his-name. So you'll have to figure out someone else to take."

"No worries on that, brother." She kisses me on the cheek.

Then I hand Fallon her gift. She looks at me in surprise. "Go on, open it."

She unwraps it to find the first edition of *Lovers Between the Sheets*. "You need to read the inscription inside."

I watch her as she opens it. She's smiling at first then her face changes to one of surprise then a bit more of a shocked look before she positively glows. She holds the book against her chest and hugs it to her.

"Are you for real?" she whispers, her eyes all dewy.

I nod slowly. She gets up and walks to me and then we're in each other's arms, hugging. "Thank you. This means so much more to me than any other gift in the world."

"Merry Christmas, Fallon." I kiss her lightly on the lips.

172

Exquisite Betrayal

Tilly is looking at us and says, "Well, are you gonna tell me what it says?"

Fallon hands her the book and she starts to read.

Dearest Fallon,

After seeing you hold this next to your heart and the way your eyes lit up when you did, I knew then it was never meant to be mine. So take this and add it to your collection. What you didn't know was that the day we spoke, I had already begun working on the sequel to this, but after hearing your thoughts, I have since scratched the whole idea. You're right. There can never be a part two to Lovers Between the Sheets *because it would spoil the purity of the words. So thank you for being honest about that and saving me from humiliating myself and ruining this story.*

Merry Christmas.

Yours,

Ryland Thomas

Fallon and I only have eyes for each other and Tilly somehow vanishes.

"You really stopped writing it because of what I said?"

"Yeah. Like the inscription says, you were dead on. It would've looked like a scheme to drag the story on and on. It would've ruined the whole thing. You made me realize that. I don't want to be one of those writers who puts things out there just for the money. I want them to be from the heart. So I trashed the whole thing. Deleted it. It will never be written."

"Willow and Jack will be so happy." She smiles and I can't help smiling in return. All of a sudden we find ourselves in each other's arms again, kissing this time. Heated kissing, like last night... sharing pieces of our souls.

She's so bloody sweet I want this to go on forever, but I know it can't. So I pull away and say, "You know I could kiss you all day, right?"

She grins and nods. "I think Tilly would feel like a third wheel, though."

I take a deep breath and then tuck a chunk of her hair behind her ear. "Have I told you how beautiful you are?"

"Hmm. Not today."

"You're not just beautiful, you're exquisite," I say against her mouth. I kiss her quickly then grab her hand. "Tilly, how 'bout another Mimosa?" I call out.

"Are you two done snogging yet?"

Fallon turns a bit pink, but giggles. "Yeah. Come here."

Tills comes in with the pitcher and tray of Mimosas, and smiles. She's happy things are straightening out between us. And it turns out to be quite a happy Christmas after all.

Fallon's excited to get into her apartment. It's more like a large studio, but it's not far from here and it's close to her office. Critics Abound located it for her so this is the first time she's seeing it in person. Everything else has been done online.

We're moving her in today and she's almost bursting. It doesn't take long because she barely has anything. Her bed is being delivered this afternoon, so we go and buy sheets and towels and then make a stop to stock up her kitchen with some extra things she needs.

After her bed arrives, I help her make it up with her new things while Tilly heads home. It's just the two of us now and we smile because we haven't had much privacy since she's arrived here.

"What are you thinking?" I ask.

"Do you have to ask?"

We both laugh right before we collide with each other in a heated kiss. However I've decided before we go any further—before we take this to the next step—I have to tell her about my past. I don't really want to because Iris burned a hole so huge and so deep within me that I dread the mere mention of her name. To avoid discussing it with Fallon, though, is too unfair, and I cannot leave it another minute.

"Fallon, before we do anything, there's something we need to talk about... something I need to tell you. It's about why I was such a jerkface to you."

Seventeen

Fallon

His eyes bore into mine and he licks his lips for a second. "Fallon, there are so many things I need to say to you, but first of all, I must apologize again. That day on the deck was the best moment of my life and I ruined it when I left. But the truth is..." he looks away for a moment and then grabs me and says, "it scared the piss outta me. I felt so close to you and I didn't know what to say... to do. So, of course, I did the worst thing of all and I ran. I know, very noble and all. The proper thing a gent would do, right? But I have this issue with..."

He stops and breathes then he rubs his face. "Fuck. You know I told you my mum and dad were killed? Yeah, well, shortly afterwards, I got involved with the girl who would fix it all. Save me from everything. Happens that she and I were together for well over a year and then one day I come home because I forgot my notes for a class. I was still in uni at the time. And well, I catch her in bed— *my bed*—with my best mate. They wanna know if I wanted to join them, too. It messed me up for a while and my sister found me a couple of weeks later. She had to straighten me out. I was really broken up… depressed, and then I started sleeping around. I was acting out, telling myself I wasn't hurt and all.

"You know the story, I'm sure. It was all rubbish. The deal was that my parents' death was still an issue and then my best mate and finally her. Then came the girls… I think I was trying to prove to myself that I didn't care about what they did, so I tried to erase it all by using women. Of course, that was stupid. I finally went through therapy and that pushed me back out of the black hole I'd been living in. So now, I'm a bit gun shy, you might say. When you and I were on the deck, I felt an anxiety attack coming on. I hadn't had one in years, so I clammed up. I should've talked to you, however I didn't know where to start or what to say. It was wrong because not saying anything hurt you and I—I wish I could do it over… you know, change the way I acted."

When he finishes, he's taken his lower lip into his mouth and I worry he's going to bite through it because he's clamping down on it so hard with his teeth. So I tug it out with my fingers.

"Look, Ryland Thomas, I'm sorry. That's a rotten betrayal if I've ever heard one. You were really screwed over and I'm sorry. And I thought mine was bad, but it was nothing in comparison."

His tilted head tells me he's waiting to hear my story now. There's absolutely no use in keeping that Bryce The Dickface story a secret, so I spill that one out. When I'm finished, he's chomping down on that lip again.

177

"You're gonna put a hole straight through this if you don't stop," I tell him as I ease it out from between his teeth.

"What a bloody asshole."

"Yeah, right? And I was so stupid." I shudder at the thought of that scene again.

His arms cocoon me, and for a minute, he's silent. "You weren't stupid. You put your trust in someone you thought deserved it. I'm just as bad as that wanker. And it doesn't negate the fact that I should never have treated you so dreadfully."

I look at him. "I'm not gonna lie and say it's okay. I had every intention of telling you to fuck off when I saw you. But, I don't know. There's something between us. I mean, at least I think there is."

"Yes! You know I feel it, too. I'm not making excuses for my bad behavior, but what I'm asking for is a chance to prove myself to you, Fallon. I promise not to act like such a bloody bastard again, if you'll only give me that chance."

"Um, Ryland Thomas, aren't you the one I've been with for the last few days?"

"Well, yeah, why?"

"Because, that's me saying I'm willing to give you another chance. But don't mess it up this time, okay? I don't think my ego can take another one of those—"

"You don't have to worry about that, Fallon."

Then, the next thing I know, I'm in his arms and my body's on fire for this man. I'm consumed with him, but he says he wants to take it slow, so I let him.

He takes me to dinner that night and I'm disappointed when he leaves to go back to Tilly's. "You're not staying?"

"Uh-uh. We're not ready for that yet. I know I slept with you that one night at her place, and you wanna know something?"

"What?"

"I didn't sleep all night with you next to me. We need to wait until it's right. I've already messed it up once, Fallon; I don't want to fuck it up with you again. I want it to be perfect with you. Do you understand what I'm saying here?"

"I do. I'm not sure I'm gonna like it, though."

"I'm not sure I will, either, yet I think it's the right thing to do."

He hugs and kisses me and then he's gone. I feel so empty without him here. It's the first time since I arrived in San Francisco that I'm alone and it's a strange feeling. I've lived alone for a while, but it was so great having the two of them around for company. Now, I'm plunged into silence and it's a bit eerie.

With nothing to really do, my new bed calls to me, so I head that way and read for a time. Before long, I'm fast asleep.

The ringing of my phone awakens me. It's Ryland Thomas. "I have coffee and scones. I'll be at your door in three minutes." No sooner has he ended the call than I'm out of bed and brushing my teeth. By the time I finish, the doorbell rings.

"I love your nighties," he says as he pulls me into him. "But most of all, I love the way you look when you've just gotten out of bed. You're terribly sexy." He slides his thumb across my lower lip and I catch it with my teeth and bite it gently as I look at him. "Now you're

179

fucking dangerous." His arms are then immediately wrapped around me and he lifts me against him as he backs me into the wall. His mouth crushes mine and he steals every last bit of oxygen I ever dreamed of owning.

I'm reeling when he releases me, touching his forehead to mine. "My body is telling me to throw you over my shoulder and carry you to your bed where I can fuck you silly, but my heart is telling me otherwise. What do you tell me, Fallon?"

Shit. I can't say a thing because my throat is so tight with need for him. I want this man like I've never wanted anything before. Yet I wonder if it's the right thing to do. Will it ruin things between us?

He senses my hesitancy. "You've just given me your answer, love."

He steps back from me, but his eyes don't release mine. They're melting me, deep pools of emerald green, as they stare at me.

"It's not that I don't want to."

"Oh, trust me, I know. I can feel your response. And you know how much I want you, right?"

I nod.

"Right then. Shall we have our coffee and scones?"

I move from the wall, my legs still a bit shaky, as he covers my hand in his and smiles. "Fallon, we'll get there."

"I'm hoping I don't explode in the interim."

He gives me a quirky smile.

While we're eating, he suggests some sightseeing things for the day. He wants to take me up to the wine country. I'm excited because I've read amazing things about how wonderful it is.

"Really. We can do that in a day?"

180

"Well, would you like to do an overnight?"

"No." I'm unwavering about this because he's done way too much for me already. "Maybe in a month or so."

"Then a day trip it is."

After I quickly shower and dress, we hit the road. It's a great day as we stop at a couple of wineries and enjoy the scenery. He's an exceptional tour guide who takes special care in making sure that my walking is kept to a minimum. After a wonderful day, we stop at a quaint café in Tiburon for dinner and don't get home until late.

He's been snapping pictures left and right all day, so when we get home, I ask to see them. All day I've assumed he was taking pictures of the scenery, but I'm astonished to see they're all of me. Sitting, standing, looking out at something in the distance, he's caught me in a multitude of candid shots.

My expression says it all. "You're surprised?" he asks.

"Well, yeah."

"Don't be. I take great pleasure in watching you. And now I have these to look at when you're three hours away from me." His eyes are so soft, I dissolve. My hand reaches for his and I bring it to my lips and smile.

The next night is New Year's Eve and he's made a reservation at some fancy restaurant. I'm embarrassed because I don't have expensive clothes to wear.

"You don't have a little black dress?"

"Of course I do, but it's not very elaborate."

"Fallon, you could wear a paper sack and knock it out of the park."

I shoulder bump him. He promises to pick me up at six, which leaves me with the whole day to myself. Hmm, what'll I do? Read, I suppose.

What I really want to do, though, is have a group online chat with all my blogger girls, so I make the arrangements and we do exactly that. I really need their opinions on what to do about Ryland Thomas. Of course, they can't know who he really is, so I plan on only giving them the old story.

Once we're all online together, I realize just how much I've missed them.

"You should just go for it," Amanda says.

Andrea and Kat agree.

"I don't know. What if it's too soon? Besides, he's all for taking it slow."

"I think Fallon's right. They need to take their time on this. At least her heart won't get crushed again," Kat says.

Mandy pipes in, "But he's promised not to do that, so why do you have to have a plan? Why not just let things flow. I mean, if the timing is right, go for it. You'll know when it is."

"Thing is, it's always right. I'm ready for the man right now," I say.

"Do you realize how lucky you are?" Amanda asks. "What I would do to have your problem."

"Amanda's right. I'd trade places with you right now. Besides, he's committed to making it right this time. He already knows he acted like an arse. He'll be doubly careful not to do a repeat," Andrea says.

"Yeah, I guess so. I think I'll simply play it by ear. You know, if it all works out, I'll go with it."

"So, are you psyched about the new job?" Kat asks.

"Nervous is more like it."

They all pshaw me and tell me I'll be fine. We chat like this for another thirty minutes or so then wish each other a happy new year and end the call. By now I need to get showered and ready for dinner.

Still unsure of what to do, I push it out of my mind and get dressed. Soon my doorbell is ringing and Ryland Thomas is there, collecting me for dinner.

He looks divine. He's wearing a dark suit with an emerald green tie, and it makes the green in his eyes glow. His hair is messy and it makes me want to thread my fingers through it. I can barely pull my gaze away from his mouth as the corners of it lift up.

"Fallon, you're lovely this evening."

"Oh, yeah, especially my lovely boot." I motion to my foot, still encased in that atrocious thing I have to wear.

He smiles. "I never noticed." He presses a soft kiss in the palm of my hand.

Whoa. I'm melting already. This is going to be a heated night.

"Shall we go?"

I grab my coat and we head down the stairs. We go to a quaint restaurant called Fire where everything is cooked in a wood-fired oven. The food is excellent. Ryland Thomas orders up an array of food and we share all the dishes. It's quite a culinary experience for me. I can tell he's enjoying himself as he watches me eat.

"I thought you were dangerous before, but now as I watch you eat, I know you're going to be hazardous to my sanity. I can hardly stand sitting here as I observe your mouth. I keep thinking about what your lips would feel like on me if they were moving like that."

Thank heavens there's a glass of water in front of me because I nearly choke on the food I'm swallowing. He grabs my hand and asks if I'm okay.

Once my throat is clear, I finally say, "I'll never just be okay around you, Ryland Thomas."

He doesn't respond. He simply stares at me with those intense eyes of his. His mouth opens and closes before he, at last, speaks. "I want so much with you, Fallon. This thing, whatever it is between us, I want it to work."

"So do I. Then you think we have a chance?" My question is bold, yet I want to know.

"Yes, I do. I think we have so much more than a mere chance." Our hands are still clasped together as I smile.

"Good. Great."

Then he raises my hand and kisses it. Those damn eyes of his suck me into his soul. My appetite has gone straight out the door and the only thing I can think of now is the unbearable ache that's blossomed between my thighs. I squeeze my legs together and sigh.

"It'll be okay, Fallon."

Not until I get home, I want to say. I keep my naughty thoughts to myself, however when I look at him again and see his little smirk, I know he's discerned my thoughts. I smirk back.

"This is difficult."

"That it is."

"What are we going to do about it?" I ask.

"Take a lot of cold showers, love."

"That's it?'

"Uh-huh."

We finish dinner and head back to my place to do the countdown to New Year's on TV. When the ball strikes midnight, Ryland Thomas grabs me. "Happy New Year, Fallon." Then we kiss like there are no more tomorrows. His mouth is fire and ice, heating me and making me shiver, sending ripples of goosebumps all over me. Flames of desire lick every inch of my flesh, scorching my skin until I'm begging him to touch me, to taste me, but he doesn't. He just kisses me.

We're on my couch and he's pushed me onto my back while his body is between my thighs. He's flexing his hips into me, dry humping me while I want our clothes to be off so badly that I start to rip at his shirt, but he traps my hands in his and won't allow it. I'm whining in desperation, yet still, he only kisses me. No hands, no touching other than rubbing against me with his hips.

I pull my mouth away from his and beg, "Ryland Thomas, I want you. Now. I need you inside of me."

"I need to be inside of you, too, Fallon. But not tonight."

"Why not?"

"Because I want it to be right."

"Does being right include torture?"

"Maybe. It's not easy for me, either. Look at me, Fallon."

I do as he asks. His eyes... God, they're so full of something, but I can't quite define it.

He frames my face with his hands. "I fucked it up so bad with you before, I'm swearing to you and myself that this time, I'm gonna get it right. Physically and emotionally. You're that important to me."

185

My heart reacts so fiercely my body jolts. I grab his shoulders and all I can do is nod. He places a light kiss on each corner of my mouth and looks at me again.

"Fallon, are you with me on that?"

"Yeah." My hoo-hah is not going to be a happy girl for a while.

RYLAND - THOMAS

I'm not sure which of us is more disappointed when I leave. I have to return to Lake Tahoe first thing in the morning. I have a deadline to meet and an aggressive schedule ahead of me. I'm so far behind as it is with all the time I wasted during the fall months while I was nursing my wounds and acting the fool. Neither my agent nor my editor are exactly pleased with me right now since I've already missed several deadlines.

Even though we'll only be able to see each other on weekends, it will give us time to immerse ourselves in our work without distractions. I need this to catch up. One manuscript needs to be at my editor's by the end of January and another one is due in April. I will be pushing it to get both done in time.

As we say our goodbyes, we kiss and both try to stretch it out for as long as possible.

"Are you sure you don't want to stay with me tonight?" she asks.

"It's not a matter of wanting. You know that. It's a matter of sticking to my plan and what I think is right this time. I'll be damned if I screw it up again."

"You won't."

I grab her and kiss her, hard. We're against her front door saying goodbye, and it's the hardest goodbye I've ever known. "This is very difficult."

"I know," she says into my mouth. "Don't go."

"Stop tempting me, dangerous girl." I've tangled up her hair during our time making out on the couch and she looks so damn delicious, I want to taste her all over. "Bloody hell, Fallon, you are so fuckable right now. If you could see yourself." I run my finger from her forehead down between her eyes, over her nose and down to her lips.

"Then why don't you fuck me, Ryland Thomas?"

"You know bloody hell why. Now stop tempting me so I can get out of here." I kiss her once more and release her. "I'll call you when I hit the road in the morning, gorgeous. Sleep well."

"As if." She grins.

"Dream about me, then?"

"As if I have a choice."

I catch a taxi back to Tilly's. It's going to be a sleepless night for me.

It's not quite light out when I get out of bed. I should've simply left last night, but I didn't trust myself with the alcohol I'd consumed. Tilly and I say our good-byes and then I'm heading back to Tahoe by seven a.m.

My hand is itching to call Fallon, but I want her to sleep another couple hours or so. She probably won't sleep tonight, since tomorrow is her first day on her new job.

Visions of us kissing keep popping into my head, and seconds later, I have a raging hard-on. Dammit! I'm going to have to start wearing baggy pants because this is getting most uncomfortable.

Leaving the congestion of the city behind, I'm on the open highway with my head wrapped up in scenes for my latest novel when my phone rings. I look at the Bluetooth console and see it's Fallon calling.

Tapping the button I answer. "Hey, gorgeous." When her voice echoes through my car over the sound system, it makes me smile.

"How come you didn't call?"

"I wanted you to catch some more rest. I figured you'll need it with your first week ahead of you."

"I miss you already."

"Same here. Wish you were sitting next to me in the car right now."

"Me, too."

We're both silent for a moment.

"Ryland Thomas?"

"Hmm?"

"Do you want me to drive out this weekend?"

"I'm thinking about coming in on Thursday night, depending on how busy your week is and how much I can get done. I can stay at Tilly's if you're swamped."

"No! You're staying with me."

"Slow, remember?" I'm not sure if I'm reminding her or myself.

"I'm trying," she sighs.

"Okay. I'll call you as soon as I walk in the door."

189

"Be careful."

"I always am."

Fallon is so occupied with her new job, I barely speak to her all week with the exception of a few texts here and there. The good news is that she loves it. I'm ecstatic for her and I've been getting loads done on my own things. It's Thursday when she realizes she won't be free until tomorrow night, so I postpone leaving until the next afternoon.

When Friday hits, I get everything done in the morning, the car's packed and I'm on the road around three. The metro rush hour looms ahead of me, but Fallon won't be home until after six anyway, therefore I'm in no hurry. I pull into the city around six thirty and still no word from her. Since I haven't heard from her yet, I don't know if I should head to her place or Tilly's. At the last minute, I decide to go to hers.

Scanning through some emails while I'm parked and waiting, I finally spy her walking home, still wearing that damn boot. I need to ask her when she gets to take that thing off. When she sees me, her face lights up, but I can tell how worn out she is.

"Am I ever glad to see you," she says as she wraps herself around me. "I feel like I've run a marathon every day this week."

"Well, I'm here to spoil you rotten the entire weekend. Come on." I grab my things and we head inside.

She looks at me and asks, "You're staying here?"

Smiling, I say, "Yeah, unless you don't want me to."

"You know I do and thank God."

"I didn't say we'd do anything. I'm just gonna sleep here, love."

"That's enough for me."

She asks for a glass of wine, so I get her settled and pour her one before I check out her food and drink supplies. After seeing that she needs some things, I inform her I'm headed to the market. "Won't be long." I kiss her and head out the door.

At the store, I pick up food for dinner and things to cook her brekkie for both mornings. I also grab some snack items and lunch things. It only takes about forty minutes, however when I return, she's asleep. That's good; I let her catch a quick nap while I cook us up some dinner.

As I cook, the aromas of the chicken sautéing must've awakened her because I feel her arms slip around my waist as she presses herself next to me. My body instantly responds and suddenly we're kissing to the sound of poultry sizzling. One kiss and I'm quite lost in her.

"I missed you, Fallon."

"I missed you, too."

I switch my attention back to the dinner in the pan while she stands next to me as I cook.

"You spoil me."

"I haven't even begun. So tell me about your week."

"Oh, God, it was amazing. I love my job. But I don't have time to *breathe*." I love the way she emphasizes the word "breathe." It's so cute I want to kiss her again. I smile as I listen to her.

"So they have you running then, huh?"

"Yes! Kristie, my boss, wants me to get a feel for how the entire business works before I start my focus on critiquing. They're going to keep me in the romance genre, thank God. They even want me to go to the Romance Today Con in Atlanta in April."

"Excellent. You know Tilly and I are going. The three of us can go together." Plans are materializing in my head.

"I'll probably have to travel with the Critics Abound team, though, just to keep up the pretense. Ryland Thomas, I don't want to exploit our relationship."

Turning to her, I put my cooking utensil down and grab her. "Fallon, I never thought you would."

"I just want you to know that. I'm not even sure I want them to know that Tilly and I are friends. You know. It might give them ideas or something. They already want me to do a spotlight on you because they know you're my favorite author."

I see where she's heading with this. "Tilly needs to weigh in on this, Fallon. We trust you to do the right thing where we're concerned. But it's okay if people know that you're friends with her."

"I don't know. We'll see. Tilly knows they want an interview."

"Either way, it's great you'll be in Atlanta."

We sit down to our dinner and as we eat, I ask her about the boot. She looks at me a bit sheepishly. "The doctor back home said to wear it for six to eight weeks. I was supposed to follow up with him after four weeks, but I never did because I don't have insurance. I was just gonna wear it until next week and see how it feels. My insurance through work kicks in on February the second, so I can get it checked out after that."

When I'm visibly upset, she grabs my clenched hand and unfolds it. "Don't be angry with me, Sinclair."

"Angry isn't the correct word, Fallon. I'm upset." My voice is soft. "You should've told me. You need to see a doctor. What if it isn't healing properly? Now it may be too late to do anything about it."

"It's fine. If it wasn't, I would know."

"No, you wouldn't. You wouldn't know until later when other problems develop from it. Please don't wait until February. I'll pay for you to see a doctor. I *want* you to see one. Please do it for me."

"Okay. I'll ask Tilly if she knows of anyone I can call."

"Thank you."

As she nods, I'm not satisfied with that, so I pull her from her chair right into my lap. "The thought of you having issues that would require a surgical procedure to fix it worries me, Fallon. I don't want that for you, love. Okay?"

She smiles. "I haven't had anyone looking out for me in a while."

"Get used to it."

Now she laughs. I like that much better. I clear off the table and we settle in for the night, watching a bit of TV.

"You like your new flat screen?" I had Tilly purchase one for her this week. It's a small one, but it fits her apartment.

"Yes and thanks. But you *have* to quit buying me things."

"Says who?"

"Says me, that's who."

"Right then. We'll see about that."

"Ryland Thomas, you don't have to buy me anything to make me happy."

193

I turn to face her. "Is that what you think I'm doing?"

"I'm not really sure."

"It's not, Fallon. The reason I'm buying you things is because the thought of you coming home to an empty apartment, saddens me. It's a lonely thought and you're new to this city, in a new job, so I thought a TV would help. I'm not trying to buy your happiness or make you feel indebted to me in any way."

"You're very kind, you know, but I *do* feel indebted to you."

"Don't. Think about it. Tilly and I bought you a bed. Between the two of us, we spent three hundred each. It's not like we bought you the cream of the crop. And the TV… it put me out a couple of hundred bucks. I have the money, Fallon. You're going to make car payments to pay off the Fusion, therefore I don't want to hear it anymore. And, I'm not kind. I can be rude and an asshole. You've been on the wrong side of it, too, so you know that."

"I don't think you're like that as a rule, though. I think I struck a chord with you and you swung back in self-defense. Or something like that anyway. People do terrible things to each other when they're hurting."

"Yes, they do. And say terrible things, too. I'm just sorry it was you that took the brunt of it all." I shake my head because I hate the memory of it. "Our beginning was so messed up on so many levels that… I don't know. You affect me, Fallon. And I'll admit, it's a bit daunting."

She grabs my hand and places it on her cheek. "I know how you feel, although I've never experienced the pain of having my heart broken like you have. I don't want to ever hurt you, Ryland Thomas. I'll never be unfaithful to you. That goes against every fiber of my being. If there ever comes a time when things don't work between us, I'll tell you. But I won't cheat on you."

First her eyes pull me in and then her mouth, and the next thing I know, we're making out like teenagers. We're both moaning and rubbing against each other, trying to get as close as we can, but our damn clothing keeps getting in the way.

When we stop for air, we're both sucking wind. We laugh. "I feel like I'm in junior high," she says.

"Don't you dare tell me you made out with a boy like this when you were thirteen."

"Ha, you're right. I would never have let one of those nerdy boys touch me like this back then." She giggles.

"Your laugh even gets me hard, Fallon." I take her hand and put it on me to show her.

"That wasn't my laugh that did that, you goofball."

"Uh-huh," I say as I start to kiss her again. The truth is, I'm about to bust through my jeans, yet I can't get enough of her mouth. I'll never get enough of her mouth. She kisses me like the world is going to end and she wants to remember every single nuance of me so she can take it with her when it does.

"Ryland Thomas, are you going to torture me forever?"

"Only as long as you torture me." I get up and pull her with me. "I think it's time we go and get some sleep."

"I like the way you worded that. Sleep and not bed."

"Ah, you caught that, didn't you?"

"Uh, yeah."

We go to her room and I undress her to the point of her sexy underthings. "Fallon, where are your nighties?"

"I don't know what you mean, Ryland Thomas."

"Ah, being a bit cheeky, are ya?"

195

"Maybe."

I rifle through her things until I find what I'm seeking. And, damn, if it isn't the sweetest thing ever. It's a light gray, short nightgown that barely covers her ass. It's designed to be cute rather than sexy, but it fails miserably. The sleeveless thing has a neckline that dips to a V and shows off her lovely cleavage, and doesn't that just want to make me put my mouth right there and start licking her? She's positively edible in the thing.

"Fuck it all, Fallon." I swallow, with great difficulty as she smiles sweetly at me. I turn around and head to the bathroom.

When I return about ten minutes later, she's lying in bed, smiling. "Are you feeling better now?"

"You're a little imp, you know?"

Her arm reaches for me. I divest myself of my clothing except my boxers and clasp her hand as I slide in next to her.

"You know you fit perfectly right here," I tell her as I pull her into the curve of my body. She feels like she has been made for me and I wonder if she was.

"I miss not sleeping with you, Ryland Thomas. Would it be bad for me to say I want you here every night?"

I smile against her hair. "No, it would be very good, Fallon." I breathe her in, letting her scent wash over me. *No, this would not be bad at all*, I think as I fall asleep with her in my arms.

Fallon

There's nothing I love more than to wake up in Ryland Thomas's arms. Well, maybe there is, but since *that's* off limits for the time being, this is my next favorite thing. I roll on my back so I can look at him. His face is nothing short of perfection to me. The sculpted cheekbones that dip to slight hollows where I love to press my lips. That adorable nose of his, and how it has the tiniest bump on the bridge, which makes me wonder if he broke it in a fight or something. Then there's his mouth... I can't even get started on it because I'll go off the deep end in naughty thoughts about what it does to me. But if I were to have to name one favorite thing, I would have to choose his eyes; intense, yet sometimes soft. Vivid and bold, but at times shy and timid; emerald pools with golden lines radiating from his pupils that bewitch me. I can fall into them and stay lost for days.

I must've made some kind of noise, probably a sigh, because his thick, caramel lashes flutter open, and there I am, looking right into those perfect pools of green.

"Mmmm. Morning gorgeous." His voice is thick with sleep.

"And the same to you." I brush his hair from his face and he catches my hand, pressing a kiss to it. Then I find myself pulled on top of him and he's grinding his hips against me.

"I'm resigned to the fact that I will be forever stiff around you."

I snuggle into his neck. "You're just saying that. My friends say that all guys wake up that way."

"Uh-huh. And I don't just wake up this way, gorgeous. It's an all day thing, love." He wiggles a little more. So I wiggle back. "Uh, Fallon, that might not be such a grand idea."

"You started it." I lift my head and look at him. I wiggle again, but his hands clamp on my hips, stilling me.

"Yes, I did. And I made a mistake. If you keep moving, I'll make a mess."

"Who cares? I don't." I start to slide my hips against him again, and he lets me. His eyes slip into that half-closed position so I know he's getting into it.

"Jesus, Fallon," he groans, so I keep going. I'm as turned on as he is because he's hitting my spot just right. I straddle his hips so the contact is better and now I groan, too. I rotate and move up and down him. Damn, this is feeling so good. He grabs my hips and presses me tightly against him as he rocks against me.

"Ah, yeah, that's good right there," I tell him and he continues with that motion. The feeling is building in both of us now. Our breathing is fast and my hand is squeezing his shoulder. I'm going to come. My thighs start pressing against his.

He knows it somehow because he says, "That's it, love, let it go."

It happens. I'm tightening all over, inside and out, and I'm crying out his name. I feel him shudder then hear him groan as he calls my name and we both lie there, breathing hard as we come down from our orgasmic high.

"Wow," he says. Then his mouth takes mine and I'm feeling the heat build in me again. I'm flipped to my back and my panties are gone as his hand finds me, fingers sliding into me, stroking in and out. It doesn't seem possible, but I'm right back in the middle of the biggest turn on where my need for him is incredible.

"Hey, can you, please? I need you. Inside of me. Please."

He kisses me instead and his hand is what I'll have to settle for. The climax is great. I mean, whoever had a bad one, right? But I want *him*. I want to feel *him* inside of me, not his hand, so I tell him.

"I want that, too, love. But not yet."

"Then when?"

"We'll know."

"I already know. Seriously, we're coming all over each other. What difference does it make?"

"A huge one. When we take that step the next time, it'll be with love, Fallon. Not lust."

Well, fuck me. I'm speechless.

He looks at me and smiles. "Now do you understand?"

I nod. I have to know. I think I already do, but I have to know for sure. "Do you think it will happen?"

"I *know* it will. I just don't know when."

I then kiss him with everything I have.

That afternoon we're sitting together on the couch, both typing on our laptops. He's working on a scene in his book while I write a review.

"Can I ask you something?"

"Sure," I say as I look up at him.

"When you read a love scene, what draws you in?"

The question throws me because it's unexpected. "I think the sexual tension at the beginning, but then the plain, old heat gets me every time."

He grins at my answer. "Okay. Do you want to go down to the wharf?"

"Now?" I ask and then laugh at his randomness.

"Yeah," he says. "Let's get out and enjoy the afternoon. I want to walk around and look at those silly shops down there, while holding your hand. Maybe buy some candy... you know, that awful stuff that's really bad for you and sticks in your teeth."

"You hate that stuff."

"No, I love it," he confesses. "I just never buy it 'cause it's so terrible for you. What do you say?"

How can I turn down an offer like that? "Only if you promise to take me by a chocolatier."

We spend the afternoon doing touristy things, eating sweets and other junk until my stomach aches from it all. When we make it home, it's dark and almost seven o'clock.

"What would you like for dinner?" Ryland Thomas asks.

Groaning, I say, "Nothing. I'm sick."

He laughs. "You didn't have to eat all of it." He's referring to the giant chocolate bar I demolished. And the funnel cake. And the hot fudge sundae.

"I couldn't help it. It was so good," I squeak.

"Come here."

He sits on the couch and I lie next to him with my head in his lap. He starts to rub my tummy.

"Feel that?" I ask. "That's the belly of a glutton."

He laughs at me, continuing to rub.

I'm just beginning to relax when the sound of my phone ringing interrupts my belly rub. I dig in my back pocket and pull it out to see it's my mom calling.

"Oh, hell," I mumble then look at Ryland Thomas. "It's my mom."

"Hi, Mom."

"Fallon, you never call me anymore."

"It's because I have a lot going on, Mom."

"Well, you'd think you could spare a few minutes for your mother."

"Yeah, like you always spare a few minutes for me?"

"Don't get smart with me."

"I'm sorry, Mom, but I work a lot. You know I have a new job."

"Well, if you'd call me sometime, you might find out how much the creditors are after you. I'm having to fend off calls left and right, so you need to pay that credit card off. I'm tired of dealing with them already. And why are you in such debt? You should be more responsible. I thought I taught you better than that."

Rage threatens to explode from me, yet worse than that, I want to break down. I can't get past how uncaring she is. Why does she do this to me? Why can't she see

201

that I'm trying and that my finances have been stretched to the limit?

"I'm sorry you're having to deal with them, Mom. I'll take care of it as soon as I can." My voice is cracking.

"See that you do, Fallon."

She makes a few other remarks to me and that's it. She never asks how my new job is going, how my new apartment is, how I like living in San Francisco, nothing. Every time I talk to her, I tell myself I won't get upset, but I do. It kills me that she doesn't have a caring bone in her body for me. My hands go to my face and I rub my eyes. Sitting up, I take a deep, cleansing breath, trying to will myself not to cry. Will I ever get over this feeling of abandonment?

Ryland Thomas's hand covers mine and at first I'm shocked. My mom's cruel selfishness has been so encompassing, I've forgotten about him.

"Everything okay?" he asks.

"Nothing is okay that involves my mom."

His hand rubs my tummy again and I sigh.

"What happened?"

Thoughts race through my head. Should I tell him? I know if I do, he'll want to take care of everything for me and I don't want that. I want to handle this on my own. However, I know if I don't tell him, he'll feel left out and hurt. So I just go for it and explain the whole thing. As I do, his body tenses.

"How much?"

"I don't want you to…"

"Fallon, you can repay me. I don't want your credit tarnished or your nasty mum on your back. How much?"

Immediately, I start making excuses for the amount, but he takes my face in his hands. "Love, I don't need those. You needed to live. You had no money." Then those warm arms are embracing me, letting me know everything's going to be just fine.

"Thank you. For everything."

"Fallon, I'm here for you. You know that, right?"

I nod as I look into his beautiful eyes.

"I'm sure I'm not the best one to give advice here because my relationship with my folks was damn good, but it seems to me that she causes you an immense amount of heartache. We don't have a choice who are parents are. You've lived with this hurt she forces on you for far too long."

His words settle into me, but I'm not quite sure what to make of them. "So what are you saying?"

He gets up and drops down in front of me so he can look at me. He's reaching for my hand when he says, "Maybe it's time to cut your losses."

"She's my mom. How can I do that?"

"Let me ask you this. You're her daughter. Does she treat you with respect?"

"No," I murmur.

"Sweetheart, I'm not asking you these things to make you hurt more. I'm trying to help you."

"I know, but it hurts when I think of how she treats me. And honestly, she couldn't care less about me."

"Being a parent is a two way street, love. You are supposed to respect your children as much as they should respect you. She shows you none. But my point here is that it's not going to change. The hurt will keep on hurting unless you stop allowing it."

"So, are you saying I should just walk away from her for good?"

"No, I'm saying that you had no choice in who your mum is. She is who she is. She's not going to change. So you need to change the way you deal with her. Change your expectations, or don't deal with her at all."

"You make so much sense. And you also make it sound so easy."

"Oh, Fallon, don't mistake me. It won't be easy. If you decide to walk away from her, it may be the hardest thing you've ever done. And not letting her words and actions get to you will be equally as hard. But lowering your expectations would help a lot. Like when she calls, don't ever expect her to ask about how things are going for you. You already know she won't, so why build yourself up for a huge disappointment?"

How can this man know so much? I throw my arms around him and hug him. "You're absolutely right. I always have this tiny spark of hope that, one day, she'll see that I'm not a worthless girl."

"If I ever think for one second that you believe that, I'm going to personally knock some sense into that beautiful head of yours. Understand?

"Yeah, and thank you for that."

The weekend flies by until the point when Ryland Thomas is leaving. I hate it, yet it's the way things are. It's late on Sunday and he has a three and a half hour drive.

"Be careful and call me as soon as you get home. I'm serious. I'll worry about you. And call me every thirty minutes. In fact, we can stay on the phone the entire trip if you want."

"Fallon, we can't do that. Besides, you have things to do. Don't be such a ninny. I'll be fine. Now go on about your night. I'll give you a ring on the way and when I get home."

I hug him so hard. I just hate for him to leave.

"I think I like this," he says then walks out of the door and is gone. I feel empty without him.

He calls me when he's halfway home and then when he gets there. I'm relieved he's arrived safely so now I can go to sleep. I hug the pillow to my face that he used and smell the lingering scent of him. It soothes me and I fall soundly asleep.

The weeks are buzzing by, and before I even realize it, spring is busting loose. Flowers are blooming, and I have to admit, I love the west coast. Being a born and bred South Carolinian, I never thought I'd find myself anchored anywhere else, but the beauty of California has me hooked. I've been to Ryland Thomas's several times and love it there, too. There's something to be said for this state of such diverse climates.

Romance Today Con is three weeks away. Since Critics Abound is hosting the huge hospitality event for some of the top authors, and R.T. Sinclair is one of them, I'm trying to wrangle a ticket for Ryland Thomas. Critics Abound is selective in whom they give their tickets to because they want to make this event one of the most sought after ones at the convention.

Kristie and I meet for lunch one day so we can lay out our plans for the event at the upcoming convention.

"Thanks for taking time out of your busy schedule, Fallon."

"Hey, no worries. You're the boss," I joke.

Her face turns serious. "Yeah, no kidding. Sometimes I don't like that role so much. Like now. I'd rather be getting ready to go to Atlanta as a participant."

"Kristie, this is going to be great. Our party will turn out just fine."

"I wanted you to know that Ruth will be there, and she's got you targeted. She's starting to focus on that spotlight thing again. The other thing is that she has her eye on you because your reviews shine. You've gotten her attention in a big way."

"Really?" I ask. I'm pretty shocked because, as close as Kristie and I work, she's never mentioned this before. "Why haven't you said anything?"

"Fallon, Ruth is not the best person to have notice you. Do you follow me?"

This statement puzzles me. "Give it to me straight, Kristie."

"It's just that, when she notices you, she ends up dumping a lot of stuff on you that you don't need. I'll try to manage that, but sometimes it's out of my control."

"Is this what you wanted to see me about today?"

Kristie looks surprised. "Oh, no. We need to make sure we have everything lined up right for the hospitality party. So, let's go over everything."

We finish our lunch, however I have this nagging feeling that Kristie is leaving something out regarding Ruth. We spend a lot of time together at the office, so I think she'll eventually tell me. At least I hope she will.

I'm headed to Lake Tahoe this weekend and I can't wait to get there. It's my birthday on Saturday, and

Ryland Thomas says he has a big surprise planned for me. I'm excited to see what it is. I'm hoping it will be... well, you know, but I'll have to wait and see. Kristie has given me Friday off, so I'll be leaving on Thursday for a nice, long weekend.

On Wednesday, Kristie and a couple of her friends that I've become fairly close to—Kelly and Brandy—take me out to dinner to celebrate. We go to this Vietnamese restaurant I've been dying to try in the Embarcadero. The food is mouthwatering, and I'm in heaven.

After we eat, Kristie pulls out a small gift bag and hands it to me, saying, "Happy birthday," with a wink.

"You weren't supposed to get me anything."

When the table erupts in giggles, I know something's up. I open the bag and my face fires up with heat. "Holy hell." I immediately close the bag.

"Come on, Fallon. Show us what you got," Brandy begs.

"No! Y'all are bad!" Then I peek in the bag again and laugh.

Brandy grabs the bag from me and pulls out a lacy pair of black panties... well, I can't even call them that. They're too skimpy to even qualify as a thong because they are crotchless. Plus, there's a see thru black cami to match except the part that's supposed to cover your boobs is missing. That's not all. There's also a vibrator with all sorts of weird attachments. I'm not even sure what they're all for.

"Y'all are crazy!"

"You can wear those on your drive over to Tahoe," Kristie winks.

"This is an inappropriate conversation to be having with my boss," I say then I start laughing as I think about my boobs poking out of the cami that's not really there.

They all bust out laughing, too. Kristie adds, "You'll be thanking me one day."

I hit the road right after work and pull into Ryland Thomas's driveway at ten thirty. He's opening my door for me as I turn off the car.

"I've missed you," he says as I'm pulled into his arms. His mouth is on mine as he leans against the car. What is it about that mouth of his that I can't get enough of? His lips suck on mine and then his tongue joins in the play. They tangle together as they taste each other.

"Your mouth should be illegal."

"Yours should be classified as hazardous, dangerous girl."

We nuzzle each other before he steps away from the car and pulls me inside, just like that.

"Where are we going?"

"I want to get you naked in the hot tub. I have this urgent desire to see you as such."

"As such?"

"I've been writing a lot."

"Hmm. I can tell. You're not gonna spring any fancy sayings on me, are you?"

"Maybe."

We're at the hot tub by now where he slides my hair to the side and bends down to kiss my neck. I shiver. "Cold?"

"No."

He lifts my shirt and it's gone. My bra follows. Then his tongue is pure heat as it glides down my neck and lands on my shoulder where he begins to nibble. And lick. And graze my heated skin with his teeth.

I shiver again. Then sigh.

Now he's moving lower, reaching my pearled nipple. He takes it gently between his teeth and teases it with his tongue. I arch my back and move closer to him. His fingers find the other one, so it doesn't feel deprived. I latch onto his head and moan again.

My body is screaming for him, but it's so much more than that. My heart wants him, too. Somewhere between Christmas and our weekends together, I've fallen in complete and absolute love with Ryland Thomas Sinclair. How do I know this? That's easy; it's right in front of me. His touch sends me to the moon. The sight of him brings me unimaginable joy. When I hear his voice, my body hums. Everything in me responds when I inhale his scent. The taste of him when we kiss is beyond anything I've ever known. Most of all, he's seeped into my heart, wedging himself within it, and I don't ever want him to leave. If he does, there will be a space so huge that I'll never be whole, never be myself again; I know that Fallon will cease to exist.

I stop breathing when this thought takes over my mind and he senses the change in me.

"Everything okay there, dangerous girl?"

"Ryland Thomas." My voice is husky and filled with all sorts of emotion.

He stands and cups my face. "What is it, love?" Concern has claimed his voice.

"I—I'm in love with you." I swallow, not knowing what his reaction will be. I don't have to wait long at all

209

because he almost immediately rewards me with the most dazzling smile.

"Damn time you figured it out. I've been in love with you pretty much since the beginning. Ever since I realized I'd been such a damn wanker. I love you, Fallon McKinley. I've loved you from a distance and now I can finally love you properly, like I was meant to love you from the start."

I'm suddenly encased in his warmth as his mouth is on mine. Our clothes are torn away by frantic hands while we rush at each other with desperation, as though we've been seeking this for centuries, even though I know that's such a silly thought. He picks me up and he's carrying me inside now.

"No hot tub?"

"Not on your life. I'm going to make love to you, in every way imaginable, starting in my bed. I want to see your face, love, as I slide into you. And I don't want the dark sky to hide any of you. You're all mine tonight, and I intend to watch every bit of you."

Whoa. My heart just broke the sound barrier and I'm not sure I'll ever catch my breath again. We enter his room and my body glides down his as he sets me on my feet. Then he pushes me backwards until the backs of my knees hit the bed and I'm forced to sit down.

He crouches between my legs, takes my hands and says, "I never believed in love at first sight, but I fell for you that day you charged into me at the airport. You were so fucking hot, with your sweet arse in the air. And then, when you stood up, I couldn't tear my eyes off your lovely nipple. I dreamed about it that night... thought about what it would taste like.

"The morning you woke up in my bed in Vegas— Christ, you looked like an angel in the shower with me. Fallon, you've unbalanced me, forced me to see things in a different light and I couldn't love you more for it." Then his lips are on mine, and my world is the one tipping over now.

The urgency we felt outside has melted away, and in its place is a relaxed sort of curiosity. It's almost as if we're getting to know each other, discovering each other for the very first time. Yes, my body has responded to him before, but Ryland Thomas is now doing things to me—and not just physical things—that are making me feel more alive than I've ever felt in my life. He's taken my heart and made it his. I know I'll never be the same Fallon as I was before.

His mouth moves over my body with a reverence I've never noticed before. It's so sweet and fiery that I can't sit still. Hands clench my thighs as he spreads them wide and then his mouth is on me and I can't help crying out his name again. I want this... I love this, but I want *him.* I've wanted him for so damn long.

I try to push him away and he lifts his head. "You don't like this?"

"Yes, but it's *you* I want. I need *you,* Ryland Thomas. I need your body inside of mine. It's been too long."

"Slow, Fallon. We need to take it slow, or it'll be over before we know it."

"I don't care. We can do it again. And again. Just... I... please..." I'm begging him. I've never ached for anything so badly.

"Move up then."

211

I don't waste any time. He's over me, resting on his elbows, my legs spread, heels resting on his hips. However, he doesn't move. His eyes—those startling eyes—are filled with love and they draw me into their depths. My breath locks in my throat because it's like I'm looking into his soul and every emotion he's ever felt for me is spilling out of those emerald orbs.

My hands slip into his hair and I say, "When you look at me like that, I can see what you feel. It's a connection."

As soon as those words leave my mouth, he plunges into me and then stays still, however our eyes never leave each other's. "Yeah, Fallon. That's what it is. We're connected. And will be forever." Then he slides in and out, easing the ache that has plagued me for months.

I'm so taken with everything, so blown away by this experience of love, that I can't tear my eyes off him for anything. An earthquake could crack his house in two and I doubt it would even register with me. His mouth is on mine and he's laced the fingers of one of our hands together.

My climax is building. He can tell; he can always tell. He whispers against my lips. I love it when he does that. "Let it go, Fallon. I want to feel your love all over me."

And that's all it takes. Those words have my muscles tightening on the length of him, over and over. His mouth captures mine as I hug him fiercely to me; I don't want to ever let him go. Now I understand why he wanted to wait; why it was so important. There is a difference between lust and love. And what a grand difference it is.

"I love you, Ryland Thomas."

Exquisite Betrayal

He brushes the hair off my damp forehead and places a soft kiss on it. "God, you're so fucking sweet. The way you feel on me, inside, when you come; so tight and bloody extraordinary." His eyes are on mine again, and there's that connection once more.

His mouth is beckoning to me and I can't resist so I pull his head to me and take his lower lip into my mouth. God, I love his mouth. His lips are completely irresistible. I lick and then bite him. He lets me, but I know he'll get me back. We're still joined together, and I want to stay that way. I wonder if it's possible to flip him over and straddle him. He must see the questioning look in my eyes because he doesn't waste time in asking.

"What's got that curious look on your face?"

My face heats. "Can you stay inside of me if we flip?"

The question has barely left my lips before I find myself straddling him. My mouth heads for my target, his nipple. I tease him by mimicking what he does to me. I'm not sure if he'll like it, yet a few seconds later, when he's moaning, I have my answer. Moving to his other nipple, my tongue repeats its little tease session. His hands grip my hips and he's rocking in and out of me, making me gasp.

I raise my head, arch my back and sigh heavily while my hands travel to his abs as we both move in unison. I lean back further and then his fingers are on my hot button. Moments later, my orgasm explodes in me and I feel him spasm as his warmth flows into me. My arms tighten around him as I crash down onto his chest. His sweet warmth smothers me while he whispers things against my neck; things I can't hear because my senses are still whirling with him. I burrow into him, wanting to

213

soak him in. One thing is abundantly clear to me now. There will never be enough of him for me. Never.

These feelings of mine suddenly frighten me. They're so potent that they threaten to take me over. He knows something's amiss.

"Tell me, Fallon. Your body just went from lax to rigid in mere seconds."

It takes me only a moment to decide that I'm going to be honest with him. "I'm frightened by the intensity of my feelings."

He chuckles, surprising me. "Now you know how I've been feeling since Christmas."

"Really?" I ask as I lift my head to look at him.

"Yeah, really. Don't be afraid. At least not of me. I'll be true to you, love. I'll never cheat on you. You understand that, don't you?"

He won't. I know that. "Yeah, I do. But what if you grow tired of me or fall out of love with me? There are all sorts of things that tear lovers apart."

"Fallon, we're more than lovers. We belong together. You feel it. I know you do. I can see it in your eyes. You and I are forever, not just for a month or a couple of years, love. Why do you think I wanted to wait? I knew it would be like this. My heart is yours now. It's in your hands to do with as you please. My hopes are that you'll cherish and treat it with care as much as I'll do the same with yours." I turn into a big puddle of nothing except love for this man and wonder how the hell I ever got this lucky.

TWENTY

RYLAND - THOMAS

It finally happened. Fallon said the words I've been waiting to hear. It's completely absurd, but as she was saying them, I felt I'd been waiting my whole life to hear them. I'm pretty sure I fell for her the day I laid eyes on her at the airport. Then, when I thought I'd blown it— when I was the king of all bastards to her—I knew I'd never get the chance to mend the rift. But now, I can't believe we're together. It will take my whole life to make it up to her, and I intend to do just that.

It's her birthday and I have a surprise for her. Well, now, there are actually three. She'll laugh when she sees one of them. The other ones… I've just decided after tonight to give the last one to her. I hope she doesn't think it's too soon. As she sleeps in my arms, there are so many things I want to do for her that I can't begin to name them. Tomorrow we'll start.

I've been awake for over an hour, though I won't move because I can't bring myself to disturb the beauty that lies in my arms. Her hair wraps around me and bathes me in its scent. Its silken strands are something I can't keep my fingers off of. Much like her smooth skin. The sun is creeping above the horizon now, and I know I need to wake her soon, to put part one of my surprises into motion. But damn, I hate it.

I decide to let my hand drift south, and soon it's cupping the roundness of her sweet ass. I'm filled with want for her. My fingers slowly slip between her cheeks, finding exactly what they seek. Just as I'd hoped, she's wet and I glide into her. She starts to move against my hand, but I'm not sure if she's awake or asleep, so I continue my pleasure play, enjoying the feel of her next to me. I'm surprised when I feel her hand tighten around me, and begin to match my rhythm in her.

"Did you think I'd let you feel neglected?" she whispers, her voice husky with desire.

"I don't really know what I was thinking, other than how damn beautiful you are. And that I'm completely in love with you."

She lifts her head and looks at me. "Ryland Thomas." And that's it for the both of us. We come together in a rush; breath mingling, mouths crashing against one another, arms reaching for each other.

This time there's no gentleness. It's fevered heat. Desperate emotion spilling out of us and into each other. She's beneath me now as I thrust into her, and she cries out my name over and over again. This rough frenzy of passion drives me to a heaven I've never known. We can't get enough of each other.

"More. I need more." And I give it to her. Her nails dig into my hips and ass as I pound into her while she tells me that's what she needs. God, she's incredible. I know she's going to climax. I can tell by the way she starts to tense up on me as well as the way she starts crying out my name. It sends me right off the edge.

When we finish, we're both catching our breath as we gaze at each other. She cups my cheek and is kissing me all over the place; my shoulder, neck, face. Anywhere she can reach and it's so damn adorable that I don't ever want this moment to end.

"Have I told you how very much I love you today?"

She giggles. "I think you may have mentioned it."

"Thank God. But I'm gonna tell you again. Fallon, love, I adore the hell out of you." I move her hair off her face. It doesn't really need to be moved, but I do it anyway, just so I can touch it.

"Can I ask you something?" She lowers her eyes, telling me it must be something she's shy about.

"Look at me, love." She does. "There isn't a thing in the world you can't ask me. You don't have to be timid about it, nor do you have to ask if it's okay. Got that?"

She nods. "I'm inexperienced at this. You know... you're my first lover and all, so I don't have anything to compare this to. Does it always feel like this?"

I see where this is going. "Never this good, Fallon. I'll tell you the truth. I'll not lie and say sex was bad with Iris or anyone for that matter. I mean, I don't think a bad orgasm is possible, but I've never had such a deep emotional connection with anyone before, like this. I've never loved anyone like I love you. So no. It doesn't always feel like this. This is extraordinary what we have."

217

I've never seen someone glow before, yet Fallon does. She positively radiates light. "Jesus, Fallon, what you do to me. You've rearranged me, love." And that is the truth of it all. She's reorganized me into something different; something better, something stronger. I'm a richer man, emotionally.

We're silent for a few minutes, but I know we need to get moving, so I say, "It's shower time if you want part one of your surprise."

"Part one?"

"Yep. Come on." I get up, take her hand and lead her into the shower. Of course, I know it won't be an in and out. Fallon loves my shower. It's huge with several showerheads that can do all sorts of magic things to her. When we finally get out, we're running late. I tell her not to put on anything except her panties, which earns me a weird look from her, however she does as I ask. Everything I need is in my closet so I dash in there and come back with my arms loaded down. She figures it out when she sees what I'm carrying.

"Oh, no! You didn't." She claps her hand and laughs.

"Oh, yes, I did. It's pretty warm today, so you'll only need these under your pants." I hand her some light tights. Then I give her the ski pants. They're a perfect fit. Next, I hand her a lightweight fleece top and a sports bra. I get dressed as she does.

"Here are your ski socks." We put ours on. I go back in the closet and bring out gloves, goggles and helmets.

"A helmet?"

"You don't think I'd let you risk that lovely head of yours, do you?" I kiss her as I hand it to her.

"But, I won't be doing anything steep, will I?"

"No, but it only takes one fall to bump your head. No arguments on that, okay?" She agrees. "I was worried about your foot when I was planning this, but you're all good there. You said the doctor cleared you for everything, right?"

"Yep, all clear."

"Good."

We're all geared up so we head downstairs where my ski pass and her lesson pass are. I grab our breakfast, which is a couple of scones I picked up yesterday, then I fill our go cups with coffee and we're out the door. I explain to her on the way that she has a private lesson for four hours and then she'll ski with me. If she doesn't like it, we'll come home after a lunch on the mountaintop.

The ski resort of Heavenly is only a ten-minute drive away, and by the time we get her geared up in rental skis and boots, her instructor is waiting on us. We head to the chairlift and she starts to freak.

"Don't worry," her instructor, Shane, says. "I'll assist you off the chair."

"I'll be on your other side, too," I add.

Her instructor shoos me away after we get off the lift. He explains that he prefers to teach his students one on one because there are no distractions.

"Shane, take good care of my girl here. You got that?" I shoot him a look, and he knows I mean it.

"Don't worry about her, Ryland. I've got her."

I kiss her, hard, and then I tell her I love her. Turning to Shane, I say, "I love this, woman. Safety, Shane."

We arrange to meet in four hours at a designated restaurant for lunch.

"That was the best!" she can't stop saying at lunch. "Shane even took me down a blue! A blue, Ryland Thomas! I went down a blue run. Can you believe it?"

I'm caught up in her excitement, super thrilled. She loves it. I've been a bit worried she wouldn't and that would suck for me because I ski a lot. So now I have a new fan, and with some practice, she can hone her skills and be on the black runs by next year... maybe.

"That's fabulous, love. I knew you'd love it!"

"Thank you. Thank you so much. This is the best birthday gift ever. So can we go and ski some more?"

"That's the plan."

We head back out. She really does have a knack for it. Her turns and stops are quite good so I move her off the greens, or beginner's runs, and we spend the rest of the day on the blues, or intermediate slopes. We take our time and she loves it so much she wants to come back the next day.

"Honey, it's your weekend and we can do whatever you want. If you want to come back here tomorrow and spend all day, we'll do just that. But let me warn you about something. It's the weekend and the crowds will be terrible. I'll leave it up to you, though."

"Like tons of people?"

Her face is shining with excitement and I don't want to crush it, but she has to know how the crowds can affect her skiing. "Tons. The lift lines will be long and the slopes won't be wide open like they were today."

She frowns. "I don't think I want that then."

"Can you stay until Monday? Sunday afternoons are usually great," I suggest.

"No, because I took today off."

My brain is churning with ideas. She loves skiing; I didn't even think about how much she would enjoy it. "Okay, I have an idea. Are there any other days you can take off... any other Mondays or Fridays between now and mid-April?"

"I can check. Why?"

"The season closes mid-April and I'll bring you back if you can get up here before then. And any weekend in early April will be good, too. The crowds tend to start thinning then," I tell her.

"That sounds like a great plan."

"I didn't know you'd love it this much or I would've thought up a way to get you out there sooner."

"But my foot. Remember?"

"Oh, that's right." I forgot for a moment. "And it didn't hurt at all, did it?"

"Not a bit. Thanks for bringing me." She leans over and kisses my cheek.

"You up for a dip in the hot tub?"

"I don't think so."

By this time we're getting in the car and I stop and turn her to face me. Her answer has shocked me. "Why? What's wrong?"

She laughs. "A dip? I want a soak, you dork. I'm sure my muscles will be screeching and telling me to fuck off by the time we get home."

Fallon gets her wish and I think we nearly empty out all the water in the hot tub with our vigorous activities.

"Damn, Fallon, you're a little firecracker."

"I am?"

"Maybe more like a hellion."

She sucks in her breath. "I am not."

My comment has offended her.

"Oh, honey, I mean that as a compliment. A man doesn't want a woman who lies there like a piece of wood. I want someone who is wild, knows what she likes and isn't afraid to enjoy herself."

"Yeah?"

"Hell, yeah." She's naked and sitting on my lap facing me, her nipples begging for some attention. I dip my head and give them some, just so they don't feel deprived. She moans. "That's what I mean. I love it when you make noise and tell me what you like, when you demand things from me."

"You do?"

"How in the world am I supposed to know if I'm making you feel good if you don't tell me somehow?"

"I don't know. I never thought about it. But Ryland Thomas, everything you do makes me feel good. You can just look at me and I go all gooey on you."

"Is that right?"

"Uh-huh. I thought you knew that."

"Perhaps, but a man likes to hear those things, too. You know, our fragile egos and all."

"Is that true?"

"You'd better believe it. Though none of us likes to confess it."

"Hey, look at me, please."

I take my eyes off her lovely breasts and look into her bottomless gray eyes. They've darkened on me now and her face is all kinds of serious.

"You are the most beautiful man I've ever known. Don't ever fear for your ego because you have nothing to worry about. I'll be nothing other than kind to it, as I will to your heart. I love you with all that I have and you're a part of me now. That means if I hurt you, I hurt myself. Where there were two hearts, there is now only one; yours and mine together." She seals it with a kiss.

I can't speak. My heart is so far up in my throat and my eyes are clogged with tears that don't fall. I haven't done this since my parents died. Why do I feel like crying now? It doesn't make sense at all to me, yet then, maybe it does. Maybe she's the only person I feel close enough to that I can drop every wall, every barricade I've ever built. And perhaps her words merely let me do that. I'm now rid of all that crap I've carried around for so long. No wonder I feel rearranged, reorganized. She's helped me put everything back to where it belongs in the first place. Besides that, she's also given me strength to face the world with open arms again.

"You've no idea what you do to me... what you've done for me. You've brought new life to my heart, Fallon."

She smiles. "As you have to mine."

"I want to rent a flat in San Francisco so we can be together more often. This three hour drive is killing me." That thought just pops into my head.

Her eyes bulge. "You'd sell this?"

"No. I'd keep it for the weekends. I can work anywhere, but you can't. I hate this weekend only thing. If I have a place in the city, then we wouldn't have to do that."

"You'd really consider that?"

"I'd more than consider it. I'm going to call Tilly and have her get right on it."

She throws her arms around me and says, "Oh my gosh. I can't wait to have you there all the time."

"Same here. The weeks are miserable without you. I'd pretty much kill to have you in my bed every night. My dream is to wake up next to you every morning."

"Mmmm, sounds so yummy." Her lips are on mine again; this love and heat between us is undeniable. I smile against her mouth and she mutters into mine, "What?"

Standing, I carry her out of the tub and walk her into the house, dripping wet. I don't give a shit about the water, but she does. "Ryland Thomas, you're going to slip and fall," she says.

"No I won't," I say as I slide and almost fall. She screams and I laugh.

"Put me down."

"Not a bloody chance. I'm giving you part two of your birthday gift." I carry her up to my room and straight into the bathroom where I wrap her in a bath sheet. "Better?"

She makes that harrumphing sound she likes to make and says, "Right. Nothing's better than your arms." Then she swats my shoulder. I pick her up and throw her on the bed.

"Now do not move. I'll be right back." I head to my closet and come out with a gift bag, which I dangle in front of her face. "Do you want your present now?"

"Yes," she giggles. I drop it on the floor. For some reason, I'm in a very playful mood. I yank her towel off and attack her with my fingers, tickling her mercilessly.

"Stop it!" She's laughing so hard and trying to scoot away from me. I grab her hands and hold them in one of mine, pulling them above her head. Then my mouth is on her stomach, blowing loud raspberries while she begs for a truce. Her laughter is the sweetest music I've ever heard.

Exquisite Betrayal

"What will you promise if I stop?"

"Anything you ask." She has to eke the words out between her guffaws. Her belly is tight with her efforts of trying to escape and now I'm seriously aroused.

"Fallon. Christ, I can't even tickle you without getting stiff." She looks down at me and then at my mouth.

"Let me taste you."

My breath whooshes out of me as she slides to the edge of the bed and her mouth closes around me. "Ah hell, love." This is the first time she's done this, and I hope it won't be the last.

"Does this feel okay?" She's unsure of herself.

I groan. "It's much better than okay."

"Tell me what to do."

So I tell her how I like it. Her tongue circles my crown and then sucks and slides down me. I'm shocked as all hell when she takes me in deep. I can't help bucking my hips when she slides up and down, pumping me, and I know I'm going to blow. When I tell her, she only sucks harder.

"Fallon, you need to stop," I cry out as I try to disengage myself. She only grabs my ass harder and pulls me against her. That's it. I explode in her mouth and she moans. That vibration against me sends me shooting off like I've never done. And damn it all, she moans again. My hands are knotted in her hair, and I'm about to collapse on top of her.

She lets me go when she feels my spasms stop. "Jesus, love." I fall to the bed and pull her up to me. She immediately straddles me and starts kissing me.

"My turn," she says and the next thing I know, she's straddling my face and I'm going to town on her. My girl

225

is certainly not shy about what she wants and when. I love to feel and hear her shatter. Her orgasms are spectacular to experience. When she's finished, she curls up next to me and snuggles into her favorite spot on my neck.

I'm not having any of that. I want her on top of me, full length contact. "I need all of you on me now, love."

"Hmm, yeah, me, too."

"I guess you didn't want your present after all, huh?"

She pops up like a jack-in-the-box and I laugh my ass off.

"I forgot."

"Get back here a minute. I need you on me." For some unnamed reason, I do need her. So I hold her on me, feeling the thrumming of her heart. "That's better."

"Yeah, it is."

After a few minutes, when I feel I can let her go, I set her aside and reach over the side of the bed to grab the bag. "For you, love."

She peeks inside and pulls out a book. It's a hard back, my latest one that she hasn't seen yet. Her eyes land on mine, questioning me.

"You know we go to Atlanta in two weeks and I release my new book the week before, right? Well, I wanted you to be the first to have it."

The smile she's wearing spreads across her face and I feel like a chocolate bar that's been sitting in the sun too long. I have it so bad for this girl I can barely look at her without doing a complete meltdown.

"You're giving me you're first copy of your first edition? Oh my God." Her voice is soft and filled with awe. She's holding the book like it's made out of the most delicate and fragile crystal that one tiny movement could destroy it.

226

"Fallon, who else would I possibly want to give it to?"

"You! Isn't that what authors do? Don't they keep the first copy for themselves?"

"I want you to have it. I want you to see the dedication."

She gently opens it and moves to the dedication page where she begins to read:

This book is dedicated to Fallon McKinley, for believing in me and changing the direction I was headed in. She knew from the start that my original idea wasn't the best, and instead of keeping it to herself, she spoke her mind like a true friend and saved me from the disgrace in which I would have found myself. So, Fallon, my best friend and savior, thank you for taking such precious care of me.

She looks up at me with tears moistening her cheeks. "That's not all. You need to read the inscription." She opens the book back up and finds it on the first page.

To Fallon, the love of my life. Thank you for saving me from a life filled with emptiness. In its place, you have created such meaning and replenished my soul with so much love that I am a different man than I was when I first met you. You've made me whole when before I was only bits and pieces of someone that had no purpose. I've learned so much from you in these past seven months, I can't begin to imagine what you will teach me in the years to come.

We are only bound by the limitations we place upon ourselves. Let's make ours endless together. Two lives... One Heart... One Love... Endlessly

Forever yours,
Ryland Thomas

She closes the book and sets it on the bed. It appears as though she's afraid she'll damage it somehow. Then she launches herself at me and I can feel her body trembling.

"I didn't mean for you to cry."

"It's the most beautiful thing I've ever received. Thank you," she whispers in my ear.

I glance at the clock on the wall and whisper, "I think we better put some clothes on because the next part of this night's present is due to arrive any moment."

"Huh?"

"You'll see."

A few minutes later the doorbell rings and I run down to answer it. Fallon follows me and gasps when she sees a whole crew come into the home. They're here to cook us a gourmet dinner. I hired them to cook her up a fancy meal so we could relax and enjoy ourselves.

"You're totally spoiling me."

"That's the plan."

The rest of the evening flies by and I hate it because I know the weekend will be over before I know it.

Saturday, we have reservations at seven. I'm downstairs waiting for Fallon to join me. My heart's in my gut right now because I'm giving her the last of her gifts tonight. I hadn't planned on giving her this until she told me she loved me, and since that happened on Thursday, here I am, feeling like a teenage kid about to kiss his first girl.

When I hear her coming down the steps, I glance up and my heart flips a few times before it slams down into my gut. She's wearing a slate gray dress that emphasizes her eyes and sets off her hair like nothing I've ever seen. She's all fire and heat in that thing and I'm not going to be able to keep my bloody hands to myself.

"Fallon." My voice catches so I have to clear my throat. "Wow! You look extraordinary." I pull her close for a kiss. My hand goes around her neck and all I want to do is run my fingers through her lovely hair and breathe her in. "What am I going to do with you? How am I gonna be in public with you looking as gorgeous as you do, dangerous girl?"

She licks her lips. Oh, why did she have to go on and do that? My mouth has a mind of its own as it zeroes in on hers, crashing into it like a damn heat-seeking missile.

"Sinclair," she says as she pushes me away, "if you keep on doing that, we'll never get out of here."

I inhale deeply. "Right then. I have something for you."

"Another gift?" She's surprised.

"Uh-huh." I'm not smiling so she knows it's serious.

"Are you okay?"

"I'm fine, sweetheart." I reach into my pocket and pull out a square velvet box. She has to know by now that there's jewelry inside. "Now, don't get all freaked on me because it's not a ring." I hold the box towards her and lift the lid so she can see the contents and then I hear it. Her gasp.

"Shit, Ryland Thomas. Are you shitting me?"

229

Now she's completely shocked. I suppose I would be, too.

"No, not shitting you, darling."

"Are these real?"

Only Fallon would ask something like that. I throw back my head and laugh. It feels so damn good. "Yes, hon, they're very real."

"Jesus-ever-lovin' C. What the hell are you thinking? These are huge!"

"They're two and a half carats each."

"What the... I can't accept these. No way. They're way too expensive and I'd be afraid I'd lose them."

"Fallon, I need to tell you something about them. About me. Come here, please." I lead her to a seat and we sit down. "My parents were wealthy. My dad owned a large printing company in Great Britain. It was before the computer age hit big. Anyway, he was extremely well invested so we had a lot of money. When my parents were killed, they had everything set up in wills and trusts so Tilly and I were well cared for. We've never wanted for anything. My mum had tons of jewelry. Tilly and I split everything down the middle. I let her take all that she wanted so she got to choose everything first and I got all the leftovers. And I was fine with that. Anyway, you're the only person I've ever met that I wanted to give anything like this to.

"I love you Fallon. More than anything. I'd give you all my worldly possessions. All you have to do is ask. I've been waiting for that special person to come along that I could give these to, and that special someone is you. So please accept them. And they're insured, so if you lose them, no worries. We'll simply replace them."

"I've never had anything like this."

"I didn't think you had, but that's not why I'm giving them to you. I want you to have them because I loved my mum. She was awesome. And she wore them all the time. She would've wanted someone I love to have them. Please take them and wear them every day. For me."

She looks at me, assessing me, and then nods. "If I lose one of these, I'll kill you, Sinclair. And then I'll go through life feeling guilty as hell."

"Listen to me right now. This is materialistic shit that is meaningless compared to you. Do you understand me? If you ever spend one day feeling guilty because you lose something like this, I'll... well, I don't know what I'll do."

"Spank me?"

"Huh? Oh, you naughty, naughty girl. Now put them on before I really do spank you." I wink at her. "I have to tell you something else, too. I don't want you to be angry with me. I did a little snooping and I paid off your student loans. Now, before you get all pissed off at me, I just want you to know that the money isn't a big deal to me. It makes me happy to do this for you and I know how troubled you were by the amount of it. It's nothing for me, Fallon. So don't give it another thought."

She stares at me a second and her face turns serious. "Ryland Thomas, thank you for doing that. I promise I'll cherish these with everything I have." Her hands quiver as she places them on her ears and I can't help noticing the shimmer in her eyes.

"Fallon, what is it?"

Her head shakes back and forth, letting me know she can't discuss it now, therefore I simply take her hand and she clasps it as hard as I've ever felt her hold it before. She's silent as we ride to the restaurant, leaving me to

231

puzzle her out in my mind. I want to ask, although I know she doesn't want me to, so I keep quiet.

Fallon

The tears threaten to explode, yet I force them back. He hasn't any idea how fortunate he is to have a piece of his mom. I'll tell him, but not until we get home, I don't want to make a fool out of myself in public. Our dinner is pleasant enough, with delicious food, however it's mired in my issues. He skirts around them, knowing he can't ask me and it makes for a weird night. His hand rarely lets mine go, and for that I'm thankful.

We finally arrive back home, and when he turns the car off, he turns to me and says, "We don't have to talk about this if you don't want."

"I do want to, but not in the car." He's such a gentleman; he's opening my door and helping me out before I'm even aware of it.

Once inside, he pours me a brandy and hands me the glass. I look at the deep amber fluid and feel the tears I've been holding back all night push their way past my lids.

233

"When my dad died, I was in such a haze I didn't realize what was going on." My voice is hollow sounding and it occurs to me that I've never told this to anyone before. "You know exactly how I felt, I'm sure. My body didn't feel like it was connected to my brain. There were broken pieces of me scattered everywhere, and I was trying to find them so I could glue myself back together again. I knew I needed to function, I just didn't know how.

"My mom was still in Spartanburg then, it was before she moved to Atlanta. She came and got me. I don't remember much of those days. I barely remember his funeral. He was an only child and both of his parents were gone so everything fell on my mom. I suppose I can understand why she was so bitter about it. I mean, after all, they weren't married anymore and there she was, having to deal with all of that.

"Anyway, when I finally surfaced from the fog I'd been living in, I realized that when she'd sold the house, she'd gotten rid of everything in it. I was left with nothing. All of his mementos had either been given away, sold or trashed. She never asked me if I wanted to keep anything. She just took it upon herself to get rid of it all. I have nothing left of him except for a few pictures of us. He had these wooden carvings he'd made for me that she just trashed. She said they were worthless. I'm sure they were, but they were mine and he'd made them for me.

"He and I would camp together and she sold all of our gear. He had an old gun collection from his father that she gave away. She tossed all his scrapbooks from high school. Just tons of things. So when you gave me these earrings, it triggered the fact that I have nothing of my dad's." I sit there and shake my head. "I'm sorry. I know

234

it happened long ago and I need to get over it already, but I just wish I had something like this. You know? Something that he loved." My hands move to my ears and I caress the earrings, not because they're valuable and pretty, but because I know how much it meant for him to have given them to me. "I'll treasure these, Ryland Thomas, I truly will."

"Fallon." He simply looks at me with that intensity in his eyes. It's as though he can't speak. His lips touch mine and my fingers are in his soft hair. I'm holding him so tight that I don't ever want to let him go. When we stop, our breathing is ragged as we stare at each other. Then he says, "Your mum's a selfish bitch."

For some reason, that strikes me as funny so I laugh. He laughs with me as we merely hold each other, the tension flowing from me.

"You don't know that half of her. Just wait. I'll never understand how my dad ended up with her. They're so different."

"Fallon, I wish things had turned out differently for you. I wish you had something of your father's. I know how important it is. I'm so sorry, love."

"Me, too. But now you know why I couldn't talk about it earlier."

He brushes my face with the backs of his fingers. "Let's go to sleep, gorgeous. I thing we both could use a good night's rest."

I'm pulled to my feet and then he leads me to the bathroom where he gently removes my make-up and then hands me my toothbrush already loaded with toothpaste. I watch him as we both brush and floss. Next, he undresses me and leads me to the bed. I curl up next to him, but he has none of that. He pulls me on top of him, and I sink onto his warmth.

"Right where you belong, love." he says into my ear. My arms wind around his torso and that's the last thing I know as I drift into a dreamless sleep.

His nose is nuzzling my cheek, but that's not what wakes me. It's the heat that is inching into my depths, and my moans. "Ahhh," I cry. His hands are gripping my hips and he's gliding into me, ever so slowly, but hitting me on that place that's going to make me climax.

My arms are still hugging his waist, but now my fingers are digging into his muscles. "Faster." My voice is hoarse from sleep, however he hears me loud and clear. I'm suddenly rolled onto my stomach. It takes me by surprise.

"Lift your hips, babe." I do and a pillow appears like magic.

"Thanks Houdini," I say and he laughs.

"The comedienne will be gone in a second," he says.

"Oh, yeah?"

"Hell, yeah," he says right as he slams into me, his hand flat on my stomach as he pulls me against him.

"Ahh!"

"Too hard?" he stops and asks.

"No," I'm panting now. "Not nearly."

He gives me a wicked laugh. "Oh, is that a fact?" He's ramming into me again and I love it. The thing about sex with Ryland Thomas is, he does the unexpected and it's always shocking. His hand slides up to my nipple and first he brushes it, but then pinches. Not hard, at first, just enough to make me moan. Between that and him pushing into me from behind, I'm filled with a multitude of sensations I can't begin to describe.

"Talk to me, Fallon. Is this okay?"

"More than okay. Fan-fucking-tastic." I can barely speak. He gives a throaty laugh that turns me on even more, if that's possible. I'm in for another surprise when he pulls me up against him, my back flush with his chest as he still pounds into me.

"Fuck, Fallon. I'm coming apart with you." He's holding me around the waist with one arm and the other hand slips down to my clit where he does that little circling thing that sends me straight into an orgasmic high. I'm crying out his name over and over as my muscles all tighten up around him and then I hear that guttural sound coming from him, telling me he's getting his own. My arms move up around his neck as I lay my head back against him, trying to gain control of my breathing.

"Sinclair, that's some kind of wake-up call you got goin' on there, honey."

His lips are moving all over my cheek and I feel his body shake as he laughs. "Glad you approve."

"I don't want to leave today."

"I don't want you to leave today."

He turns us so we can lie back down. I feel him slip out of me. "Boo, I hate it when that happens."

"Well, love, we can't stay connected all the time, now can we?"

"Suppose not."

"I think I'll follow you back today."

"Yeah?"

"Uh-huh. I need to get a jump on the apartment hunt."

"Sweet!"

We shower, pack up and head for San Francisco late in the morning. I'm loving life. Knowing Ryland Thomas, he'll have a place by the end of the week.

I was wrong. Two days later, on Tuesday, Ryland Thomas signs a lease on a house in Pacific Heights. It's unbelievably awesome with the most amazing view of the bay. He's having it furnished by a decorator and it should be ready in a week. In the meantime, he's staying with me. He's going back to Tahoe to pick up some clothes, but other than that, he's going to buy everything he needs so when he goes back and forth he won't have to pack anything other than a few items of clothing and his computer.

Work has me hustling. Ruth keeps sticking her head into my cubby quite a bit, which has me concerned because Kristie assured me I wouldn't be working with her when I interviewed, but now it seems she wants to be involved with my critiques on every book. The big convention in Atlanta is next week and we're tying up all the loose ends for that as well.

Ryland Thomas is running all over the city with his decorator, so that by the time we get home from Atlanta, everything will be done in his house. Tilly is so excited that he'll be living here full time, she can hardly stand it. Everything seems to be coming together in ways that I never would have dreamed possible.

Kristie and I are heading to the airport. She doesn't realize how close I am to Tilly, aka R.T., although I've wrangled that invitation for Ryland Thomas to attend our big hospitality function with Tilly. He's coming as R.T.'s guest. The convention ends on Saturday, but I've gotten approval from Kristie to stay until Monday, so I can squeeze in a visit with my mom. Ryland Thomas is staying with me and he's going to meet her. Lucky guy. Oh, she'll be all sweet to him, yet he knows the truth about her.

The flight is long, but we check into our hotel and then scramble around to get everything ready for our big function the next day. There are a ton of details to attend to.

"Will you make sure the hotel has the guest list?" Kristie asks. "And make sure the caterer has the proper headcount."

"I'm on it." I head out the door. We're staying in the same hotel as Tilly and Ryland Thomas, so I text them both my room number. They were on the same flight as me, but were fortunate enough to be in first class, which means I haven't had much time with either of them.

After taking care of my tasks, I head back to the room where the function is being held when someone grabs me from behind and pulls me into a darkened hallway. Then the sexiest man on Earth is passionately kissing me as he lifts me up with my back against the wall. My legs find their own way around his waist.

"How is it that I just saw you ten hours ago, and my body is going through Fallon withdrawals already?"

"Hmmm, probably the same reason mine is. I love you, R.T."

"Mmmm. Must be a special occasion for you to call me that." I never call him R.T.

"Every day is a special occasion with you."

His mouth is on mine again and I decide that I would rather kiss Ryland Thomas than eat, drink or sleep. For me, everything ceases to exist except for him.

"Do you know when you'll be finished for the night?"

"Uh-uh. Probably not until late."

"I'll be waiting up for you."

I kiss him again and he lets me slide down his luscious body. "I can't wait."

The convention is amazing! I get to see all my blogger girls Kat, Amanda, Mandy and Andrea. Simone, Heather, Terri, Alana, Jenn, Tana, Ellie and almost everyone I know from the blogging world are also there. It's so exciting, but I'm working the entire time so I can spend only moments with them. They all get to come to our big event, though, so it's phenomenal seeing them there.

By the time Saturday rolls around, I want to crawl in a hole and sleep for days. Kristie leaves that afternoon, but before she does, she makes a comment to me that leaves me a bit rattled.

"You know, Ruth mentioned to me how she noticed that you and R.T. seem to be pretty close. She knows I suggested you do a spotlight on her, Fallon. She's pushing for you to do it soon. She also wants you to use your relationship with her to get inside information."

"Kristie, I can't do that. Yeah, we're fairly close. I won't deny that, but I refuse to exploit our relationship."

"I understand. I'm just giving you a heads up. Ruth's name is pretty appropriate. She can be extremely ruthless when she wants to be, so if she gets something in her head, you may not be able to deter her from this. I'm simply giving you a warning here. And one other thing, I won't be able to sway her. She doesn't like me at all, Fallon."

"Gee, thanks for the heads up."

"You know how much I like you. I don't want you to get blindsided by her."

"Got it. And thanks, Kristie."

With that, she nods and leaves for the airport.

When I go to meet Ryland Thomas, he notices my mood. I explain what happened and he says, "She can't force you to get information that Tilly refuses to give, so stop worrying about it. All you have to say is that Tilly refused to answer you."

"I guess so," but for some strange reason, I still feel very unsettled by it all. It's the same feeling that has persisted for weeks whenever Ruth would pop into my cubicle. Ruth has never been my favorite person, and this confirms why.

It's Sunday night and we're heading to the restaurant to meet my mother and her dweeb of a husband. "Calm down, love. I've got this. I want you to remember something for me, will you?"

I nod.

"She can't hurt you anymore. Only you can allow that to happen, so don't let it. Be strong, okay? And remember, lower your expectations." He gives my hand an encouraging squeeze.

"Got it. Let's get this over with."

It starts out okay. We make all the introductions, and at first she's nice, but soon the snide comments emerge.

241

First she nails me, but then she tries to use her vicious tactics on Ryland Thomas. We introduce him as Ryland, the freelance writer. She doesn't know anything about him, however she presumes he's a nobody. Of course, she thinks *she's* all that and then some. Don't ask me why because the woman has never held down a real job in her life.

"So, Ryland, what is it exactly that you write?"

"Articles for magazines, news releases for PR companies, that sort of thing."

"Ah, a dreamer, just like my little Fallon here." She's so condescending; I have to clamp my jaws together to keep from screaming at her.

"Being a dreamer is a bad thing then, I take it?"

"You'll never amount to much. Dreams won't put food on the table or money in the bank."

"That so? That's not the way it works in my family. Matter of fact, my parents encouraged it. My granddad was a big dreamer and so was his dad. He passed it down to my dad and then my dad passed it to me. Anyway, they built quite a large fortune in Great Britain, they did. Dreaming served them quite well. You should try it some time. You might be surprised." I squeeze his hand and want to laugh at the look on her face.

"Well, look at what it's done for Fallon here."

"Yeah, take a good look. She's doing brilliantly well for someone who had no help at all from her mum. A young lady who was left to fend for herself after her dad died. Who has to pay off a mountain of school debt... oh, wait. No, she doesn't. I've taken care of that for her. Anyway, Fallon is off to a fabulous career, working for one of the largest literary critiquing agencies in the industry. Yeah, I'd say her dreams have served her quite well."

Ryland Thomas lifts my hand and presses a kiss to it and then smiles. Damn it all, I want to crawl right in his lap and kiss the hell out of him and then I want to turn to my mom and stick my tongue out at her.

Mom stammers and doesn't know what to make of him. She leans over the table and takes a close look at me. Ryland Thomas has brushed my hair off my shoulder and tucked it behind my ear. "What is that in your ear? Taking to wearing imitation diamonds now?"

I burst out laughing. "Why would I do that, Mom? These are a birthday gift from Ryland. And no, they're not fake." *So eat your heart out, bitch.*

"Not fake?"

Ryland Thomas takes over, "No, they're real. I can show you the appraisal papers on them if you'd like. But they're in the safe back at my house in Lake Tahoe."

"Lake Tahoe? I thought you lived in San Francisco."

"I do. I have a place there, too. And a place in London. Fallon hasn't visited there yet, but I plan to take her there this summer. England's quite magnificent in the summer, you know. My hopes are that after we're married she works freelance like myself, so we can travel the world together."

I choke on my wine and my mom says, "Married?"

"Oh, not in the next few months or anything. But yes, I do plan on marrying your daughter one day. She's the love of my life. Why wouldn't I?"

"Why indeed?"

I choke on my wine for the second time. "You okay, love?" He pats my back as I nod.

"Went down the wrong way."

He leans in and kisses my cheek. "I'm not joking about any of that," he says in my ear.

My hand clenches his thigh so hard, he flinches. Why the hell did he pick now to tell her all this?

We finish our dinner, making small chitchat. When we're through, the check arrives and Ryland Thomas picks it up, like he's planned all along. Then we all walk out together. That's when I realize that the selfish one's husband has barely said a word all night.

We're ready to depart each other's company when Ryland Thomas says, "Gloria, there is one thing I want to say to you before we leave. If you so much as say one more negative comment to Fallon about her life, her career, the choices she's made in this life or anything at all that she does, she will never speak to you again. All communications will be severed permanently. You are a toxic disease that she's been forced to deal with her entire life. Your selfishness after her father's death was unconscionable and you should be ashamed of yourself. Are we clear?" His tone is so icy I actually shiver as his eyes glint like chips of emeralds.

She looks at me and is ready to say something, but Ryland Thomas stops her by raising his hand. "I asked you if we were clear, Gloria. You don't have to look at Fallon; you answer to me." His lips are pressed into a thin line.

Her head swings to Ryland Thomas and I see her eyes widen as she nods. "Good. I hope you two have a nice evening." He turns to me, smiles and says, "Come on, love." My hand is encased in his as we walk to the Mercedes he's rented.

When we drive off, my mom is still watching us in shock.

"Well, how did I do?" His hands are clenched on the wheel, so I place mine on top of the one closest to me and give it a firm squeeze.

"Holy hells, Ryland Thomas. You were fabulous! But that married part. Where the hell did that come from?"

He pulls into another parking lot close to where we are and brings the car to a stop.

He clasps my face in his hands, his voice is rough with emotion. "My heart. It came straight from my heart. I want that for us one day, Fallon. Exactly how I described it. That is if you want the same thing. I love you endlessly. I want to be with you endlessly. It doesn't have to be right away, but one day I hope we get there. Traveling the world together with you writing your reviews, working from wherever we are and me doing the same." Then he takes my hand and places it on his heart and says, "One heart, remember?"

God, I am so in love with this man.

TWENTY - TWO

RYLAND - THOMAS

Could I have been a bigger fool? More lame? What the bloody hell had I been thinking of when I blurted that shit out about us getting married to her mum, the she-fucking-bitch-from-hell? I can't even answer that.

All I know is that when Fallon was telling me that story about after her dad died and the crap her mum pulled by getting rid of all her dad's belongings, it was all I could do not to get on the first plane to Atlanta and rip that bitch's hair right out of her head. I know exactly how Fallon felt, utterly and completely torn apart.

After my folks died, I felt like my body had been mutilated, my insides torn out and my bones crushed. I knew I needed to glue myself together. And honestly, I didn't do it for myself, 'cause I didn't give a shit about me. It was all for Tilly. She thinks I saved her, but it was really her doing all the saving simply by being there. I had to pull myself together and stay strong for her. I don't remember those early days, but I put the scraps of what used to be me back together and moved forward step by step.

At first the steps were mere inches, yet then Tilly made me understand that there were two of us and not one. I rearranged my scraps and made them work a little better. Everything was okay until Iris and Will pulled their shit. Then it all crumbled because, in reality, those scraps were never really glued together. Little toothpicks held them up. They were so unstable that a mere breeze could've tumbled them over, which was what happened.

What I had with Iris was nothing except a breeze. I didn't know that until Fallon. Fallon roared into my life like a hurricane, destroying everything I thought I knew, what I thought was right. Then she reassembled it into what it should've been all along, and put the pieces in their proper order. Heart was where it should be, brain was functioning the correct way, all was in order with soul and everything converged, allowing harmony to rule. Somewhere in all this, Fallon was immersed inside of it, making it even sweeter than I ever thought possible.

And that was my answer. I'd known it all along. She and I would be together forever. It wasn't a love that would last for months or years. If something happened to her tomorrow, there would never be anyone else in my life. I would always have our hearts beating as one and her soul intersecting with mine.

My latest novel hits the New York Times Bestsellers List and has been at number one for several weeks now. Tilly and I are off promoting *My Love For Her* all over the place, and I feel bad because my agent has her booked everywhere. When all this began, I promised Tilly I would travel with her to every signing and event, so here I am, on the road, and I hate it because it takes me away from Fallon. Our schedule wraps up after next week and we can take a three week breather before it cranks up again.

Fallon and I are going to spend a much needed, long weekend up in Sonoma at one of the spas. I've been promising to take her there and it's only now just worked out.

We're finally driving up on Friday morning as I hold her hand. She's taking in the scenery while I wish I had a driver so I could take *her* in. She's much prettier than the landscape she's so enthralled over.

"Would you quit staring at me?"

"Never. So get used to it." I let out a chuckle.

"Gah, the coast is magnificent, isn't it?"

"Uh-huh. Not like you are, though. I can look at the coast, but I can't fuck it."

She sucks in her breath. "Sinclair! Get your mind out of the gutter."

"It's not in the gutter. It's on you. And sorry, love, but it's the bloody truth. You're magnificent when you're naked and I'm fucking you. When that hair of yours is all tangled up and spread across the bed, your mouth is parted and sometimes you bite on your lower lip. I love it when you sink your fingers into me. You usually do that right before your orgasm hits and then I can feel all those little muscles deep inside of you, squeezing against me, holding me tight. Bloody hell, Fallon, you're loads better than any damn view of the coast line."

"Ryland Thomas." Her voice is deep and sexy.

"Yeah."

"Pull the car over."

"What?"

"I said, pull the car over. Now."

I find a secluded cove nestled in some trees, and do as she asks. "What are...?" I look over at her and she's already stripped her jeans and panties off.

She reaches for me, unzips my pants, my dick springs out, she crawls over me and then, in one fluid motion, I'm inside of her and she's riding me like it's our very first time.

I push her shirt up and move her bra out of the way so I can see her perfectly hardened nipples. They beg to be sucked, so I do and her head drops back as she moans. My hands grab her ass and we work up a damn hot rhythm. Up and down, we move together and then my thumb finds her sweet spot. This is my favorite thing because I know in a few minutes this is going to be her undoing. And God, I love this part of fucking her. I love it more that I can even say.

"Fallon, this is us, forever. Say it, love."

"Endless with you, Ryland Thomas. Ah, yes, harder. Right there."

Her fingers sink into my arms and there she goes, clenching my dick, squeezing me for days.

"Give me that mouth of yours, love." She leans into me and I lightly suck her tongue, but she's not having any of it. She's going for rough and bites my lip, so I kiss her for all she's worth. It's way more than I can even guess. I'm not quite done with her yet since I haven't gotten mine. I open the car door and get out, carrying her. Normally, I'd cringe at this thought because I'd hate to think of putting a scratch on my Aston Martin, but fuck it. I lay her on the hood, spread her legs, and my mouth meets her slit. My tongue plunges in her and then circles her pleasure points as I add my fingers to the action. She tugs the hell out of my hair, and damn it all, it jacks me up.

I pull her up and off the car, spin her around and bend her over the hood. "Hang on, love." I thrust home and it's so damn good this way... so deep.

"You good?" I don't ever want it to be too much or too rough for her.

"Oh, yeah," she pants. "More than good."

I give her all I've got and she's loud. Real loud. My arm goes around her and I find her clit. I need her to come for me again because I'm not going to last much longer with her ass pounding against me and her voice calling out my name like that.

"Babe, you gotta come for me."

"Ah, yeah. I'm close."

If anyone came by right now, I'm sure they'd think we were killing each other with the racket we're making, yet it's pure pleasure for both of us.

There comes her hand on my arm, fingers digging in hard, and doesn't that just make me soar.

"Ah... ah... yeah." And there it is, the clenching of her against me and I'm there, groaning my ass off, bent over her. When we're both finished, I'm reluctant to pull out. I don't want to move. I kiss her neck, her cheek, anywhere my lips can reach because I'm in paradise right now.

"Shit, Fallon. What you do to me. Love, I'm..." I'm speechless is what I am. I stand up, pulling her with me. We need to clean up. I wonder if I have a towel in my car.

"We need a towel."

"My thoughts exactly."

"Don't pull out or…"

"I know, love."

Then we both laugh. "What if someone comes?"

I laugh even harder. "Don't you think we should've thought of that before we ever started this?"

"I guess," she says.

"Stand on my feet," I tell her. She does and we shuffle to the boot of the car. Thankfully, I find a towel stashed back there. I step away from her, turn her around and bend down to clean her up.

"What are you doing?" She's totally embarrassed.

"Cleaning you up."

She tries to grab the towel from me.

"Fallon, stop."

"No. You can't do that."

I grab her chin and force her to look at me. "Why ever not? Most of it's from me. And besides, my mouth goes down on you all the time. What's the big deal?"

"I—I don't know. It's weird."

"Only because you're letting it be weird. I think it's totally sexy."

"You do?"

"Of course I do. As is this." I slide a finger into her.

"Mmmm."

"See. That's the same place all this comes from. So cleaning you up should really be my job, you know. I did make the mess after all."

"I helped."

"You caused it. You and your errant ways."

She laughs and her discomfort passes.

"Now kiss me." We hear a car in the distance so I tell her, "You'd better get in the car first. I'd hate for whoever is about to get here to see your lovely, naked ass."

She hops in the car like a rabbit and I laugh as I zip up my pants and close the boot.

We check into the spa and head for our first treatment, a couples massage. It's very relaxing, but all I can think about is Fallon being naked under her sheet. I wish the massage therapists would simply leave us alone in here so we could play a little. I realize I need to tame my thoughts because, when they roll me on my back, my dick's going to be making a pup tent out of the sheet over me.

The dopey expression on Fallon's face when we're finished is priceless. I want to both laugh and kiss her at the same time.

"Need a nap?"

"I'm jelly. Or noodley."

"Noodley?"

"Yep. Legs are like noodles. Will you carry me?"

I swoop her up in my arms and she laughs. "I was kidding Ryland. People are staring." She makes a point of calling me that in public, as we discussed.

Glancing around, I notice we are indeed catching looks from others. I grin and announce, "My beautiful girlfriend can't walk because her massage has made her legs wobbly." My statement earns a few chuckles from those that hear.

Fallon's face is now hot pink and matches her toenails. My grin widens. "I took you seriously. You ready for some lunch and wine tastings?"

"Sure. But, can you put me down?"

"Maybe. Or maybe I'll just carry you there."

Now she's laughing, too.

I finally set her down and she swats me on my arse.

We head on out to lunch and then we're off on an afternoon of tastings. It's a gorgeous day and we plan to end it back in the town of Sonoma where we'll be eating dinner in a quaint restaurant. So we go to our room to change without a whole lot of time, making us sort of in a rush.

The town is small and the restaurant is close enough that we can walk, therefore we stroll arm and arm to dinner.

And then it happens. The impossible. I never thought it would, but it does.

"Ryland? Is that you?" I hear my name and turn to see her. Tall, thin and blond, she's as beautiful as she ever was. Her smile plows into me like the train that killed my parents. It's been years, however I feel the blood drain from my face and everything shifts in my world.

"Oh my God, it's really you!" she says.

Fallon is squeezing my hand, as if to ask whether I'm okay. I can't speak for a second, so I nod. Finally I say, "Hello, Iris."

She runs and hugs me. I've no choice except to release Fallon's hand and hug her back. She smells the same, like vanilla, and she clings to me like she doesn't want to let me go. So I keep hugging her back because I don't know what else to do. It's completely awkward for me. I try to look at Fallon, but Iris's head is blocking my view. I finally have the sense to disengage her arms and step back from her. My head is swimming and I don't know why. I can't understand all these strange feelings that are hitting me.

"Iris, I want you to meet Fallon McKinley. Fallon, this is Iris." They shake hands and exchange a brief greeting. Fallon's face looks wounded. I know she's feeling the odd one out in all of this. Hell, so am I.

"So what are you doing here?" Iris asks.

"We're here for a getaway weekend."

"Ah, great choice. I live here now. I'm an artist trying to make it and I thought, well, this would be a great place to sell my stuff."

"I see." I don't know what else to say.

"So what about you?"

"I live in San Francisco."

"Great. That's so close."

She's talking like we're still great friends or something. "Yeah, not far. Well, we need to get to our dinner reservation."

"Oh, well, have fun then."

"Thanks."

She launches herself at me again and says, "It's so great to see you. I've missed you Ryland. So much. Let's meet soon, okay? For drinks, or you know." She does this little wiggle thing.

I don't know what to say, so I just nod and say, "Sure."

I turn away from her then Fallon and I continue on our way.

We walk to the restaurant in silence. She doesn't say a thing and I'm baffled. I don't understand why she's angry. Did I do something wrong? I'm so damn confused that I can barely eat.

When we head back to the hotel, we're like two robots getting ready for bed. And when we get in, I have my answer as she rolls to the other side. She doesn't touch me or say a word, although I can hear her sobs and see her body shaking.

254

"Fallon, we have to talk." I move to touch her and she jerks from me like I've burned her. "Please. Talk to me."

Her voice is tiny and muffled, as if she's holding back painful tears. "You ignored me in front of her. You acted like I was your afterthought, just a casual someone you happened upon, and it killed me. It's still killing me. Do you want her, Ryland Thomas?"

I'm trying to process what she is saying. Did I do that to her? In my shock of seeing Iris, maybe I did. That certainly wasn't my intention. My gravest error comes when I don't immediately respond to her question. It isn't because I want Iris. I don't. She was never true to me. Had never been. Fallon is. I never had the kinds of feelings for Iris that I have for Fallon.

As I ponder all of this, she mistakes my silence for something completely different. She gets out of the bed and walks into the bathroom where she softly shuts the door. Her sobs rip into me like a Sawzall, tearing me into bits.

I'm flying after her, knocking on the door. "Fallon, let me in. I don't want her. I want *you*. I was thinking about what you said. That's why I didn't answer you. I love you and only you. I'll only ever love you, no matter what. Iris was a shock, that's all. Please let me in." Nothing other than those awful sobs greet me. I'm a lost soul and don't know what to do. I slide down the wall and stay in front of the bathroom door all night long while sleep evades me.

In the morning, I hear the door open and she nearly trips over me when she comes out. "Fallon, we have to talk this out. I don't want her. She shocked me, yes. And blindsided me. But I never intended to hurt you. I would rather take a bullet than hurt you. When you asked me last night if I wanted her, the answer is a resounding no. I would *never* want her. The reason it took me so long to answer you was that I was processing how you said I'd treated you like an afterthought. I'm so sorry I acted like that. It wasn't intentional. You're not an afterthought. You're the most important person in the world to me. Do you understand me? Please say you do. I'm a desperate man and I'll do anything right now to make you see that."

"But why did you act that way?" Her face is puffy from crying and her eyes are red with purple half moons beneath them.

"I don't know. Seeing her hit me out of the blue. I haven't laid eyes on her since the day I threw her out. And then seeing her there, after all that time, I suppose I thought I'd feel something, anything, but I didn't. There was nothing there at all. Do you really think I'd want someone like her? Fallon, call me a wanker. Call me whatever, but don't close me out like that. Your crying was like acid on a wound to me when all I wanted to do was hold you and tell you it would be okay, but I couldn't get to you. Please don't turn away from me. Please."

She examines me, her eyes clawing into me, and then she drops down next to me and sits there, in silence.

I reach for her, but she shrinks from me. Her voice is raw when she speaks and it bludgeons me. I'll take physical pain over emotional pain any day. Physical pain is real; it's there. You know and understand the source. Emotional pain is a whole different beast. It bashes you in every vulnerable body part without mercy, over and over, leaving you defenseless with your guts exposed. Then it keeps on coming until you've nothing left to destroy.

256

"When you dropped my hand to hug her back and you didn't let go of her, I died a very painful death inside. It was something I'll never forget. I felt betrayed and I wanted to walk away from you right then, and would have, but I had nowhere to go."

"Oh, God, Fallon. I didn't mean for that to happen. I know it looked bad, but that's not how it was at all. I didn't know what to do with her. She acted like we were best pals and I kept thinking, 'What the fuck!' I'm stupid, okay. I know it. I just wasn't prepared for it." I pull her into my lap even though she struggles against me. "This is what I want. Always. Right here. Like this. Forever and without end. You, Fallon. It's always been you and it will always be you."

She finally burrows into me, and her hand creeps up on my chest. I know she's crying, but she's not sobbing anymore. I pet her hair and rub her back. I'll do anything for her not to hurt this way.

"Let's go to sleep, love." She nods. I stand and then pick her up to carry her to bed. I pull her on top of me where she always sleeps and we fall hard, wrapped up in each other.

Twenty-Three

Fallon

I really thought it was the end for us, yet when I walk out of the bathroom and he tells me everything, first I want to kick him in the balls until they're swollen and blue, then I drop into his lap and want to just stay there. I'm so damn weak from crying all night, I can't even think anymore. Is it just me or is he the dumbest thing alive? I mean, really? Right now, I need sleep and then I'll deal. When he suggests it, I don't have the strength to say no.

I'm not sure what time it is when I wake up. All I know is Ryland Thomas's arms are holding me tight and things feel right again.

He's awake. "You slept okay?"

"Uh-huh. What time is it?"

"Five."

"In the afternoon?"

"Yep."

"Shit. A lost day." My fists are balled up as they rub my eyes.

"Not for me. I got to hold you in my arms."

I inhale, smelling him. He always smells good, no matter what. My hand reaches for his face. I love to rub his scruff. I don't like for him to shave because I think he's adorably sexy with that bit of beard he wears. He traps my hand against his face and says, "Fallon, tell me we're okay. I need to hear you say it."

"We're okay, but don't ever do anything like that to me again. Understand?"

"Never." His voice cracks. "In a million years."

I'm still pissed at him, however I can't go through life not speaking or pouting. That isn't my way. My dad would always say to me, *"If you're angry about something, spit it out. Don't walk around in a huff. I'm not a mind reader."* That was one of his pieces of advice he'd fed to me, the ones I'd gobble up like chocolate covered candy. He was full of them and I think it was because he didn't want me to turn out like my mom. His biggest one was, *"Fallon, don't ever lie, honey. You can get yourself in a much bigger jam when you create a lie. It's easier to take an honest punishment than it is to take a deceitful path."* He was right. I tried it one time, and my story got so discombobulated, I couldn't remember what I said. Boy did I get in big trouble; for lying mainly, but also for trying to cover up the bad that I'd done.

"What are you thinking?"

"The honest truth?"

"Yep."

"That you're filled with all sorts of dumbassery."

His body shakes with laughter and I shake my head. "I'm serious. How can you behave like that and not think my feelings aren't going to get hurt? Buddy, you'd better start growing a brain and fast."

259

"I don't think the brain thing is the problem. It's thinking fast on my feet when I'm thrown a curve ball. I'm really terrible at it. I'm sorry you've had to deal with it more than your fair share. How can I make it up to you?"

At least he is taking the blame and not cowering away from it. That is a good thing. "By not repeating this. When we're out together and we run into an old flame, put your goddamn arm around me and act like I mean something to you. Got it?"

He rubs his face. "Yeah, loud and clear. But I don't have any more old flames. You met the one and only."

"Well, good. Then if we're out and about tonight and we run into her, act like I mean something to you then, okay?"

"You mean everything to me, Fallon."

"Actions speak louder than words, Ryland Thomas. Show her then."

"Got it." There was an edge to his voice this time, but I didn't care. He can get all pissy with me for all I care. I'm in the right and he knows it. He moves to get out of bed.

"Where are you going?"

He stops and looks at me for a second and then sighs. "Thought I'd take a shower."

"What? Without me? Like hell you are."

He gazes at me for a second. Then the corners of his mouth lift slightly and his lids half cover his eyes, indicating he's completely on board with this.

"I've always heard make-up sex is the best. You owe me some damn good make-up sex, Sinclair, and I plan on collecting." I stand, plant my hand on my hip and stare at him.

He doesn't say a word, rather he stalks towards me and the heat is rushing from him now. He drops his boxers and I'm happy to see what's waiting for me. My shirt is gone in a whoosh and then his hands are under the elastic band of my thong panties. He doesn't take them off. He snaps them off, ruining them. My mouth forms an O and his tongue is in it before I know what's happening. His hand is in my tangled hair as he pulls my head back. I'm lifted up and he impales me as he turns and slams my back against the wall.

"Ah, ah, ah..." is all I can say against his mouth as he sinks into me over and over. It's rough, hard and fast, and I'm spinning out of control. I take his lower lip, biting down on him. My nails scratch his skin, drawing blood on his shoulders, but he doesn't notice. He's intent on one thing and one thing only. My heels dig into the cheeks of his ass and he presses on, going deeper every time.

"Come on, Fallon. Come for me," he growls. It's a demand, urgent and harsh, as my back is jammed against the wall.

My teeth gouge the flesh of his shoulder. I know I've hurt him because he flinches, but I don't care. "Faster," I goad him on. He complies and then it happens.

I scream, yes, scream his name. I think I'm telling him to fuck me, too. I don't really know because I'm having one hell of a ride right now and I must say I'm not thinking properly. I hear him groan, and can feel the vibrations in his throat as its right against my shoulder and he's coming all over the place. When we're finished, we gaze at each other for what seems like an eternity.

"They're right," I whisper as I kiss him. My hands cup the roughness of his cheeks. I can't pull my eyes off his.

"Hmm?"

"Make-up sex rocks."

His voice is gruff when he responds. "You're bloody right it does. Although every time we fuck, my world rocks a little harder, a little deeper and a lot more intense. It's you, Fallon. It's always been you."

And what do I say to that?

It's around ten in the evening and we've just finished dinner. We're sitting in a quaint restaurant when Ryland Thomas picks up my hand and says, "Let's dance."

"Right here?" I look around and think how silly we'll look.

He laughs. "No, not here. In a club. Let's find a place to go dancing."

I laugh now, too. "Good. You had me a little scared for a minute. I thought you were gonna grab me and start doing one of those weird dances old people like to do."

He gets a funny look on his face and scoots his chair back. I see it coming and I'm dying in my seat. "Oh, no. Please don't." His hand is on mine, pulling me out of my chair and I'm in his arms as he moves to music that only he can hear. "Ryland Thomas," I whisper quite urgently, "everyone is staring at us."

He smiles and then lays a heart-stopping kiss on my lips. My hands are clutching his shoulders, partly because I'm trying to follow his lead, but the other part is that his kiss has me reeling. Then he embarrasses me further when he lifts his head and announces to the room, "I'm in love with this beautiful woman!" Everyone starts to clap as my face explodes with heat.

I smile to hide my acute mortification and thank the heavens the room is dimly lit, but under my breath I tell him, "You're a dead man. Just wait."

He laughs and kisses me again.

He pays the bill and we find a dance club where we can let loose. On the way there, he kids me relentlessly over the look on my face. "Yeah, well, I'll get you back one day when you least expect it."

"I wish I had it on video. You wore the funniest expression."

I stick my tongue out at him.

We enter the crowded club and push our way to the bar for some drinks. While we wait, I feel Ryland Thomas stiffen. I look up to see Iris standing a few feet from us. It doesn't take long for me to see how it will all play out.

"Ryland, it's great to see you out. You wanna dance?"

"Not interested, Iris."

Then he turns away from her and pulls me into his arms, completely ignoring her. He nuzzles my cheek with his nose and then whispers, "I'm sorry about this."

"Don't be. You can't control her actions. Only yours." He gets the message. He immediately kisses me, and not your everyday friendly peck, this is a full on, mind-blowing kiss.

"Mmmm, I like that. I love it when you fuck my mouth like that." I decide I'm going to be a naughty girl. I notice how his eyes widen slightly at first, yet then the lids drop into their half-closed positions, telling me I've just flipped his switch. I, being an extra naughty girl,

263

press myself against him, feeling him jerk when my thigh touches him. He kisses me again, roughly.

Iris isn't leaving. She wants Ryland Thomas and isn't giving up. She taps him on the shoulder. "So, Ryland, I'm going to be in San Francisco next week. Do you want to get together and maybe talk about old times?"

I feel Ryland Thomas's hold on me tighten. She's hit a nerve. I slide my arm up around his neck and thread my fingers through his hair. I want to ease his discomfort because I know this must be painful for him. She's also pissing me off, too, but this isn't my fight, it's his.

He doesn't let me go. He holds me as close as ever, though he does turn his head so he can see her. "Iris, there's no reason whatsoever for you and I to talk about old times. We have nothing to talk about." Then he turns back to me and I brush his cheek with my fingers. I want him to know I understand his pain. He blinks in understanding.

"What do you mean, Ryland? We have loads to talk about. You and I... well, we had some great times. You remember, don't you?"

Now he's pissed. Really pissed. He's trying to maintain control. He has that little tic in his jaw and his eyes have darkened to forest green. "What I remember, Iris, is throwing you out after catching you sucking off my best mate, and him going down on you in my flat. In my book, that constitutes as shit, and I don't want to associate with shit. So get the fuck out of my face."

I want to clap and cheer him on for telling her off, the little cheating slut. She sputters and then stomps off. Everyone around hears the interchange between them and they all give her a nasty look. Cheating is cheating, and she just lost that war.

264

"That was magnificent."

"What I don't get is how could she possibly think I'd want anything to do with her?"

I shrug. "She's stupid? I don't know."

His attention swings back to me. "You're a naughty girl." He kisses me again; a hot, wet, toe-curling, knee-buckling kiss. "Let's dance, love. I want to hold you and move to some music while *you* fuck *my* mouth."

"Well, darn, Sinclair. Talk about naughty."

He grins that sexy grin of his and I melt right into him as we dance. Yep, I'll never get enough of this man. Never.

When Sunday afternoon appears, we begin our drive back to the city with our fingers laced because, oddly, this weekend has brought us closer together. Earlier this morning we joked about missing our spa treatments yesterday, since we slept the day away, but he's promised me a return visit. Even though we had that terrible misunderstanding, we both feel more tightly woven than ever. Maybe it's because Ryland Thomas never really buried his relationship with Iris and now it has finally been put to rest, or maybe he realized his feelings for her were only superficial. Whatever the reason, it's deepened our bond and for that I'm grateful.

"Why doesn't Tilly go by Rose Tilly?" For some reason, that question just hit me out of the blue. "You know, since you're both R.T.s and all."

Ryland Thomas gives my hand a squeeze. "She used to. Up until my mum died. My mum's name was also Rose." The words are so softly spoken that I have to strain to hear them.

265

"Oh." My heart instantly fills with sadness for these two people that I love so dearly. I remove my hand from his and move it around his waist so I can hug him. I lay my head on his shoulder and cup his cheek with my hand. "I'm so sorry for the two of you."

He holds my hand against his face. "She said it was too hard to hear Mum's name all the time so she asked not be called that anymore."

Tears fill my eyes as I think about Tilly's pain as well as Ryland Thomas's. I want to crawl on him and hug him close just to comfort him. "Can you pull over a minute?" He does and I do exactly what I wanted to do.

"I needed to hug you. It didn't feel right not being able to do that."

"I wish I'd have had you to hold on to when they were killed." I lean back to look at him, and notice how his eyes contain such agony and how that little place between them is deeply creased. My fingers massage that tiny area, trying to ease his tension and pain. "I had to be strong for Tilly and I was busting apart at the seams, Fallon. I was only eighteen and trying to hold it together..." He stops to breathe.

"You have me now. I'm here, Ryland Thomas."

"I know."

We simply sit together like that for quite some time, me straddling his lap and holding him in my arms.

"You know, Tilly always thought I was the strong one, when all along it was really her. I only held myself together because of her. I did it all for her. If it hadn't been for Tilly, I don't know what I would've done."

"You would've done what I did. Taken one day at a time. You know our parents all died the same year. It's strange when I think of that, but you have to give it some

266

reason. I mean, for you, Ryland Thomas, all your life experiences have added to the richness of your novels. Can you honestly say you could write what you do had you not lived through the shit you went through?"

"Probably not."

"So, in a way, in dying, your parents gave you a gift. Their death wasn't in vain."

"I suppose not."

"And even though your relationship with Iris sucked... okay, bad word. Sorry. But even though she cheated on you, the pain you felt has somehow enriched your writing. I can feel it in your books. Your writing is true, Ryland Thomas. It's from the heart. So it wasn't all for nothing."

"I love you, Fallon."

"Endlessly."

Fallon

The advanced copies of novels are piled two feet thick on my desk and I'm up to my eyeballs in reviews when Kristie walks into my tiny cubby of an office.

"So how was the spa weekend?"

"Awesome. Sonoma is really unbelievable. The coastline is incredibly beautiful."

"Yeah, isn't it? I love it there. I love Mendocino, too. Get him to take you up there next time. Look, I know you're swamped today, but Ruth wants to see you."

"Sure. When?"

"Now?"

"Okay." I get up and follow Kristie to the elevator, up three floors where enter the executive level. "I've never been up here."

"Yeah, well, don't get too excited," she mumbles.

We wind our way down and around a couple of halls until we get to a reception area where an administrative assistant sits in the middle. There are four offices behind her.

"Hi, Leslie. Ruth knows we're coming."

"Okay. Let me buzz her." Leslie picks up the phone and tells Ruth we're here. "Go on in. She's ready for you."

We walk in her office. It's huge, overlooking the bay with a view of the Golden Gate Bridge. I guess I'm dazed because she looks at me and says, "Pretty decent, isn't it?"

"I'll say."

"Have a seat, ladies."

Kristie and I sit across from her in the two chairs that face her desk.

"First off, Fallon, I want you to know how pleased we are with your work here at Critics Abound. Your reviews are exceptional and we know we made the right choice in hiring you. You've been with us now for six months and we want to put into motion our author spotlight that Kristie had mentioned to you. We want you to spearhead it with an interview with R.T. Sinclair. I know you love her writing and that you two are on friendly terms, so I'm sure we at Critics Abound can count on you to do a marvelous job here. I also want to give you this." She hands me an oblong box. I take it from her and hold it a minute. "Go on, open it."

I unwrap it and inside is a leather portfolio with latest version of the iPad. It's very lovely. "Oh my. This is really nice, but I already have an iPad Mini."

"Well, this is much better than the mini and we want to reward you for doing such a great job. You can use it in your interviews so you don't have to lug your laptop around. It'll be a lot more convenient for you. We loaded Pages on it so you can type all your documents up in it as well."

269

"I don't know what to say."

"You don't have to say anything. Just go and get that interview for us. Critics Abound is ranked number two among all the literary critics and I want us to be number one. I mean it, Fallon. I'm willing to go to all lengths to get us there. Are you following me?" She smiles. For some reason I feel like I'm getting ready to get eaten for breakfast. Her pointy teeth look threatening and her eyes are not at all friendly like I want them to be.

"I'll do my best."

"I don't want your best. I want you to make it happen, Fallon."

I nod, feeling the threat of her words. Kristie and I leave. When we hit the elevator, Kristie says, "You know there are strings attached to everything, don't you?"

"I-I guess," I stutter. I'm not exactly sure what she means.

"Just do the interview as best you can, Fallon. Ruth isn't someone you want on your bad side."

"What does that mean, Kristie?"

"Let's just say that things can get pretty miserable if she doesn't get what she wants."

I look at Kristie, feeling like there's something else she wants to say, though she doesn't. We part ways as she goes to her office and I go to mine, trying to reason out what's just happened.

Two weeks later, Tilly and I are sitting in her favorite restaurant, eating a leisurely dinner that's my treat for a change. Actually, it's Critics Abound's treat because this is the night I'm interviewing her.

"I promised you I wouldn't dig for this and I'm not. My boss's boss wants me to get the real scoop on you, you know. But I told Kristie that I wouldn't exploit our relationship. Wouldn't they all just die if they knew the truth?"

We both laugh, hard and loud, and I toast her for her latest success, *My Love For Her.*

"I've never seen Ryland Thomas so happy, Fallon."

"I've never been this happy, Tilly. He's the best thing that's ever happened to me."

"He says the same about you. He told me you ran into Iris in Sonoma and what happened."

"Yeah. It turned out okay. I think it worked in our favor, actually."

"You two think so much alike. Do you realize that?"

I shrug. "I don't think about it, I guess."

"So?"

"So what?"

"When are you gonna do it?"

"Do what?"

"Tie the big knot?"

I blush. It's weird, too, because I think about it all the time, but we never talk about it.

"He ties me in knots everywhere, Tilly."

"I hope you mean figuratively because, if you mean literally, I'm just gonna say, ewww!"

"No! I don't mean he ties me up! But now that you mention it, I might…"

"Stop! He's my brother for Christ's sake. Bloody hell, Fallon. Are you trying to gross me out?"

I giggle and say, "Yeah."

"Has he asked you to marry him yet?"

"No. We don't talk about it."

271

"Ah, I see. He will," she says smugly, like she knows something I don't. "So yeah, his book is doing phenomenally well and I am so damned excited for him. I think it's you. He wrote *My Love For Her* after he met you. You do know there are so many shades of you in it."

"Yeah, I know. So, let's get this interview over with. What do you want me to write about? I know you don't want anything about your love life, right?"

"Just put down that I'm very single at the moment and looking for an incredibly hot, eligible bachelor. That will do. And then the usual. My favorite stuff to do, places to eat, things to see, etc. How's that? And you can write about where I grew up."

"I'd love that. Tell me about growing up in London."

So she talks and I take copious notes on my iPad throughout dinner. A couple of hours and a bottle and a half of wine later, I have enough to write a very informative spotlight on Tilly, a.k.a. R.T. Sinclair.

"By George, I think I've got it," I say in my best British accent.

"You're gonna have to work on that a bit. Sounds bloody awful, like Julia Child gone south."

We both laugh as we leave the restaurant. My phone beeps and I look at it to see a text from Ryland Thomas.

"Let me guess. It's my horny brother."

"You know it."

I text him back that I'm on the way.

"It must be nice to be in love."

"Tilly, I wish there were words. It's more than just love with Ryland Thomas."

We hug and I head home.

Ruth stops by my cubby-office the next afternoon to check on my progress with the spotlight on R.T..

"So when do you think it'll be ready for proofing?"

"Tomorrow."

"You have a deadline, so don't be late."

"No worries, Ruth."

"I know I can count on you."

She leaves and I'm left with the cold feeling of pin pricks on my skin. Kristie comes in right away and asks about my progress.

"What's with everyone on this spotlight thing? If you all don't think I can do it, why did you assign it to me?"

Kristie looks at me and fidgets, but then says, "I know it'll be great, Fallon." She smiles, though it's an empty one. Is it my imagination, or are things a little eerie around here?

I don't have time to spend worrying about it. I'm back to my spotlight article, honing it and making it shine. I want it to be absolutely flawless, not so much for me, but for Ryland Thomas and Tilly. I want the world to see what wonderful people they are. I put the finishing touches on it and forward it to both Kristie and Ruth.

Now I have to focus on reviews because I'm so backed up I don't know what to do. I text Ryland Thomas and explain that I'll be late tonight, so I won't be seeing him and send a sad face along with it. He sends me two back and tells me he misses me already.

It's after ten when I leave, and the office is dark and empty. I get home and crawl in bed. I call Ryland Thomas because I need to hear his voice before I drop off to sleep. We chat for a few and then it's lights off.

Two and a half weeks later, on a Thursday, I'm sitting at my desk when my phone fires up. I'll remember this day for the rest of my life. It's August and I'm thinking that it's been almost exactly one year since I've met Ryland Thomas and oh, what a difference a year makes. I glance at my phone and see it's Kat. I'm super excited to see her name because the Wicked Wenches Con is coming up in two more weeks and I get to see my girls again.

"Kat! I was gonna call you this week."

"I can't believe it! I cannot believe you never told me all of that. How could you keep that a secret for so long? Oh my God, Fallon!"

"What are you talking about?"

"You know. R.T.! Ryland Thomas."

"What!" My heart starts hammering so hard I know it's going to crack a hole right through my ribcage.

"Your spotlight is on the front page of every website and journal publication everywhere. You broke the news about R.T. being a man," Kat says.

"What did you just say?"

"The article you wrote. Your interview with R.T."

"Fuck. Shit. Motherfucker!" I shout.

"Fallon! What's wrong?"

"I didn't write that."

"What? What do you mean? It's everywhere."

I jump online and go to all my links where the published article would be and sure enough, as I start reading, the article is nothing similar to the one I turned into Kristie and Ruth.

"I gotta go, Kat."

I march into Kristie's office and yell, "What the fuck, Kristie!"

"Fallon, I didn't do it. It was Ruth."

I don't wait for her to say anything else. I'm out her door and running down the aisle, heading for the elevator. I hear her calling my name, but I pay her no heed. My finger is punching the elevator button, willing the door to open. The world is crashing down around me and I have to stop it. I ride the elevator three floors up and head straight to Ruth's office.

Leslie sits there and says, "You can't go in there."

I ignore her and push my way into her office. She's sitting there with two men and glances up at me. I don't give a fuck if the President of the United States is there. I'm having a nuclear meltdown right now and she's going to hear it.

"How could you? You took the article I wrote and created something completely different. You put my name on it and that's fucking fraudulent, Ruth. And where the fuck did you get the information?"

My chest is heaving with my breaths, and clearly, she did not expect me to barge in like this. "Fallon, this is not the place."

"No? Well, what you did wasn't the place or time either. We're having this discussion *now!*"

"This is highly unprofessional."

"And putting an article that I clearly did *not* write with my byline on it, is? That's not only unprofessional, Ruth, it's fucking *illegal*. Rescind it *now*."

"I can't do that."

"Why not?"

"It's gone out everywhere."

"Then write an article explaining it's false information and that I didn't write it."

"But Fallon, you and I both know it's not false information, don't we?"

I want to rip her into tiny pieces and crush her with my heels. I spin and head towards the door. On my way out, I yell, "Prepare yourself for the biggest lawsuit of your life."

I charge back to my cubby and collect my things. I stop by Kristie's office first and ask, "Did you know?"

She looks down and nods.

"Why didn't you tell me?"

"She threatened to fire me. She's a viper. I'm quitting. I'll testify for you. I'm so sorry, Fallon. I didn't think anything like this would come out of it. I thought it would be little stuff. Like R.T. had a secret boyfriend or was gay or something, but not this. Never this. If I had known, I would've told you."

"How did she do it?"

"That portfolio she gave you was bugged. She hired a private investigator."

"Fuck. So that's why I couldn't find my iPad that afternoon."

Kristie nods. "I swear, I'll help you any way I can."

"It may be too late. Ryland Thomas will never forgive me. Nor will Tilly and I don't blame them."

TWENTY -FIVE

RYLAND -THOMAS

I get up and throw on my running clothes. It's seven a.m. and I need to get an early jump on my writing today. I lace up my shoes, put my ear buds in and open my front door to camera flashes blinding me. There are dozens of reporters on my front steps as well as my yard, as far as I can see. I slam the door shut and wonder what the hell is going on.

Running to my computer, I turn it on and pull up the news. I see all I need to see. Every headline on every publication has it posted. "*R.T. Sinclair Identity Revealed by Girlfriend.*" I scan the article and they're all the same. The spotlight interview Fallon did on Tilly was an exposé. She's revealed all our secrets. But why? I can't wrap my brain around it.

Thirty minutes later my phone starts buzzing. It's Tilly.

"What are we going to do?" she wails.

"There's nothing to do. It's out, Tills." I feel dead inside, betrayed by the only one that ever mattered to me.

"Why? Why would she do it?"

"I don't know."

"Has she called?"

"No."

"Did you call her?"

"Why would I do that? She just fucking stabbed me to death. So she can pour salt all over me?"

"Yeah, I guess you're right."

"I'm calling my lawyer. I'm going to sue her."

"For what?"

"Slander. Libel. Breaking my bloody heart. That's what."

I hang up and sit on the edge of my bed. Then I fall back on it and put my arms over my face. I suppose I should've known it was too good to be true. Someone as good and true as Fallon seemed just doesn't exist. I've been too immersed in my own damn books for too long. Reality is hard and cold and it's a solid steel knife with a jagged, serrated edge that rips you to pieces without a care in the world. I should've remembered that and left those bloody walls up around me. I wouldn't be lying here, eviscerated right now.

I curl up and hug my knees to my chest, trying to ease the ache that keeps building in my belly. Fuck it all.

It must've been an hour or two later that my phone starts to ring. Fallon's name pops up. I don't answer. What can she say to me anyway? She keeps calling, over and over. And I continue to ignore it, over and over. I finally turn my phone off, hoping it sends a message. At this point, I don't really give a fuck.

Later that morning, I hear my front door open and close. I know it's Tilly. She always has to pick up the pieces of me and put me back together. Poor girl. She comes in my room and lies next to me, giving me a hug.

We lie there together before she says, "We'll get through this, Ryland Thomas. I promise."

"Whatever would I do without you, Tills?"

"I don't know." She squeezes me. "I brought some food. I had to buy it 'cause I know you won't eat my cooking."

"I don't think I can eat."

"You have to." She gets up and pulls on my arm. I allow her to pull me up and then I follow her into my kitchen. She's brought me a sandwich from my favorite deli.

"You spoil me."

"I try. But only because you'd do the same for me. You remember your Christmas gift to me?" she asks.

"The trip to Vietnam?"

"The same."

"What about it?"

"Let's go." I can tell this is something she really wants.

"We have the Wicked Wenches."

"Let's go tomorrow and then come straight back to that."

"I don't know." I don't want to go anywhere, I only want to curl up and die.

"No one will know you there. When we get back, we'll announce together at the Wicked Wenches the truth and go forward from there."

"Okay. Make our reservations," I relent because I know she will hound me until I do.

She claps her hands and I start packing while she makes our reservations.

Tilly loves Vietnam. Well, that's what she wants me to believe anyway. She's just putting on a show for me, though. I can see it in her sad eyes. They're filled with all sorts of sorry for me. We do it up right and she's fun to be with, yet the hole in my heart threatens to swallow the rest of me up, leaving nothing behind. There will never be anyone else in my life. How can there be after Fallon? She has been everything. Where we've been two hearts, we became one and now I don't think I can go on without her. The truth is, I can't have her, either, because the betrayal is too deep; so cutting, it severed me in half and I'll never be Ryland Thomas again.

Las Vegas is looming over me and I don't even want to go. I'm afraid she'll be there and I won't know what to do. How will I handle seeing her? What will I do? I tear my hands through my hair at the thought of it. Sometimes I wonder if my life is worth all this bloody shit, but then I think of Tilly and I know the pain it would cause her. I could never be that selfish, so I banish those dark thoughts.

The joy of living is gone for me, however. I've been bled dry and I'm like one of those unfeeling zombies roaming around. Maybe it's best this way. Less risky. I don't know anything anymore.

I simply wish I knew why she did it. If only she had asked me, I would've told her to go ahead with it. Hell, I couldn't say no to anything she asked me. She could've had the bloody interview with my blessing. But why? Did

I not make her happy? What was it? These questions are driving me crazy.

I muddle through all this, over and over until we get home. Then we have to unpack, repack and head to Vegas. My mind is all jumbled, and when I turn on my phone after we get back in the states, I'm shocked to see the number of messages and missed calls from Fallon. My first inclination is to call her, but what good will it do? It will only rip open the still seeping wound that I know will never heal.

The media is still camped out, but only with a few hearty stragglers. They yell at me as I climb into my car, though I pay them no attention. I pick Tilly up and we drive to the airport.

As we're walking towards security, she stops and turns to me. "You can do this, Ryland Thomas. You're a fucking concrete wall." Then she starts up again. I hope to hell she's right because, right now, I'm not so sure.

Twenty-Six

Fallon

I'm ruined; annihilated beyond repair. I sit here and repeatedly punch in Ryland Thomas's number, but he doesn't answer. I've gone to his house a dozen times and the media are camped there, so I just keep on going. One look at me and I would've been mowed down like a damn field of wheat. He's not returning any of my texts, either. He's gone somewhere and I don't know where to turn or what to do. Tilly's not an option, either. The scathing text I receive from her tells me in no uncertain terms to stay clear of them both.

Kristie checks on me and I ask her for a recommendation for an attorney. She gives me a few names and the first one I call refuses my case. I ask why and all he says is that it would be a conflict of interest.

"That leads me to believe that Ryland Thomas has hired you to sue me. And that's fine. I want him to sue me. He should sue me because I was careless in this whole thing. And please tell him I said all this. But Mr.

Carter, I really need your help. I did not write that interview. My name was on the damn thing, but they weren't my words. They were my boss's boss. She hired a private investigator to tap my iPad and my discussions with Ryland Thomas's sister were recorded. She took the article I wrote and discarded it. Then she rewrote what she wanted to publish, put my name on it and ruined three people's lives. Now she's traipsing around San Francisco, happy as shit, because her company broke the story. But what she really did was break three innocent people. I want her to pay. I don't want the money. The money I receive, if any, can go straight to Ryland Thomas and Tilly because I don't give a shit about me." By the time I finish, I'm shaking and yelling.

He takes a deep breath into the phone and lets it out. "Miss McKinley, I'm very sorry for your predicament, but I still can't help you. I'd be happy to recommend someone, though, someone who can do you justice."

I'm defeated. I know it. I still have to ask him while I have the chance. "Okay. Mr. Carter, may I ask you something?"

"Yes."

"Is he okay? Ryland Thomas? Is he okay?"

"Um, Miss McKinley, I..."

"Please, Mr. Carter. I have to know. I won't say anything. I promise. Just tell me he's okay. And that... and that..." I can't say anything else because tears have pushed passed everything I've tried to use to prevent them from getting through.

"He's dealing, Miss McKinley. And you should call Peter Braxton. Tell him I sent you. He'll serve you well."

"Thanks."

I cradle the phone in my arms and don't move for the rest of the day. The sun moves across the sky and shades my apartment, however I stay on my side, curled on the sofa, holding my phone and wishing I could die. Nothing could feel this bad. Nothing at all.

I'm startled when my phone awakens me. I don't bother to check the caller ID; I just answer it.

"Miss McKinley?"

"Yes."

"Hi, my name is George Patterson. I'm an attorney in Spartanburg with Patterson, Patterson and Wilkins. You're a hard one to track down and if it hadn't been for all this media attention, I doubt I would've found you."

"Um, Mr. Patterson, what's this about?"

"I'm the one that handled your father's last will and testament. He set up your trust fund and when you turned twenty-two, you came into quite a bit of money. Three and a half million dollars to be exact. However your mother moved and left no forwarding address for you, and I couldn't find you anywhere. All your records were sealed until you turned twenty-two, and since she left the state, we had no way of finding you. We were getting ready to hire a private investigator."

"Three and a half million dollars?"

"Yes indeed. He had a three million dollar life insurance policy and then some other money. It's all in your name and it diverted to you when you turned twenty-two."

I'm silent, trying to digest all of this. Then a question pops into my head. "Did my mother know about this?"

"Yes, and that's why I was surprised when she didn't let us know where you were."

"She remarried and moved to Georgia."

"Well, that explains part of it, but not why she wouldn't tell us where to find you."

Now I'm pissed as hell at her. She's allowed me to live a life in debt, fraught with worry over it, when all along she's known about this.

"So what do we need to do, Mr. Patterson?"

"All I need is your mailing address, Miss McKinley, and we're set."

I give him the information. He tells me everything will be sent express courier to me and explained in a detailed letter. If I had any questions afterwards, I could call him.

This will and trust information gives me renewed energy. First thing on my agenda—hell, the only thing on my agenda—is to call Peter Braxton. I set up an appointment for the next afternoon. When I go visit him, I give him every little gory detail I can remember. I even give him a copy of the email I sent to Kristie and Ruth with the attachment of the article I'd written. He assures me we have a cut and dry case. We'll be able to sue Critics Abound and smash them.

"Mr. Braxton, I want the entire settlement to go to Ryland Thomas and Tilly Sinclair. By the way, they'll be slapping me with a lawsuit that I don't intend to fight. They can have everything I own."

"Miss McKinley, you can't just lay down on this. You were wronged as much as they were."

"Maybe so, but they were the ones that took the brunt of it and I can't live with that."

He looks at me then, like I'm a horse that he's thinking about buying. "Tell you what. Let me talk with

285

Joe Carter. I've worked with him before. Maybe we can team up and hit Critics Abound for everything they've got."

"I want them to pay, Mr. Braxton, and we can do that. But again, whatever I win, if anything, I want it to go to Ryland Thomas and Tilly. I don't want any part of it. You can take your legal fees out of it, which I'm sure is what you normally do, but that's all I'll take."

He nods. "I'll be in touch."

After tons of begging, cajoling, threats and plain old pleas, I give in and agree to meet the girls in Vegas. I have a bad feeling about it, but they've assured me I don't have to do anything or go anywhere that Ryland Thomas will be. They want me to get out and forget about everything for a few days.

We opt for a different hotel this year, and since I've come into that money, we stay at The MGM Grand. It's not as fancy as The Bellagio, but it's a heck of a lot nicer than the Space Nugget. We laugh as we check in. It's close to the convention for the girls. For me, it doesn't matter because I'm not attending. I haven't read anything since any of this has happened. All the girls are begging me to come back to the blog, but I just don't know if I'm ready. I'm still too raw, the pain so acute; I don't think I can handle it.

I sit at the pool during the cooler morning hours and by eleven, I'm inside. I don't want to get any spa treatments because they remind me of Ryland Thomas. So one day, I wander around the strip and do a little window shopping at some of the finer designer establishments. I get my toes done in my favorite sparkly pink then head back to the hotel where I pick up my phone and hit the pictures button and start scrolling through my album of Ryland Thomas. And I cry. And cry. And that's how the girls find me when they get home.

Tonight they want to party. I don't feel like doing anything except curling up in bed. I know they're worried about me. Each of them suggests that I go home with them. I decline, but thank them. They finally talk me into a night on the town and I get drunk, which is a bad thing. A sad, drunk woman is always a bad idea because they end up crying on everyone's shoulder, which is exactly what I do that night. We go bed because the next morning, R.T. Sinclair is giving his speech... his reveal about his true identity. I *will* be in attendance for that.

I slip in at the last minute and stand in the back corner of the room. The lights are dimmed and no one notices me, or I hope so anyway. There isn't an empty seat in the house, so the fact that I'm standing isn't anything unusual. His name is announced and I feel myself die inside again and again as I watch him take the stage with Tilly by his side. She's thinner, but still every bit as beautiful as always.

Ryland Thomas steals my breath as I knew he would, but it's the cracking of my heart, and the fucking crater I feel, that kills. I want to scream with the pain. I honestly do because it hurts so fiercely. Oh God, why did this happen? How did it turn so wrong? Am I a bad person? Did I do something so terrible that I deserve this pain, and the pain it's causing the two people I love the most in the world? I can't comprehend any of it.

Exquisite Betrayal

He starts to speak, slowly at first and then his voice gains strength and resonance. He becomes more confident as his explanation carries on. Tilly is smiling at his side, her pride shining forth. I have to clench my hands to stop myself from applauding.

"You see, it wasn't that I didn't have faith in you, dear readers. I didn't have faith in myself. But I was pushed, pushed by an exquisite betrayal, a hurt so terrible, that I realized it was time to face all of you and tell the truth in person. The article told the story, not in the way I would have liked. And the truth of it all is that, if Fallon McKinley had asked to write it, I would've given her permission. I would've given her anything in the world. But for reasons known only to her, she went behind my back to tell it. So here I stand before you, the real Ryland Thomas Sinclair, and I can only hope you'll still grace me with the love for my books as you always have."

I bow my head and leave the room. The pain of the last couple of weeks has now intensified into a blinding ball of fire and it's centered in my brain as his words penetrate my mind. Tears blind me and I can't see where I'm going; I only know I need to get away from this place.

Every person in that room will think the worst of me and there is nothing I'll ever be able to do or say to convince them otherwise. But I don't really give a shit about them. The one I care about is Ryland Thomas, and those words he spoke had such finality to them that I know they will never be changed. That final sliver of hope I had held onto has just slipped through my fingers as I listened, and along with it went that tiny bit of sanity that kept me from losing it. I walk and walk and have no

288

idea where I'm going; I simply keep putting one foot in front of the other.

Time fades away from me. Images blur; all sound diminishes and the only things I'm aware of are the words, 'exquisite betrayal' and 'a hurt so terrible', which keep reiterating themselves in my mind.

There's someone tugging on my arm and I'm trying to make him stop. I want to be left alone, but he keeps bothering me. I finally look up and I have to blink several times before I can focus. Only then do I notice it's a police officer.

"Ma'am, look at me." He's moving his hand in front of my face.

I shake my head, clearing it. Lifting my eyes up to the sky, I notice it's almost dark now. My mouth is like sawdust, parched and dry, and my feet are burning with pain as though they are on fire. I look down to discover my shoes are missing and my feet are raw and bleeding.

"Do you need help?"

My hands fly to my face as I start crying. What's wrong with me? "No, sir, I'm just upset about something. Can you please call me a taxi? I need to get back to the MGM Grand."

He walks me to his car and drives me there. My feet are such a mess. I don't understand what I've done to myself.

"Thank you, Officer."

"Ma'am, maybe you should see a doctor."

"Yes, thank you." I make it back up to my room where two of the girls are frantic. They immediately call the other two and tell them I'm home. I fall onto the bed and they screech when they see my feet. "I think I'm teetering on the edge of sanity." I cry again.

Mandy asks me, "Did you hear his speech?"

I nod and they all group hug me. "Everyone thinks I'm an evil demon. Why did this happen?"

Kat sits down and grabs my hand. "You know what? You've been silent for too long, Fallon. You need a catharsis. You *have* to write the truth. You can't go on like this with it all bottled up inside. We'll put it on our blog and get everyone we know to post it. People that know you will help. You've been wronged, in a bad way. Right now, to hell with Ryland Thomas. You have to do this for your own self-preservation. Look at you. You're a mess."

"Yeah, you are. And you need to do something about it," Mandy pipes in.

I sit up. "Maybe you're right."

"You can even video yourself and maybe the damn thing will go viral. You *have* to do this, Fallon," Mandy says.

I start thinking. There are other things I need to do first; like give Ryland Thomas his things back. I'll try to talk to him again, but if he won't speak, I'll write him a letter.

Twenty-Seven

Fallon

Don't they say you have to hit rock bottom before you can crawl back up? Well, I went beyond rock bottom in Vegas. I'm back home now and I'm still in the depths of hell, the ninth ring, to be exact. I'm putting together a plan that's going to help me start my climb back out because it really sucks to be here. There may not be much left of me when I get out since I know my heart has been blown to bits and scattered around like tiny grains of sand. Besides, maybe it's not even possible to put me back together again.

I know how tough it was after Daddy died, but God Almighty, this makes that feel like a trip to Disney World. I have to try, though. I can't simply sit here and wither away. I'm pretty damn sure I tasted a bit of what losing your mind is like and I don't want to do that again. I have to at least take a stab at mending myself. I know I won't ever be the same Fallon. I'll most likely be all crooked and uneven with jagged pieces sticking out everywhere, but at least I'll be functional and better than I am now.

I call that lawyer, Mr. Braxton, and find out about writing the article. He gives me the okay. The girls are right. It is a catharsis writing my side of the story and it eases my pain somewhat. My heart isn't right, there's still a crater where it used to be, but I'm doing the best I can for now.

I'm at the point where I'm ready for the action part. I'm dreading it, however I know it needs to happen.

First, I call Tilly, but get no answer. I leave a message, asking her to call me. I don't sit around and wait. Instead, I get a nice, pretty box, filling it with the velvet box that holds the diamond stud earrings that Ryland Thomas gave me. I add to it the title and registration for my car, plus the extra set of keys. Then I sit down and write a letter, explaining my side of the story. And yes I pour out my guts, every last single bit of them. I tell him how I want him to have everything I own, including any settlement I win from the case I have against Critics Abound. Then I write him a check for sixty-five thousand dollars. That should cover the amount of student debt that he paid off for me, the cost of the car and anything he bought me since Christmas. If he spent more than that, I instruct him to let me know the amount, as I will gladly reimburse him. Finally, I explain about the trust from my dad. I tell him I will happily sign everything over to him. I know it sounds absurd, but money is meaningless to me at this point. I end the letter and stick it in the box. The last thing I put in is the original article I wrote, the one that I intended to be published on R.T. Sinclair. I put the lid on the box and hug it to my chest for a few seconds.

My phone startles me when it rings. I check to see who it is and it's Tilly. I'm quick to answer because I want to speak with her so badly.

"Tilly."

"Fallon. Don't call me again. I thought I made it clear when I sent you that text. You've damaged us enough. Neither of us want to have any contact with you from now on."

"But Tilly, please—"

The line is dead. She's hung up. She won't even listen to me. My heart has been trampled on so much by now that I'm not surprised by her reaction, but the hope I had in maybe getting her to listen to me for a couple of minutes, paralyzes me for a moment.

Tilly's call may have addled me, but it doesn't deter me. Now it's time to go to Ryland Thomas's. My nerves kick in and butterflies go to war in my belly. I pay them no attention because nothing is going to stop me from doing this.

I pull up in front of his house and park the car. I have to stop for a moment to catch my breath because I'm about to freak. I white-knuckle the steering wheel and focus on the issue here. He needs to know the full story, and if he's not willing to speak to me, I hope one day he'll read the letter. *I have a one percent chance*, I keep telling myself.

After I take a deep breath, I knock on his door. It's the first time I've been here since the media left. My feet shuffle on their own accord, and I stand there so long that I'm getting ready to turn around and leave when the door swings open and I hear that luscious voice say, "Iris, I told you it would be unlocked..." My heart, if it's even possible, plunges further into the depths of wherever the worst hell it can be. Iris. He thought I was Iris.

"Um... not Iris. Fallon. But here." I push the box into his hands. I can't bring myself to look at his face. My vision blurs with unshed tears and I need to get out of here because alarms are going off in my head like crazy. If he thinks I'm Iris that means she's on the way, and I don't want to be close to this place when she arrives. I turn to leave and start down his stairs when I remember I'm still holding the damn car key. I can't go back and give it to him so I bend down and set it on his porch. Damn it all! As I stand, out of the corner of my eye, I see a tall blond approaching. *I can do this*, I tell myself. I move to walk down the steps, but my eyes are so damn clouded with tears, I miss a step and trip. That's my undoing. I twist my ankle as I hit the pavement, scraping my palms.

"Hi darling. I've missed you so," I hear Iris purr. And then, "Fallon, is it?" I hear her say. I can't speak so I nod as I begin to pick myself up. I keep my head down to conceal my humiliation.

Then I feel his hand on my arm.

"Are you okay?"

I nod and then do my best to walk away. I'm miles and miles from okay, so much so that the question is ludicrous. I can barely walk, but I refuse to stop for anything. I keep going because I simply can't bear any more pain.

"Fallon, wait."

I keep walking, if you can call it that. It only takes him a minute, two at the most, to catch me. I mean, I'm wearing heels and sporting a sprained ankle that's inflating like it's hooked up to an air compressor. He could catch me if he were ninety and using a walker.

He grabs my arm and I wrench it free. Something suddenly snaps in me and I burn with anger. How could he?

"Don't you dare touch me! Of all the women in this city, you had to pick that slut?"

"Whoa, slow it down there."

"No, you slow it down." Suddenly, my hurt is pushed in the back seat and a ferocious anger is now at the wheel. Anger at that fuckface Ruth for ruining my life, anger at Ryland Thomas because he wouldn't even give me the chance to explain what happened, anger at my mother for making me live like a pauper for all those years, and anger at Critics Abound for taking advantage of a hard-working and honest employee.

"Yeah, you heard me. You fucking slow it down, Ryland Thomas. Exquisite betrayal, my motherfucking ass. Let's talk betrayal. You don't give me the courtesy of three lousy minutes of your precious time to explain what happened? After everything we've been through? All the things you said to me? How much I meant to you? Well, you can go to hell.

"In my world, when someone means that much to someone else, we give each other the benefit of the doubt. Did you honestly think I could betray you? Did you really think I was so mean-fucking-spirited that I would do something as low as that? Huh? Answer me, you spineless pussy!" My anger has me so riled that I'm yelling at him and spit is flying out of my mouth.

He's just standing there, staring at me like I'm an alien. "You're so goddamn stupid. And the worst part of it all is that barely a month goes by and you invite that

295

fucking cheater-slut-whore into your home. You disgust me." I turn away with a throbbing head now to go along with my throbbing ankle and my throbbing heart.

I make it to the end of his street where I break down and cry. There's a bench there so I plop down and drop my head into my hands while I wonder if I'll ever stop this ridiculous sobbing because I'm getting damned sick and tired of it.

After an unknown amount of time, my sobs turn to those dorky sounding hiccups and it dawns on me that I need to get out of this place. Out of San Francisco. Everything I love about this place centers on him.

"Feel better?'

"Aaiiiyee!" His voice scares the shit out of me because, with all my sobbing, I hadn't heard him sit next to me. I fly to my feet and end up flat on my ass, nursing my ankle again.

"Bloody hell, Fallon!"

"It's your stupid fault. You shouldn't sneak up on people like that." I'm bordering on hysteria.

"I didn't sneak up on you. I've been sitting here for over half an hour."

"Shut up." My voice is so scathing, it surprises even me.

"That looks rough."

His hand reaches out to touch it and I tell him, "If you lay so much as one finger on me, I'll twist your freakin' balls off, I swear to God."

"Jesus, Fallon. You don't have to be so bloody mean."

"Neither did you, you asswipe bastard."

"I'm not a bastard," he grits out.

"Oh no? Well, I didn't betray you, either. So there."

He blows out his breath. "So?"

"So what?"

"You gonna sit there all day or you gonna talk?"

"You've got to be kidding me."

"Hell no, I'm not kidding you."

I make my move to stand and he puts a hand on my shoulder. "You're not going anywhere until you talk."

"Get your motherfucking hand off me." My teeth are clenched and I realize I've sworn more in the past few minutes than I think I have in the past five years combined.

He doesn't move it. It just sits on my shoulder, letting me know he means business.

"Read the fucking letter in the box. Everything you need to know is in there." My voice is low and resigned. A second later, he lifts me in his arms and carries me back to his place.

"If you take me in there and that cheater-slut-whore's in your house, someone's gonna die."

"She's not here, Fallon. I told her to leave when I followed you."

"Well, wasn't that magnanimous of you?"

"You don't have to be so sarcastic."

He walks up the steps and we go inside. The place is empty. Or at least, I think it is.

"Take me to your bedroom."

"What?"

"Do as I say."

He follows orders, and once I'm convinced that the cheater-slut-whore isn't lying naked somewhere, I allow him to take me back to his living room and set me down on the sofa. He fills a bag with ice and elevates my ankle, icing it. Then he sits down and opens the box.

297

"You mean you didn't even look in it?"

"Fallon, if you recall, I didn't exactly have time."

I grunt and nod.

He rubs his face and tears his hands through his hair as he goes through everything, one-by-one, casting glances at me along the way. Finally, he picks up the letter. He looks at me first, tears it open and starts reading out loud.

Dear Ryland Thomas,

I'm writing this as a last resort. I don't know or understand why you wouldn't speak to me, take my calls or texts. With the love we both have (had) for each other, I would've thought I was worth at least a few minutes of your time. I know it all looked bad, but I swear to you on the love I have for my dad, that I didn't do it. I would never have done anything so deceitful. That secret would've gone to my grave with me and I never, ever told a soul.

I guess I wasn't careful, though, and my boss's boss became greedy enough to hire a private investigator that planted a recording device on me. And the rest, as they say, is history. I resigned immediately when I found out and I'm suing Critics Abound and Ruth. Everything I win will go to you and Tilly. In fact, you can have everything of mine, including my inheritance from my dad. It has no meaning for me without you in my life anyway.

I'm returning all your precious gifts. They are rightfully yours so they should be returned to you. I'm also paying you back for bailing me out of debt. Thank you for being so kind to me when I needed it the most.

Strangely enough, my dad left a sizable trust for me, which my mom never told me about. So don't worry about my financial state. I'll be fine (not that you'd worry about me anymore, but I thought you should know). I know you're suing me, and honestly, I hope you win. In fact, just name the price of your damages, and I'll save you your attorney's fee and simply write you a check.

The last thing in here is the real article I wrote on you... the one I thought was being published. I thought maybe you could find it in your heart to at least to read it. I know it's too late for us now, but I want you to know that I'll always love you with everything I have until there is no longer breath in this body of mine.

Yours,

Fallon

I've stopped watching him and my head is leaning back on the couch. It's so silent in the room that all I want to do is scream. Don't ask me why, however that's how I feel. I am so tired, too. Tired of feeling so sad, tired of missing Ryland Thomas, tired of everything.

"Shit, Fallon," he says as he sits next to me. "I'm sorry I didn't take your calls."

"I'm sorry, too," I cry. "Why didn't you, Ryland Thomas? Did you think I could really do something like this?"

"I don't know what I thought. I wasn't thinking, I guess. I went into damage control and then Tilly came and convinced me I needed to get out of here because the media were all over the place. So we went to Vietnam for two weeks and then we came home and immediately turned around and flew to Vegas."

"So that's why I couldn't find you." My voice is hoarse and my throat is raw from crying.

"Yeah, I was out of the country. Fallon?"

"What?"

"Can I just hold you, please?"

"Oh, God, I don't know. I..." I don't get my words out before his arms are around me and I'm being held tightly against him, I don't know what to do.

"Oh, God, Fallon. I've missed you so much."

"Stop it! I can't do this with you." I push him away from me.

He leans back, his face a mask of pain.

"You won't destroy me anymore. I won't let you and I can't snap my fingers and make all the hurt go away. You know, when I came here, I prayed on the way over that you would just give me five minutes. Then when you thought I was Iris, something inside of me snapped. For all the love you professed to have for me, when it came down to it, you abandoned me. I must've called you hundreds of times. I texted you and emailed you. I even drove out to your Lake Tahoe house, but I couldn't even get measly phone time..." I have to stop and collect myself for a minute.

I rub the wetness from my eyes and go on in a much quieter voice now. "I couldn't even get you to answer a stupid text, and the more I think about it, the more it hurts me. The same goes for Tilly. I would never, in a million years, have walked away from you so easily. I don't care how angry I was, or how incriminating the evidence may have appeared, I would've given you time to speak your peace."

I sit up and remove the ice from my ankle.

"Where are you going?"

"Home. And then I'm moving away from this town. I can't live here anymore. There are too many memories." I swipe my tears off my cheeks and rub my eyes again.

"Let me drive you at least."

I look at him for a minute. I want to say yes, though I don't. I know it will make it worse than it already is. "No, I think I've got this."

"Take the car. It's yours. You paid for it."

"I don't want it. I don't want anything from you anymore."

"How are you gonna get home with your sprained ankle?"

I laugh a crazy sounding laugh. It kind of scares even me. "Ryland, I've been to the depths of hell and back. Or at least, I'm trying to get back anyway. I think I can make it a few damn blocks from here." With my shoes in my hand, I hobble past him, out of his house and his life.

TWENTY -EIGHT

RYLAND -THOMAS

I watch her leave and it's the most helpless feeling in the world. Helpless because I love her so much, and helpless because I know she's right. Why the bloody hell didn't I let her speak, let her tell me her side? Why?

I pick up the first thing I can get my hands on, a large, hand-blown glass vase, and I sling it across the room, watching it shatter against the wall. It reminds of what I did to Fallon's heart, her life and her world.

What the fuck was I thinking inviting Iris over here? It wasn't what Fallon thought, but still. It looked bad and that makes me just as sick. I would never have anything to do with Iris in that way ever again, but I ran into her and had something I needed to give to her. Once again, a foolish mistake.

I have a lot of apologizing to do so I need to get my ass in gear. I am through with feeling sorry for myself. The only thing that ever accomplished was getting me deeper into the pile of shit I was in now.

Exquisite Betrayal

I pick up my phone and call my attorney. "Joe, this is Ryland Thomas Sinclair. I want to drop the suit against Fallon McKinley. I want to sue Critics Abound instead."

"That sounds like a better plan," Joe says. "I know Miss McKinley's attorney and I've worked with him before. I think we can make a strong case together. By the way, I didn't want to tell you this before, but she called me to represent her. I had to turn her down, of course."

"Yeah?"

"It was right after all this broke. She was... she was in a pretty bad way, Mr. Sinclair. She told me some things that, quite frankly, shocked me."

"What did she say?"

"She said she never wrote that article and that she wanted you to sue her. But she also said that if she won her case against her boss, she wouldn't take a cent of it. That she would give it all to you."

"Yeah, I'm aware of that."

"And there's something else. She was very distraught... could barely speak. She wanted to know how you were."

I rub my face for the umpteenth time that day.

"Thanks, Joe. Call me when you need me."

Next on my agenda is Tilly. She comes over and I show her the letter. As I expect, she's in tears.

"How could we have been so blind, Ryland Thomas?"

"I don't know. I can't figure out how I could ever have doubted her. Anyone else, yeah, but not Fallon. I don't think it's possible to hate yourself as much as I do right now, but I have work to do, Tills. I have to make this right. And it has to be from the heart. If I win her back in the process, great, however that's not my sole

303

motivation here. I ruined her life so I have to fix that for her, with or without me in it. It's the very least I can do."

The next day, I put a call into her blog team. I know they all hate my guts, yet I don't care. They can do whatever they want with me, but I need their help and will do anything to get it.

Kat is the only one who will speak with me. The others ignore me and Amanda sends me a message that borders on a hate crime. I don't blame her at all. I actually respect her for it.

When I call Kat, she answers with, "I promised myself I would do this for Fallon, but now I'm not so sure it's a good idea."

"Hear me out, Kat. Please."

"Go on."

"I know I'm the biggest fucking douche bag that ever lived. I know that. And I want her back. But more important, I want to set her life back on track. And I'm not sure how I can do that. That's why I need your help."

"I'm not sure I can help."

"You can get your team together for me. I'll fly to you girls, or I'll fly you anywhere you choose. But I want all of you together so we can come up with a plan. I'll let you flay me alive, I swear I will. I deserve it all. But I want Fallon to have a decent life."

She huffs, "A little late for that."

"You should know by now that we men aren't the fastest learners when it comes to women."

"Ya think?"

"Will you help? Think of Fallon."

"I am thinking of Fallon, you jerkoff!" Well, I know where I stand at least. "I'll call you back in a day or so. It's gonna take some persuading, I can promise you that."

"Thank you, Kat. I owe you."

"You owe me nothing. You owe Fallon the stars, the moon and every other fucking thing in this goddamn universe."

Wow. That was quite a tongue-lashing coming from someone who normally doesn't swear, according to Fallon. I certainly know what I'm going to be in for if I do meet with all of them, however I don't care. They can have my balls on a silver platter if they want. I don't give a shit. That's how determined I am to make this right.

It takes a bit of negotiating, but by the end of October, I'm meeting Fallon's blogger team in the U.S. Virgin Islands, of all places— St. John to be exact.

I knew they'd make me pay, but like I've said before, I don't give a damn. They all made a good point, though. It was just as far for them to fly here as it was for them to fly to the west coast, especially Andrea who was flying in from England.

I've rented two villas, one for me and one for them. We're going to eat breakfast in my villa—it should be arriving in about thirty minutes—and while we eat, we'll begin discussing my preliminary plans to win Fallon back and/or to change her life. After breakfast, we'll board the private sailing yacht I've rented for the day and sail over to the British Virgin Islands for a day of fun in the sun and some snorkeling. That was Amanda's idea, and since I fear for my life around her, I couldn't very well refuse.

Exquisite Betrayal

When I hear the knock, my gut does a flop that's perfectly synced with it. Shit, here it goes.

I open the door to four hostile faces. Not what I'd hoped for, yet it is what I expect. Right behind them is breakfast, so I tell the room service man where to set everything up. It provides a nice distraction, and the girls chat among themselves while I deal with the food set-up.

"Help yourselves, ladies."

They all fill their plates and I follow then we take our seats around the dining table and begin to eat. I don't want this delayed any longer, so I start the painful conversation.

"I know you don't give a rat's ass about me asking about your flights and all, so let's get down to it."

I'm met with four sets of raised brows; they all nod.

"We all know why we're here. You want my balls, sliced, fried and then crushed into smithereens. Fuck, I'd help you do that if I could. Here's the thing, I think we all want the same thing now. I screwed up. Worse than anyone I've ever known. I've gone over this whole thing so many fucking times in my head and I still can't figure out the why of it, other than I'm just plain dumb.

"I'm not inherently mean. At least I don't think I am. I don't really even know *that* any more. Anyway, like I said, I'm the biggest screw up in the universe. And Kat's right. When I talked to her on the phone, she said that I owed Fallon the stars, the moon and the whole goddamn universe. But I owe her even more than that because all of that is just materialistic bullshit. I owe her the dignity back that she lost. I owe her the integrity that I ripped away from her. And I owe her the life that she had when everything was in sync for her. I'm not talking about us, either, as in us together. That's a completely different

306

thing and separate from what I want your help with. Am I making sense here?"

They all nod.

"So, what I'm thinking is this…"

When I'm done, they're all grinning. Well, everyone except for Amanda.

Amanda stares me down for a second and then starts in on me. "I just wanna say something to you. I still think you're an ass and I'm gonna tell you why. Did you know that Fallon heard your little speech in Vegas… the one where you said you'd been exquisitely betrayed? The one you gave to over twenty-five hundred people?"

"I figured she had because she quoted a couple of things from it," I say.

"Well, did you know that after she left that sweet, little talk, she roamed the streets of Vegas and we didn't know where she was? She wouldn't answer her phone and she was missing for hours. Did you know that finally, late in the afternoon, a nice police officer brought her home because he found her wandering around with her feet all bloody because she was bare-foot? Can you imagine walking the streets of Vegas in the hot afternoon sun without shoes on? Well, Fallon did, and didn't even realize it. She lost her shoes somehow and didn't know it. She was so upset about that sweet little speech of yours that she nearly lost her mind. Bet that was something you didn't know. Her feet were cut, burned and bruised and she could barely walk for days, all because of that nice, little talk you gave, blaming her for all your troubles. And all because you wouldn't give her a few fucking minutes of your treasured time!"

I'm holding a stemmed juice glass in my hand, clenching it so tightly that it breaks, sending shards of glass into my palm. I don't notice the pain and only realize I've been cut when the blood starts running down my hand.

I head to the bathroom and run my hand under the water. It doesn't take a doctor to realize I'm going to need stitches. There's a knock on the door and Kat asks, "Are you okay?"

"Not exactly."

"Can I come in?"

"It's open."

"Amanda has quite a way with words."

"She should. I deserved to hear it, Kat."

"That looks bad."

"Yeah. I think I need to be sewn up."

"Want me to call the concierge?"

"Could you?"

"Sure."

While I'm standing over the sink I look at myself in the mirror. How did I get to be such a rotten fucker? I can't let myself think of Fallon wandering around in Vegas like that because I'll go as crazy as she did. Bloody fucking hell!

As I'm standing there, blood dripping into the sink, Amanda walks in and leans against the counter. "I'm sorry."

"You have absolutely nothing to be sorry about."

"Yeah, I could've been a little better about the delivery."

"How? Tell me how, Amanda?"

"Well, I..."

"There isn't a way to make that any better. I'm a nasty bloke. I did the most despicable thing in the world and I did it to the one that I loved the most and I don't have a fucking clue why or even how! What kind of a person does that make me?" I don't even realize that tears are coursing down my cheeks until she picks up a cloth and wipes them off.

"It makes you human. Now go and fix your fuck ups. You know, a very dear friend of mine once told me that someone truly special to her gave her a birthday gift, and in it he inscribed something. He wrote to her, and I think I'm quoting this correctly, '*We are only bound by our own limitations.*' Don't let *your* limitations keep you from getting what you want, Ryland Thomas."

At that, she leaves me standing there with a whole lot of shit to ponder.

I'm quiet the rest of the day. My hand took quite a few stitches, so I'm stuck on the boat while the girls enjoy the snorkeling. It's okay, though. I'm formulating my plan, and the more I think about it, the more solid it becomes in my mind. At dinner, I plan to outline it for them. I'm going to leave them to their own party after that and head home. If they have anything else they want to add, I'll take any and all of their suggestions, although the more I think, the more I know what I need to do.

That night at dinner, I tell them what my intentions are.

"Seems like when we were looking at fish, you were doing something altogether different," Andrea says.

"Yep." I'm not very verbose this evening.

"Don't give up, Ryland Thomas. Fight for it. You know, anything great is worth fighting for." This is coming from Amanda, the one who wanted to crucify me by my balls this morning.

"This is beyond great," Mandy says.

"I have one request. Don't say a word to her. If she asks you what you think she should do, stay neutral. I want this all to be her decision. Will you promise me that?"

"But why?" Andrea asks. "I mean, you want our help. If we think you deserve another shot, why not let us tell her?"

"Because this has to be her decision this time. It won't be right for either of us unless it is. Besides, I don't want just us. I want to correct all the wrongs, remember. And that comes before anything. The only thing I ask is that, if this plan does come together, make sure she sees it all. Some way, somehow. I know she'll not want to, so if you have to send her the video links until she watches them, can you do that?"

"Yeah, we'll do it all right." They all agree to help.

I board an early flight in the morning and start going to work. My hopes are to have everything in order by Thanksgiving.

Fallon

The plane lands in Atlanta and that sense of uneasiness envelops me like a soggy blanket. I hate this town. I've hated it ever since my mom moved here. I bypass the baggage claim since I'm only staying one night and head to the rental car counter where I've reserved a car. It's such a pain at the huge airports these days. I have to get on a bus that takes me to the actual place where I can pick up the vehicle.

I'm finally getting on the interstate, heading to my hotel. My mom hasn't a clue I'm in town. I wouldn't stay with her anyway, not after what she's done to me. I'm here for my confrontation. And it may be the last time I ever see her, which is fine with me.

Ryland Thomas hit the nail on the head with her. She's toxic and has been for years. She's my mother, though, and I've tried to keep things right with her. How can I after she's pulled this last little shit show with my dad's will, though? I'm done dealing with her.

Exquisite Betrayal

I check into my room and look at the clock. It's six thirty. No doubt, she'll be home getting ready to sit down to dinner. Yep, she's so damn anal. Everything has to be on her exact schedule or she blows up like a grenade. I'll always wonder how my dad ended up with her. It shall forever remain the mystery of my life.

As I make the turn onto her street, I notice that it looks exactly the same as it did the last time I was here. There sits her house with her perfectly mowed yard and those stupid lines running diagonally across it. She used to want me to mow her grass in Spartanburg for her after I moved in, so I did. I mowed it like I had mowed my dad's and she threw a hissy fit over it. The lines weren't running the correct way. Jeez, there was never any pleasing that woman.

I check out her perfect flowers; flowers that she would tend to, instead of going to my soccer games. I would ask my dad about it when I was younger and he'd mumble some lame excuse. This woman had constantly hurt my feelings over the years, but today, I was putting a stop to it all. I would have my day of reckoning with her, and it was long past due.

I park the car and walk up to the door, careful to stick to the sidewalk. God forbid I step on her precious grass. The door opens and there she stands in all her radiant glory. Dressed to the nines, jewelry and make-up on with her hair perfectly coiffed, her face registers shock.

"Fallon. What in the world are you doing here?"

"I've come to pay you a little visit. Aren't you going to invite me in?"

"Well, I guess so."

Her house is immaculate, not a thing out of place. I'm almost afraid to place my foot on her perfect carpet.

"We were just finishing up dinner."

"Great. I'm glad I caught you then because there's something we need to talk about."

"Oh, and what's that?"

"Well, can we at least sit first?"

"Oh, I guess so."

This is awkward. I know I've thrown a wrench into her nice little cog wheel and jammed it up tightly because she's already fidgeting and casting glances at me, like I'm going to steal something.

We walk into the dining room and her dork of a husband is sitting there, mouse faced, as he says hello to me. I take a seat and she doesn't even offer me water. Then it dawns on me that she's still pissed off at the way Ryland Thomas spoke to her. I want to laugh because it merely strikes me as funny. Wait until I'm through with her.

"Don't worry, Mom. I'm not staying long. I'm leaving town tomorrow. I only came to have a word with you."

Her stiff shoulders relax and sink back against her chair, which makes me giggle.

"What have you come all this way to talk about that we couldn't discuss over the phone?"

What a perfect introduction for me and I want to giggle again and rub my hands together.

"How about the fact that Dad left me over three million dollars and you never told me about it?"

I shut up then. I'm smart enough to know about the pregnant pause. My eyes bore into her like a steel drill bit. She squirms then fidgets. She looks away and won't look back at me. I still don't say anything. I'd wager two minutes pass before she finally speaks.

"I don't really know, Fallon."

"Sure you do, Mom. And I want the fucking truth."

She flinches, but is looking at me now. She knows this won't go down easy.

"Those lawyers should've..."

My hand flies up as I cut her off. There wasn't going to be any passing the buck in this conversation. "Don't you dare blame the lawyers. You were given strict instructions to make them aware of any address changes for you and me. You failed to do so, on both accounts."

"I forgot."

"Liar."

"Fallon, don't you dare call me a liar."

"I call it as I see it, Mom. And you're a liar. You've lied to me so many times I can't even begin to count them. I learned early on from Dad not to lie, so it's easy for me to spot one. And you're a liar. Why'd you do it, Mom? You let me go through college, unnecessarily so, poor as hell. Do you have any idea how many days I went without food because I couldn't afford it? Do you know how many sleepless nights I had because I was so worried about the student debt I was accumulating? And all you would've had to say was, '*Fallon, when you turn twenty-two, you'll inherit some money, so don't worry about it. It'll all be fine.*' Did you want me to suffer? Did you?"

She's really twitching now, so much so that she starts to get up. I put my hand on her wrist, clamping it hard, forcing her back in her seat. Through gritted teeth, I say, "You're not getting up from this table until this conversation is over. Do I make myself clear?"

She nods.

"Now, why didn't you tell me?"

"He loved you more than he loved me."

314

Exquisite Betrayal

"I was his daughter for Pete's sake. Are you that petty that you were jealous over your own child?"

"Yes!"

Holy shit. My mother's a freak. "You're sick."

"He paid you more attention than he paid me."

"Maybe because you're so goddamn selfish he was worried I wasn't getting any attention from you! Did you ever stop to think about that? You never had time for either of us. No wonder he paid more attention to me, and thank God he did. When he died, you didn't give a shit about me. You got rid of all his stuff and didn't even ask me. You had no regard for my feelings; that I'd lost the only person that ever cared for me."

"I cared for you."

"Really? Really Mom? And how exactly did you care for me? What did you do for me? Tell me!"

She is silent.

"Oh, why don't I remind you then, if you won't tell me? It was all those birthday gifts you sent, wasn't it? Oh wait; the last thing I got from you was a card on my sixteenth birthday, over seven years ago. Gee, maybe it was all the help you gave me when I went to college, like moving into my dorm or apartments. Oh wait, that was someone else. That was my roommate's mom. Or maybe it was the night I went to my senior prom and you wanted to take all those pictures of me. Oh, no, that was my date's mom. Do I even need to go on?"

"Fallon, I help you."

"When? Oh, yeah. I know. When you tell me that I'll never amount to anything. Honestly, that did help me. You pushed me to become something because I worked my ass off to prove you wrong. But Mom, I came here today to tell you I'm done with you. When Mr. Patterson

315

called me to tell me about the trust, you can imagine my shock. I was so angry with you, I wanted to hop on the first plane here and knock the crap out of you, but I didn't do that, obviously. That would've been stupid. I'm here now, though. I'm here to tell you that, by doing that, you put the final nail into the coffin of our relationship. It's done. We're finished. I have nothing more to say to you."

I rise to my feet, straighten my back and make the walk to her door.

I hear her voice say, "Fallon, wait."

"I'm done waiting. I waited for seven years, Mom, ever since Dad died. And I think I waited seven years too long. I won't allow myself to be hurt by you anymore."

"Oh, I see how it is then. It's okay for you to just walk out of here after you hurt me. Is that it?"

"I'd expect you to see it that way. Good-bye, Mom. Have a nice life."

My dad taught me some valuable lessons growing up and forgiveness was one of them. I forgive her in my heart for everything she's done over the years, however I'm still through with her. I won't ever be able to forget the hurt she's caused. The burden of misery disappears and I feel refreshed. She's filled my heart with such heaviness for so long that, when I drive to my hotel, I feel like a new Fallon. Now, if I could only feel that way about Ryland Thomas, I might be able to get on with my life.

Before the sun rises the next morning, I head to Spartanburg, a three hour drive up I-85. When I get here, I drive straight to the cemetery in search of my father's grave. It's been over six years since I've been here. My mom would never bring me because she would tell me I needed to focus on the future. Then, when I could drive myself, it was just too sad for me to visit. Yet, here I am, staring at the large piece of gray granite with his name engraved in it.

Moments pass before I can move. I wish more than anything I could feel his warm arms around me, telling me those things he used to say to make me feel better.

Life isn't fair, Fallon, but you have to make the most of what's given to you and never pass up any opportunities. As bad as things may seem, there's a bright star shining somewhere with your name on it.

Things he used to say crash into me and it makes it harder for me, not easier. Slumping against his tombstone, I cry, telling him how much I miss him. An hour passes and I know I must leave.

It's three hours back to Atlanta and I have a plane to catch. It's not an easy drive, but I make it in time for my flight home.

When I'm in the air again, on the way back to San Francisco, the decision about where I want to live haunts me. Going back to Spartanburg has shown me that things have changed so much, or maybe I have, that I don't feel like it's home anymore. So that's not a viable option. Atlanta's out because I hate that town. My mom's ruined it for me. Charlotte's an option, yet I just don't know.

My San Francisco friends want me to stay there, but I guess I need to start job hunting and let that be my deciding factor. I pull out my e-reader and start a new book. I haven't read a thing since… yeah, since that awful day. It's hard to believe, but I've pulled away from everything that was my life. I toss my damn reader aside and pick up a People magazine that someone's left in the seat pocket in front of me. That's a mistake. There's a picture of Ryland Thomas and Tilly at the Wicked Wenches Con. I want to rip it to shreds. Before I know it, that's what I'm doing. The man sitting next to me says, "Not a fan I take it?"

"That's an understatement." I don't want to get engaged in a conversation about it so I put my earphones on and listen to music. I've fallen in love with this new alt rock band from New York City named She Said Fire. I play all their songs that I've downloaded. The diverse sound of their music soothes me and I must've dozed off because, the next thing I know, the wheels are hitting the ground.

I'd like to say I'm glad to be back, but I can't. Everywhere I turn, I see his face; restaurants, book stores, coffee shops. You name it, he haunts them for me. The taxi drops me off in front of my apartment and I lug my bag up the steps. As I get to my door, my phone starts ringing, so I pick it up and see it's Kristie.

"You back?"

"Just walking in the door."

"Perfect! Meet us for dinner at seven. We're going to eat sushi, and then at nine, guess who's playing at The Jam Bocks?"

"Who?"

"Come on and guess."

"The Beatles?"

"Ha ha. Funny. No, and since you're such a poor sport, I'm just gonna tell you. She Said Fire."

"Seriously?"

"Yep. You in?"

"Naw. I don't think so."

"You're kidding, right? For weeks, all I hear is how great they are and now you're blowing them off? You gotta get a life."

"Yeah, tell me something I don't know."

"Well, listen, sister, it's not gonna happen with you moping around the house."

"I know, but I may have made other plans."

"You're the worst liar ever."

"Yeah, tell that to Ryland Thomas."

"Fuck Ryland Thomas. Besides, he wouldn't know his ass from a hole in the ground. What guy his age does, anyway? And I'm tired of that story. You need to make your own. Starting tonight."

I take a deep breath. She's right. I just feel like I've lost all my energy.

Damn her, it's like she has a straight line to my thoughts. "You're depressed. That's why you have no energy. Get out. Start running again. Your ankle's healed. Get those endorphins flowing. Surround yourself with positive people. Your energy will flood into you like crazy, sister. Be ready at seven because I'm coming to get you."

"You're right. I'll be waiting."

Kristie makes a good point. I'm moving on.

At dinner, I bring Kristie, Kelly and Brandy up to date about what's been happening in the life of Fallon. They applaud my actions with my mom.

"S'bout time that evil woman gets a piece of your mind," Kristie says.

"Agreed. And it was so liberating, too."

I tell them of my dilemma and none of them think I should move from San Fran.

"Honestly, where are you gonna go?"

"I don't know," I try to talk around my mouthful of sushi.

Brandy looks at me. "You know what? There's this great little studio apartment available in my building right now. I think you should move. Clean slate. Get out of your place and start here fresh."

I mull it over, thinking it's a darn good idea.

Kristie adds, "I was gonna talk to you about this later, but have you ever heard of The Erudite Analyst?"

"Yeah. Pretty influential critic, mainstream publishing. Why?"

"They're looking for two reviewers. They want me and wanted to know if I knew anyone else. It's a work-from-home job. They're all online stuff, Fallon. No commute. No office crap. No boss to report to every day."

"Seriously?"

"Uh-huh. Sound like something you're interested in?"

"Um, let me think about it... Hell, yeah!"

Everyone laughs. "That's what I thought you'd say. It'll get you out of the romance genre, too. That's, if you want that. I think they need people to do all kinds of reviews, even non-fiction."

"Sounds great."

"I'll submit your name along with a glowing recommendation."

"Um, what about the stuff at Critics Abound?"

"Oh, they know it all. I was perfectly clear about it. I told them I was above board on everything and wouldn't agree to anything unethical. When they asked why I said that, I told them what happened."

"Interesting. What did they say?"

"You really want to know?"

"Yeah."

"Well, I was gonna tell you this later, too, but they want to do a story on it with me interviewing you. You know... a your-side-of-the-story thing. I told them I didn't think..."

"I'll do it!"

"What?"

"You heard me. I've hidden the truth for too long. I actually wrote an article about it, but never did anything with it."

Kristie's grinning. "Awesome. This is the old Fallon I'm seeing now."

"Maybe so."

I look at Brandy and say, "So when does that apartment open up?"

"It's open."

"Perfect. I need your landlord's name."

They all fist bump me and I grin. Now I'm super excited for the concert.

"Oh my gosh. We're really seeing She Said Fire tonight! Do you all know their drummer's a girl?"

"Cool. Chicks rock, right?" Brandy says.

"Hells yeah we do!"

We're at the Jam Bocks having a great time. We're toasting each other and I'm actually throwing back some shooters. I can't remember the last time I've done that and I refuse to even try.

Kelly's jumping up and down, screaming out, "I'm taking drum lessons. I wanna be a drummer!" She Said Fire just finishes playing 'Funhouse' and Kelly is playing the air drums. I'm worried she's going to tear a rotator cuff with the way she's throwing her arms around.

We all crack up. I can see it now. Her husband, Kirk, I'm sure will be happy to get that piece of news, especially since they have a nine-month-old.

I start laughing so hard I'm holding my sides.

"What's so funny?"

"I just had this vision of Kelly, Kirk and little Micah forming their own band. I'm sure their neighbors are gonna love it when Kelly practices her drums."

"I don't give a shit. I'm gonna be a rocker chick drummer. Or maybe it's a rocker drummer chick." Her words are slurred from all the shooters and we laugh. It's a good thing she's not breast-feeding anymore. Little Micah would be drunk tonight if she were.

She Said Fire starts playing 'Better Ways' and the room quiets down. It's one of their slower songs, but the words trigger all sorts of memories of Ryland Thomas. The lyrics ring true for us; it's almost like it was written for us. I'm sorry to see that song is the end of their set.

While the other band sets up, some recorded stuff starts playing that has a pretty good beat. We all end up on the crowded dance floor, shaking it up pretty good. I work up a tremendous thirst, so I tell Kristie that I'm heading to the bar for some water. I get a full glass, down it and get a second. I decide I need a trip to the bathroom. On my way I send Kristie a text, just so she'll know why I disappeared. I'm not paying attention to where I'm walking and I crash right into someone.

"Aw, hell, I'm so sorry." I look up and about fall flat on my ass because I'm staring into those emerald eyes I've missed so much, but have tried hard to forget.

"Fallon." One word from his lips and I feel like I'm spinning out of control again. Everything good about this night has just turned to shit.

"Er, yeah. It's me all right."

"How are you?"

"I don't think you want me to answer that." I try to brush past him, but he grabs my wrist.

"Let me go." I jerk free of him and he drops his arm.

"I'm sorry."

"Right. I gotta go." I brush past him and go to the restroom. I'm shaking by the time I get there. How can I let him do this to me? I take several deep breaths and count to ten, getting control back. I look at myself in the mirror, satisfied that I don't look like the quivering fool that I feel I am. I use the facilities and head back out, prepared to fight if I see him. I don't, so I'm relieved.

Kristie notices the change. "You okay?"

"Yeah. I just ran in to You-Know-Who."

"Here? Tonight?"

"Yep."

"Did he talk to you?"

"Yeah, but I didn't stay to find out what he wanted. I pushed around him and went to the bathroom."

I give her the details and she says, "Nice!"

I simply shake my head.

"Hey, you're doing great."

"Tell that to my guts. They're a mess right now."

"You don't look a mess. In fact, you look damn good. Let's get back out there and shake it up some more. The next set will be starting in a few. What do you say?"

323

We dance some more and I feel better after a bit, although a part of me wonders if Ryland Thomas is still here. I'm asked by several guys to dance, yet I refuse them all. I have no interest in them. Maybe someday, but not right now. I still feel like I'm tethered to Ryland Thomas, or what's left of me does anyway.

By the time the second band ends their set, it's almost two in the morning. We exit the club and it's a fight for a taxi.

"I think I'm gonna walk."

The others look at me, protesting, "No way. You can't walk. It's not safe."

"I live ten blocks from here and it's safe. I walk around here all the time."

"Not at two in the morning."

"I'll be fine," I argue.

"Fallon, you're taking an unnecessary risk. Wait for a taxi with us."

"I'll be home by the time it gets here."

Brandy says, "Damn, you're stubborn. Then keep your phone in your hand the whole time."

"Yes, dear," I say and then head off in the direction of my apartment.

After I get a couple of blocks away, and the noise fades, the streets are frighteningly empty. I know I only have a few blocks to go, but it is a bit scary out here by myself; especially when I get the sense someone is behind me. Against my better judgment, I turn to look and there is someone there, however it's someone I know won't physically harm me.

"You shouldn't be out here alone, Fallon," he calls to me.

"You scared me." My tone is harsh and accusatory.

"I'm sorry. I didn't mean to, but when I saw you take off by yourself, I wasn't gonna let you walk home alone. You can tell me to leave, go to hell, sod off, or whatever you want, however I won't do it until I see you're safe at home."

I start to say something, yet there isn't really anything to say. He's right. I shouldn't be out here alone, so I start walking again, heading for home.

As I walk, I throw the words over my shoulder, "You may as well walk next to me if you're gonna walk me home." Why did I say that? Who the hell knows? I quit trying to figure things out anymore.

He's by my side in an instant. I glance at him and see he's looking at me.

"You looked perfect tonight, Fallon."

"I said you could walk with me. I didn't say you could talk to me."

I hear a slight chuckle come out of him.

"You find that funny, do you?"

"Not at all. Nothing about any of this is funny, Fallon."

"You got that right."

"Glad to see your ankle is better."

"Thank you. That constitutes as talking, though."

"I guess it does. I'm sorry."

"Stop saying you're sorry." He exasperates me.

"I won't ever be able to do that. I'll be sorry for the rest of my life all because of a few short minutes I didn't grant you. Sorry doesn't come close to what I feel."

"That's good, I suppose, because sorry doesn't come close to repairing the tiny pieces of Fallon that were left behind by all of that."

325

He's stopped walking, but I haven't. I continue to move with urgency down the street, getting closer to my home. When I'm finally there, I think I'm alone. I turn to walk up the steps, but I'm wrong. He's right there, next to me.

"What will come close, Fallon? What will actually make you work again?"

"Huh?" I'm confused by his question.

"You know… what will repair the tiny pieces of Fallon and make her whole again? Because I'll dedicate everything I have, everything I know to making it happen. Not for me, but for you. I want you to have a life full of joy again, and if it takes sacrificing mine, then I'll gladly do it."

He stands in front of me, waiting for an answer, but I don't have one to give.

My mouth presses together for a moment before I answer. "I honestly don't have an answer for you. I think I may be damaged forever."

"Don't say that. Don't ever say that. I'll find a way to fix you. I swear I will." His emerald eyes are filled with such agony; in the dim streetlight they look like they're about to bleed. Then he turns and walks away.

THIRTY

RYLAND - THOMAS

That meeting with Fallon rattled me to the core, so I know I can't wait any longer. Things need to move forward. My pieces are written and now it's time for a flawless execution. My agent called last week to confirm everything and I leave tomorrow for New York. I start the first of my TV appearances with early morning television then I make my way to the round of afternoon shows and finally to late night. By the time I'm finished, Fallon will have hopefully heard everything I have to say. It'll all be airing the week before Thanksgiving, which is supposed to be a good time for viewers. All her friends will be recording each segment I'm on, so even if she misses them, they'll be sure she sees them.

As part of my negotiations for this, each interviewer is aware of my intentions and how it's going to work. They'll ask some questions and then I'll have my say. It all should go relatively smoothly; that is, if I can maintain my composure.

Five shows later and I'm exhausted. I want to crawl in my bed and stay there for a week. My agent and publicist have set my phone on fire with all the calls. They're getting requests for more appearances and interviews—phone, radio or whatever I'll grant—by the dozens. I refuse them all. There's only one thing I want and that is quiet.

Sleep calls to me and I need some down time to digest it all. Fallon's friends haven't called, so I'm assuming either she doesn't give a shit, or they couldn't get her to listen. Ironically, I'm okay with that. My main intent all along was to publicly clear her name. I didn't want her to be held responsible for any of it.

Twelve hours later, I wake up at six in the morning and I can't believe I've slept that long. I pack my bag and head to the airport. The only thing I want to do now is get out of this town and go home to Lake Tahoe. A few hours later that's where I'm headed.

"Where the hell are you, Ryland Thomas?" Tilly screams in the phone. "I've been looking for you."

"In Tahoe."

"Tahoe?"

"Yes, you know that place where I used to live all the time… before I moved to the city?"

"I know where Tahoe is, dammit. But why there?"

"I needed the solitude."

"You were brilliant. I almost fell in love with you."

"Thanks. That wasn't my intention, though."

"I know. If she doesn't at least bend a little, she's not human."

"Tilly, my goal was to clear her name."

"Ryland Thomas, you professed your undying love for her to millions of people. *That* was romantic."

"She'll see it as exploitation."

"Whatever. I still say you did the right thing."

"I know I did. At least everyone knows she has rock solid integrity now and that I'm the fuck up."

"They know you're human, too. So, when are you coming back?"

"That's the thing, Tills. I don't think I am."

"What?"

"It's too hard; being back there, knowing how close she is and not being able to touch her. It's self-inflicted punishment and I can't do it anymore."

"Shit. I don't know what to say."

"There's nothing to say. Will you do me a favor?"

"Sure."

"Try to visit her."

"Oh, I don't know. She hates me, too."

"Yeah, but maybe she'll talk to you. Please."

"I'll try."

It's the first Thanksgiving Tilly and I've spent apart. It's strange, but I need my space. She does come for Christmas and we both mope around like two fools. The snow arrives early so we're able to get some skiing in. It's the second most somber Christmas since Mum and Dad died.

I'm glad to turn the New Year over. I pray that this one turns out better than the last, especially for Fallon.

Tilly tells me when she tried to visit Fallon, her apartment was empty, so I can only assume she's left San Francisco.

I send her a text wishing her a happy and healthy new year along with telling her that I hope it holds big promise for her. I don't get a response, nor do I expect one. It makes me wonder if her cell phone number has changed. If it has, there won't be any way for me to contact her anymore. Not that it matters, yet knowing I still had that one small attachment had given me a sense of security. Now, even that has slipped away.

Thirty-One

Fallon

With my move to my new apartment behind me, I'm finally settling in. My new place is great and I'm in love with it. The girls were right. This is giving me a new look on things here in the city. Kristie has worked miracles for me and I'm now employed with The Erudite Analyst. It's a dream job and I even get to work from home. Thanksgiving's around the corner and I'm a bit edgy about it.

My blogger girls keep calling me about Ryland Thomas being on TV. They say he's doing all sorts of national appearances, but I couldn't care less. I've told them to stop pestering me about it because they're not helping me at all in my cause to get over him.

Kristie invites me to spend Thanksgiving with her, so I accept. We have a nice time with her family, however I go home feeling empty and lonely. I miss that spirit of having a family, that atmosphere of closeness I briefly discovered with Ryland Thomas and Tilly.

Exquisite Betrayal

When I get home, I decide to go through my email and I'm shocked to see the number of messages. It's weird because they all contain video links. So I click on one, and it opens up to one of the network morning shows. It's an interview clip of Ryland Thomas. My first inclination is to exit out of it, yet something about him draws me in. Maybe it's the look on his face or the pain reflected in his eyes. Or maybe it's the sleeve of tattoos that weren't there before. Whatever it is, something compels me to watch, and so I do.

The interviewer asks about the breaking story of his true identity and he doesn't miss a beat.

"It's old news now. Everyone knows. What I'm here about is *how* it happened. I handled it completely wrong and I'm here to hopefully help make that right. You see, the young woman who supposedly broke that story did no such thing. She was a victim as much as I.

"No, that's not really true. She was wronged much more so than I. The company she worked for used her to get to me, and I, being the jerk that I was, didn't give her the time to explain what happened. So I let the world think she was the bad guy here. And that simply wasn't the case. I ruined her life and it's a terrible thing to realize that you've destroyed the only person you've ever loved."

I hit the replay and listen to it again. I check my inbox and see the other messages and open them. They all contain clips of Ryland Thomas saying the same thing on different shows... telling the world that he was the dickface and treated me like a piece of dirt. But on one show—the show with the largest ratings and biggest viewing audience—he reads the original article I wrote... the one I gave him the day I brought the box to him. He tells the world that this was the article Fallon McKinley

332

really wrote about R.T. Sinclair, not the one everyone saw. Then he begs the world to forgive me because I did no wrong. He tells them to place all the blame on him if they want because he should've manned up and came forward long ago.

The interviewer asks him some very pointed questions, but he never backs down. He accepts the burden of responsibility every time and admits he was a douche. In fact, he uses that exact word, even as the interviewer cringes.

The final straw is when he looks straight at the camera and says, *"Fallon, if you're out there and you're listening, please know that I'm not asking you to forgive me because I know that's not possible. I just want you to know that what I did was reprehensible and I'll pay for it for the rest of my life."* The camera fades to black.

The first person I call is Kat. "Did you know?"

"Yes."

"Why didn't you tell me?"

"He asked us not to."

"Us?"

"We all knew... Amanda, Mandy and Andrea."

"Shit."

"He loves you, Fallon. With everything he has."

"What should I do?"

"That's a decision only you can make."

"Come on, Kat, I need advice."

"And if I give it to you, and it goes bad, I'll feel responsible. I'm not saying a word here."

"What would you do if it were you?"

"Not a fair question, Fallon."

"If I go back to him, and he pulls this shit on me again, it will kill me. I mean, physically."

"After all this, do you think he doesn't know that?"

"I don't know if I can ever forgive him." Somewhere in the back of my mind, I can hear my dad's voice trying to force its way through.

"That's a pretty severe thing to say."

"You saw how I was, Kat."

"I did. And I saw how he was, too."

"So you're saying I should do it."

"I'm not saying you should do anything, but from this conversation, it sounds like you want someone to tell you that. Is that what you need? For someone to push you out the door to him? Because the time's here for you to make your own decision, Fallon. You have to determine if this is the right thing for you. I can't tell you that. All I know is that everyone deserves forgiveness. Hell, you've even forgiven your mom for all the crap's she's pulled over the years."

She's dead right. Besides, there's my dad's voice surfacing. He always said we should forgive. He also said it may be harder to forget, but that forgiveness needs to be given because no one is perfect and everyone deserves other chances. *"We're all human, and as humans, we all make mistakes. Some are horrible ones, but they're mistakes nonetheless. Forgive, Fallon. It will make you a better person."* My eyes scan the room because I swear I can hear my dad's voice.

My indecisiveness has lasted through Christmas. I've run more than I ever have, and it's helped clear my head. The week after Christmas, my feet carry me past Ryland Thomas's and I check out his place. It looks deserted. On a whim, I run up the steps and ring the bell. My heart is clanging in my chest and I'm tempted to turn around and run like hell. But after a few minutes, when he doesn't answer, my heart starts to slow down.

I peek in the sidelight and see nothing except emptiness. He's moved. There isn't any furniture in there. Ryland Thomas has left San Francisco.

My heart crashes to the porch.

I don't know why, but I never expected this.

Running down the steps, I head to Tilly's. She doesn't answer, but her decorations are everywhere so I'm relieved to know she's still here. As I jog home, I begin to breathe easy again.

It's New Year's Eve and I'm at Kristie's parents'. They're throwing a party and I'm having a good time, I suppose. At least I'm attempting to have a good time, but lately all I can think of is a tall, dark blond haired guy with emerald green eyes. I dream about him, I think about him and there isn't anything I can do anymore where thoughts of him don't consume me.

The whole thing is pointless. I've been waiting to figure out how to decide what to do when it's really been staring at me in the eyes all along. I need to see him, talk to him. We need to give it a chance and see if it works. Maybe date. Start *somewhere* because I'm drowning in him right now.

Around one a.m. I leave the party, happy to arrive home where I can put my aching feet up. Heels... I hate them. They kill my feet. Why do we women torture ourselves by wearing them? Especially to parties where we stand all night long? I rub my feet and grab my phone, seeing a missed text. I open it and gasp. I'm punching the letters as fast as I can.

Happy New Year to you. Sorry... I was at a party at Kristie's parents. Didn't get this till now. Where are you?

And I wait. And wait. And then...

Ryland Thomas: *I'm in Tahoe. You?*

Me: *SF. I moved to a different apartment. Closer to Cow Hollow.*

Ryland Thomas: *Nice. Do you like it?*

Me: *Yes. Can we talk? I mean live. In person. Face to face. Sometime.*

Ryland Thomas: *YES. Now? I'll drive in now!*

I giggle. Whether it's the champagne I've had or his emphasis on coming here, I don't know. I hit his number and call him. I'm laughing when he answers.

"What's so funny?" Oh, his voice makes me shiver. Even after everything that's happened.

"You. Your response."

"Fallon. I'll get in the car right this second to talk to you."

"Ryland Thomas. It's going on two in the morning. You need to sleep."

"Fallon, do you think I'm going to sleep at all, knowing we're going to actually speak face to face?"

"No. Have you been drinking?"

"Only water."

"You swear?"

"I swear."

"Okay. It's your call, but I'll worry about you. You'll have to call me a lot on the way."

"You'll worry about me?" His voice cracks a little.

"Yes," I whisper. "Just because you hurt me, doesn't mean I stopped loving you."

336

"Jesus, Fallon. I love you, too. And I'll call you, but don't worry about me."

"I will. You know I will." I give him my new address.

"See you in three hours and then some."

Four phone calls later, he knocks on my door and I want to swallow him whole. He's lost weight, but not much. It just makes his cheekbones a bit more pronounced. I grab his hand and walk him to my bed.

"Don't get any ideas. I'm so damn sleepy, and I know you must be, too. Let's get some rest."

I must be looking at him sadly because he says, "Don't look at me like that, Fallon."

"But…"

"But nothing. Come here, dangerous girl. Let's sleep."

He takes my hand and we get under the covers. I curl up next to him and for the first time I can remember since we've slept together, he doesn't pull me on top of him. I nuzzle close to his neck and I'm sleeping before I know it.

Thanks to my blackout curtains, we sleep until early afternoon. I stretch and feel his abs tense beneath me. I look up to see his eyes on me. Why is everything so uncomfortable the next day?

"Hey," I say.

He smiles and his hand reaches for me then stops. "You can touch me, Ryland Thomas."

"I'm afraid."

"Of what?"

"That if I do, I'll never let you go."

I take his hand in mine. "I forgive you. We have a ways to go before we get where we need to be, but I forgive you, Ryland Thomas." Then I'm on top of him, in that place that feels completely right, and he's holding me so close that I can feel every muscle in his body shake. I don't have to look at him to know he's crying. We both are. It's time for us to cleanse away the pain that nearly destroyed us and move forward again. My dad was right. People make mistakes. We all do, and we all deserve to be forgiven.

Later that afternoon, we're sitting on the floor in front of my couch facing each other. My legs are wrapped around his waist. He hardly takes his eyes off me. We're just finishing up the Chinese food that was delivered to us. He's fed me every bite, and we've laughed a lot because some of it doesn't quite make it to my mouth.

His hands are either brushing my hair back, feeling my lips or doing something else to me. He can't seem to keep himself from touching me, as if he's afraid I'll disappear.

"You're so gorgeous, Fallon. I would stare at your pictures every day, just so I could memorize every detail of you. I bet I know things about you that you're not even aware of."

"Like what?"

"Your eyes. They're this light gray, but they turn slate when you're angry. And close to your pupils, they're almost violet. I've never seen eyes like yours. And did you know you have two freckles on your nose?"

"Two?"

"Uh-huh. Right here." He touches the tip of my nose and then leans forward like he's going to press his lips there, too, but then he stops. We haven't kissed yet and I know he's taking all his cues from me.

"Ryland Thomas, how do you want this to play out?" I decided to be blunt about everything.

"Us?"

"Yeah."

"I want us to live happily ever after as Mr. and Mrs. Ryland Thomas Sinclair."

So he's playing blunt, too. Good.

"Okay. You told me you were scared of touching me when we woke up. I'm scared, too. Out of my fucking mind. Of having my heart slashed apart again. I know there are never any guarantees in this life, but I can't ever go there again. As sure as I'm sitting here, I know this much. If I have to walk in that hell again, you may as well make me an in-patient at the local mental facility. My mind will crack the next time. It's not a threat. It's not a warning. It's pure fact."

He winces, although he doesn't avoid the discussion. "I understand. I know what happened to you in Vegas and, Fallon, you know what I think about myself. I swear to you, as I'm sitting here, that there will never be a repeat of that again. I know how fragile we are, how fragile life is. There are no guarantees and we're all here on borrowed time. You and I know that better than anyone.

"I can't promise I won't make stupid mistakes. I'm a dumb shit. I'll be the first to admit I'm full of immense—what's the word you use? —oh yeah, stupidassery. Call me on it. I'll take it. But whatever I do in the future won't be intentional. You'll always come first in my life, over everything.

"I'm scared too, Fallon, but when I see your face, I want so much with you. I realize I'll do anything to make it happen."

His eyes burn into mine, compelling me to know he's being honest, but there's one other thing I need to know.

"Why Iris? Of all the fucking sluts in this town, why her?"

"It wasn't what you thought." I raise my brows and he sees it. "Really, it wasn't. I'd been out running and damned if I didn't run into her. I still had this stupid print of hers. Don't ask me why, but I did. It was in a box of my things and I didn't even recall having it until I moved into the city. When I unpacked the box, I saw the print and realized it was fairly valuable. I was gonna trash it, but then I stashed it in my closet. After you and I ran into her in Sonoma, I decided to donate it to a charity, but then I forgot about it.

"That day I was running and ran into her, I thought I'd just give the damn thing back to her. I told her to meet me at my place to pick it up. That was it. She called right as I got out of the shower. I ran down and unlocked the door and told her to just come on in. So when you rang the bell, I thought it was Iris.

"She was only coming to pick up that lousy print. That was it. Nothing happened between us. I couldn't have let it. She disgusts me, even when we saw her in Sonoma. You were right. She's a slut. Fallon, I haven't been with anyone since you. I don't want to be with anyone. You've ruined me. If I can't have you, I may as well be a damn monk."

I smile at his words. "That's good."

"About Iris?"

"No, about you being a monk." I bump him in the shoulder. "I dumped my mom."

"What?"

I tell him about my trip to Atlanta and he awards me with one of his make-my-belly-clench smiles.

"Well done, love. I wish I could've been there to see you in your glory."

"I was pretty freakin' awesome," I beam. "I went to my dad's grave, too. I hadn't been in six years. It was pretty hard. I cried. Nasty cried."

"I wish I had been there with you. I would've held you, Fallon."

"I know. I had to go... after the trust and everything."

"Can I kiss you?" It catches me off guard, but I don't care; I simply fly into him.

"What took you so long, slow boy?"

I push him back and then I'm on top as our mouths join together for the first time in months. I'm in paradise again. Our moans mingle as he's so tender with me, like I'm a precious piece of crystal. Or as though he's afraid I'll run away.

I frame his face and ask him about his new tattoo sleeve.

"It's all you. Your face. Your name is everywhere within it. You just have to look closely for the words."

My breath is trapped in my lungs, and I want to love him more, if that's even possible. I want him, all over me, outside and in. I sit up and then stand up. My hand extends and he grabs it.

We walk into my room when he turns me around and asks, "Are you sure?"

"I wouldn't be here in this place, if I weren't."

341

My fingers curl around the hem of his shirt and I pull it up. I'm now staring at his body, seeing all the new ink that wasn't there before. There are lines everywhere... down the side of his torso, across his left pec, beneath his triceps. On his left deltoid, in beautiful bold script, is my name—*Fallon Forever*. My fingers lightly dance over it as I cock my head and stare. I'm so taken by what I see. He's covered his body in images and sayings of things we professed to each other. *Two lives, one heart, one love, endlessly for Fallon*, is written over his heart. I stagger with emotion. I have to hold his arms to keep from falling.

He holds me close. I'm not aware when he lifts me and lays me down. All I know is that I'm so overcome with love for this man, I can't speak. That impossible moment passes and I look at him to see those vulnerable eyes searching mine. He must see what he wants because he smiles.

"You wear it like a badge," I say, my voice catching.

"And I will for the rest of my life. I love you endlessly, Fallon. Always have, always will, no matter where this road of ours takes us."

"I want it to take us somewhere together. I want it to be you and me, Ryland Thomas. Let's start here and now, this very minute."

"It may not always be smooth, love."

"As long as the pothole throws me into your arms, I'll be okay."

"I'll catch you. I won't let you fall. I can promise you that much."

"Just promise you'll love me and that's all I need."

"I'm overflowing with mistakes, Fallon."

"So am I."

"Your mistakes are better than mine. You made the best one with me."

"Stop talking already and kiss me."

"No, not until we've figured us all out. I'm not perfect. Tell me you understand," he pleads

"I do and tell me you understand I'm not either."

"I do. Marry me, Fallon."

"Kiss me first and then ask me."

He finally does and it's the best kiss of my life. It must be pretty damn good because he's given me some darn good kisses in the past. How he manages to top them all, I'll never know, but he does it. Boy, does he ever.

THIRTY -TWO

RYLAND -THOMAS

I stare at her as she sleeps. I'm afraid to close my eyes; afraid that if I do, I'll wake up to find it was only a dream. Can this be real? Can she really be giving me another chance? Worry rattles me because she never answered me when I asked her to marry me. I worry, too, because maybe that was another bloody stupidassery thing to do. Nevertheless, I'm going to ask her again today. I can't sit around and not know. I *have* to know. If she says no, then I'll go to work, persuading her. I know one thing. No one, and I mean no one, dammit, will ever love her more than I.

Her breathing changes. I can tell in the way it fans across my chest. It's more rapid now, like short bursts. I wonder what she's dreaming. Her legs start to twitch, slight movements at first, but then they become fierce. Now she's mumbling, like she's scared. I hold her close and rub her back. I don't like to feel her fear.

"Ssh, it's all right, love," I whisper. She doesn't hear me. She's shaking now and I can feel moisture on my neck where her cheek meets my skin. What terrible thing is she dreaming about?

"Fallon. Wake up, love." I shake her awake.

She lifts her head and searches me out in the dark. "Huh?"

"You were dreaming and crying. What had you so upset?"

"You left me."

"Aw, fuck. Do you dream of this a lot?"

"Yeah. All the time." Her voice is rough.

"I won't ever leave you. Hear?"

"Love me?"

"You know I do."

"No, I mean…"

I roll her on her back and kiss her. Her lips are salty, so I move to kiss the taste of the tears away. I lick and kiss her cheeks to erase the remnants of them there. She's naked and, I'm so in love with her, I just want to look at her. So I roll to my side, lean on my elbow and rest my head on my hand. The nightlight is casting the room in shadows and making her body glow.

I notice her pebbled nipples so I brush my fingers lightly over them. She shivers, so I do it again. She's always so responsive to every touch, soft or heavy. My fingers trail down the curve of her belly until they reach that smooth place between her thighs and I lightly dance over them. When I can't bear it any longer, I allow my lips to taste her nipples, alternating between the two. I'm encouraged by her sighs and the way she arches into me.

My finger slides between her folds as she lifts her leg. I run it along her slit to find that she's already soaked.

345

I slip inside her opening and hear her call out my name. I move between her thighs and start my play; first on the inner left one, by nibbling and sucking on her. Then I repeat that same action on her right inner thigh and end by licking my way all the way to her core.

She's moaning loudly now and those lovely thighs of hers are starting to clench against my shoulders, letting me know her explosion is near. I don't want her to come right now, though. I want her to come with me inside of her. When I stop, she protests, as I knew she would, but when I settle between her legs and then push inside of her, she urges me on. I move one hand under her beautiful ass and the other I lace with her fingers and pull it next to her head. Then I kiss her as we rock against each other, exchanging breaths as we move together.

I know she's climaxing when I feel her squeezing me on the inside. It makes me fall apart in her as I call out her name. I wrap my hand in her hair and kiss her again, loving her with everything I have.

I roll back over with her on top. "I love you, sweet Fallon. Now go to sleep and have pleasant dreams. I'm not going anywhere except with you, love."

Her arm encircles my neck and she whispers her love back to me. Then she sleeps a soundless slumber, as I lie awake, staring at her loveliness.

I must've drifted off sometime during the night because I wake up and Fallon's not on top of me. My heart kicks a bit, but I look around and settle down when I realize it's her bed I'm in. I hear the toilet flush and then the water running so I know she's in the bathroom. Then the door opens and she's crawling on top of me. She rubs her cheek against mine, letting my scruff scratch her face.

"You never answered me earlier," I say.

"What did you ask me?"

"To marry me. To be my wife. To be Mrs. Sinclair." She inhales and then says, "Yes."

"Yes?"

"Yes."

I lift her up and she asks, "What are you doing?"

"We're taking a shower. Then we're getting dressed and I'm taking you ring shopping."

"Ryland Thomas, it's late and it's New Year's Day."

"So?"

"Everything will be closed."

"Everything?"

"Everything."

"Bloody hell. I finally get the love of my life to say yes, and I can't take her ring shopping?"

She laughs. "I want you to surprise me anyway."

I must have this awful expression on my face because she really breaks out into a laugh this time.

"What?" I ask.

"Is it that bad? To surprise me?"

"Bloody damn straight. I don't know where to start."

"Start big, Ryland Thomas. Always start big where diamonds are concerned."

"Right then."

"I'm joking," she says.

"Too late. You want a surprise and you just gave me my direction. Give me your hand a second." She does and I look at her long fingers. "Hmmm."

"What?"

"Just getting some ideas. That's all."

"Tease."

"That's what you get for not wanting to help." I wink at her. "Come here. How 'bout we Christen that shower of yours?"

When she grins I know she's in.

We're all clean and shiny when I give Tilly a call to see what she's up to tonight. She said she's just hanging out and doesn't have plans. She has no idea I'm in town, so Fallon and I decide to pay a surprise visit on her. We pick up some carry out sushi and arrive with our arms laden with bags of food. When she opens the door, she nearly falls to the floor.

"Happy New Year, Tilly," Fallon says.

"Get in here, you little shit!" Then they hug for centuries. "Jesus, it's about damn time you two reconciled. Damn it all, Fallon. I'm so bloody sorry."

"Hey, let's put it to rest. Ryland Thomas and I are good, so let's just leave it at that. Damn, I've missed you Tilly."

"Same here."

I'm grinning like a five-year-old with a new toy while we set out our sushi and start chatting.

Finally, I just casually say, "Oh, by the way, Tills, Fallon and I are going to be married."

Tills inhales the wrong way, practically choking. When she can breathe again, she says, "Are you trying to kill me? Bloody hell!"

"I didn't know you were gonna go and choke on us."

"It's all in the delivery. Now, Fallon, would you care to tell me the good news?"

"Well... we're getting hitched!"

Tilly shakes her head and laughs a little. She coughs again and I ask if she's okay. "Yeah. I'm fine. But that was a bit rough." She rubs her throat.

"Can you eat?" Fallon wants to know.

"I'm fine," Tilly insists.

Tilly wants to know about our plans and Fallon tells her about the ring. Tilly is in stitches, laughing.

"You realize you're in trouble, Fallon, don't you?"

"Me? Why?" she asks.

"Let's say my brother here has a tendency to go overboard."

"No." Fallon looks at me and says, "Just don't get me something that looks like a giant plastic toy."

Tilly laughs harder and I tell her to stuff it. This turns into the best New Year's Day I've ever had.

It's now Valentine's Day weekend and Fallon and I are headed to Mendocino for a three day weekend. We take our time driving up the coastline, enjoying the clear blue skies. I've arranged for us to stay in a quaint, though very swanky, bed and breakfast that's equipped with a spa and every other amenity one could want.

We check in and head to the spa for our hour-long couples Vichy shower treatment. Afterward, we head to a couple of wine tastings and then we go back to our room for a tasting of something completely different.

Dinner is in a small bistro, consisting of perfect seafood paired with local wine. She's in heaven, and I can't take my eyes off her.

The next morning, we have our extravagant breakfast delivered to our room and take our time eating. I love to feed bites of it to her, missing on purpose, so I can kiss my misses away. I lick the syrup off her chin and move to her lips as she laughs at me.

"Oops," I say as I drop a tiny bit of French toast in the V formed by her robe. My head dips to grab it with my lips. When I come back up, she has that look in her eye, the one I love so much; the one that tells me she has something up her sleeve. Except this time, she drops her sleeves, along with her robe and stands before me, naked and gorgeous.

"Take it off," she says.

When I'm naked, she pushes me back in the chair and straddles my legs. She dots my chest with pieces of her French toast, and then follows it with syrup as she pours it from the small pitcher. Then her eyes dig into mine for a second before her head moves down to lick some of the gooey liquid up with her tongue. After she swirls it on me for a bit, she puts her lips around a piece of the toast and throws her head back, chews and then swallows. I swear to God, my dick almost explodes.

"Fuck."

"Like that, did ya?"

I swallow and nod, speaking isn't possible.

She gives me a sinful smile and drops down for round two. But this time that damn syrup is all over my nipple and she makes a beeline for it. I groan when her mouth hits it, and my hand flies down to my crotch.

"Uh-uh." She traps my hand in hers and won't let me cover myself up. "I'm gonna take care of that for you, babe." She lifts up and guides me into her. I grip her hips so hard I'm afraid I'm bruising her, however I can't help myself. God, I can't help myself.

"Ahh," I only say because that's all that will come out. I want to tell her so much at that point, but I still can't speak. I can only use my body at this time. So that's what I do. I take her hand, put it on my heart and lay mine on top of it.

My heart is in my eyes. She has to see it. I know she does because her eyes are showing me all her love. I explode, calling her name over and over.

After she gets hers, I can't stop looking at her. I take her hand, kiss her palm and then put it back on my heart.

"How did I get so damn lucky to find you, lose you and find you again and again?" I kiss her.

When we pull apart, she picks up my tattooed arm and examines it. She likes to do that. She likes to pick things out in it, usually finding something new every time. She cried when I told her I had it done in only two sittings. I told her it was the best thing I've ever done. Other than meet her, of course.

"Come on, sticky boy, let's shower." I look down and laugh. I am one syrupy mess.

That afternoon, we drive out to the cliffs that overlook the Pacific Ocean. There is a great, little secluded place where I pull off and park. Before us lies a splendid view of the jagged coast and the giant, turbulent waves as they crash into the rocky shore, creating that perfect layer of bluish white foam.

We sit there and admire it for a moment before I take her hand. "It's endless, the motion of the sea. Like our love, Fallon. I'll love you until my life ends. I think I'll even love you after that. You said you'd be my wife and you'd marry me. So now we'll complete the circle. Close your eyes, love." She does and I slip on the ring I've been carrying around with me for days now. "You can open them now.

"Fallon McKinley, we're two lives, one heart, one love, endlessly. When I look at you every worry, every fear I have, disappears. You always bring me home, love. Please marry me and be mine forever."

Her right hand flies to her mouth and then she cries. I pull her into my arms, and eventually on my lap.

"You know I will. And it's perfect," she whispers against my neck.

"Yeah?"

"Yeah."

"You can exchange it if it doesn't suit you."

"It suits me just fine."

It's a two and a half carat round diamond set on an eternity band of pave diamonds. It looks lovely on her hand.

"I wanted it to be symbolic. The eternity band symbolizes my endless love for you."

"This is perfect. We may not be perfect, but we're endless." She gives me a teary smile and kisses me. She tastes of salt, so I tell her so.

"They're the best tears I've ever shed, Ryland Thomas."

"I hope they're the last."

"They won't be."

"Why not?" I ask her.

She gives me one of her looks that tells me I'm showing my stupidassery again.

"Sorry, love, I claimed it, remember?"

"The wedding!"

"Ah, right then. The wedding."

352

"After all the shit we've gone through, you didn't think for one minute that I could get through our wedding without crying, now did you?"

"Fallon, I hadn't thought that far ahead, but now that you mention it, no."

"So?"

"So what?"

"Really?"

"You got me again, love."

"The wedding, Sinclair."

Good lord, I am a bloody idiot. "Whatever your heart desires, it's yours."

She rattles off without even stopping, "Lake Tahoe, this summer—small, intimate, close friends. That's it. Oh, and *no media*."

"Media! Did I tell you that they want *Love Between The Sheets* for a movie?

"No way!"

"Uh-huh."

She smacks my shoulder. "And you were going to tell me this, when?"

"Fallon, love, I've had other things on my mind. Like you and asking you to be my wife and giving you this ring on Valentine's Day in the most perfect place I could find."

"You did well, Ryland Thomas. Did I tell you I love you with everything I have? Because I do. Even your stupidassery."

"It's a damn good thing, 'cause you're stuck with me now." I kiss her.

"Let's go back to the room. Fallon wants to play with her fiancé. Naughty play."

There's no way in bloody hell that I would turn that down.

Fallon

Five Months Later
Lake Tahoe

I put the diamond earrings in as Tilly makes sure my lipstick is on straight. I've always hated lipstick, but she tells me I have to wear it because of the pictures. "You'll want wedding pictures," she reads my mind. "Years from now, when you have grandchildren, you'll want to tell them what a stupid ass their granddad was and you'll want to show them pictures of the day you married him."

She's right. She's always right.

"You know, Ryland Thomas will have your portrait everywhere, too. So just don't lick all that gloss off your lips."

"Yes, sir." I give her a mocking salute.

She stands back, declaring, "Well, you're..." and then she's dabbing at her eyes. "Damn you, you're ruining my make-up."

I hold out my arms and we hug each other. "At least we're officially sisters now, right?"

"Finally! That bloody exasperating brother of mine."

"Hey, that's enough."

She laughs. "You've become so damn protective of him."

"And why shouldn't I be? He's my..."

"Spare me. I've heard it too many times as it is."

I laugh at her.

"So, is everyone here?"

"Fallon, how the bloody hell would I know? I've been in here with you for the last several hours."

We're in Ryland Thomas's—make that *our*—bedroom. The wedding will take place overlooking the mountains on the brand new, massive deck he had specially built for this occasion. The reception will immediately follow. The caterers arrived late this morning and have been cooking up quite a feast. Then the hairdresser and make-up artist came right after that because Tilly insisted we needed them.

My dress is simple; a sleeveless, silky sheath with a deep V and some beading that is sewn into the waist. I didn't want anything fancy since the wedding isn't going to be fancy. As I told Ryland Thomas back on Valentine's Day, I wanted an intimate affair, and that's what we are having. Tilly's wearing a short, periwinkle blue, silk dress that shows off all her curves; she looks fabulous.

"Well?"

Tilly looks at me, gives her dress one last adjustment and says, "Right then." We walk out the door and head down the stairs where the photographer waits. He starts to snap photos and we smile.

I'm doing something quite unusual; Tilly is walking me down the aisle. There isn't anyone else I feel close enough with to fulfill that role, so I chose Tilly and she gladly accepted. She's also going to serve as Ryland Thomas's best mate, as he calls her.

My girls are all bridesmaids, and some of Ryland Thomas's mates from London are here, along with his agent, to stand up as groomsmen.

As I walk towards the deck, I gasp. It's strung with lights and colorful flowers all along the railing. It's been transformed into the most perfect garden I've ever seen. String music is playing in the background as I make my way to Ryland Thomas who looks... well, he looks as scrumptious as the wedding cake I've been dying to sink my teeth into ever since it was delivered this morning. He's wearing dark pants and a dark jacket with a white shirt, unbuttoned to his chest. He's opted to go tie-less since we've dispensed with formalities.

He flashes me one of his tummy tightening smiles, and I want to melt right into him. His arm is extended as I take his hand in mine, feeling its warmth send a tingle all the way my toes.

He pulls me towards him and asks the small group seated on the deck, "Do I have to wait until the 'I do's' before I kiss this woman?"

Everyone, including me, laughs. Then he leans in and whispers, "Much more than dangerous."

I laugh again.

The minister says his thing as we stand there. I don't hear a word of what he says, though, my attention is solely focused on the man next to me. Then it's time for us to exchange our vows. We agreed to write our own. I have no idea what Ryland Thomas has written, nor does he know what mine are.

He begins by saying, "When Fallon and I decided to write our own vows, I thought I'd have something

357

romantic and quite flowery prepared for her. Yet the more I thought about it, the shallower I thought that would sound. I didn't want to sound like R.T. Sinclair, the writer. I do that for a living. I wanted these vows to be just for her, and for everyone here that came from near and far to be with us today. So, dear friends and my gorgeous Fallon, here goes.

"As you know, I've been the worst person to be in a relationship with due to my stupidassery. Hell, I've admitted it on national tele, so I know this comes as no surprise to anyone here. But, I swear to all of you as my witnesses, and to God above, that I will try my damnedest to be a wiser man for this woman who is about to become my wife. I love her with every piece of me and I will love her until the end of time. She's taught me what it is to be complete, to be a better human being, to love unconditionally, to respect that love and to cherish it with my life."

He stops for a second and places his palm on my cheek. "I fell for you that very first day I saw you in the melting sun at the airport in Las Vegas. I started falling in love with you when you woke up in my bed, hung over and lost as hell because you'd misplaced your purse. That love grew into something so immense that I can't imagine being the old Ryland Thomas anymore. So, my love, *you* are my alpha and omega, and today, you bring me home by becoming my wife. Two lives, one heart, one love, endlessly."

Tears are bubbling out of my eyes, but I know I must speak. He takes a handkerchief out of his pocket and dabs the droplets away, being careful not to smear my make-up.

"You remembered."

"I did."

I say to the crowd, "See, he's learning already." They all laugh.

"Ryland Thomas, you're a tough act to follow."

He cups my cheek and whispers, "I'm nothing compared to you." I put my hand over his and smile.

"So, Ryland Thomas is right. He *was* filled with all sorts of stupidassery, but he's not giving himself much credit for how much smarter he's gotten over this past year." More chuckles come from the group. "He says he fell in love with me in Vegas. Well, admittedly, I took a *little* longer than that. But what I discovered in him was a generous, thoughtful, kind, caring and loving man with a heart that swallowed me whole, and I haven't been the same since.

"No, our road wasn't smooth, but someone very near and dear to my heart once told me that sometimes when you go through the rough spots, the beauty shines through, and when it does, it's much more appreciated. Ryland Thomas, you were right. You also told me so many other things, but one thing especially stands out and that is how fragile our lives are. We've both lost loved ones and we understand how precious these moments are. So I more than appreciate you. You bring me home, to where I belong. I love you beyond words, forever, in this world and the ever after. Two lives, one heart, one love, endlessly."

Then the minister says the "I Do's" part and pronounces us husband and wife. Ryland Thomas grabs me and seals our vows with a ground-shaking kiss. The crowd eventually starts to clap, which lets us know we need to break it up.

When we pull away from each other, I look at him and laugh. Hard.

"Hand me your handkerchief." He does and I wipe all my lipstick off his mouth. He pulls me into him and kisses me again. This time, just a brief one.

"Have I told you I love you?" he asks.

"I think you have."

"Good. Because I really do, Fallon. I fucking love the hell out of you."

I can't help smirking at that. "Hmm, for a writer, you sure can come up with some pretty flowery phrases."

"It's honest and straight from the heart, love." He kisses me again, leaving me no doubt he means it. "Let's get the party started," he announces.

There a big rush to congratulate us, and then champagne is being passed around along with platters of appetizers. Music is piped through the sound system and things start to crank up. Ryland Thomas's London friends are quite a rowdy bunch and it turns into a fun-filled bash.

The caterers keep the tables loaded with food and there are two small bars set up, one inside and one out. We have a car service ready to transport guests back to their hotel whenever they want to leave, but I have a feeling that this party's going to last awhile.

Ryland Thomas and I dance the first song together, alone; it's a nice and slow one. The noise of the guests vanishes, and it's just the two of us, staring into each other's eyes. I lick my lips because he looks so good I can almost taste him.

"Ah, dangerous girl. You're treading on thin ice, you know."

"Uh-huh. But I can't help it. You look awfully tasty, Mr. Sinclair."

360

Exquisite Betrayal

He wiggles his brows up and down, giving me a sexy grin. "Don't go there, Mrs. Sinclair. That'll lead to no good."

"That depends on what your definition of no good is."

"You're being a might naughty, aren't you, considering we have more than a houseful of guests?"

"Are you saying you can't handle it?"

"Is that a challenge?"

"Maybe."

He dips his head so his lips are almost touching my ear and then says, "Fallon, I'll always accept one of your challenges." His voice brushes over me and I shiver. I can feel every nerve ending react to him, including the ones between my thighs, and he knows it. Then he whispers, "Now, my lovely bride, let's act like charming hosts, but be ready because, the first chance I get, I'm going to give you exactly what you want and you're going to tell me how hard and how fast."

I quickly suck in my breath, and he kisses me before I can do or say a thing. The song ends while we're still kissing.

Amanda comes up behind me. "Think you two should just go on ahead and get a room?"

I know my face heats. I have no doubt it's as red as a tomato because I can feel the heat stinging my cheeks.

Ryland Thomas smiles. "You look lovely with the roses blooming in your cheeks." Then he takes my hand and we make our way around the room to chat with our guests. The night passes. I've had way too much champagne and all sorts of other things, but I don't care. It's a party and that's what I'm going to do. We finally cut the cake I've been salivating over, and when we feed

361

it to each other, Ryland Thomas tells me I look disappointed.

"I am. I expected it to be all kinds of good, but my anticipation over what awaits me later has spoiled it."

"Tell you what. We'll take a pile of that stuff to our room and eat it later and then we can have it for breakfast, too."

"Yes!" Everyone looks at me as I shout, making Ryland Thomas just laugh.

We finally leave the party at one in the morning and climb the steps to our room. There are some guests still hanging around, but the caterers are there until the last one leaves. They will clean up and the guests have transportation, so we don't have a care in the world. Tilly is staying in the hotel with the other guests.

We're leaving for a two-week honeymoon to the Greek Islands on the day after tomorrow. That was another good call by Ryland Thomas, making it so that we don't have to get up early for a flight in the morning.

I have a feeling this will be a night without sleep by the look in his eyes. I don't mind. I've waited long enough for this day, and the reception nearly killed me. I wanted to steal away and come up here all night long, yet he wouldn't dare. He tortured me constantly, so I'm going to pay him back now.

"You better take that dress off. Tell me how to take it off, or I'm going to tear it off you in two seconds."

"Buttons. All the way down the back," I gasp.

He starts undoing the first of twenty five. "Holy crap, Fallon. Could you have chosen one with any more buttons?"

"I wasn't exactly thinking about this when I bought the dress."

"Bloody hell, I'm just gonna tear it off you."

"Don't you dare! I'm saving this dress for your daughter."

"I don't have a daughter."

"You might someday. Now calm down and take your time."

"They're stuck, and so fucking tiny my fingers can't even grab the little fuckers."

I start to giggle. "Ryland Thomas, don't tear any of the loops."

"Oh, for fuck's sake. Lift the damn dress already."

"What?"

"Pick up the bloody dress."

I do as he asks and he tears off my panties. Rips them to shreds. His fingers find me and I'm crying out for more. He unzips, picks me up, slides in and we're riding the tide of wedded bliss. It doesn't take us long to reach that place we seek, and after we're through, we look at each other and start laughing our butts off. His shirt is unbuttoned and hanging off and his hair is all kinds of messy. He's still wearing his pants and he looks sexy as sin. My dress is bunched up around my waist and he's pulled my hair out of its chignon, well, half of it anyway.

"Damn, you'd think we were two teenagers."

"Buttons. Don't ever buy anything ever again with those bloody buttons on it. I'll tear the fuckers off ya. I swear I will."

"Right. So now that you're a bit more calm, would you mind unbuttoning me?"

"Mrs. Sinclair, I'll do anything in the world for you."

"Good, because what I really want is to get this dress off and to climb into bed so you can feed me our wedding cake."

363

"Brilliant idea."

This time he succeeds in getting the tiny, silk covered buttons undone. We lie in bed as he feeds me cake and I think about how grand life is with Ryland Thomas by my side.

Thirty-Four

Fallon

One Month Later
Las Vegas

I wake up with the sun's rays casting the room in an amber glow. I feel all warm and fuzzy as I stretch my arms. A hand wraps around my wrist and a voice roughened by sleep asks, "And how did Mrs. Sinclair sleep last night?"

"Oh, she slept just dandy. And did Mr. Sinclair?"

"Never better. You know, it's full circle, isn't it?" he asks.

"What do you mean?"

"Two years ago, we met in Vegas, and here we are, back again. The Bellagio, but in much better circumstances, wouldn't you say?"

"Most definitely. And quite a circle it was."

"So, love, are you ready for today?"

"I am. But Ryland Thomas, what do you think their reaction will be?"

"They're gonna love you."

365

"I wasn't talking about me. I was talking about you."

He looks thoughtful for a moment and then he says, "I don't know. We have a fifty-fifty chance of getting heckled, I suppose."

"You don't really think…"

"Hell no. I was just kidding. The response was overwhelming. You know what my agent, Sam, said. They want us. Bad. They're bloody dying for the Q and A."

"I'm a little nervous for that."

He grabs my chin, forcing me to look at him. "I've got you. I've got this. I won't let anything or anyone make this difficult for you. We clear?"

I nod then wrap my arms around him. "I think we need to shower."

An hour later, we head to the convention because we're set to go on at nine in the morning. We're the keynote speakers at the opening session for the day. Not only that, they've allotted us two hours, one more than the usual.

They've told us to arrive at a rear entrance due to the media coverage. Apparently, we've become quite the talk of the town, and they're expecting all the major networks to be covering this talk. I don't know why I'm not hyperventilating. I guess it's because my husband is holding onto my hand and keeping me tethered, acting as my lifeline, as usual.

We stand back stage, hand in hand, waiting for the MC to announce us and when she does, the room explodes. My heart pounds as I break into a huge grin. Ryland Thomas looks at me and grins back. "I guess we're on the good side of that fifty-fifty, love. Let's do this."

We walk on stage, and the roaring turns into thunder. I'm afraid the roof is going to come down. We look at each other and simply laugh. We can't speak because it's too loud, so we just stand there feeling goofy as all hell. Ryland Thomas raises our linked hands in the air, probably thinking it will start to quiet them down. It has the reverse effect. The crowd goes wild once more.

He leans over to me and asks, "What should I do?"

"How the heck should I know?" Then we merely laugh because, really, there isn't anything else to do. Finally, after what seems like an eternity, the audience starts to calm down, allowing Ryland Thomas to speak.

"Wow. I was *so not* expecting that. You totally amaze me. Whew." He looks at me. I'm just grinning at him. "I told Fallon, here, before we came out that we had a fifty-fifty chance of a positive response because—"

The applause breaks out again and he has to stop. We look at each other and laugh again. Then he shouts in the microphone, "I love you guys!"

They go insane with that shout out.

He puts his arm around me and yells, "Bloody hell, is this all we have to do?"

I'm almost doubled over in laughter by now because it truly is funny to me.

They quiet down again and then he grabs the microphone off the stand. We walk closer to the front of the stage.

"You blokes are amazing. But you're gonna have to calm down or I won't be able to tell our story and you won't get to ask any questions."

He gains control of the audience with that and gives his informal speech about us. Then he hands the mike over to me and I talk about our life together and how it all started right here in Vegas and how we wrote our own romance novel. They love it.

We're finally at the point of the Q and A. They want to know everything, so we tell them. The toughest question I get is the one about his speech from last year's Wicked Wench's Con. He starts to answer, but I stop him.

"Ryland Thomas did what he thought was right at the time. He left home to avoid the media because they were camped out on his lawn. How do I know this? Because I went there, dozens of times. He actually left the country and didn't know I'd been calling. So we both had obstacles to overcome. He manned up and I dealt with everything. We've made things right between us, and in the long run, it's made our relationship stronger. Would I recommend this route to anyone? Hell, no! Would I do it again this way? Hell, no! Would I do it again with Ryland Thomas? An unequivocal hell, yes!" He grabs me and then kisses me. Need I say the crowd goes wild again?

We finally finish and leave out the back entrance where my girls are waiting with tackling hugs. And we do end up on the ground... all of us, while Ryland Thomas and Tilly stand there, laughing.

Yeah, I sure did meet my goals at the Wicked Wenches Con in Vegas. It may not have been the one from two years ago, but I succeeded and then some. I happened to snag the sexiest author in the world and boy did I hit it right when I picked him to lose my virginity to. Looks like the odds were in my favor in Vegas after all.

Exquisite Betrayal

September — News Release

The San Francisco Chronicle reported today that Ryland Thomas Sinclair and Fallon McKinley Sinclair were awarded a combined ten million dollars in damages from a lawsuit against Critics Abound. The lawsuit was filed thirteen months ago against Critics Abound, claiming that they fraudulently published an article by McKinley Sinclair, when in fact, she never wrote it. It was the article that revealed the true identity of world renowned author, R.T. Sinclair.

Sinclair and McKinley Sinclair were also awarded an additional five million in a case against Ruth Conner, the Executive Vice President at Critics Abound who gave permission and demanded that the article be published. According to McKinley Sinclair, in the original suit against Critics Abound, it was Connor who planted an illegal electronic recording device on her and recorded private conversations between her and Sinclair.

"Though what Connor published was true, the fact that she used me as the byline constituted fraud, and I wasn't going to stand for that," said McKinley Sinclair.

Sinclair and McKinley Sinclair joined forces in seeking damages. The couple donated the ten million dollars awarded to them from the first suit to the local children's shelter. The second five million will be set up in a charity called the David McKinley Dream Big Scholarship Fund For Creative Writing. It will be a need base fund for students wanting to study creative writing who can't afford the cost of student loans in college.

"I struggled with student loan debt after I graduated from college and Ryland Thomas saw what a burden I was under. If we can help students alleviate that debt, we'll achieve our goal," McKinley Sinclair said.

As a side note, McKinley Sinclair and Sinclair were wed in a private ceremony in July at their home in Lake Tahoe, California.

About The Author

A.M. Hargrove lives in South Carolina with her husband and family. After spending years in the corporate world, she now enjoys writing fiction while she is fully caffeinated. She also thinks coffee and chocolate should be added to the USDA food groups. Oh, and ice cream too!

Other books by A.M Hargrove include *Tragically Flawed, Edge of Disaster, Shattered Edge, Kissing Fire,* The *GUARDIANS OF VESTURON* Series (*Survival, Resurrection, Determinant, Beginnings* and *reEMERGENT*) and *Dark Waltz* (A Praestani Novel).

Acknowledgements…

It's become abundantly clear to me that I have so much to be thankful for, it's hard to even begin. So let me start with my family… my husband Henry, daughter McIntyre, son Tac and my soon to be daughter-in-law, Jaclyn. As always, thanks for your patience. You all get put on the back burner *way* too much so thanks for putting up with me.

Thank you Kathryn Grimes, Amanda Hootie Clark, Andrea Stafford, Kristie Wittenberg and Mandy Anderson for being a part of this novel. Y'all have done more for me than I can ever say so big HUGS to each and every one of you. And Amanda, thanks for the hot dog inspiration… enough said!

This book would never have been possible without my amazing beta readers. You all are simply the best so I'd like to thanks Megan Bracken-Bagley, Heather Carver, Amanda Clark, Kathryn Grimes, Tawnya Peltonen, Alana Rock, Andrea Stafford, Terri Thomas and Kristie Wittenberg. Thanks for your brutal honesty and keeping me on track with EB. I seriously do NOT know what I would do without you amazing ladies. And I need to give a special thanks to Andrea for keeping my British slang spot on with Ryland Thomas. One of these days I'm going to make that trip across the pond to meet you in person!

And on those lines, I'd also like to extend a huge thanks to my editing team at C & D Editing—Kristin Campbell and Alizon Duckwall. Thank you for your diligence, all your comments and kind words about EB! And I would be terribly remiss if I didn't thank my proofreaders, Lynne Beta, Megan Bracken-Bagley and Heather Carver. Thank you, my eagle-eyed ladies for catching those tiniest of typos.

Now for my street team…Annie's Fan-Attics. Thank you, thank you, thank you! You all are THE BEST! And I sincerely mean that. From all the fun stuff we share (and y'all know what I'm talking about here, right?) to all the other things I ask of you, I couldn't have a better group at my back. So a million thanks to each of you because this whole show would never get off the ground without you guys. I love you all! XOXO

I'd also like to thank my publicist, Jessica Estep at InkSlinger PR. She's always hopping around doing one thing or another, along with handling my panic attacks, which is no small feat. So thank you my friend!

There is one more person that needs to be thanked, and that is Meredith *Fallon* Atkins, for whom the main character was named. Thank you, Meredith, and the rest of the gang at Foothills Allergy for all the chats and the support while I get my shots every month! You ladies (and yep, the docs too) are pretty damn amazing, not to mention fun! Oh, and keep on teasing you know who. He deserves it. *Winks*

Music plays a huge role for me in my writing, as it does for many authors. One day while I was on Twitter, I noticed I had a new follower so I clicked on their page. Much to my amazement, it was an extremely talented band named She Said Fire. So I clicked the link to their website and listened to their music and well, what can I say? It was instant addiction. Not only that, I was in the middle of writing Exquisite Betrayal, and their song, *Better Ways*, was the perfect match for the scene I was writing, so I knew I had to contact them. To make a long story short, I was fortunate to connect with Joshua

Hawksley and hence, *Better Ways*, did indeed become a part of this story. So thank you Joshua, and the gang at She Said Fire, for not only allowing me to use *Better Ways* as the introduction to this novel, but also for creating such awesome music! By the way, you'll have noticed other songs of theirs referenced in this book and they're pretty damn incredible too. And one other thing, the scene in the book, where I referenced that their drummer is a female is true. Don't forget to click on their links at the end of this section to stalk them. You won't be disappointed. You can also find their music on the Exquisite Betrayal Playlist.

And finally… I'd like to thank all the book bloggers out there who so tirelessly read and review books and put their hearts into it day after day simply because of their love for reading. Authors everywhere would be lost without you, so thank you! I would like to recognize these blogs in particular, because they have literally gone out of their way to help me. So thank you from the bottom of my heart (in alphabetical order) to: Bestsellers and Beststellars, Carver's Book Cravings, Dark Obsession Chronicles, Delphina Reads Too Much, Globug & Hootie Need A Book, I Read Indie, Kristie's Kaptivating Reviews, Love N. Books, Make My Day Book Club, My Book Boyfriend, Random Jendsmit, and Tsk Tsk What To Read. I know I've missed a ton of you, and please forgive me, but there are just so many of you, my brain went into a meltdown when I tried to remember you all.

Cover Art by Sarah Hansen at Okay Creations
Photography by Kelsey Keeton at K Keeton Designs
Cover Models: Jaclyn Baker and Matthew Samson

Follow A.M Hargrove

www.amhargrove.com
www.twitter.com/amhargrove1
www.facebook.com/AMHargroveAuthor
www.facebook.com/anne.m.hargrove
www.goodreads.com/amhargrove1
www.pinterest/amhargrove1
annie@amhargrove.com

Follow She Said Fire

www.shesaidfire.com
www.facebook.com/SheSaidFire
www.twitter.com/shesaidfire

EXQUISITE BETRAYAL PLAYLIST

She Said Fire – Better Ways
She Said Fire – Funhouse
She Said Fire – Sleeping Through the Revolution
Ellie Goulding – Explosions
Bastille – Pompeii
Lawson – Learn To Love Again
Lana Del Rey – Summertime Sadness
Train – Drive By
Imagine Dragons – Demons
Mat Kearney – Breathe In Breathe Out
Mat Kearney – Nothing Left To Lose
Radical Face – Welcome Home, Son
Pat Benatar – Fire And Ice
Lana Del Rey – Blue Jeans
The Shins – It's Only Life
Metallica – Nothing Else Matters (Live)
Three Days Grace – Never Too Late
Three Days Grace – Misery Loves My Company
Delta Rae – Unlike Any Other

Made in the USA
Charleston, SC
08 February 2014